A Notorious Ruin

By

Carolyn Jewel

cJewel Books
Petaluma CA

Cover Design by Seductive Designs
Image Copyright © Jenn LeBlanc/Illustrated Romance
Image Copyright © deposit photos/FairytaleDesign

ISBN: 978-1-937823-32-0

A Notorious Ruin

She did not retreat from him. She gazed at him, and he possessed no defense against this woman. None at all. He wiped another tear from her cheek, aware he was in a great deal of danger.

"My lord. I've no idea—"

"Don't." He moved closer. "Don't pretend to be a fool if you are not one. I take offense." He stayed close to her when he ought not. Because he did not want to lose this astonishing sense he was alive and on the verge of changing his life. She had chosen to show him the woman she really was because he was not like other men. Not easily fooled. Not so dazzled by her beauty that he did not care about anything else.

He brushed his fingers under her chin and was devastated by her distress, by her continued quiet regard of him. Most of all, however, was his awareness that she wasn't doing anything to make him think she did not want to explore the heat boiling between them. And that was a shocking thing. Arousing.

She tipped her chin toward him, and her smile changed. "You don't want this."

"Don't want what?" He leaned closer, their torsos mere inches apart. "For you to stop pretending? I want that more than you can imagine."

Books By Carolyn Jewel

HISTORICAL ROMANCE

Sinclair Sisters Series

Lord Ruin, Book 1

A Notorious Ruin, Book 2

Reforming the Scoundrels Series

Not Wicked Enough, Book 1

Not Proper Enough, Book 2

OTHER HISTORICAL ROMANCE

In The Duke's Arms from the Anthology *Christmas In The Duke's Arms*
(Carolyn Jewel, Grace Burrowes, Miranda Neville, Shana Galen)

One Starlit Night, novella from the *Midnight Scandals* Anthology

Midnight Scandals, Anthology

Scandal

Indiscreet

Moonlight A Regency-set short(ish) story

The Spare

Stolen Love

Passion's Song

Acknowledgement

My deepest thanks go out to Carolyn Crane for being an awesome beta reader and to Robin Harders for editorial brilliance. To my sister for being such a great sport and a true fan. To my son Nathaniel for having grown into a fine young man. Bella, thank you for not eating my shoes. Recently.

To my Readers

Probably some of you reading this will roll your eyes when I say that as I write this, I am tearing up. But it's true. The biggest, widest, most enduring, and heartfelt thank yous go to the many readers who loved *Lord Ruin* (the first book in this series) whether you wrote to tell me so or not. You've made all the difference.

For years, there was no hope of my being able to write the planned sequels, in part for contractual reasons, in part because, well, why would a publisher take a chance on a sequel to a book originally published in 2002? Especially since it went out of print shortly thereafter. But, between 2002 to this day, readers have been emailing me asking if I would ever write the sequels to that book. Every single month, every single year, for 12 years. Some of you even emailed my editor about contracting me to write the rest of the books. I am profoundly grateful that I was able, eventually, to take matters into my own hands.

And so, after far too long, after a really rotten 2013 when I got behind in my writing while life was...difficult, here is the first of the sequels. The others will follow. Thank you, thank you, thank you, to everyone who wrote to me. I hope you enjoy *A Notorious Ruin*.

About A Notorious Ruin

A Notorious Ruin
The Sinclair Sisters Series, Book 2

All the widowed Lucy Sinclair Wilcott wants is to save enough money to move to a cottage of her own and keep her younger sister safe from the consequences of their father's poor judgment. No one is more aware than she how thoroughly her first marriage ruined her. She could not remarry if she wanted to. Then the Marquess of Thrale comes to visit and long-absent feelings of desire surge back.

Everything Lord Thrale believes about the beautiful Mrs. Wilcott is wrong. The very last woman he thought he was interested in proves to be a brilliant, amusing, arousing woman of deep honor who is everything he wants in a lover, for the rest of his life. If only he can convince her of that.

Books in the Series:
Lord Ruin, Book 1

CHAPTER ONE

L
ucy sat in the bow window of the second parlor and gazed at
the scene unfolding below. Their new groom, looking smart in
the suit she'd bought him from last week's winnings, continued to
struggle with the step to the carriage in the driveway. Oh, dear. She
had hoped for a better debut from him than this. "Well, Roger, old
boy." The elderly hound at her feet rose and placed his head on her
lap. She rubbed his shoulder. "This does not bode well."

The dog, a wolfhound, if one squinted just so, did not reply.

The mechanism of the step defeated the groom still. She hoped
and expected he would improve rapidly. At last, he managed the
trick, but then he struggled with the carriage door. High atop the
vehicle, the driver watched with disdain.

Outside, her father arrived to greet their guests. He stood a few
feet away, hatless, arms held wide in greeting. Yesterday's excellent
weather had given way to clouds and enough of a breeze to riffle his
iron-gray hair. She'd locked the door to the wine cellar three hours
ago and was hopeful he was not drunk. He'd have found his way to
the port and sherry, though. The groom held the door.

A gentleman exited; Captain Niall. She did not want them here,
her father's guests. Papa entertained like a man with ten or twenty
thousand a year when, in fact, his income was far less and his debts
far greater.

Captain Niall buttoned his greatcoat against the wind. He was a
man of immense charm and refinement whom others had hinted

would be a good match for her. As if such a thing were conceivable or in comportment with her desires.

This would not be, no matter anyone's wishes.

The second occupant of the carriage emerged.

The Marquess of Thrale swung his arms and glanced at the sky a moment before he shook out his coat and wrapped his scarf around his throat. Despite his being unmarried and in possession of a title, he had not been a dashing figure in Town last season. Thrale, however, had made a friend of her sister Anne, and that was enough to recommend him to anyone. Though she appreciated his height and brawn, she did not find him interesting.

Captain Niall put his hands on his hips and arched his back. Thrale said something in that somber way of his, and Captain Niall laughed. They seemed unlikely friends, those two, yet they had traveled together from London all the way to Bartley Green. A month or more at The Cooperage and then another at Rosefeld after her brother-in-law and the others arrived.

She did like Captain Niall's quick smile. Who did not appreciate a handsome, amiable man? She resented his being here. Lord Thrale, too.

The groom now held the head of Thrale's lead horse. Here, he displayed the expertise that had made her hire him over an older man. He had his mouth by the horse's ear and gave every appearance of whispering secrets while he stroked the animal's neck.

Roger settled his head on her lap as she absently rubbed his ears. Outside, her father and Lord Thrale shook hands. The same exchange occurred with Captain Niall. The men continued to converse, and then Papa went to the lead coach horse and ran a hand down its front leg. They were fine horses. Not ostentatious, but one saw the quality. One of the hunting dogs wandered from the stable, and her father gave its shoulders a pat. Lord Thrale did the same. Conversation turned to the carriage, for Lord Thrale thumped the side of the vehicle. The marquess's carriage, since that was his coat of arms on the door. *Talbot passant*, and his coronet of rank.

Captain Niall, Lord Thrale, and her father remained in the driveway chatting. The groom rode postilion while the coachman drove the rig to the stable block. She continued with her excellent view of Thrale. He was a man of restraint and reserve who rarely extended his friendship to others. One must earn his regard. Her sister Anne, now the Duchess of Cynssyr, had done so. As if anything else were possible.

Papa gestured, describing, most likely, the general bounds of the property. He then pointed in the direction of Rosefeld, the home of her brother-in-law, Baron Aldreth. Not, at present, in residence, though he soon would be.

The two men were here to ride and to hunt and fish, and do all the sorts of things gentlemen did in the country. Lord Thrale's presence was due, she suspected, to the fact that Bartley Green was a fertile location for a Sporting man to spend his time. Exhibitions and battles between talented and renowned prizefighters were frequent here owing chiefly to the presence of Johnson's Academy of Pugilistic Arts in town. The Academy was one of England's finest arenas for training and improving one's skills in the art and science of pugilism.

At last, all three men turned to the house. Papa was grinning. No one could say Mr. Thomas Sinclair, Esquire, was not a congenial host. Because he never bothered to square expenses with income, there never was a guest who went away complaining of his experiences at The Cooperage. The best food, the best wine and spirits, cigars of rare and exotic tobaccos. Constant entertainments.

Roger came to attention when the front door closed. Voices he did not know meant new people to admire and pet him. She leaned over and stroked his head. Five minutes more of freedom. Five minutes in which she could be herself. So much grey around his muzzle. "We shall meet them presently, and you will be your noble self, yes?"

Most everyone believed the Sinclair fortunes were beyond reproach. After all, there were now two noble sons-in-law, one of them a duke, and long outstanding debts had been settled within days of Anne's marriage.

In reality, he'd had a year to run up new debts and had done so with disheartening rapidity. Lucy kept the books now that Anne was married and was now intimate with the hopelessness of their finances. Papa had only to say; *My second daughter's husband is Baron Aldreth, and my eldest married Cynssyr. Yes. The duke.* And credit was extended for more foolishness and waste.

She stood and ran light fingers over her hair, securing an errant pin or two, then adjusted her shawl and smoothed her bodice and skirts. If all one had was one's looks, then appearing at one's best was vital. Time and again she'd been told beauty did not matter, that what mattered was one's mind and heart. The evidence for that, in her experience, was not persuasive. The exception proved the rule; her sister Anne's marriage to the duke.

With Roger at her heels, she walked down the corridor to the stairs to meet her father and their guests, fully armored, to paraphrase the great Boswell, with perfection.

"Lucy." Her father extended a hand and kissed her cheek when she met them. Captain Niall and Lord Thrale stood behind and to one side of her father, expectant. Smiling. Well. One of them was smiling. "Look here, it's Lord Thrale and Captain Niall come to visit."

She despised meaningless conversation. She did not wish to be cheerful or amusing or, worse, interesting. She had made an art of never being the latter. Subjects ladies were expected to find interesting seldom interested her. Sometimes, oftentimes, too often, she missed the bluntness of her old life. "Sit, Roger."

Roger sat like the magnificent dog he was. *He* had no trouble meeting people. She remembered to curtsy to Lord Thrale first. She'd been away from London only a few months, and already she'd fallen out of the habit of genteel manners. Disaster awaited if she forgot herself. "My lord. Welcome to Bartley Green."

Few men could stand silent and be so terribly present as the marquess. How had she forgotten that about him? His silence made her worry she'd already misstepped. He was taller than Captain Niall by three or four inches at least, much broader across his shoulders and torso, too.

In her time away from London, she'd not had to pretend she was a delicate and fragile woman. From the corner of her eye, she saw her father frown. He took it as a point of pride that men found her desirable, as if she were a pet dog who mattered only when it performed the requested trick.

Everyone falls in love with Lucy's beauty.

Sometimes she wondered if her father kept a tally of the men he felt had fallen in love with her face or figure, and whether his satisfaction with her depended upon an ever-increasing list.

If she had managed to offend Lord Thrale so soon, well, there was nothing for it. He would have to live with his disappointment in her and she with his disapproval. Quite manageable, in her opinion.

At last, the marquess bowed. "Mrs. Wilcott."

The next several weeks stretched before her, a desert of emptiness that must be crossed no matter how desiccated she became. With a smile, she turned to the captain. Ah, yes. This was the trick, wasn't it? A smile that meant nothing at all.

In contrast to Thrale, the captain was *a la mode*; everything a man of taste and fashion could hope to be and more. "Good afternoon, sir. I hope we find you well."

"Yes, thank you. Is Miss Sinclair at home?" Captain Niall had been one of her sister Emily's most ardent admirers last season.

"She is visiting a dear friend, but never fear. She will be home presently." Roger bumped against her thighs, and she came near to losing her balance. Lord Thrale was close enough to steady her. "Thank you, my lord." There was unexpected strength in his grip. "Before tea I expect."

Roger left his sit to sniff Captain Niall's boots and then his knees. He gave the dog a gentle push away with one leg. Thwarted in his quest for admiration, Roger turned to Lord Thrale.

"Now, Lucy, m'dear." Papa's frown deepened. "No one wants a dog coming up so bold as that."

"My apologies." She moved to pull Roger away, but Lord Thrale had already bent to give Roger's shoulder a rub.

"This is your dog, ma'am?"

"Yes."

Captain Niall's mouth twitched. "I don't know that I've ever seen a dog of such uncertain antecedents. Are you certain he's yours, Mrs. Wilcott? I thought ladies kept dogs they can hold in their arms. This one is a monster."

"I'm sure some do." A thread of panic pulled tight. Such ironic words were not expected from her, for she did not miss Lord Thrale's cocked eyebrow. She pasted on another smile. She would defend Roger to anyone, including charming, happy, Captain Niall. Even to the king himself. "Nevertheless, he is mine."

Lord Thrale found the spot behind Roger's ear the dog loved best, and Roger groaned in ecstasy, dignity abandoned.

"I hope you had a pleasant journey here, Captain Niall. My lord."

Papa spoke over her. "Now, Lucy, that mongrel of yours—"

Lord Thrale gave Roger one last pat and straightened. "Yes, ma'am. We did."

Her father clapped Thrale on the shoulder. Roger, meanwhile, plastered himself against the marquess's legs, tail wagging. "I'm going to show you the billiards room, had it put in last winter. What do you think of that?"

"Papa." Careful negotiations were required with her father now that he had the stimulation of guests and spirits. "Lord Thrale and Captain Niall might first like to change from their travel clothes."

"Are you saying our guests do not look presentable?"

"Not at all." Anne knew how to deal with him when he'd been at the sherry. Anne knew the words to say and how to say them, and Lucy failed at that. She always had. Even before Lucy left Bartley Green, Anne had managed everything.

Thrale and her father both were watching her. Captain Niall, too, and her panic blossomed. She was to be unnoticed for anything but her appearance. She had not made an auspicious start.

She took a step back, and her elbow bumped a marble bust of Aristotle. A recent purchase of Papa's she had been unable to prevent. He'd had the statuary sent all the way from Athens. She doubted it was genuine. For several seconds, she lost the feeling in her arm. *Damn.* She resisted the impulse to cradle her elbow. "Had I been traveling all day, I should want a moment to put myself to rights."

Her father guffawed. "If there's a light breeze, she wants to put herself to rights, ain't that so, Lucy?" He shook his head and shared his merriment. "I never saw a girl so worried she might have a hair out of place. From the day she was born, I own."

"I'm sure," she said, "quite sure Lord Thrale will enjoy the billiards room." And there was Captain Niall, standing here, so handsome and charming. "Captain Niall, too."

"A moment to neaten myself would be welcome." Whether Thrale said this because she was floundering so horribly, she had no idea, but she was grateful he had. "Thank you, Mrs. Wilcott. Sinclair, shall we find each other later?"

"Yes, yes, of course," he said. "I'll show you your rooms, then, my lord. Captain. We'll have a friendly game afterward."

"I look forward to it," Thrale said.

Captain Niall's gaze lingered on her, and she gave him what she called her *drawing room* smile. "Will we see your sister later, Mrs. Wilcott?"

"Yes, certainly." There were two of her. The woman she presented and the woman inside who wished these men gone. How was she going to survive the coming weeks?

CHAPTER TWO

"This is a pleasant town," Thrale said to his valet, Flint. They were on the cobbled main street of Bartley Green, ostensibly in search of the florist. Per the directions he'd been given, they ought to have turned right two corners back, but Johnson's Academy was located on the far side of the Crown & Pig, and that excellent establishment was in sight. The florist wasn't going anywhere.

"Tis, milord."

The Crown & Pig stood as the transition between the older, Tudor-era section of the town and more recent structures, which, it happened, included Johnson's Academy. With luck, he would soon be seated in the tavern with a warm beer in hand, the fire at his back, and a firm engagement with Johnson himself.

Johnson was a former pugilist who, since his retirement from the ring, had trained more than a dozen prizefighters of some repute. He organized regular exhibitions and provided a respectable place for gentlemen to learn or hone their skills in the art. He was eager to see the place first hand, note who was in training, and meet the proprietor himself.

They passed the Crown & Pig without a word spoken between them. Not five minutes later they stood before a nondescript building with the words *Johnson's Academy* painted above the door in bright yellow letters. Thrale gazed through the window at the wall with its display of ropes and unframed prints of fighters. Anticipation snaked through him. "Well," Thrale said. "Here we are."

"I should think, my lord, that you ought to ask after Mr. Johnson." Flint opened the door and made a *come in* gesture.

"I ought to leave a card at the very least."

"Right you are."

They returned to The Cooperage three hours past when he'd thought to be back. Flint was barely visible behind a mass of pale pink roses. At one point while they were climbing the stairs to the front door, the wag pretended to stagger under the weight. His servants, all of them hired in the last year—it having been necessary to let go the majority of his London staff, had come to him recommended by the Duke of Cynssyr. Flint had been the first to be sent with the duke's personal character, and the first Thrale had hired.

From behind him, Flint said, "Not too late to save yourself, milord."

He didn't regret the decision in the least. Flint was an excellent valet, but the man had a sense of the absurd Thrale could do nothing to eradicate. He ignored the theatrics. The door, he noted, was a cheerful blue. This was one of the delights of a woman's touch on one's home. A brightly painted door and window-boxes of blossoms.

"Abandon the roses and decamp before the ladies of the house see you, milord."

He stared at the snarling lion knocker then opened the front door since Flint had his arms full. "No."

"I could pitch them into the hedge."

Thrale turned. "Captain Niall brought them a box of pralines. Each."

"And?"

"While I do not wish to appear extravagant, neither do I wish to be a thoughtless guest."

"Roses, milord. Roses." He adjusted the flowers. "And young ladies in the house. Beautiful young ladies."

"Roses are an appropriate token of my esteem. They delight the senses. Brighten a room." He touched one of just-opening buds. "They are impermanent. Like pralines, they pronounce a man's regard for a lady, and yet, some days later, there is nothing left but fond memories of the delight taken."

"Unless the lady dries them or presses them, or one of those things ladies do to amuse themselves."

"Such as saving the box the pralines came in?"

"Aye, sir." Flint had been in the recent hostilities with the French. Infantry, and his personal habits reflected the discipline of his time in that rough trade. "Their father will be wanting another noble son-in-law, one deep in the pockets, if you take my meaning. I advise you to retreat. Now. No shame in that."

He stepped into the entryway. "Roses are not an offer of marriage. Or do you believe Sinclair will think I'm offering for both his daughters?"

"He'll wonder which of them you'll take."

He turned again. "It's not as though there's any disgrace in marrying one of the man's daughters. He's a gentleman. They are ladies. Their sisters are Lady Aldreth and the Duchess of Cynssyr. If I were to marry, not that I intend to do any such thing, I could do worse than one of them."

Though he said either would do, if he were to decide it was past time he was married, which in point of fact it was, only the youngest Sinclair daughter was of interest to him. Her elder sister, the widowed Mrs. Wilcott, was more to his physical preferences, but Miss Sinclair had the intellectual spark that mattered most to him. Alas, Niall had his matrimonial hopes pinned on Miss Emily Sinclair. If anyone could captivate her, it must surely be Niall. The captain, with his perpetual good mood and elegant looks might well succeed where all others had failed.

"He paid last quarter's wages only a week ago."

He stepped further into the entryway. "What the devil do you mean by that?"

"I mean, Mr. Sinclair might well be looking for another son-in-law to pay his debts. And here he's got two pretty daughters in the honey pot."

Thrale frowned. Six weeks in arrears? It was not well done of

Sinclair to leave his staff so long unpaid. He was himself punctilious to a fault about paying his servants. His father, God rest his be-damned soul, had let wages go months past due. Thrale, having lived under the consequences of that neglect, had dedicated himself to being as different from his father as possible in that regard and every other. "Sinclair's debts, if he has them, have nothing to do with me giving roses to his daughters."

From behind the flowers, his valet made a faint *tick-tock* sound. The closing seconds of his doom, one supposed. As if he could be compelled to marry where he did not wish to.

Footsteps echoed inside the house, coming nearer. He took off his hat and hung it from one of the pegs above the doorway to the pantry. The Sinclair's home, while modest, as befit its name, was a charming place. More charming than Blackfern, his country seat. From the flowers outside, to the arrangement of daisies on a side table, he felt a woman's gentle influence. Miss Sinclair's most likely. So he fancied.

The Sinclairs did not have a butler so it was the housekeeper who came in, a cap on her iron-colored hair, and with a steely gaze to match. She dropped into a curtsy. Flint made that *tick-tock* sound again.

"Milord." Her gaze flicked to Flint and then back. Thrale dropped his umbrella in the stand by the door then slipped out of his coat.

"Roses," he said to Mrs. Elliot after he'd pressed a coin into her hand. He did not stint on vails. Then, because it was obvious there were, indeed, roses, he added, "Two dozen each for Miss Sinclair and Mrs. Wilcott."

Mrs. Elliot remained solemn. Or was that disapproval? Servants gossiped as much as anyone. "They will be delighted by such thoughtfulness, my lord."

"Are they home?"

"Miss Sinclair is out, my lord."

"Is she?" Now there was a pity. He'd hoped to have the luck to be found arriving with the roses.

His valet eased into the foyer with a sideways slide and just the top of his head visible above the flowers in his arms. This close, the scent of roses was at the very edge of overpowering. Some indefinable signal passed between Flint and Mrs. Elliot, for his valet, arms full, headed toward a back staircase.

"Captain Niall and Mr. Sinclair are out as well." She smoothed her apron and smiled. He liked the woman for that smile. "We expect them back before tea."

"Such are the perils of stepping out to obtain roses."

"Indeed, milord." She was a rail, wrapped tight, precise in her words and movements. Easy to imagine her running the house with ruthless efficiency.

"While you wait for the others, my lord, you might find the second parlor a pleasant place to explore. The duchess, when she lived here, always enjoyed that parlor best. The view there is much admired."

"Thank you." He remembered the room from his previous tour of the house, and she was right. The view was striking.

"Shall I bring refreshment?"

"No, thank you."

Mrs. Elliot retreated, and he proceeded to his quarters. Here, one saw the back of the property; fields sloped away to dense trees to the east, to the west, sunlight glinted off the water in a distant canal. Flint came in when he was washing up. "This is a nice bit of property."

"Aye."

He allowed Flint to retie his neckcloth and brush every possible speck of lint from his jacket.

With his clothes arranged to his satisfaction and Flint's, he made his way to the second parlor. Like the rest of the house, this room was inviting and comfortable. He pondered what made The Cooperage so pleasing to the eye and spirit. He suspected the duchess, the former Miss Anne Sinclair, had had a hand in that. Not until Thrale was well into his majority had he understood his father had abominable taste. What, he wondered, as he studied the parlor, might he do at Blackfern to further eradicate the ponderous imprint of his predecessor to his title?

Here, shelves of books lined two walls. No doubt the room served as library and parlor. Along another wall was a long table, and there he found Mrs. Elliot had arranged the roses. They looked exceedingly well here, placed as they were against the backdrop of a lilac wall. There were no lilac rooms at Blackfern. His father had handed over the last round of renovations to a man with an excessive love of gilt and an unending supply of oxblood paint.

He sat by the fire and imagined himself at Blackfern and that the credit for his surroundings belonged to him, or perhaps to a wife of refined taste. He would write to the duke and ask for the name of his architect. Damn the expense if the recommendation was that he should pull Blackfern down to its foundations. He would, by God, now that he had the money.

Thrale shifted his chair to face the tall windows and picked up a well-thumbed copy of *Paradise Lost* that Sinclair must have been reading. One could imagine him here with the two daughters left at home, entertaining family and select friends, perhaps reading from this very book. Most every volume in the library at Blackfern had uncut pages. Every book but the ones he'd cut himself.

He opened the Milton. Not only had Sinclair read the work, he'd made an Oxford don's study of it. Whole passages were underlined in pencil. He and his host, it seemed, shared a similar opinion of the work. This was more erudition than he'd have credited Sinclair with possessing. Book in hand, he walked to the window and gazed down on the lawns.

The prospect invited the eye. One wanted to walk the grounds and explore what lay over the hill to the right. He ought to have the grounds at Blackfern redone as well. His father had preferred the formal, geometrical lines of the previous century. What was needed was a modern touch, a more natural one.

While he gazed out the window, a woman appeared on the path that emerged from the trees to his left. A maid walked behind her, a paper-wrapped parcel in her arms. The wolfhound mongrel with the improbable name of Roger paced at her side. Mrs. Wilcott, then. A parasol hid most of her face from him, but even if the hound did not announce her, he'd seen that languorous stride too often not to know her. There was a softness to her, a gentleness. A lack of spirit, he thought, that instantly identified her.

And yet. She was physically nothing less than his ideal. A face to make a man weep for her beauty. A figure no less admirable or stirring.

Watching her walk was a sensual delight. Her gown caressed her limbs as she strolled. She moved slowly because the dog was old. Roger, Thrale suspected, was the sort of hound who would keep pace with his owner if it meant he dropped dead of it. It spoke well of her that she was aware.

He stayed at the window until she was out of sight. Notwithstanding his high opinions of the other Sinclair women—the duchess, Lady Aldreth, and Miss Sinclair—Mrs. Wilcott was, in his opinion, the loveliest of them. She'd been married young and widowed early and wasn't much more than twenty-three herself. Left destitute, one heard, or near to it, by a husband of whom no one in the family would speak. One heard vague accounts; very little that was specific.

He did not hear the front door open, but he remained unconcerned by that. If she'd come in a private entrance, the housekeeper would see she was told he was here. He went to the table and inspected the roses for imperfections. He found none. While he waited, he took out two calling cards. With pen and ink from the writing desk, he wrote *Miss Emily Sinclair* on one and *Mrs. Wilcott* on the other. What had her husband's Christian name been? He did not recall that he'd ever heard. He set a card in each of the bouquets.

Not long after, rapid footsteps descending stairs had him turning from the window. Not Mrs. Wilcott, he thought. No, this was someone spirited. Her younger sister, or one of the maids, perhaps. He adjusted his coat. Perhaps he'd give Niall some competition for Miss Sinclair's affections.

"I left it in the second parlor," a woman said to someone, breathless and not loud enough for him to identify the speaker.

"Ma'am, Lord—"

The parlor door, left ajar, flew open.

The third of the Sinclair sisters swept in, and this was a surprise, to see her full of life and energy. Roger trotted behind her. She did not see him yet, and he stood, book in hand, bereft of coherent thought.

Her air of abstraction was gone and in its place was focus and deliberation. A stranger to him. This creature was another woman entirely. Vivid. Intense. Aware. He stood, dumbfounded, wordless.

"Where the devil is it?" She headed for the chair by the fire.

Her language took him aback.

She was halfway across the room before she became aware of his presence. Her eyes widened, and a woman he did not know looked straight into his soul, took his measure, and found him lacking.

What a fancy, to think a woman like Mrs. Wilcott had that spark in her. "Ma'am."

All the life in her vanished, and she was the Mrs. Wilcott he knew too well. His brain filled with thoughts that were no credit to him. Her gown was dark blue, and ribbons in her hair pulled her curls away from her temples and the nape of her neck. He returned to her face, ethereal, angelic, devastating. He drew in air but nothing helped, and over her shoulder he had a disconcerting view of himself in the chimney glass; a man stunned into imbecility by a woman who was so beautiful it hardly mattered that he did not care for her.

"Oh," she said, looking at the roses. She curtsied. So young to be a widow. Roger left her side for him, and without thinking, he rubbed the dog's head. "Lord Thrale. Good afternoon."

"Madam." He decided he was mistaken that she sounded sorry to see him.

"My sister is not here. She'll be back in time for tea, though."

Mrs. Wilcott was no intellect, he was certain of it. He would have discovered it before now if she were. He was not often fooled by the people he admitted into his acquaintance, and that eased his mind enough that he smiled during his bow to her. He was still smiling when he straightened, but she wasn't looking at him. Her focus was on the book he still held. In the instant before she met his gaze, something behind her eyes flickered with awareness, and then it, too, died. Killed? Nothing but vapid beauty remained.

Her sisters were intelligent women. All three of them women of wit and discernment. The possibility that Mrs. Wilcott might be their equal stupefied him. Surely, no. No woman played so deep a game. Not her.

She waved with no sign that any thought of substance had ever entered her head. "Captain Niall has gone for a walk with my father. Their destination was the river. Something about fishing." Her eyes flicked again to the book he held. "Your errand in town was successful I gather. It must have been, since you have returned."

Thrale lifted the book. Mrs. Wilcott blinked. "Yes, madam. It was."

She tipped her head to one side, and his impression of her as vital and formidable slipped away like mist. There was nothing in her eyes. No spark of understanding, no sense that she'd seen through him and was disappointed. She smoothed her skirts, an unconscious gesture, and that part of him that remained aroused took in the way her gown settled around her body, the perfection of her bare arms between her sleeves and the tops of her gloves, the curve of her bosom. That disgraceful, lusty part of him whispered he could as easily fuck a stupid woman as an intelligent one.

He swept an arm in the direction of his roses. "For you, Mrs. Wilcott."

She turned her head in that direction. "So many. How generous and thoughtful you've been." She walked to the vases with his two cards propped against the petals in each arrangement. "Thank you, Lord Thrale. They're lovely. Wherever shall I put so many flowers?"

"For you and your sister."

She looked over her shoulder at him with the distracted expression that was so familiar to him. There wasn't a complicated thought in her head. He was certain of it. "Shall I order tea, my lord? A bite to eat?"

What he ought to have said was no. His apology for not obliging her would take him half a minute, and then he could be back in his room with Milton, or walking to the trees and a shady spot in which to read. What came out of his mouth was, "Yes, thank you."

He watched her walk to the door and call for a servant. Instructions for tea were conveyed to the maid who appeared. When she turned back, an empty smile curved her perfect mouth. A thousand miles away.

"Do sit, my lord." She returned to the fireplace, lowering herself to a chair with exquisite grace.

He sat, legs crossed, the Milton balanced on his thigh. "I am delighted you are here, Mrs. Wilcott, though I could not help but overhear that you came here not to entertain me but to search for something." He scanned the room and then picked up the book and fanned the pages. No reaction but disinterest and then—his heart sped up because of that flash of something through her eyes again. "Perhaps I might help you find it."

"I think not."

"No?"

"No." She lifted a hand in a dismissive gesture. The back of her knuckles hit the candelabra on the table. "Goodness!" She steadied the candles, but not successfully, for she knocked it over entirely. It was a mercy for the household that no one had lit the candles.

A footman tapped at the door, and Mrs. Wilcott waved him in. "Tea is here. How lovely." She rose, and when Thrale came to his feet, she said, "Please don't stand on my account." He remained on his feet while the footman arranged the tea and set out plates. At the sideboard, she rearranged the roses meant for her.

"A fine day, don't you think?" he asked.

She glanced out the window, then back at the roses. Her fingers moved quickly, touching each of the flowers in turn. "I wonder if it will rain. I do like rain when I am not in it."

She was counting them. For God's sake, why? "There are forty-eight in total, Mrs. Wilcott, across both vases."

She went still, and that quiet had an edge he recognized. It pained him, that understanding, almost as much as his dismay. He did not want to feel anything for her more complicated than his appreciation of her beauty. This pinch of his heart was as unwelcome as his curiosity. Had he not arrived at his opinion of her in London? That despite her beauty, she was a woman of little consequence.

"So many?" she said in a light voice. Having touched every rose, she now rearranged them until they sat in the vase with perfect symmetry. "I'm sure it matters not a bit whether there are twenty-four or thirty-seven. They're very pretty. Emily adores roses." She faced him, and she was as pleasant and empty-headed as ever. "As I'm sure you know. She'll be very pleased you brought them. They are her color."

"I hope you like them just as much."

"Like all roses, they are as beautiful as they are dangerous."

Thrale forced himself to take a mental step back. Had those words come from any of her sisters, he would have appreciated the hidden thorn. But Mrs. Wilcott? Was that possible? He'd long ago concluded she let her intellect lie fallow. A pity.

And yet. He could not shake his conviction that he knew nothing about the woman behind those so-blue eyes, and that worse, the woman he'd glimpsed was worth knowing. Roger sat near her, eyes on her as if he, too, found her beautiful beyond understanding.

She put her back to the roses. "Tea, my lord? Before the water is cold." She gave him an empty smile. "I don't know about you, but I do not care for tepid tea."

He retook his seat after he saw her to her own. He ought to have been comforted by that smile that spoke of nothing, but he wasn't. While she scooped tea from a box carved with a fanciful chevron, he watched her for any sign she was capable of the deception he suspected. He set the Milton on the table beside him.

She paused with the tongs over the sugar bowl. "One lump did you say?"

"Thank you, a smaller one if you don't mind."

"Not at all." She used the edge of the tongs to search the contents of the sugar bowl. "I find that my day is quite destroyed if my tea is not perfect. This one?"

"Yes."

She held out his tea and a spoon and beamed at him. He knew what he'd seen when she came in. He knew it.

"Thank you, Mrs. Wilcott." He stirred his tea.

"Perfect, I hope."

Deliberately, rudely, even, he held her gaze. "Yes." No reaction to that. None whatever. "Tell me, Mrs. Wilcott, do you read?"

"Oh, yes my lord." She leaned against her chair, her features smooth. "I adore novels. Particularly historical novels. And ghosts. I adore stories with ghosts. Mrs. Sleath's *The Nocturnal Minstrel* is a particular favorite of mine."

Thrale tapped a finger on the Milton. "I am not familiar with that novel. Ghosts, you say. What would you say about a novel with devils?"

"Blasphemy, sir." She spoke without the least sign of irony, and he sighed. Defeated.

He liked her dog. There was that.

CHAPTER THREE

A handful of weeks more, Lucy told herself, and she would never have to endure another overcrowded assembly with more people than chairs. She loathed the Bartley Green assembly. Loathed it as much as Emily adored it. She endured it for her sister's sake alone. She did not want to dance or smile or pretend to have a good time when she did not enjoy crowds in the least. Nor did she care to drink weak lemonade or be obliged to smile at anyone.

If all went as planned, she would soon be signing a year's lease on her own home, and she would live on her own, as befit a widow. She would not have to leave her house except to walk to the subscription library and back. She would see Emily moved in with Aldreth, and her and Roger ensconced in a charming cottage nearer to Little Merton than Bartley Green. Close enough to visit her father from time to time. Far enough away that he was unlikely to call.

She would never have to endure another supercilious look from Mrs. Glynn or a leer from Mr. Charles, who ought to be persuaded to step down from his duties of introductions at the assemblies. She would never be made to feel unwelcome, or responsible for her father's behavior, nor endure an improper remark from a gentleman who knew or thought he knew, some portion of the story of her marriage.

For now, though, she was here with people who left her alone so long as she smiled and flirted—not overmuch—and behaved as if she hadn't a thought in her head. She was happy to oblige. She headed toward the chairs where the older ladies sat, her stomach in a knot the size of the ocean. So much noise. Too many people. So many frowns in her direction, familiar looks askance from the people who would never forget or forgive the scandal of her marriage.

She recited Milton in her head because she needed a distraction. Poetry, often Milton, but sometimes Pope, or Dunne, or Dryden, helped keep her thoughts from rushing off to fearful continents.

At the last moment, she did not take a chair. Mrs. Glynn sat among the matrons, a hard smile on her face. Lucy would not be made welcome there. Instead, she continued around the perimeter of the room. Save her from pretentious crowds like this. There was no air to breathe. None at all.

When she reached one of the pier-glass mirrors that hung at opposite ends of the room, she looked away. She took perverse comfort in her triumph over refusing to indulge qualities she'd been told made her so weak and imperfect a vessel. The accusation that she was over-proud of her looks had been floating around long before Mrs. Glynn said the words to her face.

I will not have my son involve himself with a chit who thinks to marry above herself on account of her face.

If her husband were alive, she'd not be in this room, among people who questioned her respectability and who thought her vain. Nor would she be exhausted from the strain of not giving life to gossip. Here, she must be perfection itself and empty inside. She missed her husband with a soul-deep ache.

More than the usual number of gentlemen who were strangers to the village were present tonight. Understandable since Bartley Green was a sporting town. The Flash came here frequently because of The Academy and its pugilistic events. Whatever one thought of such men, the local shopkeepers, innkeepers, and tavern owners relied on the income.

Some of the strangers were gentlemen of good family. Naturally, they were present tonight. Others, thankfully not here, were less reputable. In town, she'd recognized a few of the men from her married life; sporting men and members of the Flash. Gentlemen or otherwise, they were here for one thing and one thing only; the rumored Clancy/Granger battle. To take advantage of the crowds, Johnson had scheduled a series of exhibitions between the best fighters in England. No fewer than three battles had been privately arranged from among the fighters present.

The rougher sort of the Sporting set would never dare appear at the assembly—there were other establishments for their nocturnal amusements. The gentlemen were another matter. Though she did not doubt that they, too, made their visits to less respectable venues, they were here tonight in force, adorned in evening clothes that would not have been remiss in London. They presented cards to Mr. Charles, these Flash gentlemen, reciting the names of prominent acquaintances and relatives, or, in a few cases, identified themselves as such. So long as they left her alone and made themselves agreeable to the young ladies of Bartley Green, she was content.

Lucy pressed her back to the wall and wished she were invisible. Her father was at the other side of the room from her, a glass of wine in one hand, in heated discussion with several other gentlemen who were strangers to Bartley Green. The Flash, all of them.

She caught a glimpse of Captain Niall. The eyes of most every lady who was not dancing followed his progression through the room. Candlelight sparkled off his hair and off the diamond stickpin in his cravat. Lord Thrale was beside him. He was not as splendidly dressed as Captain Niall, but he was a compelling man, with his dark brown hair and gray eyes. Not unappealing, if one liked men of physical prowess.

A wave of reaction followed their progress. The young ladies of Bartley Green and Little Merton knew these two were from London, one a hero from the wars and the other a marquess, and both unmarried. Their parents knew, too. What parent of an unmarried young lady would not make a point of knowing which eligible men were present?

Emily was in conversation with Harry Glynn and his sister Clara. Though she had to admit Harry had grown into a handsome man, she could not see him now without resenting that his mother had decided Lucy was in love with him when she never had been. That was so even though there had been a time when she'd been in love with someone new every month. She'd never fancied herself in love with Harry. There'd been no convincing Mrs. Glynn of that.

The sound of slippers and shoes chasseéing and tapping on the floor made a lovely contre-point to the music. There was a great deal of conversation as well, of course, with the occasional laughter or shout that rose above the general noise. If she stood silent, who would notice her? No one, she hoped.

After the set ended, there was a break for the musicians and the usual refreshments for the attendees. Lucy headed for Emily. What a crush. She counted backward in her head to settle herself. So many people here. Too many, and could not someone open a window? Her shawl drifted off her left shoulder and floated behind her until she slowed enough that the end fell to the floor. She turned right, half way around, waving her hand to catch the trailing end, and with about as much success as a dog chasing its tail.

A Dungeon horrible—

She'd know the lines better if that dratted Lord Thrale hadn't taken her copy of Milton. In the same spin that had her missing the end of her shawl, Lucy looked over her shoulder and saw Emily and Clara Glynn had left Harry. The two were now, predictably, at the center of a group of at least eight gentlemen seeking an introduction. Lucy, still turning and attempting to catch a corner of her shawl, finished her impromptu pirouette.

Someone grabbed her shoulders and steadied her, and she gasped, startled, but prepared with an expression of cold unconcern. Lord Thrale released her shoulders and took a step back.

"You," she said. She lost her place in the lines of poetry she'd fixed in her mind.

"Madam."

A dungeon horrible, on all sides something something...

He handed her the wayward corner of her shawl. Nothing ever

ruffled him, did it? She took it from him and then remembered to smile. "My lord. Forgive me."

"For?"

Captain Niall joined them and gave her an excuse to make Lord Thrale no answer. The captain beamed at her. "Mrs. Wilcott. I hope you are enjoying yourself at this splendid assembly."

"Yes, thank you."

"I think I never saw so many pretty girls in one place." Captain Niall surveyed the room. "Did you ever see prettier girls at an assembly, milord?"

"Indeed, never." Which words Thrale uttered without an ounce of enthusiasm. His attention shot sideways. To Emily, it happened, who was approaching with Clara. Was that not interesting? She'd always thought Thrale and Emily would suit, but she had never had the impression from either that a nudge in the other's direction would be welcome.

"Lucy, there you are." Emily pressed a hand to her forehead when she and Clara reached the spot where she stood with Lord Thrale and now Captain Niall. "I am absolutely all in. Aren't you, Miss Glynn?"

"What?" Captain Niall asked. "But there will be at least one more set. Do you mean you will not dance? Not either of you?"

Emily tugged on Lucy's sleeve. "I'm parched, and I cannot abide the orgeat here. You know how sour it is."

Lucy knew very well what her sister was up to. Emily was no more ready to leave the assembly than any other young lady of spirit. But she knew Lucy did not like crowds. "You have hardly danced at all."

"But I have!"

Captain Niall leapt into the breach of this impending disaster. "Miss Glynn, you shall dance with Lord Thrale here while I partner Miss Sinclair. If we are lucky enough to persuade these delightful musicians to play a reel, why then we shall swap dance partners after. What say you, my lord? Is that not an excellent plan?"

Thrale glanced at Lucy. Was that a smile? She thought so, and that worried her that he should look at her as if she were in the least interesting to him. "I don't believe I've seen you dance, Mrs. Wilcott."

"I'm sure I did." Some devilment made her add, "Once."

"I'm sure you did not." His mouth twitched the slightest amount. "Tonight."

Emily squeezed Lucy's arm. "You ought to dance, Lucy. You used to love dancing."

This would not do. Not at all. "If you and Miss Glynn dance with Captain Niall and Lord Thrale, I shall count this evening a complete success."

"Captain Niall. Ho there! Here's where you've got to."

Lucy froze at the sound of that familiar voice. She'd known it was possible, perhaps inevitable, that Arthur Marsey would be one of sporting men here for the Clancy/Granger fight. He was one of the Flash; a lifelong aficionado of boxing who had attached himself to her husband's fortunes. She had hoped they would not meet.

"We've not got anywhere, I daresay." The captain lifted a hand in greeting to someone behind her.

"I told myself I would find you here, and I have."

She knew that laugh too well.

"Come, come. Join us," Captain Niall said.

And so he did.

Her first thought was that Arthur Marsey had changed little in the three years since she'd seen him last. He remained a striking man with a hearty smile. Now that she'd been to London and met men like Anne's husband, or Captain Niall, or Thrale, even, now that she'd had the opportunity to see Aldreth in anything but country clothes, she saw Marsey was not quite the man of fashion she'd imagined.

He sent a quick glance in Thrale's direction, and she saw him dismiss the marquess as of no consequence. He surveyed Emily and Clara. And then her.

Seeing him here brought back memories of the days when every action available to her had come at an intolerable price. After her husband had died and she'd listened, grief stricken and unmoored, to Marsey say nothing while the lawyers and bankers explained why there was no money, she'd packed what few possessions were hers and, with Roger at her side, walked out of that horrible place. If not for one of her husband's friends taking pity on her, she'd have had to walk all the way home to Bartley Green. She would have done so, too. She would have.

Thrale touched her elbow, and she flinched.

Marsey's attention stayed on her with unwarranted boldness. With a start, she realized he knew nothing of her life here now or before she was married. He knew her as a wife and then a widow whose departure had no doubt been a relief to him.

Captain Niall thumped Marsey's shoulder in a manner that suggested the two were not just acquaintances, but men who knew each other well. As he spoke, Captain Niall turned to Thrale. "My lord. May I introduce Mr. Arthur Marsey? We're old friends, Marsey and me."

Marsey's eyebrows shot up, and Lord Thrale got another, longer, assessment.

Thrale nodded.

"My lord, Mr. Arthur Marsey. Arthur, I present the Marquess of Thrale."

Marsey bowed with that open, friendly smile that had so deceived her husband. "My lord. I once had the honor of meeting your father."

"Did you?" As Lucy well knew, Thrale did not warm to people easily, but even so, his reply was notably cool.

"A most excellent man, your father." He bowed. "Please accept my condolences for your loss."

"Thank you."

Captain Niall put a hand on Marsey's shoulder. "Here, sir, is one most beautiful women you'll ever meet."

He smiled slowly. "Charming, charming."

Lucy stood frozen. From his smug expression, Marsey believed she would say nothing. Do nothing.

"Mrs. Wilcott." His smile turned her stomach. "I never expected I would see you here."

She hated his smile. She hated his smile with all her soul.

"You know Mrs. Wilcott?" Captain Niall asked.

Marsey gave Niall a look of condescension. "I was acquainted with her husband."

"Were you, now? No introduction necessary then." Captain Niall lifted a hand in Emily's direction and said in his golden voice, "The Divine Sinclair. Miss Sinclair..."

She refused to drown in unhappy memories. Nor would she say nothing. Not again.

"...may I introduce Mr. Marsey?"

Lucy, who had never in her life been unkind, and who had transformed her very nature out of pure desperation to maintain her sanity, looked Marsey straight in the eye, and he had the gall, the colossal nerve to smile at her with the expectation that she would let him pass.

She turned to Captain Niall and said, "No, sir. You may not."

The silence was sharp enough to cut to the bone, and while that blade sliced through the gathering, she took Emily's arm, and Clara Glynn's, too, and walked away.

CHAPTER FOUR

Lucy's stomach clenched into a hard and painful knot, but she stood before her father, a cheerful smile on her lips. She wore her good nature like armor. No one, absolutely no one, would ever guess resentment was two inches from shoving her off a cliff. Not any of her three sisters, nor her two brothers-in-law, nor anyone else who had met her since she came home a widow. She settled her shawl around her shoulders and prayed she would not betray herself. "Yes, Papa?"

Her father remained slouched on the chair closest to the fire, feet stretched to the fender as if the room weren't mortgaged twice over.

"My dear. My dear." He waved a hand at the ceiling. "Have you seen the invitation from the Glynns?"

"Emily has it, I think. You may expect she has taken her reply to Mrs. Glynn herself." Her chest pinched. Why, why, did pity overwhelm her when she needed to be strong? The answer was before her. She'd believed for years her father was impervious to the predations of time, and now, with resentment and anxiety near choking her, she could see he was not, and, my God, she did not want to live here with him. She wanted that cottage and a home that was her own.

He'd always looked younger than his actual years. When he began to gray, the change made him the more distinguished. Now his hair was more gray than black, and though he remained a distinguished man, his shoulders stooped where they had not before, and the lines of his face cut deeper than she remembered. He was thicker around the waist, and the vitality about him that had made him more youthful than other men his age seemed lessened.

He wriggled his fingers at her. "I've had a letter from Mary in the morning post. She and Aldreth will be here soon. A fortnight she says. She hopes you and Emily will stay with her at Rosefeld. We ought to plan a gala when she's here. That would show those Glynns a thing or two about a party, I daresay."

She smoothed one of her sleeves. He mustn't guess how he tugged at her. He had no tolerance for weakness. None at all. These moments, much as they tore at her sympathy and pity, did not balance out what he'd done. "You know we want to see Mary and the children."

"Not that I expected anything different."

She never knew any more what he intended nor what she would have to endure when he asked to speak with her in private. Without Anne's mastery of the household to steady him, he was at sea. They all were. All the behaviors that had kept him less extravagant, less insensate with drink, less inclined to dark moods in which he struck without mercy; she could not manage as Anne had.

Lucy's failings in that regard were the more obvious because Anne had been so dreadfully capable. They hadn't any of them realized how brilliantly she'd managed the house and their father, and that was so despite Lucy knowing how much Anne had endured. She continued smiling. What did he want? She did not believe he'd called her here to discuss parties and how long she and Emily would stay at Rosefeld once Aldreth and Mary arrived.

He settled on his chair. "Thrale, Captain Niall, Mr. Glynn and I, and perhaps another fellow or two are to dine in town tonight. You and Emily will make do without us, I hope."

"We shall, Papa." Was that all? Her anxiety eased. "Have you told the cook, or shall I?"

"I leave that to you." He waved in a peremptory manner and nearly overset the bottle of wine on the table beside his chair. "Sit down, my dear."

She did, though her foreboding redoubled.

"We are obliged, I hope you know, to have a fête here as well."

"Why, Papa?" Her heart clenched. There was no money for such an event.

"The Glynns. We can't let them make all the noise. They mean to have the marquess to dinner. A grand affair as if they were the family related to a baron and a duke." He snorted. "We Sinclairs can entertain, too."

"We are not obliged." She spoke too sharply, for her tone turned him mulish. She'd done it. Made everything worse. Now he was set on this course.

"We'll have dancing, too."

"No, Papa."

"Find out who Mrs. Glynn hires to play and have them here. And that fellow who chalked the floors at Rosefeld last year. Mary will know his name." He pulled a sheet of paper from his pocket and handed it to her. "I've made a menu, for I won't have it said Thomas Sinclair does not entertain as well as a Glynn."

"Papa. It's not a competition." She glanced at the menu and held back a groan. The wine list alone would cost more than she had on hand.

"The deuce it isn't. Write to Anne. She'll tell you how it's done. She always managed. There's no reason you can't as well."

"Yes, Papa." There was so much for him to find fault with now that she had stepped into Anne's place in running the household. She hadn't her sister's patience. Nor her gift for organization nor for financial improvisation. She had a mind for figures, but that was of no use when she looked over the household accounts and saw no way to balance monies owed, monies spent, and income received.

"You've been a good daughter," he said. "Never mind that you are not Anne."

"Thank you." Her stomach ground down on itself. At least he wasn't very drunk. This late in the day, it wasn't unheard of for him to be worse off than he was. She knew better than to argue, though he was wrong. Once, she'd bent to his will, but in the days and months after her marriage she'd learned to resent her father for what he'd done—before and after.

"The only obedient one."

When he did not dismiss her, she knew there was worse to come. "Is something the matter?"

He took a long drink of his wine. "I'm in a bind."

"I'm sorry to hear that." Rebellion stirred her in ways that ate at her soul. He was her father, and she ought not resent him for his failings. She ought to be a better daughter than she was. Let her be better than she was. She had but to endure until she had saved enough for that cottage. She would have violets, pansies, and geraniums.

"No more than I, my girl." He laughed too heartily. Everything amused him when he was drunk, and he was drunk most of the time.

She waited him out, stifling the urge to tell him she did not want to see him, nor speak to him, nor have anything to do with him. Her life had been upended once, and that was enough. Enough. He had no right to ask more of her.

"Lucy. My girl." He got that faraway look that came over him whenever he talked about their mother, and that made her heart constrict again. Every year on the anniversary of their wedding and again on the anniversary of her death, he visited her grave. "My dear sweet girl." His words had a familiar maudlin ring. "You look so like your mama."

"I look like you."

"You're dark like me. You and Mary." He touched his head. "But you've your mother's smile. If I close my eyes and listen to you speak, why, she could be here in this very room, you sound so much like her." His mouth trembled, and Lucy battled tears at his heartbreak and hers. "God rest her, Lucy. God rest her."

She knew what it was to love someone like that, to face the rest of one's life with that loss. Her bitterness eased, pushed aside by her father's sorrow and the softness of his encroaching old age. "What do you need?"

His eyes snapped open, and there was no fond gaze now, no lost love recalled. With Anne beyond his reach—Mary had been safe a few years now—he'd moved to her as the cause of all that inconvenienced him. "Delaney was a certain winner, you said. Miller is vulnerable to a right cross, you said."

She cocked her head, and her anxiety roared back, hidden behind an empty smile. She ought to have guessed. All the men, Captain Niall, Thrale, and her father, had been up with the dawn to arrive in town in time for this morning's exhibitions at the Academy. The featured battle between Delaney and Miller had been much anticipated. "Nothing is certain, you know that. Delaney ought to have beaten Miller easily. Did he not?"

"No. He did not."

Delaney had lost? A shocking result, if true. It meant she'd lost the ten pounds she'd put on him when she ought to have won four times that. "What happened?"

"Miller landed punches to his face." He mimed several strikes. "By the fifteenth round Delaney's eyes were swollen shut. He had to forfeit."

"A forfeit?" Delaney was by far the better fighter, but perhaps Miller had found a weakness or merely been lucky. Such things happened. Johnson would tell her when next they met, but she wished she'd been there to see for herself.

"Now I'm in difficulties."

Such an odd bifurcation of her mind went on between the danger of her father's mood and the details of the match between those two men. "Delaney has better defense than Miller. Miller lacks art. It's shocking he won."

"I'm not the only one to say Delaney was bribed."

"No, never." She could not deny the possibility, even with her father in spirits and his mind sailing seas of faulty logic. "Delaney? Johnson trains him. He wouldn't."

He poured more wine. "The bookmaker has my two-hundred

pounds, so there's the proof Delaney lost."

The announcement jerked her out of her thoughts of what had happened between Delaney and Miller. "Two hundred pounds?"

He pointed at her. "On your say so."

She opened her mouth to protest then did not. What would be the point? He was rarely amenable to reason in the matter of wagers he ought not have made. "Oh, Papa. So much?"

"I've another three hundred owed on the side."

"Three hundred." Now she did feel sick. Three hundred pounds? How was that to be repaid? She wracked her brain for bills that might be left unsettled and, of those, singly or together, that might come close to that amount. The arithmetic did not give a satisfactory result. "Papa. No. Three hundred?"

He scowled. "You're not deaf, my girl."

"So much?"

The lines on either side of his mouth deepened. "I meant to put money on Miller, but you dissuaded me. I should have made a tidy sum if you'd not steered me wrong."

Mightn't she be at fault? He *had* asked her opinion. And she *had* given it. "Papa, no."

"It's a debt of honor." He wiped a hand across his face, and he looked so tired, so emphatically old, that she thought with a flash of guilt and dread, *one day, he will leave this earth.* "The debt must be paid. Honor, you understand. I'm a gentleman. I've never not paid my debts. But this one? This one is beyond my reach just now."

She handed back the menu he'd scrawled out. "There will be no party."

"Damn my soul if I'll let the Glynns put us to shame again. We will have a party if I have to write every damned invitation myself."

She fought for composure. They'd always found a way, hadn't they? Anne had. Anne had always managed. For years, her sister had worked miracles running the household on almost nothing. Lucy and her sisters had spent most of their lives never knowing if there would be money to pay the bills or whether their father would come home with pockets of cash and presents. Lucy hadn't known, not really, how Anne had coped in the face of their father's porous pockets. She just had, and no one had ever wondered about the cost to Anne.

Wine sloshed in the glass as he lifted it to his mouth. "There's appearances to keep up. We must. We shall, and besides, when Aldreth arrives, all this will come right."

"We cannot spend money we do not have."

He waved her off to take another drink.

"I'm sorry." Her stomach hurt, but her smile did not waver. Five hundred pounds in new debt, and she'd no idea where the money would come from. "So sorry you find yourself caught short."

"Anne always found the money. She always saw us through."

Protest choked her. She wanted to shout, to scold. *I am not Anne. I cannot work miracles.* More than anything, she wanted to remind him that he'd begged her to marry a stranger because there was no other way to recoup his ruinous losses. And she had done so. Had she not paid and repaid him more than enough? On that day, she'd given up every expectation of happiness to keep him and her sisters from penury.

She'd paid enough. Too much. She'd paid with her happiness. Her future and her security. All that to see him back in debt as deeply as ever before she became a widow. She had done her best by her husband. Her best, and she thanked God he'd proved a decent man, but she had lived a life bereft of all the people and places she loved best; her sisters, friends left behind in Bartley Green, the life she'd once imagined for herself.

He gave his wine a swirl and drank what was left in one long draught. "A hundred pounds would do."

"What do you mean?"

"You can get the money." He made a dismissive gesture.

"I cannot."

"I'd have had the money to pay the debt if you'd not said Delaney was sure to win."

She closed her eyes. She'd not said Delaney was a certain win. A probable one, yes. But not certain. Never that. "I don't know where you think the money will come from. I've not got a hundred pounds, let alone five hundred." It was a lie. She had the money, but giving her father that much would leave her with almost nothing left of her savings and depleted of hope.

"You're not as clever as Anne, but you're a sight more beautiful. All you need do is smile."

She hid her fists in her skirts and came as close as she'd ever dared to laying blame at his feet. "I don't know why you think I've that much money to hand. I haven't."

Not even a blink of recognition. No shame. No remorse. "A hundred will barely do until you get the money from Aldreth. Or the duke."

"I do not understand." Marriage had given her backbone she'd not had as a girl. "The debt is yours. Not mine."

"It's your fault and only fair that you help me recover. I won't abase myself to them again. I can't. Not for the world." He sat forward, eyes alight with passion. "I've my pride, you know."

"Again? What do you mean, again?"

He stood and walked to the fireplace, bottle and glass in hand. Unsteady. "I came up short once or twice these past months. I can't ask again. They'll think I've been imprudent when it's really you to blame."

"You can't mean that." He did. She could see that he did.

"Ask them, Lucy." He put an elbow on the mantel, but his arm slipped off the edge. "Give them a smile, the way you do, you know it strikes men dumb. They'll open their pockets to you and thank you for it, too."

"How am I to explain the need for five-hundred pounds?" She couldn't. She couldn't ask anyone for such a sum.

"A new season. New gowns. You've a reputation for a love of fripperies and other such useless things. Tell them you've over-spent." He gripped the mantel with one hand to steady himself.

"Shed a tear or two. They'll see you the money if only to stop the heartbreak. There's not a man alive can resist your tears."

"Papa."

"If you don't, I'll have to defend my honor when the debt is called in, and it will be. It will be." His hand shook as he refilled his glass. "I don't see as well as I used to." He drank three-quarters of his wine. "Ask the duke, Lucy. Tell him you need new gowns and such. He'll give you the money."

"He'll wonder why I have nothing new."

"Ask for more, dear girl. Enough to buy yourself a new frock or slippers or a bonnet or two. Remake some of your gowns. No one will know the difference, and in the event, the duke won't miss the money. A thousand pounds is pocket money to him. Ask him. If you love your dear Papa, you will." He winked. "I daresay we'll both come out ahead."

Lucy's ability to speak vanished, and that was for the best. She would have regretted whatever words she'd trapped inside her. She stood, counting a silent ten, and he took that as her agreement.

"You're a good daughter. The best of the lot."

She wasn't. She wasn't at all. No longer.

"You don't scold like Anne." He drank more wine. "Write to the duke. Call on Aldreth when he's home. You'll have money from them both."

"I can manage fifty."

"Fifty." He made a face. "That's not enough. Not near enough."

"That's all I have."

He poured the last of the wine into his glass. "Borrow the rest. Aldreth will give more than you ask for. Or Cynssyr. There's a good girl, Lucy. You'll have new gowns and all the useless things you like so well." He winked again. "Hell, you could ask Captain Niall, and he'd give you enough to make me whole. Or Thrale, for that matter."

"You can't be serious."

"All you have to do is smile. There's no man can resist you then."

"Is that all that matters? How pretty my smile is?"

He snorted. "What else would they care about?"

CHAPTER FIVE

Though he heard rapid footsteps in the corridor, Thrale remained in the chair where he'd been reading while he waited for Niall to join him. The Cooperage was a house of cozy rooms, each one decorated and furnished with comfort in mind. Whoever was heading toward the parlor where he sat couldn't be Sinclair. The cadence of the steps was all wrong. A woman. Moving quickly. Running.

The door opened with a bang.

In the time it took him to realize he ought to stand and his actually doing so, Mrs. Wilcott whirled to the door and slammed it shut. With both hands.

He stood, but, she, as yet unaware of his presence, pressed her palms flat to the door and hung her head. Her shoulders shook as she whispered, "Bloody, bloody, bloody horrible—"

Thrale cleared his throat.

Without turning, she went motionless for a count of five. She straightened and faced him, perhaps not composed but with a smile of impenetrable cheer that made him want to weep. Or gnash his teeth. She gazed at him as if she had swept into the parlor expecting to find him here so that she might entertain him with weak tea and anecdotes of mind-numbing dullness.

Even he, who considered himself indifferent to her, could not help his visceral reaction to her. She was, arguably, though not by much, the most beautiful woman in England. Some men swore her younger sister outshone her. In his opinion, no.

Thrale bowed. "Madam."

One could count on Mrs. Wilcott to take command of a conversation and strip it of any particle of interest. He did not doubt that she would do so now. And, indeed, she began with a sugary smile and empty eyes. It was a talent she'd honed to deadly sharpness. She pressed her back to the door, that vacuous smile in place. Her wasted intellect was one of the great tragedies of the age. If it was true. If not, then this was farce, and he did not care to be the butt of her joke.

"Oh, it's you," she said.

"I expected Captain Niall to be joining me. Not you."

"I'm sure he's on his way." And yes, she was smiling, and he fancied her smile was rather what it would be like if Aphrodite came to life and deigned to notice a mortal man. Men lost their souls over a smile like that. He was not immune.

"No doubt."

"Yes." The word was clipped, and—could it be so? Her smile turned brittle, on the brink of shattering, and that was alarming to see her crumbling. She pressed her mouth closed as if she did not trust herself to speak. But then she did, and the words flowed. Empty of meaning. Stripped, even, of any fluctuation in emotion. She swallowed hard. Just the once. "Only a moment's delay, my lord."

"I am content to wait."

"Yes." Her smile was nothing but treacle. "You must be content to wait."

He watched with alarm as she blinked several times and drew a long slow breath. The silence went on and on, with her saying nothing. Not about the weather nor any inquiry about his health, nor a recitation of her most excellent breakfast, wasn't Sinclair's cook a genius in the kitchen? Which whoever held the position most assuredly was not.

Thrale coughed once. If this were her sister, Anne, they'd be discussing politics. If it were Mary, Lady Aldreth, he'd be having an insightful exchange about estate management. With the youngest, Miss Sinclair, God only knew. Something outrageous. He had no notion what to do with Mrs. Wilcott. They had nothing in common. "Your sister is well, I hope?"

At last, her expression smoothed out, and thank God, all was as it should be. "Very well, thank you. I shall tell her you've asked after her."

But no. All was not as it should be. The woman looked as if she were drowning on the inside. He told himself that was nonsense, that impression of his. Mrs. Wilcott had no great passion in her.

"And you, ma'am?"

She lifted her chin. "Quite well, my lord."

Silence fell again.

He had no friendship with her as he did with her sisters. No claim to her affection, nor had she any claim to his. And so he stood by his chair, mute until the quiet reminded him of the reason one gave meaningless responses to meaningless statements. Such words prevented awkwardness like this. And so, he could not fault her for empty conversation, though why, if she had lost her capacity for inanity, she did not take her leave was beyond him. Could the blasted woman not move away from the door?

Against every inclination, he said, "Is aught well?"

She let out a breath and stared at the floor. Head bowed. And then, God save him, she made a motion suggestive of a surreptitious attempt to wipe away a tear. He considered allowing them to march their separate, solitary paths. But not even he was proof against tears she did not wish him to see. Her fingers swiped her cheeks again. No. Not this. Not pity. He refused.

Her mouth quivered, and her eyes were too bright. "Yes of course." She laughed, and the sound was a perfect imitation of nothing. "I am quite well. Thank you so much for asking."

She examined the skirt of her gown, smoothing the drape, realigning the ends of the ribbon tied beneath her bosom. His way out of this damnable situation was clear. Bow and take his leave. She'd have to stop blocking his way to the door, then. As simple as that. Doubtless she'd be as glad to be quit of him as he would be to leave her here.

Except, one single drop glittered on the sooty black of her lower lashes. He watched, helpless, as it slid down her cheek. She brushed it away as she had the others. Too late for either of them to deny it.

He hadn't a reputation as a man of warmth, but he was not cold enough to leave a woman in so unhappy a state. She was a lady, and, more, the relative of men he considered friends. Besides, Anne would never forgive him if he left this room knowing her sister's despair and having done nothing for her. One had a duty to one's friends.

"Mrs. Wilcott."

She spread her arms. "My lord. As you can see, I am well."

"Yes." He filled that word with full doubt.

She blinked, and more tears balanced on her lower lashes. Save him. Please God, save him from the lurch in his chest at the sight of this woman valiantly battling for control.

"Shall I call someone? Your sister? Your maid, perhaps?"

"No." And now, she was fascinated by the floor. Her refusal to acknowledge her tears struck like an arrow to his heart. He did not want to feel sorry for her, to have his emotions knot up like this.

"Ma'am."

She turned her head, and the world tilted on its axis. Awareness shone from her eyes. Intelligence blazed there, fierce. So fierce. A woman he could have fallen madly in love with stared at him, and there were still tears. More of those bloody damned tears.

"You need not pretend," she said.

"I beg your pardon?"

"I know," she said with devastating clarity in her eyes and in her voice, in the very way she stood, "that you do not like me."

He could deny it, but she'd know it for a lie. This woman would know. He gave her a different truth instead. "I do not like the woman you pretend to be."

"There is but one of me."

Again, a crossroads loomed before him. Agree and go on as they had been. Or not. "That is not so."

"Do not be cast down, my lord. I am in perfect charity with your dislike of me. I consider it a compliment to your good taste."

He walked close enough to hand her his handkerchief, but she refused to take it. Stubborn. Where, for all that was Holy, was the woman who would have accepted a gentleman's handkerchief as if it were a prize due her? "For now, while you are not that other woman, tell me what is the matter."

She shook her head.

Thrale took a step closer and touched her cheek. He'd taken off his gloves to read because he'd expected Niall not her. His bare fingers brushed her skin, so soft. It was true. He could fuck a stupid woman as easily as any other sort. If she, a beautiful young widow, was agreeable to that, why not? "What's happened to bring you to this state?"

She did not retreat from him. She gazed at him, and he possessed no defense against this woman. None at all. He wiped another tear from her cheek, aware he was in a great deal of danger.

"My lord. I've no idea—"

"Don't." He moved closer. "Don't pretend to be a fool if you are not one. I take offense." He stayed close to her when he ought not. Because he did not want to lose this astonishing sense he was alive and on the verge of changing his life. She had chosen to show him the woman she really was because he was not like other men. Not easily fooled. Not so dazzled by her beauty that he did not care about anything else.

He brushed his fingers under her chin and was devastated by her distress, by her continued quiet regard of him. Most of all, however, was his awareness that she wasn't doing anything to make him think she did not want to explore the heat boiling between them. And that was a shocking thing. Arousing.

She tipped her chin toward him, and her smile changed. "You don't want this."

"Don't want what?" He leaned closer, their torsos mere inches apart. "For you to stop pretending? I want that more than you can imagine."

"You don't want to kiss a woman like me."

The knowledge behind those words stirred his every carnal instinct. He shifted his hand on the door until it was by her ear. "Is that a dare?"

"It is a statement of fact."

He brushed the backs of his fingers across her cheek. "You don't want to challenge me."

"Why not?"

He laughed, a low sound. Ironic. "Some of the rumors about me are true."

She tilted her head, and if she'd put her hand on his prick, he would not have been more titillated. "And yet I trust you."

"You shouldn't."

"I know what you did for Anne last season. I know what you endured." She rested the back of her head against the door.

"What has that to do with anything?"

"Everything. Shall I prove it to you?"

He laughed, entertained. Intrigued. "Please do."

She gave him a slow, heated smile that showed him a woman who had been in a man's arms and enjoyed herself whilst there. "My Lord Thrale." Her eyes went wide. "My Adonis Lord Thrale. Do whatever you like right now. Anything. I won't say no. I won't object. Do the very worst you can imagine, and I'll never tell a soul."

"They'll hear you scream."

Her mouth twitched, but he did not mistake that for scorn. "I shan't make a sound."

He kept the distance between them close. He knew damn well when he was being played, but whatever she'd heard about him, she seemed to have guessed which parts were true, and that aroused him, that she might know that about him. "If I leave marks on this pretty skin of yours, what then?"

She paled, but that was all. "Obviously, you ought not leave them where anyone but my maid will see. She is the very soul of discretion, I promise you."

"Now?"

"*Only* if you do as you like right now. This very moment." She leaned closer; pure seduction in her voice and smile. "Whatever you like."

He imagined what he might do. He imagined a great deal that he should not. He imagined her soft skin and the perfection of her face and figure, and he imagined he was the sort of swine who would take a woman like her up against the wall, even if the encounter would have been the hard, fast, fuck he liked.

He pushed away.

"Precisely," she said.

He narrowed his eyes at her, affronted by her victorious tone. "What is that to mean?"

She did not flinch at his sharp retort. "Whatever else is true about you, so is this. No matter what anyone says, I am safe with you."

"What if I'd gone ahead?"

"Why, I would have let you."

His chest tightened. "Foolish woman."

"You may think so. I believe the evidence suggests otherwise."

A door banged somewhere in the same corridor as the parlor they were in, startling them both.

A man bellowed from the corridor. Thomas Sinclair. "Where have you gone, Lucy?"

There were more footsteps.

The man shouted again. "I'd not done talking to you, you know."

Their gazes collided. She was cool and remote, and it was as if he stood before Cinderella at the stroke of midnight, because she changed back. She changed from the fascinating, aware, beguiling creature who could tell him with full irony she did not despair of his dislike of her, back to the empty-headed creature of the ballroom.

"No," he said. "No."

Sinclair continued. "Five hundred will see me through the month. Ask him. Give him that pretty smile, and he'll open his wallet for you." The man called out in that over-loud voice so common to drunks. He was coming closer, and then he was outside the door. The hardware rattled when he tried to open it, which he could not because Thrale pressed his hand to the door above Mrs. Wilcott's shoulder and leaned in.

"Your father?" Thrale said in a low voice, hand still on the door. Cynssyr said very little about his father-in-law, but he'd let slip a few words that made him think this incident was not as rare as it ought to be. "Your father is asking you to pay *his* debts?"

Color rose in her cheeks.

Her father, for that was her father, pounded on the door. "Is that where you've got to? Open the door. I'm sorry. Sorry, my girl, but there's nothing else for it. Nothing else to be done. Ask for six hundred, they'll give it you if you smile the way you do. Six hundred, and you'll have enough left to buy yourself a nice gown or two."

Thrale pushed hard on the door. He wanted to open it and tell the man to go to hell.

"It's your fault. Your fault." Sinclair said from the other side. He rattled the door. "You steered me wrong, and now you must make it right."

"Papa." That was Miss Sinclair's voice, a shade too hearty, a touch pleading, but direct. Nothing like her sister. She was not close, but not so far away, either. "Here, Papa. Allow me—"

The conversation outside devolved into an unintelligible exchange as Miss Sinclair led her father away. Mrs. Wilcott pushed his hand off the door, and he allowed himself to be moved aside, but no more than that.

"What the devil did he mean?"

Hand on the door, she bowed her head. Defeated? Aware he had seen and understood too much? "Nothing."

"Do not lie to me." He had no right to make that demand. They were not lovers. Nor friends. They were scarcely acquaintances.

She walked out, as was her right.

CHAPTER SIX

The shop door closed with a clap when Lucy swept into the bookshop. She breathed in the papery scent and was transported. The smell was almost as wonderful as the sight of floor-to-ceiling shelves of books. Her maid took a seat on a bench by the door and settled in for the customary wait.

"Mrs. Wilcott." The shopkeeper positioned a book on a sheet of the red paper he used to wrap purchases and leaned to one side to see around his customer. "Good day to you, ma'am."

"Likewise." She perused the shelves and wished she had more ready money, for here was a volume of poetry she would have bought under better circumstances. She wandered to the counter with an array of the latest fashion prints. Several issues of various ladies magazines took up the counter, most unbound and full of instructions on how a woman might perfect her appearance and properly comport herself in society. As a girl, she'd read every issue of *Le Beau Monde* and *La Belle Assemblée* from cover to cover, breathlessly absorbing the advice.

While she flipped through the pages, the shop door opened to admit Johnson. He carried himself with a familiar physical confidence. Even at the height of his fighting career, he'd never been more than nine stone, so he'd never faced any of the heavyweights in battle.

She moved away from the fashion prints to examine a book of maps, one of several on another counter. There was a new edition of *The Gazeteer* that she'd have loved to take home with her. Eventually, Johnson joined her at the counter, engrossed, one might think, in his perusal of the books there.

"Owen and Neimiah?" she said in a low voice.

"Six to one."

"Neimiah, five pounds to win." She had to wager more conservatively than she liked, but she'd take those odds. Neimiah was a small fighter, but fierce, with exemplary technique backed by strong legs. Owen relied too much on his size. Five pounds, not seven or eight or even ten because of her outlays in advance of Lord Thrale and Captain Niall's arrival at The Cooperage. No more the stark fact that the hundred pounds she'd given her father had set back her hopes for a removal.

Johnson made a tick in his notebook. "To win, then. If you're sure."

"I am. I understand Eliss and Kirkland battle Wednesday next."

"Aye. Location to be arranged." He gave the current odds, and she made the wager she'd derived from studying her information on the two prizefighters and their respective battles. So long as she did that, over time, she stayed in profits. Her strategy of caution was even more crucial now that they had the expense of a noble visitor, and her with a hundred pounds to recoup.

"Dutch Jim against Isaacs."

"Pass."

There was another difficulty arising out of having visitors who could be counted on to attend the local battles. It would be more difficult for her to see the fighters and assess their fitness and talents. Her goal, her only goal in her wagers, was to have a source of funds about which her father knew nothing. Money she'd been laying by since her return to Bartley Green.

She had, as it happened, plentiful sources of information about fighters and their battles, historical and recent. Her father subscribed to several Sporting magazines in which the results of battles were described in florid detail. She had spent six weeks updating and expanding her painstaking compilation of information about battles and outcomes, noting size and weight and the sorts of hits recorded, the number of rounds, and from those records there had emerged a set of general predictions that might be made about certain fighters.

A betting man, she'd been told, could use her figures to turn a profit. The money she won she used to pay the most pressing of the household expenses. She set aside as much as possible for the cottage where she would one day live.

She and Johnson ran through the battles set for the coming days, many of them exhibitions at the Academy—no prizes publicly offered so as not to run afoul of the law. Purses would be held separately and informally. Competitions and bouts were arranged in secrecy and on short notice so the authorities would not discover the engagements until too late to intervene. Many a time, the constabulary looked the other way on account of being in attendance themselves or being unwilling to arrest men of rank. Here in Bartley Green they'd long turned a blind eye to the goings-on. Nevertheless, one never knew.

There were battles in neighboring towns she could wager on, but she preferred to place money on engagements where she knew who was likely to officiate. Bottlemen, seconds, and timekeepers had been known to collude to affect the outcome, and worse, as with that infamous match with Dutch Jim, there had been allegations of collusion between fighters.

Lucy had no illusion the noble sport was entirely pure. She'd seen and heard too much to think anything so naive as that. For all the appreciation by admirers of a battle well fought, followers of the great sport sometimes conspired. Wherever men crowded to watch a battle, there were pickpockets, thieves, and cheats eager to send the flow of money to the illegitimate. Such was ever the case where there was money to be had.

She gave Johnson banknotes to hold for her. Having lived too many years with a father who bet with funds he did not have, she had always paid over her bets. There would be wagers aplenty at the scene, with monies held by third parties, Johnson or one of his sons, if they were local fights.

While they concluded their business, the shop door opened again. She glanced to the front. Her stomach headed to the center of the earth, for who should be holding the door but Captain Niall. Behind him were Emily, Miss Clara Glynn, and her mother. The Marquess of Thrale came in last.

Johnson moved away, and Lucy was grateful for his discretion. His livelihood depended upon the patronage of men like Mr. Glynn, Captain Niall, and the nobility. Men such as Lord Thrale.

Emily gave a delighted grin. "Lucy, see who came to call on us at The Cooperage! How fortunate that we've found you here. We were wondering where you'd got to."

"You see, Mama?" Clara headed for Lucy, too. "Lord Thrale was correct. Mrs. Wilcott is here."

Mrs. Glynn did not reply, but Lucy had no expectation of a warm greeting from the woman. There was a longstanding and mutual dislike between them. Not even Anne's marriage to a duke could erase Mrs. Glynn's dislike of Lucy. She was tolerated for the sake of her sisters.

Through the still-open shop door, she saw Roger on his feet, tail wagging, unaware he'd betrayed her presence, and ready to follow Lord Thrale anywhere. Lucy watched the tableau as if she were an onlooker and not a participant. Captain Niall made no secret of his regard for Emily. Lord Thrale and Clara Glynn made a striking couple, though no one but her and Mrs. Glynn seemed aware of that. Once the door was closed, Lord Thrale took Clara's arm, a deft method of leaving the field clear for Captain Niall. Emily, however, did not cooperate in that pairing off, for her sister walked away from the captain. Was there not to be a match between them, then?

Emily drew Lucy's arm through hers. "Did you know Roger is in love with Lord Thrale?"

"He's shameless." She refused to meet Lord Thrale's gaze.

Clara reached them. "Mrs. Wilcott, good afternoon." Her smile was too set, too determined, and Lucy was sorry Clara was in the difficult situation of displeasing her mama by being polite. She did not wish to be rude, but neither did she want Clara, who had been a friend before Lucy's marriage and was the sweetest creature to this day, to be in trouble with her mama because she refused to cut Lucy.

"I was disappointed," Clara said, "when we called at The Cooperage and found you were not at home."

Lucy did not know where to look nor what to say. If it were possible to vanish, she would have wished herself away from here. She did not care to manage with so many people. This was too complicated, her desire to be cool to Mrs. Glynn at war with her regard for Clara, and then the challenge of maintaining her drawing room smile when Emily and Clara knew better. Possibly Lord Thrale, too. Now there was a man she must keep at a distance.

Johnson slipped his betting book into his pocket and headed for the door. Lord Thrale exchanged a look with him. Yes, of course, Thrale of all people would know who he was. He'd already been to the Academy and impressed Johnson with his abilities. "He's a right Count," Johnson had told her when the subject arose. Among the Flash, a gentleman who boxed was referred to as a Count. Sometimes fondly, often not. Johnson had been too impressed for her to think he intended scorn.

"Thank you, Clara. How is your sister?"

"Very well, thank you. In her last letter, she begged that I would tell all the Sinclair sisters hullo, so you must accept this hullo from her through me."

Thrale and the others came farther in. Mrs. Glynn refused to acknowledge her beyond a curt nod in her direction. Captain Niall gave her a penetrating look that included a sweeping consideration of her person. She'd had that look from enough men not to be overly alarmed. She could imagine what he'd heard from Arthur Marsey. Nothing to her credit.

"Mrs. Wilcott." Lord Thrale bowed.

She addressed him with a degree of naturalness. "My lord. I hope Roger did not accost you."

"I was greeted with due respect." Thrale had more reason to think ill of her virtue, yet she saw no sign he had any recollection whatever of their encounter.

"No one knew where you had gone." Emily gave her hand a squeeze. "You should have told us you were walking here. We could have come together. What fun that would have been."

Mrs. Glynn was dreadfully quiet. Disdain dripped from her every pore and syllable she spoke. To Mrs. Glynn, Lucy would always be the girl who'd had her cap set at her beloved son. Mrs. Glynn would always believe Harry had made a narrow escape, no matter the truth.

Lucy locked away her anxiety. "If I had, Emily, you would not have been at home when the Glynns called."

"Oh, well." Lucy was baffled by Emily's ability to be so infernally at ease no matter the circumstances. "I am quite certain I would have insisted we should wait a while to see who might come to visit The Cooperage on such a splendid day."

Captain Niall came to stand beside Emily. Like Thrale, he glanced at the prints scattered across the tabletop. She did not care much for men who were so slender, but she had to allow his eyes were the softest brown imaginable. He had a cleft in his chin and thick hair that curled when the air turned damp, as it had now. In London, men like him filled the ballrooms and drawing rooms.

Mrs. Glynn moved to the counter to inspect the plates there, placing herself between Lucy and Captain Niall. "Is there a gown you admire, Clara?" She glanced at Captain Niall and Thrale, and no woman in all of creation could smile as warmly as Mrs. Glynn. "My daughters and I are always eager to know what fashions Miss Sinclair admires. My eldest is married now, but her letters to me beg for descriptions of our Sinclair sisters. They have always been our inspiration for all that is perfect in a woman. Is this the one?" She turned with one of the plates in hand, a dreadful gown with too much lace and not enough bodice.

"What do you make of this, Clara, my dear?" Mrs. Glynn examined the plate up close then held it at a distance. "Miss Sinclair?"

Clara smiled brightly. "Mrs. Wilcott's taste is beyond reproach, as everyone knows. May we hear your opinion?"

Emily leaned in to look at the print then gave Mrs. Glynn a narrow look. Lucy's breath caught. "Not very much, ma'am. Lucy, is there anything new in the subscription library?"

Still focused on the print, Mrs. Glynn shook her head. "I cannot declare this gown a success. It would not suit you, Clara. Nor you, Miss Sinclair, not with your coloring. If others find something in it, why, there is nothing one can say to that, is there?"

Lucy could not imagine that gown suiting anyone. It looked to have been conceived by someone with a deep dislike of the female form, and drawn and painted by someone half asleep.

"Now, Mama." Clara took the plate from her mother and returned it to the counter. "Mrs. Wilcott was not looking at any particular plate when we came in. I hope you'll tell us which, if any, of these caught your eye, Mrs. Wilcott. My sister, Mrs. Briggs, will want to know every detail."

She fixed a smile in place, for she would never want Clara to feel ignored or dismissed. "I hadn't time to look through many, and I'd not found this month's plates yet."

Mrs. Glynn shifted around other sheets that were loose on the counter then abandoned that to flip through pages in one of the magazines. "Ah. *La Belle Assemblée*. I adore this publication, don't you, Clara? So many uplifting and elevating articles."

"Yes, Mama." Clara returned Lucy's smile. "With so many new fashions, it's no wonder you hadn't the chance to assess them all. Shall we look now, Mrs. Wilcott?" She glanced over her shoulder at her mother. "I have been hoping to consult our Oracle of Fashion."

When she and her sisters had learned of Aldreth's plan to take them to London, Lucy had been the one to take charge of their wardrobes, and, as it turned out, she had a talent for fashion. Anne had given her fits, with her refusal to accept anything new.

"Come, Clara. We ought to show Lord Thrale and Captain Niall around our little bookshop."

"Yes, Mama." Her attention shifted from her mother to Lucy. "Another time, Mrs. Wilcott?"

"You've no need of advice from me."

"Come with us, Emily? And you, Mrs. Wilcott. Won't you, please?"

Mrs. Glynn made a shooing motion. "My dear Clara. Not everyone comes here for books. Let us leave fashion to those who do not care to elevate their minds."

This Lucy met with a practiced, stolid silence, though her stomach had turned into a knot. Lord Thrale cocked his head, but that contemplative expression was nothing new for him. Best if he paid her no attention at all. Her gloved fingers slid over the illustrations, happy to retreat behind the familiar engagement with fashion. It was expected of her. "Do go on, Emily."

"Shall we?" Captain Niall held out both arms, one to Emily, the other to Clara. Mrs. Glynn beamed at him.

Thrale came nearer to where Lucy stood, close enough that she breathed in the scent of his cologne. Was that ambergris? She closed her eyes. Very pleasant. Behind her closed eyes, she saw him as he had been in the second parlor. Leaning over her with that wicked, carnal smile. He was built along the same lines as her late husband, as she could not help noticing. If he boxed, and if, as Johnson claimed, he was not without skill, then this was no soft man.

"Which frock were you admiring?" Thrale sounded as if her answer mattered, which was rather sweet of him. She pulled her thoughts from wondering what would have happened if he'd taken up her dare. Would they have ended up skin to skin?

"All of them, of course."

While she'd been entertaining wicked thoughts of Lord Thrale, Captain Niall had detoured and brought over Emily and Clara. They crowded around the counter, looking at fashion prints. Emily sidled away and that left Captain Niall beside her.

"What, all of them?" Captain Niall said.

Mrs. Glynn's smile was a veneer of cheer over scorn a mile

deep.

"Even this one?" He pointed to the print of the dreadful gown Mrs. Glynn had picked up.

No. Not that one. The words stuck in her throat. He was standing beside her, his upper arm practically touching her shoulder. She edged away from the contact.

He tapped another of the prints. "Do ladies not consider whether a frock suits them? I think no. Fashion is all. This gown because it is new and in the current season's colors."

Let him think what he liked. He cocked his head at her, and Lucy could not deny that he was attractive. Men like him did not appeal. He was too slender. Too polished.

Captain Niall leaned a hip against the counter and took up the print. "It seems to me, Mrs. Wilcott, that a woman either admires a frock because it would suit her or she does not, because it would not."

Emily, who had all this time been examining the fashion plates herself, had been listening avidly, since she said, "As if a woman could not admire a gown that looked well on someone else. Honestly, Captain Niall, do you mean to say a woman only cares for that which suits her, all else be dashed?"

Clara took the print from Captain Niall. "Here is the proper test. What do you think, Mrs. Wilcott? Does this gown meet with your approval?"

Responding to Clara was no difficulty at all, thank goodness. "One may admire a gown without believing it would suit one."

"In that event," Captain Niall said with that brilliant, joyous smile of his. "You must admire all gowns, Mrs. Wilcott."

What a nonsensical thing to say. "Why is that?"

His smile softened, and that was a shocking thing, that he would look at her that way when he'd come here because of Emily. "Why, because it is impossible to think you would be anything but perfection itself, whatever you wear."

The pinpoint of dread over what Arthur Marsey had told him blossomed.

CHAPTER SEVEN

Thrale reached in and took the print from Captain Niall, giving him a dry look as he did. He wanted to take the man by the shoulders and give him a good hard shake. "I should think, Niall, that you would know better than to interrogate a fashionable woman on the subject of fashion."

"Who better to ask?" Niall shrugged, but he wasn't stupid. He'd eyes in his head. A brain beneath that thick pate. Mrs. Glynn's dislike of Mrs. Wilcott was no secret to anyone. Niall had no business stirring that pot. If he thought those words would impress Mrs. Wilcott, then Niall understood her even less than he did himself.

Miss Sinclair picked up another of those blasted prints. "I rather like this one. What do you think, Clara?"

He hoped Niall felt the ice in Miss Sinclair's words, for he deserved to pay for his careless words.

The young lady's odious mother laughed. "By all means let us hear from our oracle on the matter." The woman examined the plate, then looked at Miss Sinclair from over the top of the page.

Mrs. Wilcott had that abstracted expression again. There might not be a thought in her head for all the life there was on her face. How many times had he seen that exact reaction from her and taken it for disinterest? She moved away, nearer another counter where there were no bloody, be-damned, fashion plates. "Miss Glynn looks very well in greens and blues, as I am sure you are well aware." She gave them a smile so cheerful it hurt his soul.

She went on. "How fortunate. This month's colors are apple green, primrose, apricot, and blackberry. However, neither Miss

Glynn or my sister need my advice. Their taste is impeccable."

"Thank you." Clara curtsied.

Emily rolled her eyes when she thought only her sister was looking. Mrs. Wilcott retreated farther yet, and it was only because he'd begun to pay attention that he knew she felt the tension.

Miss Sinclair put one hand to her bosom and waved the other beneath her chin. "I do not know about you, but I live in horror of any gentleman or nobleman proposing that we ladies adorn our forms in clothing we do not like merely because the color is *au courant*. That, Captain Niall, is my nightmare."

Niall bowed and winked at the company. "It is my wish that all ladies adorn themselves in a manner best suited to their forms."

Mrs. Glynn simpered. "My dear Captain, we shall endeavor to ensure she does."

Miss Sinclair was not smiling. Nor was Miss Glynn. Thrale looked at Mrs. Wilcott, but she'd walked away, and now her attention was locked on the books stacked on another of the counters. She had her elbow on the counter and her hand pressed to her mouth. Whether that was to hide a smile was impossible to say.

Miss Sinclair marched to her sister and left Niall to contemplate his setback. "Shall we see what new books have arrived since last we were here? Miss Glynn?"

The longing Mrs. Wilcott sent the book she'd been looking through was by far the most genuine emotion he'd seen from her since they'd come in. She closed the book, newly bound from the shine of the leather, and swept her fingers over the gold lettering on the cover. "Yes, let's."

"I hope there are new novels," said Miss Glynn as the three strolled to the shelves without Niall. "There were none when I was here last week. Do you believe it, I'd read them all?"

"Does that mean you have finished *The Lost Heiress?*" Miss Sinclair bumped shoulders with Miss Glynn. "You did say you'd lend it me when you had."

"I'll send it over. You'll never read a more thrilling story in your life, I promise you. The Count of Diomanti is too horrible. I could not sleep for thinking he was on his way to Bartley Green, all the way from Tuscany."

Thrale examined the volume that had so absorbed Mrs. Wilcott. *The Gazetteer.* He flipped through the pages. The volume was full of maps and pages that listed the names of cities and other notable locations the world over, each with a description and other details about that locale. Hardly fascinating for a woman who cared only for fashion.

"What a pity it is, "Mrs. Glynn said, "when a woman neglects her mind. Do you not agree, my lord?"

"Hm?" He unfolded one of the large engravings included and compared the map to the locations described. The young ladies, including Mrs. Wilcott, were now examining the shelves of newly arrived books. Many were still in the blue-gray boards of books shipped unbound.

"My Clara," Mrs. Glynn said, "has had all the very best tutors. She speaks Italian, German, and French, she draws, sings like an angel, and plays the piano-forte. I insisted that she learn mathematics, history, and the natural world."

He left the map open. "Miss Glynn is an accomplished young woman."

Mrs. Glynn sent a sour look in Mrs. Wilcott's direction. "Clara understands more than fashion, I promise you that. She is not the sort of young lady one finds in London, one who cares for her appearance above all else that is proper."

"I confess myself unable to agree that only women become obsessed with fashion."

Her gaze slid to Mrs. Wilcott. The Oracle of Fashion. Yes, that was what he knew of her, and it did not fit the woman who'd as much as dared him to take her up against the wall. She continued. "Among women of a certain ilk we find an unhappy lack of education and refinement."

"Are there not men in whom we might observe the same imbalance?" He had himself had little formal education. His father had either engaged tutors who did not care whether their charge learned anything a'tall, or engaged one who did and failed to timely pay him. The damned vicar had done more to educate him than his father had.

"Hear, hear, Lord Thrale," Miss Sinclair said from the other side of the shop. "Lucy, do help us find something to read. I feel the need to improve my mind."

Thrale held up *The Gazetteer.* "Here is a worthy volume. Full of facts to improve any mind, as Mrs. Wilcott will no doubt confirm for us."

Mrs. Glynn snorted, but everyone, even her daughter, ignored her. Niall had found a sheaf of sporting prints and was examining them while watching the ladies when he thought he was not observed.

"Pray my lord, watch the map." Mrs. Wilcott took a step forward. "The page will tear."

Indeed, the map he'd been examining was not properly refolded into the book. He placed the book on the counter and folded the map to its creases. "There. Disaster averted."

"My sister is mad about maps."

More than a hint of panic shadowed Mrs. Wilcott's features. "I'm sure I am not. One worries about damaging a book for which one has not paid."

Miss Glynn coughed gently. "We ought to have dancing at Withercomb Hall. What do you think, Mama? It's been an age since we have had dancing anywhere but at the Bartley Green assembly. Harry is home, you know, so we will have extra gentlemen for once."

"An excellent idea." Mrs. Glynn clasped her hands. "You must have a new gown, of course, Clara. Is there one here that you like?"

At this, both the younger women returned to the prints. Miss Sinclair summoned her sister with an imperious glance. "Come help us decide, oh Oracle of Fashion."

Perhaps, Thrale thought, Niall had a point.

Mrs. Wilcott replaced the book she'd been paging through with rapt attention and returned to the prints. "If there is to be dancing at so elegant a home as Withercomb, then here is something that will look well on you, Emily. Gauze sleeves, gold tassels—" She sorted through the plates. "Violet silk would suit."

"Violet? Oh dear, no." Mrs. Glynn leaned over her shoulder. "That is not a color for this season. Not a'tall. What do you think, Captain Niall? My Lord Thrale?"

Thrale knew better than to reply to such a question with any degree of specificity. "I know nothing of ladies' fashion and have no opinion of purple."

"Violet," Mrs. Wilcott said, still searching among the plates.

"Does it matter whether a gown is purple or lilac or violet?" Niall walked to the counter and stared at the prints. He rested a hand on Mrs. Wilcott's shoulder. Under cover of reaching for another print, she moved away from Niall. "Or any other color so long as it looks well?"

"There is something to that." Emily leaned in, too. "That's your color, Lucy."

"This for you, Emily. And for Miss Glynn, perhaps this one?" She held up a plate. "Brussels lace, I think. And not so many flowers here." She pointed to the hem.

"I like that gown exceedingly."

Mrs. Wilcott gave Miss Glynn an assessing look. "Yes, yes. Have you slippers that will do?"

"I believe so, Mrs. Wilcott."

Mrs. Wilcott put a finger on the plate in question. "This gown, I submit, has just such a pleasing confluence, with the alterations I have suggested. Provided one pays the proper attention to execution, that gown, in violet, would be an excellent addition to most any woman's wardrobe."

Mrs. Glynn coughed delicately. "Violet will not suit anyone this season. Pale green for you, Clara. And for you, Miss Sinclair—" She touched Emily's cheek. "Sky blue would suit, I declare it absolutely."

"Here is a gown that will look divine on my sister." Mrs. Wilcott found the print she meant. Thrale again found himself attempting to reconcile this quiet, uninteresting beauty with the woman who had looked at him and seen more than he liked. "I've a particular shade of blue in mind. Some of the trim here." She pointed. "The hem ought to be reduced for a young lady who is not tall."

Miss Sinclair leaned in to look. "What do you think, Captain?" she asked with a sly grin. "In your opinion, which of us will it suit?"

Niall moved closer. "I must suppose that you would look beautiful in anything you choose to wear."

"A philosophy without flaw," Mrs. Wilcott murmured.

Niall laughed. "I can offer no more cogent opinion than that, I fear. Though I daresay, it is enough."

"Quite enough, Captain Niall," said Mrs. Glynn. "We women, even those of a lower rank, must strive to impress the opposite gender by all possible means. A gentleman need only know whether he admires a young lady or not."

"A gentleman hasn't the need to fuss about his clothes," Miss Sinclair said.

"You've never heard of Brummel, then?" Niall opened his arms wide. "As I hope you will agree, I am a devotee. What say you, Thrale?"

Mrs. Glynn settled a hand over her upper chest. "You are masculine perfection, sir. No improvement necessary."

He lowered his hands. "Ah, but what is the opinion of the woman who knows all of fashion. Mrs. Wilcott?"

She gave him a serene gaze and said not a word.

Miss Sinclair filled the silence. "One can say nothing that is not to your credit, sir."

"Thank you, miss." He bowed.

"In my experience," Mrs. Wilcott said with her attention on the prints, "gentlemen are rarely aware of the precise reasons for their admiration of a lady, while ladies of any age are aware of the importance of detail and understand the necessity of a toilette that results in myriad details converging into a pleasing whole."

Niall plucked the fashion-plate from Mrs. Wilcott's hands. He walked to the shopkeeper. "The ladies must have their patterns of perfection. And you, Miss Glynn and Miss Sinclair. Do chose what you mayn't live without. Our night of passionate dancing must be one without flaw."

"How very kind of you, Captain Niall." Mrs. Glynn bent a knee. "Beyond kind."

Not to be outdone, Thrale laid a banknote before the shopkeeper. "Ladies, while we are here, is there a book you'd like? I would be pleased indeed if you allowed me to purchase something for each of you. So that you will have the continued improvement of your intellect as well as your wardrobes. A novel, if you like. Or poetry or some other uplifting work."

"Clara will have a book of sermons." Mrs. Glynn fixed the shopkeeper with a stern look. "Have you something improving for a young lady's mind?"

"I enjoy novels." Emily tugged on one of her gloves. "Don't you, Lucy?"

"Oh, lah, Miss Sinclair," said Mrs. Glynn. "You are a lively, intelligent young lady. You may well enjoy a range of works. Not every woman is as accomplished as you, nor does every woman enjoy the benefits of reading."

"Beauty," Niall pronounced, "Needs no improvement."

"Lucy reads vastly more than I."

Mrs. Wilcott stared at nothing at all. But her cheeks were pinker than they had been moments ago.

Miss Sinclair pointed at the other counter. "Lucy would adore that book. The one Lord Thrale was looking at."

Niall picked it up and shook the pages hard enough that one of the maps came partially unfolded. "A dashed bore, I say. This is the sort of reading to put a man to sleep at any time of day."

Thrale cocked his head. "Come, ladies, if you will not have a novel, then permit me to choose something for you. A volume of poetry, perhaps?"

Miss Glynn shot a glance at her mother and then at Mrs. Wilcott. "*The Ghost of Monkston Parish* is a thrilling read. You might enjoy that, Mrs. Wilcott, for I know I did. I saw as well a copy of *The Mad Man of the Mountains.*"

Miss Sinclair draped an arm around Miss Glynn's shoulder. "*Mad Man of the Mountains?* I think I should like that very much. Either sounds delightful."

Mrs. Wilcott returned his tilt of the head and softly said, because she meant it for Miss Glynn and her sister's ears alone, "We've only begun to look for something to read, and already he says Dunne."

Miss Sinclair stifled a laugh and pointed to *The Gazeteer.* "Were you not looking at *that* book, Lucy?" She went to the counter and plucked the book from the stack. "It's full of maps, Lucy. You adore maps."

"Maps?" Mrs. Glynn laughed. "Oh, gracious, I do not think so, Miss Sinclair. A novel is more to her sensibilities."

This was intolerable, the woman's constant digs at Mrs. Wilcott. "If no one wishes to have the *Mad Man,* then I shall have it." To the shopkeeper he said, "The sermons, please. All four volumes of the other. Pope for you, Mrs. Glynn? I assure you, you will find much inspiration in the pages."

"So generous of you."

"Miss Glynn, when you have read from your sermons, I shall expect you to tell me your favorites."

Miss Glynn curtsied while her mother beamed at him. "She will be delighted to, milord."

Before long, Thrale's additional purchases were wrapped in red paper and securely bound with heavy twine. Doubtless Mrs. Wilcott would have preferred to return to The Cooperage by herself. He could not blame her for that if she did.

Roger trotted beside him the entire way.

CHAPTER EIGHT

Despite the modest size of The Cooperage, two rooms had been allocated to Thrale's use; a bedchamber and an anteroom with a writing desk, a small table, and an armchair set before the hearth. Flint was quartered above stairs, but, true to pattern, he'd come down in advance of Thrale's rising. This Thrale knew without leaving the warmth of his sheets because the fire had been brought up. When he entered the anteroom, Flint handed him his morning tea, prepared precisely to his taste.

Steam rose from his cup while he gave himself a quick wash, heedless of the cold water in the basin. The fire was up in here, too, but he never minded the morning damp unless it was dead of winter. Flint handed him a plate of rolls, fresh from the kitchen. He carried both tea and rolls to the window. Not wearing a stitch of clothing, he sipped his tea and ate two rolls with butter and jam while the sky brightened.

The view from his window was striking. The rear of the property followed a gentle downhill toward a river. In the distance was a meadow surrounded by more trees. Across the river, a hill blocked a view of Aldreth's property. The Cooperage, he decided, was not much like its name. Plenty of trees and cover for game, that pretty river for fishing and pastimes to delight the country Squire. The house might be small, but it was well tended inside and out.

A vision rolled over him, so vivid he paused with his tea halfway to his mouth; him at Blackfern listening to children racing up and down the stairs, knowing that somewhere in the house was the mother of those children. His wife, for the children were his, and he was much satisfied with that state of affairs. As if he'd ever been satisfied with anything at Blackfern. The Cooperage had been like that once, with Sinclair and his wife, and four girls.

He drank more tea, unsettled by the images and the clench in his chest. The house was silent, with most of the inhabitants abed. In his limited experience, young ladies were rarely early risers. They'd not be up anytime soon. There were but two Sinclair women in the house, and neither of them would race up and down the stairs.

Niall wouldn't be stirring for hours, and he didn't yet know what hours Sinclair kept, which meant he would have welcome time to himself. With Johnson and his Academy, there was excellent fighting and better training. Considering he now had several upcoming engagements at the Academy, he needed to keep his wind.

"I'll have a breather this morning." By which he meant, a half-speed training run. "Then see who's stirring."

Behind him, Flint went about the business of getting him dressed for his morning's exertions. "Good weather for an outing, if I do say so myself. Not too warm, cold enough to keep you moving, milord."

"Yes." He stepped into his small clothes.

"Good battles to be seen whilst you are here, milord."

"I'm devising excuses now." Sinclair would understand if Thrale begged off certain engagements in order to be at the Academy or some remote location for a battle. In the case of a battle, Sinclair would surely be with him.

"I heard a rumor you'll find interesting." Flint handed him clothes as they were needed. Stockings, his fighting britches, with no fall and but two buttons at the waistband, a shirt. He blessed the day he'd taken the duke's suggestion that he hire the man.

"The rumor?"

"Clancy versus Granger."

"That's not news." He yanked his shirt down a tad too hard. Anyone who followed the sport of pugilism would do murder to be here if that fight came off. "The Flash have been filling the villages for miles around in the hope it's not just talk."

Flint tapped the side of his nose. "Before the end of the month."

"Gad." He sat to put on his shoes. Flint set them on the floor for him. In three week's time, then. "Any truth to that?"

"I heard it from one of the prizefighters at the Academy. He swore Clancy has increased his training."

Johnson had not said a word about a battle like that, but then the final details of some of the greatest matches had been closely held secrets until the last possible moment. "I'd move heaven and earth to see that battle."

"Indeed, sir." Flint pressed a hand to his heart. "Who would not?"

"Remind me to send letters to the usual set." The duke would want to know. Aldreth, too, and if he failed to inform Bracebridge, why, he'd never hear the end of it.

"Milord."

Five minutes later, Thrale stepped into the morning air and set out in the direction of the river, not at top pace, but a brisk one. He saw no reason not to make double use of this morning's route. He'd use the outing to make a study of the water where Sinclair had promised good fishing.

All thoughts of fishing or glorious battles between heavy-weights were dead by the time he'd left the immediate grounds for the well-worn path to the river. His recent lapse in training cost him. His breather became less than half-pace, and more effort than it ought to be. Long before he reached the river, his thighs and lungs were in revolt.

His planned walk along the bank to study the river enforced a welcome break. There was good water here, with shade and vegetation that suggested Sinclair's boast of good fishing had been no boast at all. As he walked, he saw more than one likely spot. One of them had fat trout just waiting for him to return with pole and creel.

He came around a corner and was no longer alone.

A woman sat on an outcropping of rock that overlooked the kind of shaded, quiet water that promised excellent sport. He recognized the hound at her side, its head on her lap. If he'd known he would find her here, he would never have come round that corner, but there she was, Mrs. Wilcott and her elderly dog, and she had seen him. Too late to feign that he had not noticed her.

It was a rare occasion when he was at a loss as he was now. He'd behaved badly with her. Beyond anything a lady ought to tolerate from a gentleman. If Cynssyr or Aldreth were to find out what he'd said and done and thought, he'd be deciding between a meeting at dawn or one in the chapel.

He bowed, once, guilty of relief that his state of undress provided an excuse to avoid her. She remained where she was. Her dog stayed on its stomach, ears forward, at attention.

"Forgive me, ma'am. I did not mean to intrude." He remembered how she'd cut Marsey dead, and he prepared himself for a similar response.

"You are in training, I take it." While she did not avert her gaze, neither did she look at him.

"I am."

"The hill there." She pointed to her left where the land rose. "There is a path to the top recommended by many of the fighters."

What did a woman know of such things? He bowed again, cautious, yet with a drop of hope that he'd been forgiven. "Thank you for that information."

She considered him dispassionately. Her aloofness now was a better result than the cold steel of her reaction to Marsey, and more than he deserved for what he'd said and done. "If you wish to increase your wind and your bottom, a five times repetition of that hill is said to be most efficacious."

"Indeed?"

Her dog thumped its tail on the rock. "You'll realize great benefits to the large muscles of your legs, as well."

"Is that so?"

Her cheeks pinked up, and her expression smoothed out in that so familiar look of abstraction. "I've heard, that is."

"Thank you for the advice." He could not presume forgiveness. He was Thrale. And a guest in her household. She might well feel she must extend an olive branch against her private inclination. Very well then. If he was not forgiven, he would accept peace.

"If you're in training, you'll want to spar with Mr. Glynn. Were you introduced at the assembly? If you've not met him, no doubt you soon will. The Glynns are one of the leading families of Bartley Green. He is a member of Johnson's Academy. A true gentleman, I assure you."

He heard the irony this time. Undeniable. "Already I've heard the name."

"A neighbor of ours." She glanced away. "They live five or six miles east of The Cooperage."

"I will be glad to know him better."

She hesitated, and Thrale waited her out while she considered what she would say. Nothing, as yet, which surprised him not at all, considering his offense.

"Mrs. Wilcott." He spoke with deliberation so that she would hear, he prayed, the sincerity of his apology. "I beg your forgiveness. You need say nothing in response, just know I am aware of my transgression with you and deeply regret that I behaved in so ungentlemanly a manner. It will not happen again."

"Thank you." She rested a hand on Roger's shoulder. "I suppose."

What the devil did she mean by that?

She stood with languorous care. "Harry Glynn was born dexter-handed. Though he was forced to change that preference, I have observed that he never lost his facility. If you step into the ring with him, he's a good right. Don't discount that, but watch for his left."

He'd no idea what to make of this conversation. None whatever. These details of Mr. Glynn's abilities were so specific that he wondered, stupidly, absurdly, if she could have seen Glynn fight.

Impossible, that. The better explanation was that, with sporting men here with such frequency, even ladies must hear conversations that were not entirely proper.

"Thank you for that information."

She patted the side of her leg. "Roger." The dog went to her. "You are welcome. My lord."

Thus far, the weather had been their most controversial discussion, and here they were speaking of training and another man's fighting habits. Belatedly, he realized she was not merely repeating what she'd overheard knowledgeable men say. "Your father has taught you something of the science, I take it."

"My father? No." Her fingers smoothed along the dome of the dog's head, and she focused all her attention there. In these past days he'd learned to watch for minute changes of expression that gave away her true state. What he saw now was the kind of sorrow from which one never recovered. "My husband."

CHAPTER NINE

Her husband. Thrale did not know if he ought to follow that fascinating trail or leave it be. The subject of Mrs. Wilcott's husband was nothing short of mystery, and he was curious beyond what was proper. "He was a Sporting man?"

"After a fashion, yes."

While he was not yet willing to conclude he was forgiven, his measure of hope grew. Any confidence from her about her late husband must be taken as a sign that she did not despise him. "This explains much. Mr. Wilcott was a student of the art, I take it."

She smiled, and that distracted him. "There was very little on the subject he did not know. I could not help but learn a thing or two myself."

How odd that pugilism would prove a common ground for them. "I ought to have asked the bookseller if he has Wilcott's great treatise on the subject. You might like a copy for yourself. Mine has pride of place in my library, though if your husband was a student as you say then he would have had a copy as well."

"He did."

Now there was a coincidence, that Mrs. Wilcott's husband shared a surname with the writer of the finest treatise ever written on the subject of pugilism. Aside from that concordance, there was no reason for her to care about a St. Giles-born fighter and scrivener, but he found himself unable to let the subject drop. "Perhaps you know the author was a prizefighter himself. By the name of Jack Wilcott."

Her fingers paused in their stroking of Roger's head, then resumed. "Yes."

The name Wilcott wasn't uncommon, but if her husband had been a Sporting man and the treatise had been in her home as well, she would have remarked the surname she and her husband shared with Jack Wilcott.

"Six foot six," he said. He came closer, but not, he hoped, so close as to offend. "Arms like trees. Never a better student of the science. They called him—"

"Devil." Her frock was white sprigged with lilac. Nothing spectacular. This was a gown to wear when one did not expect admiration. The woman made it spectacular.

As a young wife, had she felt it was her duty to read Wilcott's treatise because her husband held the subject in esteem? That was not the action of a woman whose marriage had been unhappy. "You are familiar with the work, then."

"I am." This she said with a smile, not a grimace. He could not conclude she had read the book unwillingly.

"Devil because as a boy he sold matches near London Bridge."

"He didn't, though." She brushed her skirts with both hands. "That was the story he told, but he was the tenth of eleven children from a farm in Cornwall. He made up the story about the matches in the hope he'd be called Lucifer."

"Did he now?" He crossed his arms over his chest. Plainly, she had read parts of Wilcott's treatise, but not all, since the story of the author's life in St. Giles was scattered throughout the work. Had she read to the end, she'd know the entire story of Jack Wilcott's life.

A smile flashed at the edges of her mouth, not the least coy. The tedium of their previous conversations was gone with this discovery of a shared interest. "He was never anywhere near London Bridge until long after he ran away to fight. I suspect the nearest he got to London Bridge was the Five Courts."

Five Courts being London's premier location for exhibitions and battles of pugilism. Wilcott had fought there many times. As to Wilcott's birthplace, that was definitively documented and recorded in writings too numerous to name. There could be no dispute.

"The history of his career is well known, ma'am. Jack, The Devil, Wilcott grew up in St. Giles where he sold matches and brawled on the streets until the day someone told him he ought to fight for prize money."

"Yes." She walked off the rock, the dog at her heels. Thrale moved forward to help her to firmer ground. Her fingers tightened around his hand. He was too aware of the state of his undress, she, however, seemed not the least concerned. When she reached the path, she released his hand. "Thank you, my lord."

"Ma'am."

She glanced at the sky. He braced himself for a remark on the promise of rain. "He did not write the entire truth." Her attention returned to him, and he was caught unprepared by her sharp focus. "He wasn't less of a fighter because he came from Cornwall and not St. Giles."

"No." Was he charmed by her provably wrong beliefs? He thought he might be. She looked at him full on, and his breath caught. The woman before him was not the woman he'd known in London. This woman was formidable.

"Anyone who knew him heard the truth in his voice." She took a few steps away from the bank. "He was no more from St. Giles than you or I."

"Every word written of his life prior to his taking up the art says otherwise. Including his own, ma'am." They stood close since she'd not moved far from him after he'd escorted her to the path. He ought to put some distance between them.

She waved a hand in her familiar, lazy, manner, as if it cost her everything to move even that much. And yet, there was nothing of that enervation in her words. "The story suited him."

Very well then. "Why?"

"At the time he published, he had business affairs he wished to succeed."

He considered that for several seconds; her certainty about facts no one could know without having known Wilcott himself. The unusual, for her, assurance.

No. Surely, not. He wracked his brain for any information he might have heard about her late husband and came up with nothing. Even her sister the duchess had said next to nothing about Mrs. Wilcott's marriage, other than to imply it had not been a happy one. It was inconceivable that this woman, a lady born and raised, had been married to a prizefighter.

"For all that he was lowborn, there was never anyone more aware of the importance of reputation than him." She smiled, and he could not get his bearings. Impossible. "He used to say he lied like the Devil Himself to avoid being called The Farmer."

"Your husband was Jack Wilcott." The words came out hard. Incredulous. An accusation.

Her expression stayed smooth, and he saw it now for a hard-won defense. "He was."

"Jack Wilcott. The Devil?" Wilcott had been a great battler. A warrior. Among the best. Strong, fast, determined he would not lose no matter whom he faced. It was said upwards of a million pounds sterling had been wagered on his last battle.

"Yes."

Over the course of his career, Jack Wilcott had turned his winnings into a fortune. He'd a knack for investment, it seemed. In his fighting prime, he opened his Atheneum and penned the first of various writings on pugilism, its history, its notable battlers, and then the work that had made his name golden to lovers of the art. A combination of all his writings into a comprehensive history and a guide to techniques for the modern fighter.

During that great match, it had looked as though The Devil would lose for the first time in his career, he'd taken so many terrible blows. In the fiftieth round, he'd struck his opponent a nobber that dropped the man to his knees, and then another to his face, and that was the end. A convincing victory.

Afterward, there were rumors the timekeeper had been bribed

and that one of the referees had been paid to throw the match to Wilcott's opponent, or that The Devil Himself had been paid to lose. Whatever the truth, three days later, Jack, the Devil, Wilcott was dead of the injuries he'd suffered during the battle. His name was celebrated among the Sporting set and revered among those who knew their fighting history. He made a fortune with his fists and hands, but one thing Jack Wilcott had never been, and could never have been, was a gentleman.

"Jack Wilcott. The owner of the Atheneum Sporting Arena and the author of *Wilcott's Guide?*"

"The very same." She replied without inflection, and yet there was something there in those words, some note of ironic comment.

He cast back in his memory for details about her marriage and came up blank. He was stunned. Horrified. Repelled. This delicate woman, a lady born, had married a prizefighter? No wonder her family never talked about a marriage so far beneath her. No wonder Arthur Marsey had behaved as he had when he saw Jack Wilcott's widow at the Bartley Green assembly.

Had she eloped? She must have. The scandal must have been unspeakable.

"There are newer books now," she said. "It's only men who are mad about the science who know his name."

His thoughts spun in his head. Devil Wilcott had married a lady and taken her to his bed? "I saw him fight once."

Her face lit up. "Did you?"

That smile. Pure joy. Did she have no understanding of her ruin? Wilcott had been his age, or a very few years younger. Eight or ten years older than she. "Near Blackfern. He was a young man at the time. Just starting out."

"That must have been his battle against Bill Ramsey."

"Yes."

She plucked a leaf from a willow tree and folded it over and over until it could be folded no more. "Devil won that thirty seconds into the fifteenth. A ribber, a facer, and then a nobber, very fast, and

Ramsey went down."

"How is it I never heard your husband was *that* Jack Wilcott?" The question burst from him, inappropriate. Incapable of response. Of course, she would not speak of it. One simply did not.

She shrugged. "We Sinclairs have agreed silence is the wisest course."

"How did you meet?" Appalled that he'd given voice to his curiosity, he lifted a hand, palm out. "Your pardon again, that was unforgivably rude."

"He came to Bartley Green when Johnson opened the Academy. For the first exhibitions. He and Papa struck up an acquaintance, as sporting men will do."

"Ah." Her dog ambled to him and pressed against his leg. He crouched down and rubbed his ears. He could not imagine Thomas Sinclair inviting a prizefighter to his home nor introducing a lowborn man to his daughter. What sort of girl had she been to have met and run away with Devil Wilcott? He kept his gaze on the dog. Had he not heard from someone that Mrs. Wilcott's husband had paid her father's not inconsiderable debts? Had not the duchess implied that her sister had married to save the family from a notorious ruin?

Her pleasant smile never changed, and he was both chilled and impressed to see her so adept at disguising her feelings. "We were married soon after."

"I see."

"Roger was his dog." That was affection in her words. She adored the animal, that was plain to anyone with eyes. "Devil took great pleasure in owning a dog like him. They were both mongrels, he said."

Thrale watched her walk away from the river and failed, again, to match the woman he thought she was—vain and scatterbrained— with this woman. A few feet from him, she turned, and their gazes met. His heart twisted again. What was he to do with the knowledge that she'd been married to a prizefighter? That she had kept her late husband's dog? That she maintained an acquaintance with her husband's associates?

"You'll find the gentlemen who train with Johnson have excellent technique. He'd not accept anything less of them, but Mr. Glynn is the best of them."

"Thank you for the information."

She laughed, and his breath caught. "You cannot imagine what facts are stuck here in my head. I am as Flash a woman as any man."

"I cannot doubt you." Jack Wilcott. Good God.

She curtsied, still with that devastating, empty smile. He could understand any man falling in love with her; young, old, or infirm. But what made a young lady of good family fall in love with the likes of Devil Wilcott? "Last month, Dutch Jim was seen to be drunk the morning of his battle with Nate Booker—"

"You saw that battle?"

She shook her head. "Johnson told me. Dutch Jim's state that morning was a sham to sway the odds. His second, the timekeeper, and several compatriots between them, lay down five hundred pounds and came away a winner at ten-to-one odds."

Astonishing, this, having with her the sort of conversation he only ever had with men. "One hears of such things."

"Indeed, my lord, a disgrace to the art." She curtsied. All very proper. You'd never look at her and think, *here is a woman who has ruined herself beyond redemption.* "Now, I've taken enough time from your training. You'll grow too cold if you stand much longer so ill-dressed for inactivity."

"One question for you, if you will."

She quirked an eyebrow at him.

"Clancy versus Granger before the month is out. True?"

"All but settled."

"Clancy's been training here?"

Another smile flitted over her mouth. "He has been."

"I thank you, madam." He bowed, and, as he watched her walk away, he remained unable to reconcile the fact of her marriage to Devil Wilcott to anything he'd ever believed of her.

CHAPTER TEN

Lucy stared at the book sitting atop her dresser. This was Emily's doing. There was no other way for *The Gazeteer* to have made the journey all the way from the bookshop in Bartley Green to her room. No one else would have thought of purchasing this book for her. For all her headstrong ways, Emily was generous to a fault. Her sister's gesture was beyond thoughtful. She owed Emily a long, hard embrace and heartfelt thanks.

With her Milton in Lord Thrale's continued possession, *The Gazeteer* would provide her hours of enjoyment. She not always been an avid reader. As a girl, anything but. Their governess had despaired of her reading without constant prodding. She was ashamed, now, of her failure to apply herself. The one exception in her lack of educational success was her fascination with maps and globes. In this one arena, she had excelled.

With a fond smile for her sister's generosity, Lucy opened to the flyleaf, enjoying the sound and feel of the leather binding and the crisp, newly cut pages.

There was an inscription. Arrogant black ink dominated the page.

Not in her sister's hand.

Not signed by Emily.

MRS. WILCOTT—

MAY YOU HAVE MUCH ENJOYMENT FROM THE MAPS.

YRS, THRALE

She slammed the book closed, but the words she'd read continued to accuse. She could see the bold strokes of the letters still.

The Sinclair family had achieved a balance of sorts by never speaking of painful subjects. The loss of their mother so many years ago. The rarity of their father's sobriety. How the house had been stripped of objects that could be sold for ready money. Merchants and tradesmen seeking payment. The fact that she was responsible for Anne being forced to marry the duke. Her marriage.

She should never have told him about Devil. Never. But she'd encountered him at a time when she'd been feeling the loneliness of her widowhood. Devil, for all his faults, and hers as well, had been her husband. They'd had a difficult beginning, yet had found physical satisfaction together. There were times she missed that dreadfully.

Peace between them had come only after Devil's discovery of her research into his livelihood. He'd stood there with her pages and pages of compiled matches in hand, and he had so plainly studied what she'd done. His silence had terrified her. And then he'd said, "According to this, I don't do as well against a left-handed fighter."

"You don't."

"I'll have to do something about that, then."

"You ought to, sir."

His acceptance had transformed her life. They'd become close, but this had changed everything. Everything. His reserve with her vanished even from their intimacy. He'd made her pulse race, and she hoped, believed, knew in her heart, that she had learned to do that for him. She missed Devil's physicality. She missed having someone to talk to, to listen to, to listen to her.

In the middle of a moment when she'd been missing the physical closeness of her marriage, Lord Thrale had come along the river path. A pugilist in serious training—that had been her first thought, for no man who wasn't serious about his fighting condition had a body like his or went out in the early morning on a breather. When she saw him, she'd thought, foolishly, with bittersweet longing, *here is someone who will understand what I lost.*

Too late for circumspection. She was forever bared to him be-cause she could never take back her disclosures. Because of her indiscretion, Lord Thrale knew more about her than anyone still living. Including her sisters. How foolish she'd been, telling him about her husband, conversing with him about pugilism and training or discussing which fighter might prevail against another. She feared his gift of the book. If he expected her to continue such disclosures, he'd flay her to the bone.

He wasn't Devil. He was a nobleman, and she'd been stupid, beyond stupid, to forget that.

She picked up *The Gazeteer* and went in search of Lord Thrale. This book must not be in her possession a moment longer than necessary. As she walked, her shawl trailed off one shoulder and threatened to catch in her feet. Roger, following behind, did step on it, and she had some moments to untangle them from that.

She found him in the second parlor again and strode in, Roger at her heels. "My lord."

"Mrs. Wilcott." He rose, addressing her with no particular in-flection. He dressed so plainly it was easy to forget he was a marquess, not a commoner. She would not make that mistake again. Despite his careful speech, his lack of superiority in manner, the way he cheerfully petted Roger, he did not inhabit the same world as her and never would. He'd not grown up with a father who squandered every penny or drank himself into oblivion every night. He'd not been coerced into a ruinous marriage for the sake of paying off the family's debts.

She gathered her emotions and shrank them to a manageable size. Her heart misgave her for what she was about to do, but that was all the evidence she needed to know she was right. His attention focused on the book she held. "Good afternoon, my lord."

"A good afternoon to you, as well." His eyes were gray. The col-or of a dawn sky, and when he looked at her, his calm regard lodged in her bones. Behind his aristocratic exterior was a man who could say *they'll hear you scream* and make those words a promise of bliss.

Roger, the traitorous hound, loped across the room to greet the man. The marquess obligingly bent to rub Roger's back and shoulders.

She did not trust him. Not one atom. Not one fraction of an inch. Never mind how much Roger adored him. The dog had lost his mind over someone who knew where to scratch. "What do you mean by this?"

He glanced at her but did not stop petting Roger. "Your sister said you liked maps. She made a particular point of that. Several times."

"What has that to do with anything?" Damn him. Damn him for listening and hearing beneath the words.

"It's how I knew that was likely to be a book you would be pleased to have."

"I did not ask you to buy me anything." He was a large man, and there was always a threat implicit when a man was made like that. She responded to the possibility that he would use his strength for her pleasure. In her imagination, he was in bed, naked. His cock hard and inside her, *yes*, and him looking at her, willing and able to give her what she needed. What she wanted and missed; the raw, hard, physicality that Devil had brought to their bed.

He sighed. "Mrs. Glynn treated you abominably."

"Did you not stop to wonder if she had reason?"

"I assumed she did not." He quirked his eyebrows. "Was that wrong of me?"

"You know why she finds me objectionable." She never talked about this, never. The guilt of allowing the words to be said tore her apart. Her marriage was not a subject for discussion. He must know that. He must feel that as deeply as she did.

"Because you married The Devil Himself." He spoke matter-of-factly, but she saw the flicker in his eyes, his curiosity. She could *feel* his restraint, and that intrigued her against her will. She'd heard the gossip. The Marquess of Thrale had superior physical endowments. A woman who did not mind a man who was not a gentleman in bed would find herself well sated—if, if, she did not mind a bruise or two.

Mrs. Glynn was right about her nature.

"Because she believes her son admired you too much when you were practically children."

"He didn't. He never did."

"I do not doubt that. But she believes it."

He was dangerous, Thrale was. The very best of fighters combined physical prowess with mental acuity, an insight into their opponents. In less than a second, a fighter read his opponent's body and saw weaknesses to exploit, strengths to avoid or turn to his advantage. Thrale studied that art. The science. "I don't want this," she blurted out.

"Madam."

The word was polite enough to have teeth.

He went on in the same manner. "Captain Niall bought a fashion plate for each of you. I bought a book for all the ladies but you."

"I did not want his gift either." She had made a life for herself here in Bartley Green. A space carved out in which she disappointed no one, and Thrale meant to pierce the veil. He would destroy her.

"Why?"

"It is enough, sir, that I must deal with Mrs. Glynn. Miss Glynn is a dear friend of Emily's, and of Anne and Mary, too. Harry gets on with Aldreth, and if he meets Cynssyr, I daresay they will like each other as well. I don't wish to be the cause of a break in their friendships."

"I had good evidence you would like that book." His pale eyes held hers. "You will not have to pretend to enjoy it."

"I do not pretend to enjoy anything."

"You make my point for me."

"I enjoy a great many things, my lord, but—" Roger butted Thrale's chest, in search of more affection, the poor deprived dog. "Roger, no. Come here. Pray, sir, do not be difficult. My express desire was that you not purchase any book for me. You cannot purchase one later and presume it is my desire now. On what grounds is that logical?"

His gray eyes stayed steady on her. Her drawing room smile had no effect. None whatever. "My apologies. I was out of bounds. I did not intend to offend you."

She extended the book. Perverse creature that she was, she was sorry for his retreat. "I cannot accept this."

"Understood." He straightened from petting Roger. "Leave it here, then. There's room on the shelves for it. No one need know."

She gripped the book with both hands. The pages were filled with maps. Intricate, detailed maps that folded out to a sheet three times the size of the book, and she had, when at the booksellers, imagined the hours she could spend perusing the pages, absorbing all the places in the world one could visit. "I did not ask you to indulge me. I did not ask for a gift."

He smiled, a grin that reminded her he wasn't a man who often smiled. That curve of his mouth made her stomach flutter. It was true, she thought amid the panic swirling in her head. He did not often smile. "I prefer to think I was indulging myself rather than you."

"I cannot leave it here."

"Why not?"

"You inscribed my name in it. And yours. What if someone sees it?"

Lord Thrale extended a hand and wiggled his fingers until she gave the book to him. He opened it to the inscription and scanned what he'd written.

He walked to the fireplace, and she followed, horrified.

"No. You cannot. You must not."

"Must not?" He moved aside the fire screen.

She put a hand on his arm. "It won't burn in there. You'd need a much bigger fire than that one."

He ripped the page from the book.

"What have you done?"

He crumpled the page and tossed it on the coals. "True. If I meant to burn the book, that is. One page, however, burns quite well."

Lucy froze with her hand on his arm. "Why? Why would you do such a terrible thing?"

"The volume may now safely rest on one of those shelves."

She stared at the curling ashes. "You've murdered it."

"Murdered it." He laughed. "I say I've solved the problem."

"You haven't at all."

His grin faded, and her stomach fell to her toes when he held her gaze. She saw in his eyes an echo of how he'd looked at her when she'd been mad enough to challenge him to do to her whatever he wished.

He said, "You fare poorly when someone is kind to you."

"It is not kind to deface a book." She could not stop thinking of that encounter, nor her belief that he was the sort of man who put a woman's back to the wall and took her hard and fast.

"We have a difference of opinion, though I apologize sincerely. It was not my intention to upset or insult you."

His words, the way he said them, the sincerity of them, dampened her temper, but her visceral reaction to him intensified. He'd been thoughtful. Observant. Oh, indeed, he was a dangerous man.

"Do you mistrust kindness in everyone?" He touched her cheek with the side of his smallest finger. A feather-light caress.

CHAPTER ELEVEN

Lucy froze, caught between the need to protect herself with whatever wits she had and the fact that he'd shaken her enough to crack the facade she showed the world. "I'm sure I don't know what you mean." She turned her cheek, and the contact between them broke. The silence became intolerable. "On those rare occasions when I encounter it from people I do not know, yes, my lord. I do mistrust kindness. And so ought you."

He cocked his head, and her foreboding deepened. "I will solve you."

"I'm no great puzzle, my lord." Men fell in love with her beauty. Lord Thrale was a man and, therefore, could be distracted from the mistake she'd made with him.

"You are."

She laughed, and it was a sound that had come from her during dozens of gatherings in London. Bright, airy, frothy and impermanent. Meaningless and empty. "There is nothing to understand." She spread her arms at waist level. "See me, and you know all there is to know about me."

He gazed at her and during that moment, it struck her anew, harder and more viscerally than before, that beneath his clothes was a body of muscle and sinew. "That is not so."

Before her marriage, when she had no experience of men or what mattered in life, she'd preferred men like Captain Niall. Slender men. Elegant ones. Devil had proved to her that charm was well and good, but a man who did not shy away from the rough and physical spoke to her so imperfect soul. The sort of man who would take a morning breather up a hill and back.

"It is so." She laughed again, but he refused to be repelled. "It could not be more so, my lord."

"So say you. I do not believe it."

"You are free to have whatever fanciful notions suit you."

"You are kind to humor me."

"You're most welcome."

"Sit a few moments with me?" He patted his coat pocket. "I've got Milton here. Let's be dazzled by the iambs and imagine we could write half so well ourselves. When you're done indulging me, you may borrow the Milton of me, and we'll not speak of maps or kindness again."

As if bespelled, she sat on the nearest chair. As if she had no sense. When she was seated, Roger eyed her and then Thrale. "My own dog loves you more than he loves me."

"I am mere novelty to him, adept at scratching him." Thrale placed *The Gazeteer* on one of the shelves then brought a chair close to her and sat.

"We've not a large library here," she said. Her head filled with images of him leaning over her, eyes locked with hers, and desire boiling between them. Would he be a rough lover, as he'd implied? Did she want that from him?

"It suits the house."

"It's why Emily and I go so often to the bookseller's and the subscription library."

"You have a decent collection of books. The Milton, for example."

She waved a hand, glad for any subject that distracted her. "Most of the books that are left were favorites of our mama. The rest are new."

He lifted his eyebrows. "I see. What of the ones that are not here?"

Thank God, he did not ask her *before when*. A man like him, he'd make a picture of that, and an accurate one. Likely he already had.

"Papa sold them. The ones we had before."

"She had excellent taste, then. Your esteemed mama. I presume the remaining books reflect the tastes of your mother and her daughters."

"My lord."

"I wish very much my home had a library as inviting as this one."

On the floor between her and Thrale, Roger flopped on his side, eyes closed. "Your home in London?" Her uneasiness settled. "Or do you mean another of your other vast, palatial estates?"

"I was thinking of Blackfern. The family seat." He stretched his legs to one side of Roger.

"Have you a large collection of books there? I suppose you must."

"No." There was a grimness to his smile.

Here was the Thrale from London. A severe man who did not care for her. "I find that difficult to believe."

"Why, when my father and yours have so much in common?"

"There is a tragedy. You poor man." She regretted her informality the moment the words were said.

"Your father emptied the library here. Mine gutted the library at Blackfern."

"I'm sorry to learn that happened. I know how devastated we were here when we found dearly beloved books gone."

"Even you, the young lady who would not read?"

"Yes. Even me." She shook her head in mock sorrow, but she remembered too well the shock of that day. "All the geography sold off. Not a single map left behind. It was worse for my sisters, of course, for they lost much more than I. Did you have a large collection of books? Before?"

"The original library? Yes. But most all of it was for show, but for a few well-used volumes. Ones I'd hidden from him."

"Poetry?" She eyed the bulge in his coat pocket that was her Milton.

"I was not the sort of boy who read poetry beyond what my tutor managed to force before my unwilling eyes."

"I shan't believe that of you."

"As you wish." He was a lion at rest, she told herself. It would be fatal to forget what happened on the hunt.

"What did you prefer?"

"Geography." He lifted his hands, but she was not deceived by that dismissive gesture. "I assure you, it's true. Treatises on farming. Mathematics. They were useful to me at the time. I wanted to save them when I discovered he meant to sell the whole lot."

"He sold them?" She curled her fingers around the edge of her chair. "Why?"

His gaze darkened. "The sale funded a fête in which the library was turned into a woodland scene, complete with the accouterments of a Bacchanalia."

Her breath caught, but not with offense. "You mean an orgy."

He flushed, and Lucy was charmed. "Forgive me. A gentleman ought not speak of such subjects to a lady."

No never, she ought to say. "I was married, my lord. Do you imagine I learned nothing of men and what they find entertaining?"

"No."

"Before I became a wife, I constructed absurd scenarios in which my future husband and I would read to each other from favorite books—that I had not read, mind you—and discuss them afterward."

He nodded. Not agreement, nor encouragement. Merely acknowledgment.

"We would share an intellectual life, have interests in common, thoughts, hopes, and fears told to each other. We would have children and love them dearly. Our life would be idyllic."

"The future is seldom what we imagine it will be."

"True. So true." Her chest tightened. "I never once imagined my life as it is now, nor the path that brought me here." She thought of that silent carriage ride away from Bartley Green, with hardly a word between her husband and her. Every time he spoke, she heard the vast difference between them. "We began so badly, Devil and I."

"Did you?"

She adjusted her shawl, and Thrale got up long enough to add a few more coals to the fire. "Barely speaking to each other, and Lord, his housekeeper so jealously guarded her domain. Devil wanted to show me off to his friends, the lady he'd married, and at the same time keep me from them. I own, I was the unhappiest bride there ever was."

"You did not stay unhappy, that much I know."

"All because one day, from boredom or possibly out of spite, I've never been sure which it was, I read his treatise on boxing."

"Then?"

"I came to know him through the book, and he wasn't what I thought at all. Nor was what he did every day what I'd thought. After that, I read the magazines he left everywhere, and followed his career. They wrote about him in those pages as if he were a hero or a god, even, and I know you are thinking, he was a prizefighter, a commoner, but when he discovered what I was doing, he did not forbid me." She leaned forward, her eagerness to tell him of her triumph incapable of restraint. "We talked. In a way, it was everything I'd imagined as a girl. He told me more about pugilism and his study of what he did in the ring, and he did not think me incapable of understanding."

"A happy circumstance, then."

"He loved me. With all his heart, he loved me." She wanted to cry, again, and again, and all over again, for the hole that losing him had left in her. "He loved me, and I cannot tell a soul for the shame of loving a man like him in return."

He said nothing, and it was just as well she could not speak. She counted the pleats in her skirt. When she came to eleven, she was once again blank inside. She would win this contest of silence. She always did.

She leaned an elbow on the arm of her chair and propped her chin on her closed fingers. "When I was a girl, I painted the maps in my geography texts, either after the original or with my own scheme."

"With watercolors?"

"Anything else obscured the lines."

"I can see you now, bending over your table tracing and coloring maps. Engrossed as only the best student can be." He interlaced his fingers and clasped his hands over his stomach.

"I assure you, I was far from a good student. When I ought to have been practicing my German or Italian, I was tracing maps or painting them."

"My gift to the Sinclair library is a useful one then. You've a whole book of them to work from."

"Will you read more of the *Mad Man* to us?" Last night after dinner he'd read from the novel he'd bought in town, and she and Emily both had been enthralled by the tale.

"I don't see why I shouldn't." He crossed his legs the other way. "Unless you are unhappy with the story."

"I'm not. Not at all." She narrowed her eyes at him. "You've read ahead, haven't you?"

"It's a perfectly horrid novel."

She laughed. "Emily would be devastated if it weren't."

He took her Milton from his pocket. "Do you care for poetry?"

Passionate assent leapt to her lips, but she bit back words that would betray her more than she had already. "Does it matter?"

"I suppose not, though that is no answer to my question." This time, his smile was smooth, a thing of confident beauty that she distrusted. That smile reminded her he was the Marquess of Thrale, as far above her in rank as any man could be. She picked up one end of her shawl and began to count the strands of wool in one of the tassels.

"You do, I expect." Was he a man who made reckless love? Did he laugh during the act or was he formal and somber even then? Or was he the sort of man who lost himself and took his partner with him?

"Do?" she asked.

"Like poetry. Now. Confess, Mrs. Wilcott." He leaned over and tugged on her shawl.

"Very much." She shrugged. "I am older and wiser now."

"I am happy to read Milton to you. You're familiar with his work, I take it."

"He is a poet."

"Of a certain renown."

She adopted her drawing room smile, but this time in jest. "I believe I've heard the name."

He opened her book, flipped several pages and glanced up. "Make yourself comfortable. Please."

She stayed perched on the edge of her chair. "Thank you."

"You do not look comfortable."

"I've nothing to do with my hands." She lifted them from her lap. "A lady must always have her hands occupied, and here I have no sewing or knitting or embroidery. I don't think I can listen and do nothing with my hands. It's wicked to be idle."

"Indulge me if you won't indulge yourself." He tapped the book. "One must be fully present when listening to Milton. No distractions." He opened the book. "Shall I begin?"

CHAPTER TWELVE

Thrale came down from that damned hill the second time with his thighs screaming at him and his feet complaining of hard treatment. His lungs had air and, though he felt the effort, he remained in control of his body. He could, if he pressed, take his breather a step faster. He could, if he wished, continue at this pace for some time yet. He came off the path worn smooth by the fighters who trained here, heading for The Cooperage rather than Johnson's Academy.

He crossed the footbridge over the river and continued along the bank toward the path that would return him to the Sinclairs. The weather had cooperated this morning, as it had most mornings he took a training outing; cool enough for him not to feel the sun.

By personal preference, he ended his excursion at the pool where he'd encountered Mrs. Wilcott on the day she'd advised him to run at the bloody hill. Like a horse in need of a cool down, he walked beside the pool waiting for his breath to calm and his pulse to slow. Presently, both happened in sufficient amount, and he headed toward The Cooperage. He'd not got ten yards along the path before Roger came around the bend, tail wagging. That somewhere in his antecedents there was a deerhound was as indisputable as the many other facets of his mixed lineage.

Roger loped toward him with that gait so peculiar to the breed predominant in him. This could only mean that Mrs. Wilcott was not far off, and, indeed, by the time Roger reached him, she appeared on the path.

Once again, he was in no fit state to be seen by a lady. He'd stripped down to his shirt for his breather, and the material was plastered to his skin. He wiped his forehead with the side of his arm. His shirt stuck to his forearm. She was, as she had been before, unaffected by his indecent state. He found that unbearably arousing.

Those were no thoughts for a gentleman to have about a lady.

She arrived at the part of the path where he and Roger were. Not close. Not far either. She wore white muslin sprigged with blue and a blue cashmere shawl around her shoulders. Her attention was on the dog, and though she was more natural with him now, he could not help thinking she continued to hold back some essential part of herself.

"He adores tall men and must always make their acquaintance."

"I shouldn't wonder. Such men are superior in every way." Roger pushed into his arms, a big enough dog to have knocked him over if he hadn't been solidly planted. Her husband had been tall, too. Taller than he was. A prizefighter had carried her away from her family and made a life with her. Ungentle hands had been on her body, and her still so young. Thomas Sinclair had much to answer for in respect of his neglect of his daughters. His lack of vigilance had led to a ruinous elopement.

"I always wonder," she said in a soft voice, "if he is looking for Devil. They were devoted to each other."

"Who would not be devoted to this dog?" He straightened and remembered, then, that he was not fit for the company of a lady. Thank the Lord he'd not peeled off to bare chest. Though, how would he know she would be offended if he had? She hid her emotions too well.

She closed her blue parasol, a tiny thing more decorative than useful, and balanced the handle against her shoulder. "How was your breather this morning?"

Again, he wiped his face with his sleeve. When she talked about boxing she became another woman, confident and more knowledge-able than many men he knew. This had the peculiar result of him conversing with her as if she were a man. She wasn't. God knows, she was not. "Twice to the top of the hill."

Her eyebrows rose. "Impressive, my lord."

She understood, she did, what such a feat meant about his physical condition and his mental fortitude. "Tomorrow, I spar at the Academy."

"Well, Count, you are diligent in your training." She knew the cant, and he wondered what other rough words she'd heard.

"With one of Johnson's fighters."

"A true enthusiast."

Enthusiast. That was not how he felt when he faced another man, fists raised. Or what he did when he was in the ring, and that was so even though he did not, and could never, fight for money. Enthusiasm did not touch the intense satisfaction of having control over his body. Enthusiasm had nothing to do with the way his mind focused in the moment. Nor the importance, to him, of control.

She amended herself before he could voice an objection. "No, much more than an enthusiast, I'd say."

He bowed. "I'm no Devil Wilcott." He spoke lightly, but he saw a shadow fall across her face. No. He was not The Devil Himself. What had Wilcott felt when he stepped into the ring with his body fashioned into a weapon? Alive? Eager? Blood and breath singing through him? Eager to test himself or just determined to best his opponent?

"Don't despair of that, sir. There was only ever one."

Her smile betrayed her in every way. He'd never again be fooled by a facsimile. Lust whispered to him; The Devil Himself, that prime physical specimen, had come home from battle to fuck his beautiful wife, and Thrale had reason to believe she had not objected. Far from it. "Art, science, and strategy," he said.

"There's no harm in size and strength, too."

"Not at all." What art was lost when one stepped into the ring to vie for that two-thirds of the purse allotted to the winner? Had Wilcott thought of the art when he had a wife to support by dint of his fists? "He never merely pummeled his opponents, did he? Your husband. Even as a young man, he devastated the best with science and strategy backed by strength."

"Tactics matter," she replied. "You know that."

"I do."

"Devil studied his opponents and learned his own weaknesses."

"He turned them to advantage." A baseborn prizefighter, and yet he'd had the intellect to write a definitive treatise, and the wit to make a fortune long before he married. That told of ambition and intelligence; a man looking into the future and determined that it would belong to him.

"Pugilism was Devil's passion. He lived and breathed it." She turned her parasol.

Her beauty distracted from the mind behind those lovely blue eyes. What had Wilcott been thinking when he married a Sinclair sister of Bartley Green? He could not possibly have believed she would get him entrance through the front door of her home or any other. Had he seen Lucy Sinclair and been determined to possess her at any cost?

"I own," she went on, "he learned the names, talents and weaknesses of every prizefighter of the last dozen years, whether he fought them or not."

"Walk back to the house with me?" He dropped a hand to Roger's head. "Or were you and this handsome boy intent on a longer ramble this morning?"

She eyed Roger. "This is about as far as we go these days. So, yes, thank you. We will escort you safely to The Cooperage."

"I won't offend you by offering my arm."

"That's kind of you." Her frock was trimmed with ribbons and bows and the sort of whatnot ladies put on their gowns, and she was fetching in it. The color and fit highlighted her delicacy, and his head filled with images of her husband sliding roughened hands over her body, and then, instead of Devil Wilcott, it was him in that place.

"Did he take you to matches?"

"He did." Roger walked by her side. What kind of life had she faced, married to Wilcott, necessarily estranged from her family?

"I only saw him fight once. You must have seen more battles." Many more. Why, she'd helped Devil in his training what with her detailed and meticulous study of his battles and those of other fighters.

"Not all of them, but more than a few."

"Any match involving Devil Wilcott would have been a battle not to be missed." There would have been hundreds of men present, lowborn and high. The money that changed hands when Wilcott fought had often been dizzying. Two opposing thoughts stayed in his head as they walked; envy of her experience, and the knowledge that no lady would attend a battle. Her reputation would be shredded for such a thing.

"The best I saw was his battle with Carter," she said. "He won in the fifty-third round."

"A famous battle."

"Yes. The first battle I saw, though, wasn't one of Devil's but Goldberg versus The Stoneman."

"You attended the Goldberg and Stoneman battle?"

"I did." She nodded. "Devil made me stay in the carriage, but we had an excellent view, and while we watched, he told me what to look for and what made the match a good one."

There was more, of course. "And?"

"It was brutal." She slowed, pacing herself to Roger. "I was repelled at first. I did not understand why anyone would wish to see two men beat each other or why anyone would cheer at the sight of blood."

"Your opinion changed, I gather."

She nodded "A trained fighter knows how to attack his opponent and how to defend himself. He has learned to withstand the punishment. Naturally, he will be hurt, but he will be less damaged than an untrained man who brawls."

"Just so."

"There is an art, yes. And science, as you've said." She turned her parasol in another slow circle. "Devil mastered both."

"Best prizefighter in England in his day," Thrale said. "Bar none."

"He was."

Her soft, sad reply hurt his soul. She'd lived a life no proper young lady ever did. Going to battles, watching men train. Discussing fights with her husband, and no doubt, the many sporting men or fighters who must have come to the house. She let out a short breath, then checked herself. When she did speak, it was softly. "I never talk about my marriage." She glanced at Roger, waiting patiently for them both. "It would make no one happy if I did. I don't know why I've talked to you about Devil. I shouldn't." She rushed on. "I know what you must think of me as a result. My family is ashamed, too, though they'd never say so to my face."

"They are not ashamed of you."

She met his eyes, this time, and she was hard. Brittle. "The price of a roof over my head is silence about my marriage. I don't want to pay forever."

This, too, was a puzzle. Devil Wilcott had amassed a fortune and here was his widow, destitute. "Did he make no provisions for you? There must have been something for you. What happened?"

Her mouth tightened. "Arthur Marsey stole every penny of it from him. Investment after investment, never bought. Devil tried to bring an action, but no lawyer would hear him without money to pay. Besides, Marsey was a gentleman, and Devil was not. He fought that last time because there was no money. He never thought it would be his last battle. Nor did I."

Wilcott's death had been even more tragic than he'd believed. He'd left behind a devastated widow who mourned him still, and that tugged at him. "I am deeply sorry for your loss."

"We were happy. I know that seems impossible, but we were." She shot him a glance. "I am grateful for the time I had with him, and I would not give that up for all the money in the world." She touched his arm. "Come now, my lord. Let's speak of something joyful for us both."

"Do you miss the battles?"

She laughed. "What a question."

"Do you?"

She gave him a sideways look and faced him on the path. Initially, he expected her to remonstrate with him for the indelicacy of his question. She did not. "He taught me to box."

"He never did."

"So you believe, my lord."

"How did he come to teach you to fight? Why?"

"I made a joke of it one day. We were discussing his battles and how he had trouble with a certain fighter. One of the Americans, and I told him I'd seen him flinch. He wouldn't believe it at first, but I showed him." She was smiling at the recollection, proud and fond, and then she dropped her parasol to the ground and, one foot forward, dropped her weight on her back leg, fists raised. "I showed him, and he allowed as I was right, and from there, he taught me to box. In private of course."

The moment she raised her fists, anticipation pulsed through him. When he boxed, no matter who stood across from him, he wanted to win. Even when he faced a woman.

"I am the last student of The Devil Himself." She jabbed at him, a motion both precise and measured. If she'd meant to connect, he'd have felt it. "He said I was his best."

"You're quick."

She grinned at him and crossed with her right. "Indeed, my lord."

"Is that a challenge?"

"What do you think?"

He tipped his head to one side. "Did you spar with him?"

"Not in the way you mean." Her joyous smile brought an answering smile from him. "He was twice my size, and many times stronger."

"A given. He'd not punch you."

"Not a nobber, a ribber, or a facer." She punctuated each word with a feint to his head, his ribs, and his face. "He'd never have harmed me."

Though he did not take the classic sparring position, he traded a few feints with her. "Did you punch him?"

"I was fast enough to." She jabbed, and it was sharp and crisp. If she'd not pulled her punch, she'd have landed him a decent ribber. She jabbed again and this time he caught her fist. His hand fit easily around her clenched fingers.

"That's no answer." He released her and raised his fists.

Her eyes sparkled. "I did not wish to bruise him, sir."

He came at her with a quick left, then a right. Neither touched her nor had he intended any such thing. He had control of himself. Once, she had to bend back—he'd meant that, testing her.

And again. But her heel caught in her gown, and he grabbed her shoulder and hauled her toward him and immediately released her because, for the love of God in heaven, he was stripped down to his shirt, and he had no business touching her like that. He took up her parasol and handed it to her. "Those are no fit clothes for boxing, Mrs. Wilcott."

"I shall start a fashion for ladies' boxing attire." She shook out her skirts.

Sparring with a woman. Who would have thought such a thing was possible, even in jest? In London, from time to time, he'd sparred with prizefighters in training. He was nothing like the fighter Devil Wilcott had been, and he was aware the fighters he faced pulled their punches. Yet he well knew his ability significantly exceeded that of the typical amateur. He wanted Mrs. Wilcott's acknowledgment of that. And would never have it.

They continued to the house in relative silence and went in by the back entrance, Roger behind them. As they came in, a small mirror on the wall opposite them flashed into his peripheral vision. She put her shoulder to it as they passed.

He put a hand on the wall, barring her way to the stairs. This was not the first time he'd seen her avoid a mirror. "Why do you never look at yourself?"

She glanced at his arm, and he dropped it to his side. "I know what I look like."

"That isn't what I mean." There was no one here. Just them.

"It's what I mean."

With a firm grip on her, he turned her around until she was in front of the mirror. She closed her eyes. He devoured her reflected image. Heartbreaking to see her, this woman, "Have you always been beautiful?" He stroked fingers across the nape of her neck. His fascination with her threatened to become obsession. Such tender skin. He willed her not to move, and she did not. "Like this? As you are now?"

"I cannot help the way I look."

"Yes, then. You have always been like this." His fingers moved from her neck to the line of her cheek. "It's true you cannot help your looks. So, why won't you look at yourself?"

"I am not vain." Her voice was tight. Curt. Another piece of the puzzle for him to arrange in his head.

"True yet again." She smelled like lilacs. A faint scent. "I never met a woman less vain than you."

"It's my reputation." She looked away from the mirror she'd refused. From his face, also reflected in the glass.

He frowned. "Who made you ashamed of your beauty? It can't have been your husband."

"Devil married me for my looks. He was proud of me for that."

He turned them around, both of them, away from the damned mirror. She opened her eyes. They stood inches apart. Her gaze was so aware she scorched him. He could not act on his desires. Not with her. He could not betray Aldreth and Cynssyr or any of her sisters. He struggled for safer ground and found he had no reserves of fortitude to see him there. She'd burned all that away.

"Would you fight me?" He meant *fuck. Will you fuck me?*

She searched his face. "Do you want me to?"

He heard the challenge there. His body came to attention. This was a dangerous game to play. So be it. "Yes."

"Why?"

"You'd be a worthy opponent," he said.

"Tomorrow, then? Or another day?"

Again, he touched her cheek with the tips of his first two fingers. "I'd be afraid to bruise you."

In the silence, she said, softly, "Do you want to?"

Anticipation turned the world more vivid yet. Satan sat on his shoulder and whispered that he should accept what she offered. If she was willing, why not? "Don't bring me down that path. I can't. Not with you."

"Why?"

Roger whined and that broke the spell between them.

CHAPTER THIRTEEN

A t the moment, Lord Thrale was unaware she'd taken root in the parlor doorway or that she was not master of herself. It was nearly midnight, and he sat reading by the fire, one foot braced on the fender. He'd moved one of the lamps to a nearby table to increase the steady light. His informal attire unsettled her more than seeing him stripped to a shirt and fighting britches. In his loose coat, striped trousers, and felt slippers, he was undeniably a gentleman at his leisure.

She had a three-quarter view of him from where she stood. In repose, there was an appealing solidity to him. A calmness. Beneath that restraint was tightly leashed violence. Devil had been like that. He'd had that same restraint. He'd been able to face another man and, without mercy or compunction, use mind and body to send his opponent to his knees. Johnson had confided to her that Thrale had done just that to one of his most promising young fighters.

Roger left her to join Thrale. After stroking the dog's head, he looked to the doorway. She registered his surprise, then pleasure—could that be so?—at seeing her. He stood, a book in one hand. "Madam."

"My lord." Last season she'd wondered why Anne had been his loyal supporter. She understood now. He was an honorable man. Alas, friendship between her and Thrale was neither wise nor safe. He seemed to have come to the same conclusion, for he had avoided her most of the day. But they got on, she and Thrale, and like Anne, she was now his staunch defender.

His expression did not change. There was nothing in his attitude or the way he looked at her to suggest he'd said or done anything improper with her. They'd skirted that line, no more. Nothing irrecoverable. "Come in, please. Don't let me prevent you from finding something to read."

She walked halfway to where he stood with Roger. Words tumbled around in her head, and rather than allow the silence to turn uncomfortable, she plucked words that leapt to mind. "Did you spar at the Academy today?"

"Yes." He touched a spot at the head of his right shoulder. His grimace was mostly feigned. "I was well instructed."

"I used to put liniment on Devil's bruises." The house was quiet. The servants were abed. Before she came here, Emily had retired for the night. Her father, too, since Captain Niall had gone into Bartley Green to dine in town. "Basilicum powder on his cuts, if he had them."

"Such tender mercy."

"Johnson says you are strong."

"Does he?"

"Quick, he told me. With a hint of the vicious."

Thrale cocked his head.

"You hit hard."

"I mean to."

"A little weak to your left."

"I am addressing that."

"Yes. He told me that, too." She considered him as she would any fighter. He had Devil's build, the physique of the great Jim Belcher. "If you weren't a nobleman, Johnson said he'd have you training for a career in the ring."

"Rank flattery."

"No, sir, I say emphatically now. Johnson might flatter you, I suppose, when he speaks to you. But you were not there, and there are reasons—" She kept her back to the chimney with its mantel-to-ceiling mirror. She could hardly tell him about her wagers or that Johnson was one of the ways she kept abreast of which battles might go one way or another.

"Yes?"

She got a look at the book he held and lifted a hand to forestall any more from him on the subject of bruises. "What's this? Do not tell me you are reading *The Mad Man*."

With a smile, Thrale hid his book behind his back.

"Emily and I turned the front parlor upside down looking for that."

"Whatever for?"

"Why, to read ahead, of course. You stopped at a most thrilling moment."

"I stopped at the end of the chapter." He shrugged with feigned innocence. "You must endure the suspense, ma'am, as does everyone else."

"Except for you. You know if the *Duc* survived the *banditti* attack."

He laughed. "If you want a good reading from me, I must have some idea of what is to come." Roger demanded attention and, to oblige the dog, he set the book on the floor beside him and crouched to pet him. "Good evening, old man."

"Roger, come." She hurried to him and would have hooked her fingers in the dog's collar, but Thrale waved her off.

"This magnificent boy? He's not bothering me. Never." Roger sighed, and Thrale reached around to scratch his belly. Devil's dog was in love with him, slavishly in love.

"Since you cannot read *The Mad Man*, Mrs. Wilcott, is there another book you would like?" He glanced at the shelves. "A volume of maps, perhaps? Or would poetry be more to your tastes?"

She shook her head. The silence required of her here had carved a place for her memories of Devil. There was a wall around that hollow built to impenetrable thickness. Until Thrale. Her heart raced at the thought that with Thrale, she had been given a small space to give voice to herself. The woman she was, not the one she had to be.

"I won't believe you don't care for poetry." He went back to petting Roger. The dog lay at his feet in a state of utter relaxation.

She should not tell him anything. Not one more confidence about her marriage. "Once..."

"Yes?"

"Once, I read Wordsworth to my husband. Early in our marriage, but not so early that I did not think there was a hope he'd listen. He wasn't an educated man, but he wasn't stupid."

"He was not."

He agreed as if Devil's intelligence could not be in doubt. Lucy, accustomed to the assumption that her husband had possessed no redeeming qualities, was taken aback. Relief and gratitude overcame her. "He read a great deal, you know. He wrote, too, and well. You have read him, those words were his." Indeed, she was Thrale's loyal supporter. "Still, I ought to have known better than to read poetry to him."

"Because?"

She clasped her hands behind her back, remembering the days before they had found solid ground beneath them. She could smile about the incident now, but at the time, she'd been angry and devastated. "Before I'd finished the first poem, he snatched the book away and pitched it out the window and into the gutter."

"Good God, why?"

Thrale's outrage brought another smile from her, and she was glad to have shared the story with him, even though it was foolish of her to do so. "He was too pragmatic for poetry. If I'd paid more attention to him at the time, I'd have known that. In the event, I never again attempted to convince him of the beauty of words for their own sake."

"I expect," he said, rubbing Roger's belly as he spoke, "that had he lived, you would have found poems that spoke to him."

A different silence filled up the room, and it terrified her, burned behind her eyes, closed off her throat. Would they have? She would go to her grave never knowing.

"Mrs. Wilcott?"

She pulled herself from the morass of what might have been. She and Devil had made their peace, but, in truth, she did not believe he would have come to love poetry as she had. Instead, verses for her became a secret, solitary indulgence. "Forgive me, my lord. What did you say?"

"You have no interest in reading Milton?" His hand rested on Roger's shoulder. "But of course not. You came here for *The Mad Man*. I fear you must abandon all hope of that."

They were friends. They were, as foolish as that was. They were friends as he and Anne were friends; within the bounds of what was proper. She would be as loyal to him as Anne. More. She returned his grin. "Perhaps one day *The Mad Man* will vanish from your quarters."

"Unlikely. He is permanently ensconced in my life." He scratched behind Roger's ear and then stood, retrieving his book from the floor. He dropped it on the table beside his chair.

"It happens I am a renowned sneak thief in the Sinclair household. Ask any of my sisters which of us could be counted on to find or liberate an item not currently in our possession."

"You underestimate my resourcefulness." His stern delivery would have been more terrifying if the corner of his mouth had not twitched.

"My lord." She held both sides of her skirts and curtsied. Never mind that she found him physically appealing. Never mind that. His friendship was too precious to jeopardize. There was no one else she could talk to about her past. About Devil and boxing. She couldn't bear to lose that. "You underestimate mine."

"I think not." His smile flashed again. He was built like Devil, but there the similarities ended. With Devil, there had never been wordplay like this. Conversations never slid along on multiple levels. "That was not meant as an insult. I am wholly on guard where you are concerned."

"I might trip and knock you down a flight of stairs?"

They referred to the events leading to Anne's marriage to the duke, which had begun when Lucy had tripped and knocked her sister down half a flight of stairs. She had been the cause of that accident, and that accident had led to a marriage that had, for some time, seemed certain to doom Anne and the duke to a life of unhappiness.

"Such mishaps occur from time to time."

"Too often to me. Don't deny it's so."

He held her gaze. She did not want to acknowledge the shiver that went through her. "I continue to work out the puzzle you present."

"There is no puzzle."

"Mrs. Wilcott." His gaze flicked over her, and it was shocking, the jolt of her response to his look. Disaster would result if this went beyond words. "I will unravel you."

She drew a breath, for there were too many meanings in his words, and in his eyes. Too many, and it was wonderful and wicked. "Here I thought I would make off with the *Mad Man* and be on my way."

"You might yet." His slow smile sent another spiral of heat through her. "If you are quicker than I. And cleverer."

"Oh, but I'm not clever. Not at all."

"I disagree."

"I can't think what you mean, sir."

"Since you cannot have *The Mad Man*, allow me to suggest something else. To be sure, material improving to your cleverness."

How daring she felt, engaging in such banter. "I daresay there is much in me that needs improvement."

He bowed. "If only you knew something of literature, ma'am."

"If only I'd paid more attention in the schoolroom."

"I did not read much as a boy. Like you, I had scant familiarity with literature. Like you, not until later in life did I take up the poets."

She looked at him sideways. "Do you prefer your poets dead or living?"

"It depends on whether I'm having them to dinner."

"A dead poet makes for stiff conversation."

He let out a bark of a laugh, and she joined him in that. He took a book from the pocket of his coat. It was her Milton. "This is a favorite poet of mine. A shame you have no interest."

"Hm." She rocked back on her heels. This was novel for her, that anyone would engage with her as if he believed in her wit, or that she could reply in kind. She would not dare with anyone but him. "The fellow who wrote that book seems a poet of some talent."

"So they say."

"But he wrote of Hell, sir. Or did I mishear?"

"You did not. Blasphemy of the worst sort."

"When would a work with the devil in it not be blasphemous?" she asked.

He crossed his arms over his chest. He was teasing her, and she was amused. "Do you mean to suggest, ma'am, that the Bible is blasphemous?"

"The Bible is not a novel." She'd thought of him as stern and colorless, a man who would never interest her. How wrong she'd been.

"True enough."

She strolled toward the window by a circuitous path. The curtains were drawn against the night. As she ambled, one hand slipped over the top of the chairs and tables. Roger, though he remained by Lord Thrale, watched her progress through the room.

She walked toward his chair. "What was the name of the other novel you said you enjoyed? I can't recall from one moment to the next what I've read or only read about. I read Papa's *Sporting Magazine* this morning." She touched a finger to her chin. "And *The Times.* I read the advertisements every day, or as often as I can, at any rate. As to poetry, why, I mayn't have read a poem in an age." She picked up the volume of *The Mad Man* and flipped the pages without looking at them. "Pentameter, iambs, couplets, stanzas. I can't keep them straight."

"Tut, tut, Mrs. Wilcott. Do you think I am so easily fooled?" He took the book from her.

"What do you think of Wordsworth?" She tapped the tabletop.

"He is no Milton, but I find him compelling for different reasons." He held up the Milton. "One is safer with Mr. Wordsworth's scenes from nature, I think, when Satan might appear in these pages at any moment."

"I don't know how you expect me to sleep tonight, with talk like that."

He pressed the Milton to his chest and grinned at her. "I should hate to think of you awake at night, unable to sleep for the terror. Allow me, Mrs. Wilcott, to prevent this book from disturbing your tender sensibilities. I shall take it with me to my room. In order to spare you a sleepless night."

"You are all that is generous." She bent a knee.

"You may safely retire to bed without a mad man or a devil."

They locked gazes. "I'll never sleep, now," she said.

CHAPTER FOURTEEN

Lucy's heart beat a tattoo against her ribs when Arthur Marsey planted himself in her path a few steps past the Bartley Green stationer's. Roger stayed close to her side. She had made it plain, she thought, that she wished nothing to do with him. If he had any decency, he would let her be.

"What a delightful surprise to see you here."

"I cannot say the same." Ice coated her reply. She wrapped herself in that same frozen response. Roger pressed against her thigh, and she rested the tips of her fingers on his shoulder. She glanced at Arthur and he at her, and then, without a word, she moved past him.

He caught her elbow, and she whirled, offended that he dared accost her. "Unhand me."

His grin sent a shiver down her spine. "Mrs. Wilcott."

She dislodged his hold on her. Roger's whine evolved to a snarl.

"Keep that beast under control."

Oh, that familiar scorn. During her marriage to Devil, she'd often seen that arrogant dismissal from people like Marsey. She'd become inured, as she had likewise become inured to those who had not welcomed her in Devil's life. More than one gentleman who'd met her believed her status as the wife of a fighter made her fair game.

She walked away, but he matched her stride. "What cause have you to be so proud, I should like to know?" He kept his tone light, but Lucy heard the nasty undercurrent.

"Leave me be, sir."

"Quite a come up in the world for you, isn't it?" He edged in front of her and blocked her way. Roger growled. Marsey patted one of his pockets. "I won't hesitate to shoot that monster. Damn me if I won't."

Lucy hooked her fingers in Roger's collar. "I have nothing to say to you, sir."

He touched his upper chest in a half-bow. She knew that smile too well. That charming smile had been present all the while he was robbing Devil. "Don't play the grand lady with me. I know better. Captain Niall has become your ardent admirer. What he will think when I tell him the truth?"

"Even if you have already, he can think nothing others don't." She tried again to get around him and failed.

"What? No interest in the captain? I'll say that speaks well of you, that you know you should have none. But who have you set yourself to capture if not him? Never say it's that young fellow, Mr. Glynn? A sly dog if it is."

"Leave me be."

"No. It can't be Glynn." He had her backed against the wall of a shop. Roger growled, and she soothed him. "Not with that dragon of a mother."

"No, of course not. She dislikes me heartily." She tried to walk around him, but he continued to block her way. She gave him a poisonous look. She'd spent time with a rougher sort of crowd and had not crumbled then. She would not now. He didn't know the woman she'd become since she came home. Hard inside. Hard as iron.

"Is it Lord Thrale?" He kept his voice low. "What a coup that would be to have him among your admirers. Your protector. Better him than Glynn or the captain. You're wise to set your sights on a higher rank this time."

"Yes, that's it precisely. I've had no luck so far. Alas. He is too much a gentleman for me, I fear."

"Don't be disrespectful to your betters."

"Never." She gave him a frosty smile.

"I am to meet with Captain Niall tomorrow." His supercilious smile deepened. "It seems I may be of assistance to him in certain ventures."

"I shall warn him."

He checked himself, and, in that moment, she saw what not even Devil had suspected; that he was filled with hate. He'd despised Devil for having money, for his success, and for making a life that was not the one he'd been born into. "That would not be wise."

"I have never been a particularly wise woman."

He blocked the walkway and stood too close. She said nothing. Refused to look at him or speak to him. Was there no one to see that she had been accosted? She glanced across the street where several men spoke in excited tones. One of them hailed Marsey.

"You are wanted there."

Marsey looked her up and down. "I had rather be wanted here."

"Do not think, Mr. Marsey, that I have forgotten anything. I have not."

He tipped his head the merest amount while his smile dripped treacle. She endured his slow, insulting, appalling, consideration of her person. "Nor have I. Believe me, nor have I."

"It has been too long since last you saw me. I fear you find me greatly changed."

"If anything, you are more beautiful."

"I will warn everyone." He could not do worse to her than had already happened. "If not for you, my husband would not have returned to the ring. He would still be alive."

"A woman has nothing but her reputation." He glanced at his gloved hand and adjusted his cuff. "An observation."

"One may observe the same of men."

He flushed. Marsey had always been quick to take offense in that regard. *Men* not *gentlemen*. "What do you suppose Glynn or his lordship would say if they heard the rumors about us?"

She made certain her smile did not falter. "I cannot fathom how you live with yourself."

He looked her up and down again, and then sneered at her. "Do not dare lecture me."

"You are no gentleman."

"You play at being a lady. You are not. If you're not careful, others will learn the same."

"I have spoken to you this once. To be certain you understand that I do not give a fig for you or what you say about me to anyone. Tell all the lies you like, and I'll still have no complaint of you. But if I discover you have done to anyone dear to me what you did to my husband, I am your unrelenting enemy."

"As if you've any idea how your betters get on."

"Good day, sir." She walked around him again, and this time he let her pass. She increased her pace, paying no attention to the direction she went. Not home. Not yet. Not when she was shaking with anger. She took the path toward the river rather than The Cooperage, walking as fast as she dared with Roger at her side. She walked long past the time when she'd left Bartley Green behind and did not stop until she realized Roger's gait had altered.

Panic rolled through her when she saw he was limping. His mouth was open, his ribs heaving, and he was panting. Appalled by her inattention, she dropped to her knees and threw her arms around the dog. "Roger. Roger, I'm sorry."

He licked her cheek and lowered himself to the path. What had she done?

"Roger, I'm sorry, so sorry, oh, my poor noble boy." He groaned and lay flat on his side, ribs heaving. What if he was dying? What if in her absorption with herself she'd walked Roger beyond his endurance? She knew that was a danger with him, and she'd walked and walked and kept walking anyway. She kept her arms around him, stroking him, willing him to be better.

She lost track of how long she stayed with him, not daring to leave while he was in this condition. If she left him to get help, he'd only follow, and that would make him even worse off. She was terrified he might die no matter what she did. "What have I done?"

She held back tears. She couldn't lose him. Not Roger. She couldn't bear it if she lost Roger, too. "What have I done?"

"What's this?"

Her father, Captain Niall, and Lord Thrale stood on the path, staring at her. She'd been so caught up with worry about Roger, she'd not heard them heading her way. Thrale, in boots and a battered coat, balanced a fishing pole on his shoulder. Behind them was Thrale's valet. What was his name? The servant held another two fishing poles, a creel, and a wicker basket. The tail fin of a trout poked from under the closed cover.

"Is he all right?" Thrale asked.

"No. No, he's not." She burst into tears of self-hate and relief that someone who could help was here. "I walked too fast for too long, and he would have let me walk him to death—" She became incapable of speech. What sort of selfish, insensitive woman was she to lose track of Roger like that?

Her father lifted his hat, ran his fingers through his hair, and replaced the hat. "Lucy, my dear. Perhaps it's time you put him down."

She threw her arms around Roger. "Never! Don't you dare say such a thing. You'll never take him from me. I won't allow it. He's walked too far, that's all."

"Sinclair." Thrale spoke sharply. "Show Captain Niall to the house, won't you? Flint and I will assist your daughter and her dog."

Captain Niall cleared his throat. "Mrs. Wilcott."

She looked up, ready to do battle again. "Sir?"

He flushed. "I know how fond of him you are. I hope he recovers."

Lucy burst into fresh tears. His kindness made her feel worse. She did not deserve his consideration. She pressed her fingers to her eyes and willed herself to calm. "Thank you, Captain. I hope the same."

"Gentlemen," Thrale said. "I'll see you at the house in short order."

When her father and the captain were on their way, Thrale handed his fishing pole to his valet and bent down. "Fetch a dogcart or wagon, Flint. We'll wait here for you." He spoke firmly. "Quick on it, if you don't mind."

"Straightaway, milord." The servant tucked all three fishing poles under his arm and hurried off in the direction of The Cooperage, one hand on his hat, the other on the creel to keep it from bouncing. He made a wide arc around her father and the captain.

"I thought—" Words jammed in her throat. Roger remained stretched out on his side, panting, eyes closed.

"He needs rest is all." He stroked the dog's side. "A loyal beast."

"I might have killed him."

"You haven't." He sat on the other side of Roger with one knee bent. Without comment, he handed her his handkerchief.

"I don't deserve a moment's kindness. None."

"You are too hard on yourself." He took her hand, squeezed it, and let go. The contact, brief and undeserved as it was, helped. "He'll be fine."

"You don't know that."

"I'll ask your father's kennel master to look after him when we get him home."

"Thank you. Thank you. An excellent idea."

Before she expected Flint's return, the servant appeared with a ramshackle cart. Between Thrale and the valet, Roger was lifted onto the back. When he was settled, Lucy sat on the open end of the cart, one hand on Roger who, though listless still, showed signs of recovery. Thrale walked alongside the cart. By the time they reached The Cooperage, Roger jumped down on his own. He landed with a limp and a whimper, though.

"Oh, Roger." She dropped to her knees beside him, and did not object when Roger licked her cheek.

"Flint, please ask the kennel master to check on Roger as soon as he has a moment to spare."

"Aye, milord." Flint bowed and dashed away.

"Thank you. Thank you. That was an excellent idea," Lucy said.

"Mrs. Wilcott. Allow me." Thrale picked him up and carried him inside. At the top of the stairs, he waited for her to point the way to her room. She hurried ahead and threw open her door. Thrale came in and set Roger down, waiting to be sure Roger was steady on his legs. When that proved the case, he straightened. Roger walked slowly to his favorite spot by the fireplace and lay stretched out by the fire screen.

"You were so kind. Are so kind to help." Lucy grabbed his hand and lay her cheek atop his fingers. "Thank you, my lord. Thank you, thank you, thank you."

"You are welcome."

She released his hand and hurried to the hearth to bring up the fire. As she did that, Thrale said, "What happened to upset you so?"

She rose and stared at the ceiling. She counted the scallops in the plaster. "Nothing that matters."

"Mrs. Wilcott." He scrubbed a hand through his hair, and she was at sea. Thrale had earned the right to her family's undying appreciation and now hers a thousand times over.

She crossed the room to fetch the pitcher by the basin. At the fireplace, she poured water into the bowl she kept there for Roger.

"Not nothing." Thrale fixed her with a glance that bespoke annoyance and some hurt. Her heart lurched. "If someone has made you unhappy, then, Mrs. Wilcott, I hope you would turn to me for protection."

The unsavory connotations of that word slammed into her. She knew he'd not meant that—not a mistress, not as Marsey had meant when he accused her of setting her hopes on an illicit relationship with Thrale.

This time he stared at the ceiling. "Mrs. Wilcott. Please."

"I know you did not mean *that.*"

Under his protection. Her mind raced away with the indelicate notions such as no proper lady ever had. But heavens, would he not be a magnificent lover?

He gave a rueful smile. "I hope you believe you might turn to me for assistance. In such a case as someone making himself obnoxious to you."

"Thank you."

"I do mean that."

She went to her side table and pretended to be enthralled by the flowers there. The roses he'd given her and Emily were long dead, but fondly remembered. She turned her head to one side so as not to have her back to him, but she was aware enough to wonder if there was significance to her not facing him.

"Marigolds," he said.

She touched several of the blossoms. "They are a cheerful flower."

"They are."

She peeked at him. Johnson had described him as tireless. Merciless in the ring. He liked to have his newer fighters face Thrale, he'd told her, for they learned to take punishment from him. Here he stood in her room, present in that way he had that made it impossible for her to see or think of anyone else.

"I don't know why you are so kind to me." Ten marigolds and less than a third of the arrangement counted. "Because of Anne, I suppose."

"I would do near anything to keep her sisters from harm's way, that's true. As would Aldreth or Cynssyr."

"Anne deserves that." Twenty. "So do Mary and Emily."

"You believe you do not?"

Twenty-six. She tried to distance herself from him and failed. She faced him though, because she was no coward. "I married a man who fought with his fists and took money for it. A man who betrayed his class in every word he spoke."

"So you did." He adjusted the cuff of his coat, the comfortable sort that a man wore in the country. He'd been fishing in it and the pockets bulged out, doubtless stuffed with string and a knife and, even, bait. "You needn't answer this impertinent question, but did you wish to marry him? I have no need to know the answer, only curiosity. Silence is answer enough if I've overstepped."

She curled her fingers in her skirts. She liked him in these rough clothes and had to fight a mad, mad urge to walk to him and twine her arms around his neck and see where they ended up. She never could. Never. She'd rather have his friendship, her only friendship since she'd returned to Bartley Green without her husband. "When he asked me to marry him, I said yes."

"I'd wondered if you'd eloped with him because you were in love."

"No. I mean, no, we did not elope." Her silence on the subject was so ingrained in her by now that the words resisted her saying them. They weighed her down, made her feel she was betraying her father and sisters, yet, at the same time, Lord Thrale listened without scorn, and she could remember those days and the ones following and remind herself she had made a good life with her husband. "Devil had a special licence, and the vicar married us. In his front parlor. The vicar's parlor." The more she talked, the more confused everything became between guilt and shame and memories she cherished. "I did love him," she said. "You know I did."

"Before, Mrs. Wilcott." He held her gaze. "Before you married The Devil Himself. Did you love him before then?"

She glanced away, then back. She touched the petals of one of the marigolds. "I agreed to marry him."

He crossed to her and took her by the shoulders. He was gentle and did not hurt her in the least. "Why?" His eyes bored into hers. With him like this, it was too easy to forget he was a marquess. Too easy to think of him as she had Devil. "Did your husband pay your father's debts? Is that the reason you married a prizefighter?"

She squeezed her eyes closed. "He cried, Papa did, when he told me."

"Crocodile tears."

Her eyes popped open, and he was still staring at her. His scorn was not meant for her. His fingers tightened on her. "He never said I had to."

"Bah." He released her, and she took a step back, prepared for the worst. "What sort of man asks his daughter to marry so far below her station?"

"You don't understand."

He shot back an answer. "I do. Don't think for a moment I don't."

"He would have lost The Cooperage. The lawyers had been to the house twice. The bailiff would have been next." She looked at him, stripped again of emotion. "We would have had to move away from our only memories of Mama. Our home. He'd already arranged to send Emily to a relative in Bath. Mary was to go away, too. And I was to be sent to yet another relative. He meant to keep Anne with him. Emily was a girl too young to lose everyone she loved, and Mary—I knew she meant to do something drastic, and I could not let that happen."

"It was not your dilemma to solve."

"But it was." She was a rival for Thrale's reserve. "To keep my sisters together in this house, all I need do was marry Jack Wilcott." She swallowed the lump in her throat. The truth was not something she could change, and she would not lie to him or make what had happened sound less dreadful than it hand been. "He cried when he showed me the letters about Emily and Mary. The mortgages and the dunning letters, nearly a hundred of them, and correspondence from the lawyers and bankers. I knew what I was doing. You mustn't think I did not."

"Lucy—"

"He wanted me. He didn't want Anne or Mary." Why had she thought his eyes were the color of fog when they were cold, sharp steel? "I did not want to marry him, that is true." If, somehow, Thrale did not understand what she'd done, how thoroughly she'd ruined herself when she'd married Devil, then he must be made to understand, or there was no use thinking they were friends. "I knew what it meant to marry a man like him and what others would think of me for it." She clutched the sides of the table behind her until her fingers ached. "No matter any of that, sir. Devil was a decent, honorable man, and I will never say I'm ashamed of having loved him."

Still too close to her, he spoke in a hard voice, at the edge of indelicate. He touched her cheek, and her soul clenched at the contact. "What else could you have done?"

She sat on the nearest chair, undone by his pity. She covered the top of her bowed head with her palms. "I could have let him send us away."

"Another girl might have submitted to that fate." He'd come closer while she was bent over, and she was still, still hopelessly at sea. He did not despise her. He didn't. Yet. When he'd had time to reflect on what she'd done, he would. She remained bent, for she could not bear to look at him. "Again I ask you," he said in a steely voice, "what happened today that made you so distraught?"

She straightened because she was no coward. "I ask you again, does it matter?"

His expression softened, and that broke her to see that he wanted to be kind to her. "That is not a question you ought to ask me."

"I do not mean to offend you."

He crouched, hands on the arms of her chair. "Whatever you say I will not betray your confidence to anyone. Not to your father. Nor to any of your sisters."

She let out a breath, unsettled. She could trust him. If he made her a promise, he would keep it. "I saw Arthur Marsey in town."

"Marsey." He pushed away, standing now.

"He knew me before."

"Meaning?"

"As Devil's wife."

"He insulted you."

"No more than Mrs. Glynn or others like her." She sat forward. "I do not blame any of them. They are rightly appalled. As you are."

"What's appalling, Mrs. Wilcott, is your father having the gall to put such a choice before you."

"I'm glad he did." She wiped her eyes of tears. There was no possible way to make the truth anything but what it was. She accepted the consequences of what she'd done. Devil had not been a gentleman. Nothing like it. "Glad, my lord. I'll never not be. We'd have been sent away if he hadn't."

He gave her a curt bow. "If Marsey makes himself unpleasant to you, tell me."

"No."

"I'll see he never does again."

CHAPTER FIFTEEN

At half past twelve in the morning, fewer than three feet separated Thrale from Mrs. Wilcott. "Afraid, my lord?"

Her gaze locked on him. Determined. Focused. Her bare fists were up, one slightly in front of the other. A table and several chairs had been pushed to the side of the room. His coat hung half off one of the chairs. She'd kicked off her slippers. Her shawl lay abandoned on an ottoman.

"Of a slip of a woman like you?" He kept his loose fists high, too, but he was aware now, having had a painful lesson, that he needed to protect his torso. "Never."

His neckcloth was wrapped around her waist in order to hold her skirts high enough to avoid her tripping on them as she had before. Pale-rose material bunched above, and he had told himself more than once now that he would not look at her ankles. He could not afford the distraction. Besides that, her informal gown was cut loose enough to give her less restricted movements of her upper torso.

The damn woman was fast. Blindingly fast. They could not face each other in earnest, and yet her speed required his vigilance. No matter what he did, she anticipated him so easily he'd begun to think even if wanted one of his punches to connect, he'd not succeed.

There was no hope of her landing a facer, and she wasn't trying. He was too tall for that. But six times now, she'd tapped his torso; ribs, stomach, chest. She came in close, jabbed. His rapid twist to the side avoided contact.

In his defense, he had strikes of his own to count. Not punches;

loose-fisted touches. The presence of bosom was an adjustment. He had no experience with bosoms when he was within the ropes.

Left cross.

To no avail. She wasn't there to for him touch and, bugger him, her knuckles grazed his side. Her follow-up was lightning. If there was anything to be said in praise of his performance, it was that she was breathing hard. Her cheeks were flushed from exertion. He focused and deflected her next punch, a ribber. Her right connected with his belly.

He lifted his hands and stepped back. "What am I doing wrong?"

She dropped her hands and shook her head as she steadied her breathing. "It's been too long. I'd not realized."

"Mrs. Wilcott. You anticipate my every move. How?"

"Your body tells me."

"Damn me. I have sparred with prizefighters who saw nothing of the sort from me. They couldn't all have been allowing me to beat them at will."

"You're close to Devil's size."

He bloody knew that. "Your point?"

"I am used to sparring with a man your size." And that man had been The Devil Himself. "You, however, are not used to a match with someone my size. You're holding back too much."

"I'll not fight a woman. Not in earnest. You can't expect for a moment that I would."

Her smile reached her eyes, and she was transformed. The effect was...bracing to say the least. "Advantage, Mrs. Devil Wilcott."

"There's more. Tell me."

She relented. "You're faster than this."

"I outweigh you by ten stone or more." He extended an arm. "I've twice your reach."

"Of that I am aware." She moved in and touched his right shoulder. "You lead here. If you'd peeled off, I'd see more." Her fingers traced down the side of his chest. She didn't mean it as anything but an illustration of what she was telling him. He kept his lust to himself. "This tells me all. If you continue to spar with me at half or three-quarter speed, I'll have all the time in the world to see where you mean to strike."

"I won't risk hurting you."

"You insult me."

He crossed his arms over his chest. "How so?"

"You think I've not held back with you."

"The devil you say."

"I do." She lifted her fists again. "Faster, my lord. See if you can make me scream."

Enough, he thought. Enough. He'd had enough of her getting the better of him. "That will do, ma'am."

She lifted her eyebrows. "Whatever do you mean, my lord?"

"You bait me. Deliberately."

"Am I succeeding?"

He lifted loose-fisted hands, and while he kept rein on himself, he gave her the credit she was due. This time while they sparred, that she was a woman ceased to matter. She *had* been holding back. She came inside his reach, and, before he could reset, she landed three crisp punches. Chest, stomach, ribs.

He took the blows. He'd had far, far worse. She came back to position, and he crossed with his left, fast enough to send a jolt of anxiety through him at the possibility that he would connect too hard. She evaded, but he touched her midsection, and then was obliged to slide away to avoid that fast right of hers. She still anticipated him.

Methodically, he tested her. How fast could she react, and how fast could he punch and jab and stay within the bounds of necessary control? This forced him to consider his technique, and then he understood the movements of his body that had conveyed to her his intentions. The dip of his shoulder. That his head tipped.

At last, she skipped back several feet, hands lifted, panting. "I've not the bottom for this."

He strode to her and put his hands on her shoulders. "By God, you've taught me more in twenty minutes than I learned these past two years."

She was breathing hard. So was he, and the room went away. They could have been at the Academy or out there by the river, or anywhere where there wasn't another soul near. He wanted her. His blood was up, lusts aroused as he'd not been in some time. They were alone. He could take her in his arms and happily spend another twenty minutes dedicated to making her scream.

Once, not so long ago, she'd dared him, knowing the whispers about him, she'd invited him to do whatever he wanted. Anything. A sexual *carte blanche*. Tension zinged through him.

"You're welcome, my lord."

She had no such thoughts about him. He forced himself to release her and step back. He could do nothing when he was in this state. Should do nothing. He bowed. "I owe you a debt."

"I owe you one, too."

He retrieved the table he'd pushed to the side of the room and returned it to its place. Next, he fetched two of the chairs, carrying one in each hand. Mrs. Wilcott returned another, and he finished by putting on his coat and replacing the final chair. In the meantime, she'd unknotted his neckcloth from her waist and returned her clothes to order.

"Thank you." He shoved the linen into his coat pocket. "Good night, Mrs. Wilcott."

She curtsied. "My lord."

When he reached his quarters, he found Niall waiting with one shoulder against the wall by the door. He had a grin on his face and an open bottle of brandy in his hand. "My lord Thrale. Had a good night, then?"

"I have, thank you." He held out a hand, and Niall gave over the bottle.

CHAPTER SIXTEEN

Lucy fished out her ledger and pencil and added twenty pounds eleven shillings to her two hundred and six pounds. The amount was still less than what she'd had previously, but this addition made back a portion of the hundred pounds she'd given her father. Her goal was four hundred pounds. Five hundred would be better, but with the smaller sum, she could live modestly on her own, as a widow must often do.

She looked down. "A fair penny, Roger."

The dog thumped its tail on the floor.

A fair penny, yes. But not enough. Counting up her savings and finding the sum lower than it had been turned her stomach. What if she'd lost some, or even all, of her wagers this past week? Her strategy was to win more than she lost over time; this she had done. Nevertheless, each loss, every occasion on which she dipped into her savings put her planned removal that much farther off.

She touched her lockbox. Granger and Clancy would meet, that was certain. All but the date and location were settled. If ever she was going to leave here, she would do so by boldness. Therefore, bold she would be. If the match came about, she intended to make a significant wager on that battle.

Her father would never reform. He would always spend more money than he had. She would always be his target for ready cash and miraculous economies or imagined tearful appeals to Aldreth or the duke. She would always feel obligated to use her own money to make ends meet or pay bills her father did not. She replaced her ledger and pencil and turned the key in the lockbox just as the door opened.

"Lucy, my dear."

She jumped, and that was a mistake, for there stood her father, his attention fixed on the box in her hands. She willed herself to have no reaction. "Yes, Papa?"

"Emily asks when you are coming downstairs."

"Momentarily."

"Not a bad tactic, my girl, to keep them waiting. All eyes on you."

She drew on her calm. "Thank you, Papa."

"Captain Niall tells me he finds you charming."

"Oh?"

He examined one of the buttons on his coat. "Young Glynn has a bigger fortune, and he's a neighbor. I'd have you close by when you leave us."

"Papa."

"It's right that you'd want to." He broke out of his melancholy. "So, I advise you, it's Thrale you ought to smile at more often, for he has a larger fortune yet, and a title."

"Yes, Papa."

"You may find the captain more dashing, I daresay most women do, but it's Glynn or Thrale will make you a better husband."

What was she to say to that?

"Your mother would be easy knowing a man like Thrale had her daughter to wife. She'd want the best for you. She wanted the best for all you girls."

"I know." Marriage would not be the means of her leaving here. No man of rank would have her, not Harry Glynn. Not Captain Niall, and certainly not Lord Thrale. More than anything, she wanted a solitary life, as befit a widow with time to read all the poetry and novels she could buy or borrow. She wanted her own garden with roses and daisies and lavender. She wanted free of the silence that bound her here.

"Thrale it is, then." He nodded as if his deciding the matter made it inevitable.

She did not move until he was gone. He'd seen her lockbox and the open drawer. Her desk was no longer a safe place to keep it, but where could she hide it from him? She looked around her room, considering and then discarding several alternatives. She settled on the back of her wardrobe.

"Lucy?" This time it was Emily who'd come to her door. "Did Papa not find you?"

"He did." She would see Emily removed from here, too. Leaving Emily behind was unthinkable. Her sister could live with Aldreth and Mary, or Cynssyr and Anne. Papa could not object to that. If Lucy was nearby The Cooperage, then all the better.

"Everyone's waiting."

She stood and smoothed her skirts. This morning's walking dress kept her reputation for fashion intact, as it must. She took her mantle from the chair where she'd left it. Every ensemble a new disguise. For this morning's outing, an apple-green muslin under-skirt, pale jade tunic with pearl fastenings to her knees, a darker green hat with ribbons around the brim, and a yellow mantle lined with swan's down. Her boots matched the mantle, her parasol matched her tunic. Yellow kid gloves and a yellow-and-green reticule made her *tout ensemble*.

"How do I look?"

Emily swung her reticule. "You are stunning, as always. I wish I had dark hair like you."

"I wish I had golden hair like you."

"I don't know why. Have you tied your laces?"

She lifted the hem of her gown to show her boot laces tied and double-knotted. "No one will trip."

"Excellent." Emily clapped her hands. "Hurry now."

They were engaged to call on Clara Glynn's married sister, who'd wed last year. She and her husband lived on the other side of Little Merton, the next village over, on a property renowned for its view of the valley. They had a cook who, Emily swore, served an incomparable tea. On her way out, Lucy bent to take Roger's head in her hands. "You must stay here, old man."

Roger whined.

"It's too far, my darling boy. You must rest. When I am back, I shall take you for a walk, just the two of us." She rose and remembered, at the last moment, to pluck her reticule from the dresser. "We're off, then. Be a good boy, Roger."

Emily led the way downstairs, chatting the entire way about their engagement in Little Merton. "I own, their cook is almost as talented as Cynssyr's."

"We are in for a delightful repast if that's true." At the bottom stair, Lucy readjusted her mantle and avoided the pier glass on the opposite wall. Captain Niall stood beside Clara Glynn. There wasn't another gentleman in the whole of England whose smile made others so cheerful. There, as well, was Harry Glynn whom she now thought might be enamored of Emily, not that it mattered, for Emily did not seem to be in love with anyone.

In the shadows of the entrance to what they had always called the butler's pantry—though there had never been a butler at The Cooperage—Lord Thrale held his hat in one hand. Such a serious expression. Dark corduroy breeches, a tan greatcoat, and boots suitable for a country walk. He nodded, and she curtsied.

"Mrs. Wilcott." Harry Glynn pushed off the wall he'd been leaning against. "Enchanting to see you after so long."

"Likewise, Mr. Glynn." They'd been such friends when they were young. She did regret the loss of that acquaintance.

Since his youth, Harry had grown from a gangly boy to a solid man with broad shoulders and a wide chest. Not a little handsome, either, with his dark hair and eyes. His mother had sent him away the summer she turned seventeen. She was married not long afterward and far gone from Bartley Green. He'd been away when she'd returned after her husband's death and was only recently come home. They had studiously avoided each other at church or the Bartley Green assemblies. Given the accusations laid at her feet in respect of him, that seemed a wise course for them both.

Captain Niall looked her up and down, and she pretended not to notice, but in truth, his attention unsettled her.

Emily held out a hand. "Do come, Lucy."

Clara smiled, too, so genuinely that Lucy was reminded of happier days when they had tramped through the fields and had adventures and when they returned home it was to no care greater than whether they would like the dinner put before them.

"Clara." She must be circumspect, even among past friends. "I'm looking forward to seeing your sister after so long."

"I as well," Harry said. "It's been an age since I saw her."

"Hah." Clara jabbed her brother in the side, and he feigned injury, as he had done when they were children. A pang of regret went through her for the days when they met to make up lovely, fey games to be played indoors or out. "You're looking forward to tea at Nan's is all."

"No more than you, little brat."

Clara laughed. "The first true thing I've heard from you since you came home."

"Are we ready, then?" Captain Niall put on his hat. "My lord?"

"Indeed, Captain." Thrale nodded. "These last long minutes."

"Three beautiful women." Captain Niall grinned at Clara, Emily, and her. "My lord, Mr. Harry Glynn, I challenge us to think of a happier predicament than ours."

Emily gave her arm to Harry, interesting that, and Clara to Lord Thrale—there was an excellent pairing, Clara and Thrale. Captain Niall put a hand to his chest. "Mrs. Wilcott?"

She did not move, despite that the others were already outside. He was a guest here. He was Lord Thrale's friend. She could not fail to warn him. "You have an acquaintance with Mr. Arthur Marsey."

"I do." A wary expression came into his eyes.

"Have you known him long?" She used her drawing room smile, and his eyes widened. She recognized in his reaction a comforting dismissal of her as anything but a woman whose appearance he admired. She embraced the safety of that.

"A most excellent man, I assure you. One of the Wessex Marseys."

"I don't wish to speak ill of anyone."

"You do not approve of him. You made that plain." His smile sent dread coursing through her. "Never fear, Mrs. Wilcott. He explained your situation to me."

"Did he?" She was too late, then.

"That there was once a...friendship between you. Gone awry as such friendships sometimes do."

The pit of her stomach knotted. "We were never friends. He did my husband a great wrong, and I think, sir, that you should be cautious."

He held her gaze. "In the time I have known him, he has never been anything but a gentleman." He gave the word *gentleman* a subtle emphasis.

"No, of course not." Marsey had told him about Devil. Captain Niall would never see her as anything but a woman who had compromised herself without hope of redemption. He was not wrong. "If you wish to avoid ruin, have no financial dealings with the man."

"Thank you," he said without sounding at all thankful for her warning.

There was nothing more she could do. She headed for the door and was halfway down the front stairs before he caught up.

"They'll not leave us behind, Mrs. Wilcott." He took her hand and placed it on his crooked arm with a firm pat as if their unpleasant exchange had never happened. "If they did, why, I daresay we would enjoy a private promenade."

She pulled away from him. "They have not got far."

On the path ahead, Harry waved his hat at them and called out, "We were about to leave you to catch us up on your own."

They set out, heading in the general direction of Rosefeld, though they would pass only a corner of Aldreth's property before they turned toward Little Merton. Captain Niall and Harry were soon conversing as if they'd been friends their entire lives. They'd been to the same college at Oxford, albeit a few years apart.

As they walked, Harry elicited a few comments from Captain Niall about his military service, and when it was clear there were memories Captain Niall had rather not relive, Harry adroitly changed the subject. Well done of him. From there, conversation turned to matters agricultural. Soon all three men were debating methods of farming.

Lucy walked ahead with Emily and Clara, and allowed her conversation with Captain Niall to fall away. Her sister was right. It *was* a lovely day to be out and about. Only a few clouds floated in the sky, though one felt the promise of rain in the air.

The path went from well trod to narrower as they veered toward the hill that would give them a panorama view of Bartley Green, the very hill that she had sent Lord Thrale to ascend that morning when he'd appeared on the path and reminded her of Devil.

CHAPTER SEVENTEEN

As they walked, Lucy raised her face to the sun. She didn't care that it would ruin her complexion. The warmth felt good. Her father and The Cooperage were in another world. Arthur Marsey was nowhere near. If Captain Niall now thought the less of her, well, then he did. There was beauty and friendship here, and she wanted always to remember this carefree afternoon.

"This hill," Thrale said as they began the climb. They were all of them now walking together. "This blasted hill. I broke my lungs here."

"I deduce, my lord," Harry said with a look over his shoulder at Thrale, "that the illustrious owner of the Academy praised this hill to you."

"He has."

"He must think you're worth something, for he would not otherwise advise you to take that training."

Captain Niall clapped a hand over his heart. "He's not given me that advice, and I am no slacker, I promise you."

"Johnson wasn't the first to tell me," Thrale replied.

Captain Niall's look in her direction turned her blood cold. She stumbled, but Emily caught her elbow.

"Who was it?" Harry asked. "Another of the fighters?"

Lucy's heart pounded so hard she had to concentrate on breathing calmly.

"Goodness." Emily slowed. "This hill shall be the death of me!"

"Mrs. Wilcott," Clara said, "why did you not bring that dog of yours? I should think he would have enjoyed the walk."

"To Little Merton and back is too far for him." Harry's question to Lord Thrale was forgotten.

Clara continued in bright tones. "Your Roger has made me wish for a hound like him."

Captain Niall belted out a laugh. "That mongrel? Miss Glynn, why?"

"I have observed that Roger is loyal and even-tempered. He adores Mrs. Wilcott. I should like a dog with those qualities."

"I'll take a good birding dog over any other."

Emily skipped ahead and cried out, "Was there ever a grander day than this? Clara, race me to the top. Lucy, come! Come! We must take the hill before the gentlemen."

Clara darted after Emily. Lucy stayed where she was, remembering a time when she'd have not have hesitated to race away like that. Emily pulled her bonnet from her head and ran bareheaded, and she did not care, Emily didn't care at all. None of the gentlemen appeared to mind or otherwise be shocked.

The hill was too steep for the two young women to keep the pace they'd set, and before long they slowed. Emily, hair bright in the sun, turned and waved. "Lucy! Have you abandoned us?"

She wanted to run. She wanted to forget the need for dignity. She wanted to fly to them. She saw herself racing up the hill, laughing, calling out the danger.

"Lucy, do come!" Clara cried out, half bent over, hands on her knees. "Do not desert us in our hour of need."

Thrale said, "Gentlemen, two such girls as that cannot defend the hill against us. Not when we have a military mind among us."

And then she simply did. She might never again have such a moment of pure happiness. She picked up her skirts and ran. The wind caught her bonnet, and the loose bow came undone. She let the hat soar to the heavens, if that's where the breeze would take it. She sped toward Emily and Clara, calling out to them as she had when they were girls, her words flying away, "To arms, ladies. They plot against us!"

When she reached Emily and Clara, she grabbed their hands and together they ran, walked, and lurched, gasping, to the very top of the hill. They turned as one and stared at the men forty yards distant.

"Gentlemen." Lucy cupped her hands on either side of her mouth. "My lord. We have the high ground. Abandon hope, for we shall not yield."

"We stand fast." Emily put her hands on her hips. "Always."

The men went different directions. Harry and Captain Niall to the left and right respectively, Thrale a circuitous route away from other two.

"Ladies." Lucy raised her voice. "I claim this land as ours and christen it Butterfly Hill." She gave Emily and Clara her most serious gaze. "Let no one take what belongs to us. We do not, my comrades-in-arms, bestow friendship upon those who think they shall defeat us."

Clara giggled and then saluted. "Unity!"

"Sororité!" Emily saluted, too.

Captain Niall and Harry were halfway up the hill. Thrale was yet some distance from them. If he did not wish to join the fun, then, let him not. *She* had a hill to defend.

Clara pointed to a spot five yards from them. "If you value your lives, do not cross that line."

Lucy wrapped an arm around Clara's waist. Emily moved closer, and Lucy put her other arm around her sister's waist. "At your great peril, sirs."

Harry stopped. He, too, pointed. "This line? Are you certain it's this one?"

"Yes, Harry. That one."

He stroked his chin. "Have you terms for your surrender?"

"Our surrender? Are you mad?" Emily scoffed. "What of yours?"

"None," Lucy said.

Captain Niall approached. His eyes sparkled with laughter, and there was surely never a man more joyful than he. "Never mind the line, Mr. Glynn. The line means nothing. We shall obliterate it."

"Miss Sinclair?" Harry set his hands to his hips. "You're a reasonable young lady. What say you to a peaceful surrender?"

"Trust nothing my brother says. Look at his eyes. I always know when he's not truthful."

"Yes, Clara," Lucy said, "I have seen that look myself."

"Mr. Glynn." Captain Niall sent a fiery look at Harry. "You can't mean to treat with these usurpers of The Battery Fortress."

Emily gave a dramatic sneer. "Butterfly Hill."

"I say we lay siege." The captain's gaze flicked to Lucy. She lifted her chin. Silently, she told them, think what they would of her, she would never surrender to anyone's contempt.

"Caution," Harry said. "You don't know what my sister and Miss Sinclair are capable of."

Captain Niall stood tall. "Defensively, they hold a superior position. I will allow that. But we gentlemen have determination and courage."

Clara ran the toe of her slipper in a line before her. "Sacred ground here, Captain. Concede defeat now, for we, too, are determined to hold our position."

Harry examined the terrain and his three opponents. "Perhaps this is not the battle we wish to fight, Captain, sir."

"Three women? We can take them."

"My sister is pitiless," Harry said. "There might be consequences in not making peace."

Clara pointed at him. "I'll tell Nan not to serve you tea."

"No tea." Emily punched a fist in the air. "Solidarity!"

"Courage, my brother," Captain Niall said.

Harry put a hand to his stomach. "You never in your life had a better tea, Captain Niall. You won't want your life if we find ourselves denied."

"Hunger means nothing to me. Why, I've had a two days march with nothing to eat or drink but a dried biscuit and a mouthful of brackish water."

"Food such as you have never tasted." Harry patted his flat belly.

Captain Niall walked perilously near the line of demarcation and studied it.

"Think of it, Harry," Clara said. "No apple tarts. No Geneva wafers."

"My sister Nan would take their side in a single beat of her black heart."

"There is always a cost to war," said Captain Niall.

Harry pretended to stagger. "Have you had Geneva wafers?" He kissed his fingertips. "Bliss that melts in your mouth."

Lucy tightened her arms around Emily and Clara. "I believe you were speaking of terms?"

"Gentlemen." Lord Thrale appeared in the gap between Harry and Captain Niall. Hands clasped behind him, he took several steps forward and propped one booted foot on an outcropping of rock.

Emily pointed. "Cross that line, my lord, and it shall be your Rubicon."

Still with a hand behind his back, Thrale braced his forearm across his thigh. "Terms, you say?"

"My lord." Emily straightened.

"Brave lass," Lucy said. "Brave lass. The very best of sisters. My lord, Captain Niall and Mr. Glynn were about to capitulate. Are you wise enough to join them?"

A smile spread across his face, and then he brought his hand from behind his back.

Clara gasped.

"Infamous," Emily said.

He tapped one of the silk flowers on Lucy's hat. "I confess, ladies, I do not know much of fashion, but this seems a striking bit of headgear. Am I right, gentlemen? Did this not, when it sat upon Mrs. Wilcott's head, seem the finest sort of bonnet a lady could wear?"

Harry nodded. "That it did, my lord."

"Can't disagree there," Captain Niall said.

"Shame if she were never to wear it again."

Lucy looked to Clara and then to Emily. She drew herself up. "Stand fast, gentle ladies. If I sacrifice the most cunning hat there ever was, I shall do so."

Emily giggled.

Clara looked directly at her brother. "You will never taste another Geneva wafer. I promise you."

"Suppose," Lord Thrale said, running a finger along the brim of Lucy's hat, and without looking up, "I bought Miss Glynn and Miss Sinclair two such hats. Would that not be an inducement to peace on our terms?"

"Two hats?" Emily tightened her arm around Lucy's waist. "We scoff at your two hats."

Thrale looked at the other men. "What say you?"

Harry folded his arms over his chest. "The recipe for Geneva wafers must be made safe. I say if they're to have new bonnets it must be in return for peace and Geneva wafers for all posterity."

Lucy tapped her foot on the ground. "Don't be greedy, Mr. Glynn. We cannot promise what is not ours to give."

"Ah," said Captain Niall. "What delights are in your power to grant?"

"What is a hat to possession of the hill?" Emily said.

Thrale pretended fascination with Lucy's bonnet. "You have misunderstood. Two hats for each of you, of course."

"And for Lucy," Clara said. "Two hats for Lucy as well."

"But of course." He made a half bow.

"At the milliner of your choosing," Harry added.

"I hear nothing but empty words." Clara shook her head. "By what date shall you be bound to comply with our treaty terms?"

A smile twitched at Lord Thrale's mouth. "We cannot, I am sure you can imagine, guarantee the date of delivery. That will not be in our control. But we three"—he gestured to Harry and Captain Niall—"will escort you to the shop no later than Friday next. Agreed, gentlemen?"

"Agreed." Captain Niall gave a curt nod.

"That is acceptable." Harry did the same.

Emily swung her arms free. "Six hats? Why, I daresay, we've profited more than any of us dreamed when we took Butterfly Hill for our own."

"Battery Fortress," Captain Niall said.

"Butterfly Hill." Lucy bent to pat the ground. "Or there will be no recipe for Geneva wafers put into the hands of your cooks, sirs."

"Mrs. Wilcott." Harry put a hand over his heart. "Have mercy."

Lord Thrale smoothed one of the ribbons of her bonnet. "Sir. She has none."

CHAPTER EIGHTEEN

Thrale leaned against his chair, a plate of Geneva wafers in hand. He had but three left of the original five he'd been served, and he was eyeing the larger plate on which the remainder had been arranged. He did not mean to be greedy, but they were a devilishly good concoction. A buttery wafer cone filled with jam and fresh cream that melted in one's mouth. Harry Glynn had been right to insist that the recipe be shared.

The ladies were seated near Glynn's elder sister, Mrs. Briggs. Her husband sat beside her, one arm around his wife's shoulder while she leaned against him, head toward his shoulder. Her son was fast asleep and limp against her body, his head resting on her shoulder.

He had never been one to think much about the domestic state except in the most abstract terms. He must one day marry, yes. He must one day have children; also the case. So why, when previous encounters with other people's offspring never made his chest tighten, was he now enrapt and enthralled by the Briggs's infant?

The child was so thoroughly helpless and dependent, and he wanted all at the same time to brush a finger across the child's cheek, be nowhere near him, and to hold the infant himself. He envied Mrs. Briggs and her husband to the point where his own unmarried and childless state seemed intolerable.

"A handsome boy," Thrale said.

"Isn't he just?" Mrs. Briggs beamed at the child and kissed his soft forehead. "So much like his father, yet such an easy, good-natured boy."

"There's a bit of the devil in him." Mr. Briggs patted his wife's shoulder. "Is that not so?"

"Didn't I say, Mr. Briggs," said Mrs. Briggs in all fondness, "that he is like his father?"

"That you did, my love. That you did." Mrs. Briggs met Thrale's gaze then stood and crossed the three steps to his chair. "Would you like to hold him? It's easy when they're sleeping."

Before he could object, she settled the boy in his arms, and he, somehow, had moved his hands to accept the burden. The boy was transferred to his care as if he weren't a delicate, helpless, creature who ought to be protected from brutes like him. Mrs. Briggs pushed one of his arms underneath the baby's bum. He put the other across the boy's back, and the child hardly stirred. The blind trust of everyone involved shattered him, from the baby, to Mrs. Briggs and her husband, and everyone else who didn't think he'd drop the poor thing.

"One day, you'll have one of your own." Mrs. Briggs stayed close. Thank goodness for that. "Just think, when it's yours you'll say to yourself, 'I've held a baby before!' and I shall tell everyone that a marquess held our boy."

Young Mr. Briggs slumbered on, unmindful of his present danger or of a future where he would be proud—heaven make it so—to have been cradled by Lord Thrale himself.

"Well now," he said. "I'll have to make something of myself, won't I?"

Briggs laughed. "There, sir, you had better, for that's my boy you've got in your arms."

At that moment, Thrale wanted to be married. He wanted a wife who thought he set the sun in the sky and whom he could fondly tease. A woman with whom he could share words and looks only the two of them understood. A woman he could tease like that, and who could tease back with words that carried a meaning known only between them. Children. A boy as soft and sweet as this one. His own children, to be loved fiercely and joyfully. Sons and daughters he could hold fast and say *isn't she just* with the same joyful pride and awe as Mrs. Briggs.

His father might have been a hard and neglectful parent, but that did not mean that he would be the same, if the day came that he was a parent. When that day came. That choice was his, to be a different sort of father. To be a different sort of husband, too.

The nursemaid leaned in. "Let me take him. He'll mess your coat, milord."

He cupped a hand over the back of the boy's head. "He's fast asleep, can't you see?"

Captain Niall shuddered. "What unspeakable domesticity."

Thrale stood, the boy snugly in his arms. Mrs. Briggs misunderstood the reason he'd left his seat and came take her son into her arms once more. "We can't have that, can we?" she said.

"You promised I could hold him." Mrs. Wilcott held out her arms.

"So I did." The infant was passed, still sleeping, to Mrs. Wilcott, who did not seem the least terrified by the responsibility. Then again, had he expected she would dash up a hill, fast as a rabbit, too, and take the lead in defending captured territory? He felt he'd been given a private glimpse into the sort of woman who would unhesitatingly sacrifice her future to save her family. And had. She had. She'd kept her family together.

Captain Niall tilted back his chair and beamed at his plate of wafers. He was also, naturally, gazing in the general direction of Mrs. Wilcott. Whatever else one thought of her, she was, at this moment, quite the Madonna-like beauty. "Now, the scene is perfection itself."

Eyes on the baby, Mrs. Wilcott smiled. "Why would it not be, with so perfect a child?"

"The best child in the world, I daresay." Glynn ate his last wafer. "The best nephew there ever was in the world."

"Thank you, Harry." Mrs. Briggs pushed the plate of Geneva wafers toward her brother. He took half a dozen.

"I'll buy him a pony." He ate one of the treats. "I saw a nice one t'other day when I was at the stockyard in Bartley Green."

Mrs. Briggs laughed. "He's not yet crawling."

"I think his father can buy him a pony." Briggs put several Geneva wafers on his plate, too. "When it's time."

"How else am I to spoil the best nephew a man ever had if not with a pony?"

"Visit him," said Mrs. Briggs. "Come see us and dandle him on your knee."

Glynn extended his arms. Thrale wondered whether there hadn't been something to Mrs. Glynn's worry, not on account of Mrs. Wilcott, but on account of Harry Glynn.

"Lah, Harry, not when he's fast asleep."

"You allowed Lord Thrale to hold him."

"I knew Lord Thrale would not wake him."

"I'm not giving him up yet," Mrs. Wilcott said. "He's too sweet."

"Why should you have all the delight of holding him?" Glynn wriggled his fingers at Mrs. Wilcott. "Think what you can tell him, Nan, when he's old enough to understand his uncle held him in his arms."

"Don't listen to a word he says," Miss Glynn said.

"Another time for you, sir," said Mrs. Wilcott. "I am too selfish to give him up, as everyone knows."

There was the briefest silence, full of discomfort because, as he realized now, that was very much her reputation. Everyone here knew that.

In the silence, her cheeks went pink. "You will see him more often than I, Harry. Who knows when I shall have the chance to hold him again?"

"That's the truth," Mrs. Briggs said too brightly. He applauded her for her unfeigned warmth. "You Sinclairs do not come here often enough."

Thrale wondered then whether Mrs. Wilcott was sorry she'd not had children. Perhaps she had, though. That was a melancholy thought, that she might have borne and lost a child. She and Wilcott had been married long enough to have expected children, with her so young.

"Does he sleep well, Mrs. Briggs?" Mrs. Wilcott asked.

"Oh, yes. He's very regular, isn't he?" Mrs. Briggs consulted the nursemaid.

"Yes, ma'am, he is. He's an easy baby."

Thrale went to the parlor window. As promised, the view was breathtaking. This was disconcerting, that from nowhere this desire for a wife and children sprang up. He'd always had in mind that it would serve his father right if he never did. Now, he could think of nothing he wanted more.

Before long, Mrs. Briggs joined him in admiring the prospect. Like her younger sister, she was a pretty woman. Were there nothing but beauties born in Bartley Green and environs? "I never tire of the view, my lord."

"Nor would I, were this my house."

She settled herself on the window seat. "I'm glad to see Mrs. Wilcott and Miss Sinclair here. It's been too long."

"They are agreeable callers to have, ma'am."

"Allow me to tell you what an honor it is to have you visit us. I must thank Harry and Clara for bringing you."

Young Mr. Briggs remained sound asleep, with Mrs. Wilcott showing no signs that she wished not to be holding the infant. Indeed, while he watched her, he saw her finger brush lightly over the boy's cheek. "The honor is mine, I assure you."

"Thank you, my lord. You're very kind."

He said, "You've known them a long while, the Sinclair sisters?"

"Oh, yes," Mrs. Briggs said. "Since we were children. We were great friends and have remained so, though we see each other less often than we would like."

"You must be pleased to have them back from London." He was curious about Mrs. Wilcott and that mad, mad dash up the hill that was unlike her. The sparkle in her eye and the wit, yes, the damned wit, of her demands for peace.

"We miss them when they are not here." She settled her skirts. "I think my brother was in love with all of them at one time or another."

"Understandable." Damn Harry Glynn, too.

"Have you met Anne? The duchess, I mean."

"I have. A most excellent woman."

"Harry and Anne were friends, but he was always fondest of Lucy. Mrs. Wilcott. To the point, I believe, that he wished to have an understanding."

"Oh?" Harry Glynn. Yes. That fit with the man's behavior. And his mother's.

"She never did cooperate in that. Harry made calves eyes at her with no success."

Had the proud Mrs. Glynn known more than she let on? Had her son's desires been the danger to his mother's expectations? He could not find it in him to fault a youthful Harry Glynn for falling in love with a neighboring beauty, but he could fault Mrs. Glynn for laying blame where it did not properly belong.

"I don't know if he might have convinced her to agree, but a great uncle of Mama's became ill, and that was that. Harry was sent to assist him, and from there directly to university." She nodded and leaned a shoulder toward him. "It was a difficult letter for me to write, telling him that Lucy had married. But he wrote back and said he wished her every happiness, and so, I suppose, all was well. I can't help wishing she hadn't disappointed him. I would have liked her as my sister." She glanced at Emily. "Perhaps another Sinclair."

Thrale followed her glance. He doubted Miss Sinclair was anything like in love with Glynn.

"I suppose," she went on, "that it would never have come off. Mama did not feel the Sinclairs were entirely the right sort. She objected to them all, and then—" She winced. "I'll say nothing of Lucy's marriage."

Thrale made no reply.

"We think of youth as a time to make mistakes and recover from them the wiser for our heartbreak, but there are mistakes from which one cannot recover. She married, and then Lord Aldreth fell in love with Mary, and I suppose you know Lucy came home a widow, and not long after that, Aldreth took them all to London. Even Lucy. I thought sure Mrs. Wilcott would return from London in a better situation than the last, swept off her feet by some fancy lord."

"Not for lack of suitors."

"Her and Miss Sinclair both. The duchess. Miss Anne Sinclair. To think of Anne, married to a duke!"

"Quite so." He returned his attention to Mrs. Briggs, glad she spoke so eagerly. Defending Mrs. Wilcott and her sisters at every turn. "Did you meet her husband? Mr. Wilcott?"

Her eyes went wide, and her cheeks turned pink. "I saw him once, when I heard the news and went to The Cooperage convinced I would discover it was not so. But it was. It was, every bit of it. They were already married by special license when I got there."

"As bad as that."

She did not answer immediately and, when she did, it was in a low, wondering voice. "For all his brash roughness, he had a kind look about him. I thought... however unsuitable—unthinkable match." She lowered her voice. "I thought he treated her with great respect, as he must. How could he not when she was so much his superior? The daughter of a gentleman, and him...."

"She married against her father's wishes?"

She lowered her head and her voice. "One hears so many things. Her sisters were devastated, I know that. Anne especially. She took it hard, Lucy marrying like that."

He made a sound he hoped would be taken for *please continue.* Was it possible he'd not heard the truth from her? She couldn't have been with child, could she? With Wilcott agreeing to be the father of another man's—Jesus. Glynn? Had Devil Wilcott seen her out of a desperate situation?

"She came home a changed woman. Who would not be changed?"

"Indeed."

"I don't care how much money he's said to have given her father—" Mrs. Briggs turned white as ash.

He pulled a figure from the air. "Ten thousand pounds, I heard."

"Oh, lah, my lord." Some of her alarm faded. "Forty thousand to pay her father's debts, though fifty changed hands, is what I heard. That can't be true. I won't believe it. Not even of Mr. Sinclair, and I'll believe a great deal about him. A gentleman wouldn't sell his daughter to a man like that."

Thrale stared out the window. If Sinclair were here right now, he'd be sorely tempted to thrash the man and demand answers, he was that angry on Mrs. Wilcott's behalf.

"Even at seventeen, she was the most beautiful creature you ever saw."

"That, I believe." Jack Wilcott had bought a beautiful wife for fifty thousand pounds sterling. The Devil Himself meeting Sinclair, seeing Lucy and falling in love. Wanting to possess the one thing a gentleman could have that he could not. There would have been a compliment, with The Devil telling Sinclair he had a beautiful daughter. Carefully, though. A man of his class had to be careful what he said and how he said it.

Perhaps they'd been at the Crown & Pig. Sinclair standing the great pugilist a drink. The subject of money could have come up. The innkeeper might have refused Sinclair more credit. Perhaps Wilcott had seen Sinclair lose and fail to pay a wager. Sinclair, drunk, half drunk, all drunk, might have blurted out that he'd sell his daughter for fifty thousand.

"She came home," Mrs. Briggs said, "and all she did was take long walks with that dog of hers and never speak. No one here who knew about her marriage spoke to her, that's so. Then Lord Aldreth took them all to London." She lifted her hands and let them fall to her lap. "And now Anne is a Duchess and a mother, and Emily, I daresay, won the hearts of everyone who met her."

"You are not wrong."

Glynn called out, "Nan. Nan. Are you done filling Lord Thrale's head with nonsense over there?"

The baby stirred in Mrs. Wilcott's arms, awoke, and looked around, and Mrs. Briggs jumped to her feet. Before she left his side, she said in a low voice, "Lucy Sinclair was my dearest friend. Maybe she did disgrace herself, but she hadn't a mother to guide her, and we all knew her father may not have been the best influence. Think what you will of her or of me for speaking out of turn, but I want nothing but happiness for her. She's had so little."

"Whatever my sister is telling you is nonsense, my lord." Glynn waved a hand.

She curtsied. "Forgive me if I've talked your ear off."

"Not in the least." He escorted her to her son, now in the arms of his nursemaid. There was a great deal of fussing and cooing.

"My lord," Briggs said when Thrale had retaken his seat. "My brother here tells me you follow the great sport of pugilism."

"A fair bit. You?"

"I like to see a battle from time to time, my lord, that's no lie. Harry here's a brawler." Briggs dandled his delighted son on a knee. "Don't be fooled by his talk of art. There's no art in him."

"I don't brawl." Glynn fell serious, as befit the subject. "Shall we meet at the Academy then, and see what we shall see? There's the Thursday exhibitions. We might attend those and have a go in the ring afterward. Bring Niall and Mr. Sinclair along."

There was no question. No question at all. He was eager to face Glynn. "I consider it a positive engagement."

"Will you come along, Mrs. Wilcott?" Niall asked.

"Why would she?" Mrs. Briggs said, as astonished as everyone else by the question.

"I hear there are lady boxers. Are you one, Mrs. Wilcott?"

"No, Captain. I am not." She gave her attention to the shoulder of her gown. "I'll need to wash this out. Mrs. Briggs, do you mind?"

Thrale gave no sign that he understood what was behind Niall's query of Mrs. Wilcott. He'd been indiscreet, sparring with her in the house. Evidently they had been seen, and now Mrs. Wilcott would pay the price. Women always did.

CHAPTER NINETEEN

O n the rear terrace, Lucy moved closer to her sister so she could hear what she was saying. Emily leaned against the stone fence that separated the garden from the field. The noise from the guests remained considerable. "It's all any of the gentlemen can talk about."

"What?"

Emily shifted so the backs of her elbows were atop the fence. "The fight, of course."

"You'll soil your gown, Emily."

"Pish." But she straightened. "I shall be glad when this nonsense is over. It's never been this bad before."

"I'm sure there are many who agree with you."

"Mrs. Leverton says she's complained to the constable about all the men who are here. She says whoever is foolish enough to attend the event will find themselves taken up, and good riddance to them."

"Does she, now?" That was an alarming thought, that the local officials might do something to prevent the battle.

"Do you suppose we ought to warn Papa?" Emily scanned the company. "Harry, Captain Niall, and Lord Thrale, too. I should hate for anything to happen to them."

"They rarely arrest the gentlemen."

Emily returned her attention to her. "But sometimes?"

Lucy didn't know what to say. Other than their father, none of her family had said a word to her that touched on any subject that involved her marriage. They'd gone three years without once broaching the subject, and here was Emily confronting it headlong.

If it were anyone but one of her sisters, she would refuse to be drawn into such a conversation, but this was Emily. The sister with whom she was closest. Admitting she knew anything at all about the subject sent her pulse racing. "Sometimes. Yes."

"Will—"

"Emily." She spoke sharply. Too sharply, she saw. "This is not fit conversation for a young lady."

"My pardon." She frowned and then gave a sigh that was pure Emily. Her sister was often frustrated when anyone hinted she might be more circumspect. "I was—We never talk, Lucy. The way we used to, and I miss that. If you'd rather not say anything, I don't—Why don't you talk to me anymore?"

She drew her sister into her arms. "Oh, Emily. You haven't any idea, do you?"

Her sister hugged her hard, and for the first time in years, she wondered if it was possible to repair the break with her sisters. Emily pulled back. "It's true. I haven't an idea. I ask you, whose fault is that? I love you. I miss you. I miss us talking. I won't love you less no matter what you tell me."

"What do you want to know?"

She lowered her voice. "Were you ever at a battle where spectators were taken up?"

"No. I wasn't." She tweaked her sister's nose. "Don't look so disappointed."

"Will the constabulary try to stop the battle, do you think? It can't be any great secret that something massively big is going to happen here. Do you suppose anyone will be arrested?"

"The chief Constable will certainly be at the battle. As a spectator with money on the line, unless I am much mistaken." Her sister was so earnest that Lucy found herself fighting a lump in her throat. There had been an ocean between them. Emily was so young yet. She knew so little of men and their ways, the demands they placed on a woman. There was so little she could say that was proper.

"We ought to warn them."

"I assure you, they are already aware." She held out her arm. "You are so pretty in your new bonnet."

She touched her head. "The spoils of Butterfly Hill."

"Let's rejoin the party, shall we? Captain Niall and Mr. Glynn are there. With Clara."

"Harry is mad about this business of fighting, isn't he?"

"Like many of the men here in Bartley Green."

"I've five pounds to risk." She folded her arms beneath her bosom. "Upon whom should I put my money?"

Her pulse stuttered. "Do not say such a thing, not even in jest."

"I wouldn't be the only woman to risk a little money."

"You will not be one at all." She faced her sister and spoke more sternly than she'd intended. "Has not Papa set an example for you on the evils of gambling?"

"I have five pounds saved. I may spend it as I like."

"How will you wager?" Panic threatened. "Whom will you approach with your wager? Some Flash man on the street? A stranger? You cannot. You cannot!"

"You'll tell me, won't you?"

"No."

She lifted her chin. "I'll ask Harry."

"Most certainly you shall not."

"Then Bracebridge, when he arrives."

"You won't. I forbid it." Anne would have stopped this with but a look, but she hadn't that talent of their elder sister's, either.

Emily took her arm in hers, the very picture of docility. Lucy instantly mistrusted the change. "As you say, there is Clara. We must say good afternoon to her."

She did not move. "Emily, you mustn't. Have nothing to do with this."

Her sister rubbed the bridge of her nose. "Very well. I shan't. Whatever it is you think I will do that I ought not do."

"You don't fool me. Not for a moment. I'll talk to Aldreth. I'll tell him to forbid you."

"You would." She linked arms with Lucy again, and they strolled arm-in-arm along the perimeter of the terrace. Many of the leading residents of Bartley Green were here.

Lucy nodded to their right. "Tell me which gentlemen you admire."

"Captain Niall is handsome and amusing."

This was not an answer that she cared for. "He is."

"You've nothing to worry about. I do not like him as he wishes me to. Nor do I like the way he speaks to you. Or looks at you. You ought to marry Harry."

She stopped walking, but Emily didn't, and so Lucy was pulled along. "What?"

"He fancies you."

"Can you imagine what his mother would say of that?"

Emily laughed evilly. "Yes. Yes. You should marry Harry. Please. It would serve her right."

"Mrs. Glynn for a mother-in-law? I shudder." She stopped and lowered her voice. "Now, darling Emily, since we are telling each other secrets, are you in love with anyone?"

"No." An emphatic answer.

"Not at all?"

"No. What about you?"

She shook her head, and she saw a cloud pass over her sister's face. That was unmistakable heartbreak. "There is someone, I see it in your eyes."

"It does not signify."

"You used to tell me whenever you fell in love." She took Emily's arm again. So many men had loved her. Heavens, the duke himself had planned to marry Emily before events left him with no choice but to wed Anne. "Is it Lord Thrale? I know he admires you."

She made a face. The sun came out long enough that both of them adjusted their hats. "If I had any sense, I'd fall madly in love with him. But then I admire any man Anne admires."

They'd been walking the main gravel path, working their way

toward Harry Glynn and his sister, but now Lucy took Emily to a portion of the garden where they could speak in privacy. Emily and Thrale would be an excellent match. He deserved a woman as noble and strong-hearted as Emily. And Emily deserved an honorable man. "Why aren't you in love with Lord Thrale?"

"Don't ask after the state of my heart. It will not make either of us happy." Emily had grown up a great deal. Almost twenty and no longer a girl. When had that happened?

"Who would not love you?"

She let out a dramatic sigh. "Perhaps I will fall in love with Lord Thrale. He *is* handsome."

"Indeed so."

"He is too severe for me." Emily shook her head. "Now that I can marry whom I prefer rather than the man most able to save Papa and us from ruin, I intend to be particular." She referred, of course, to her debut in London. Yes, Aldreth had been behind that season, for Lord knows their father would never have thought of it, but all three of them, Anne, Lucy, and Emily, had been vitally aware that one of them must make a marriage. There had been no other hope for a reversal of their father's increasing losses.

"Marry after your heart, Emily."

Emily plucked a marigold from the landscape that formed the borders of the path here, and tucked it behind Lucy's ear. "Yellow looks so well on you."

"Thank you."

She broke off another bloom. "I wish it looked half so well on me." She tugged a petal from the flower and let it drop. "He loves me not." Another petal floated to the ground. "He loves me."

"Who, Emily?" Her sister was not a girl anymore.

"He loves me not. He loves me."

Lucy counted petals as quickly as she could. "Superstition. A flower cannot predict the state of a man's heart."

"It will do as well as anything else. He loves me not. He loves me." She lifted the stem with its single remaining petal. "Not. And so, you see, I am doomed to perish of unrequited love."

"Nonsense."

Emily pulled back to get a better look at Lucy, and Lucy gave her sister her full attention. They'd been close enough in age that as girls, before Lucy was married in such haste, they'd whispered to each other about the gentlemen they admired and hoped to marry. Kings and princes. Dukes and lords. Men of fabulous wealth and heroic character.

Her sister gazed in Lord Thrale's direction. "You are correct, you know. He's very handsome."

"Agreed."

Emily tilted her head. "If I'm not to marry him, perhaps you should."

"We're talking about the state of your heart, not mine." The gulf between them was too wide, and that saddened her. Emily knew nothing of the woman Lucy had become. In fairness, Lucy knew almost nothing of how her sister had changed, and she had.

"Do you mean to say you have no opinion of Lord Thrale?"

"Of course I have."

"Well?" Emily plucked another marigold and then another and began to weave a chain.

She reached for a marigold and gave it to Emily to add to her yellow necklace. "As you say, he is handsome."

"That's all?"

"Severely handsome."

Emily laughed and added another flower. "Aldreth?"

"Handsome." Lucy added the next while her sister took another marigold and worked it into Emily's chain.

"Lucky Mary, to have found a handsome man to fall so madly in love with."

"I concur."

They took turns picking marigolds and weaving their chain of gold. Emily looked at her from beneath her lashes. "What do you think of Harry?"

"Handsome, if you like a dark-haired man."

"Mm. Yes. And doesn't his mama know it too well?"

Lucy broke into laughter, and it was quite undignified. She did not care. "Doesn't she?"

"It's a shame so agreeable a man has such a disagreeable mama."

"I'll say nothing about that, thank you."

"Cynssyr?"

"You know he's too lovely for words."

"What of Lord Bracebridge?"

Lucy worked in the next flower. "I don't suppose anyone would say he's handsome."

"No one at all?" Emily dropped the chain of flowers and left Lucy holding it. Emily put her hands on her hips. "Why do you suppose so many women pursue him, then, if he's not handsome? It can't be because he's an earl."

"No?"

"Not only that. It's maddening the way women fawn over him."

"I don't suppose his title is the only reason he is admired." Thank goodness her sister was too innocent to understand the appeal a man like Bracebridge held for some women. She fastened in the last flower and turned the chain into a circle.

"He has a married lover."

Lucy's heart stilled. "You can know no such thing."

"He does."

Gently, she removed Emily's bonnet and placed the finished flowers atop her sister's fair head, a crown of brilliant yellow. "You're wrong that yellow does not suit you." She adjusted the garland and handed Emily her hat. "How I would love to be as dainty as you."

"You wouldn't."

"All the gentlemen swoon over you."

"They swoon over you, too. I wish I were tall like you. And stop changing the subject. Do you find Lord Bracebridge attractive?"

"Not as anyone would define the word, no." She smoothed a

lock of Emily's hair. She knew the game, this back and forth discussion of the men they knew, but this time, it was dangerous. Bracebridge was dangerous that way, and she was concerned that Emily seemed fully aware of that. Her innocent, beautiful, younger sister. "You do look well in blue and marigold."

Emily frowned at her bodice. "I hate blue. This shade of blue. It's insipid. I have decided I will never wear this blue again. Indeed, this is the very last blue gown you shall see me in."

Lucy laughed, glad to leave behind the uncomfortable subject of the Earl of Bracebridge. "You sound determined."

"No more pink, either. I don't care what Anne or Mary say. No one takes me seriously when I wear such colors."

"Not so."

"You don't think there's something devastating about him?"

"About whom?"

"Lord Bracebridge."

"I did not say that." She set herself to adjusting the tiny bows along Emily's neckline. Emily was old enough to know her mind. If she was old enough to find a man like Lord Bracebridge interesting, perhaps it was not too soon for her to be married. To a steady man like Lord Thrale. "If you've decided to avoid pastels despite how well they suit you, you might try darker hues. Deep blues. Do not make faces at me. Dark blue will flatter you. Red, perhaps, if you are bold enough. Green with gold trim would do. A gown of forest green. With pearls and pewter trim."

"What do you think?"

She considered her sister. She was exquisite, but it was true that the colors she wore, those pale shades, emphasized her youth, and what young woman wants constantly to be reminded that the schoolroom was so recently in her past when she noticed a man like Bracebridge? "Perhaps you're right. Banish girlish colors from your wardrobe. Banish them this instant."

"I meant about Bracebridge."

There was an inscrutable sadness in her sister's words, and it made her heart fold over. "Yes, he has something, that is undeniable."

"He speaks Italian. Did you know that?"

"Italian, you say."

"And Latin."

"What gentleman is not conversant in Latin?"

"You see what I mean, then."

"Not precisely."

"He's hardly less eligible than Lord Thrale. They are the two most handsome and eligible men we know. No one else compares."

"I agree." Was this possible? Had Emily fallen in love with Lord Bracebridge? If so, she foretold heartbreak for her sister.

"Would you marry him, Lucy? Lord Bracebridge, I mean."

CHAPTER TWENTY

Lucy linked arms with her sister again and got them strolling in the direction of Captain Niall and the others. "I haven't thought about him that way. He's done nothing to make me believe he might be so inclined, so I must question why you think he might think anything of me at all."

"I overheard Anne say he ought to marry you."

That brought her to a halt, to hear that Anne had said any such thing. Emily lifted her chin, but of all her sisters, Lucy knew Emily the best. They'd shared a room for years. They'd whispered secrets to each other in the darkness. Despite Emily's nonchalance, she heard a different truth in her sister's voice, in her eyes, in the set of her face.

"She told Mary so. I heard them talking about it. You'd get on well together, you and Bracebridge. That is my own opinion, by the way, though it mirrors Anne's."

"You are entitled to your opinion. As Anne is entitled to hers." Bracebridge and her? What could Anne have been thinking? She could not think of anyone who would suit her less.

"Mary agreed."

"Mary is entitled to her opinion as well."

"Do you not find him appealing?"

Lucy caught her sister's fleeting look of misery. "Do you?"

"He's not handsome like Cynssyr or Aldreth. Or even Thrale. No, I don't care for his looks at all."

"That's not been my impression."

"Then you have mistaken me."

She studied Emily, peering into her sister's face. "I had thought perhaps you had a fondness for Mr. Glynn."

"He's agreeable enough."

"Are you in love with him?"

Emily's chin firmed. "I'm not in love with anyone."

They continued toward the other guests. The more she thought about this situation, the more she worried about her sister's attachment to Bracebridge. Carefully, she said, "Do you think he's recovered from his disappointment over Anne?"

"No." Emily adjusted her crown of marigolds. "I don't think he has."

"Nor I," Lucy said, relieved by that admission.

"When I marry, it will be for a grand passion. Nothing else will do." She clasped her hands to her bosom with deliberate drama. "My future husband will marry me because he loves me desperately and cannot take one more breath without my love." She turned in a circle. "If I thought a gentleman felt that way about me, and I felt the same for him, then, and only then, would I marry him."

"What wouldn't I give for a life with a man who thought a grand and fatal passion was a fate to avoid."

"Oh, Lucy, how can we be so much alike and yet so different?"

Someone called to Emily and then one of the Leverton girls emerged from the crowd and hurried to them. "We are in need of your assistance. Good afternoon, Mrs. Wilcott. Do you mind if we take Miss Sinclair away?"

"Go along, Emily." She watched her sister's departure with Miss Leverton. There was a trail of admiring looks in her wake. Lucy was near enough now to Captain Niall and the others that they were already making room for her to join them. Well. There was Emily safe with the Leverton girls.

She scanned the crowd for her father. With so many sporting men here she hoped he was too busy to drink himself into disrepute. One edge of her lace shawl slipped off her shoulder, and she fished for the end before it could hit the ground, a feat that entailed her walking forward so as to put air between the ground and the lace.

She caught the end and collided with someone.

"Careful, Mrs. Wilcott."

She looked up. Thrale had his hands on her shoulders, gripping tightly enough to keep her from tumbling to the ground. The sun was in her eyes, so bright she couldn't see anything but his face. She refused the image that came to her, of that night in the parlor, when they'd cleared the floor and sparred.

"I apologize, my lord. I don't know why I am constantly knocking you over. One day I'll do you a great harm."

"No need to apologize." He didn't smile. He so rarely did, and it calmed her, the solidity of him. His steadiness.

"Forgive me, nevertheless. I'm forever losing track..." She waved a hand as if she could hardly remember the end of her sentence let alone the reason she'd walked into him. He went along with her charade.

"As long as you've not injured yourself. Have you?"

"No."

He did not reply. Or release her shoulders. An oversight on his part. The moment stretched out. He touched her temple, and there was an elongated moment during which her stomach dropped to the other side of the earth. The possibility that he meant something by that touch devastated her. He didn't. He couldn't. She did not want that between them. "Very pretty."

Lucy froze. They had in silence agreed that their improper meeting in the parlor had never happened, but she could not forget the light in his eyes nor her reaction to him. No coat. No neckcloth. More than a glimpse of his upper torso.

"There are marigolds at Blackfern."

"Marigolds?" She could not fathom why he was talking about marigolds or how that had anything to do with her.

"Such as the one in your hair."

She touched the side of her head, and yes, of course. Emily had put a marigold in her hair. "Oh. I'd forgotten. Emily has a crown of them."

"That's what you two were doing. Captain Niall was certain you were plotting something nefarious that would cost us a dozen fetching hats."

"I don't know why you are so suspicious."

Seconds before the following silence would have stretched for too long, Thrale spoke. "They were a favorite flower of my mother's. Marigolds. I grow them at Blackfern as a remembrance to her."

"Blackfern."

"A rather dreary name for an estate, but it is the Thrale seat. I'm dashed if I know if there's a black fern anywhere near." Whatever the state of things between them, uneasy, yes, very much that, he knew the worst about her and, so, she was less anxious that she might otherwise be.

"Blackfern summons the most Gothic images, don't you agree?"

"No."

"You should be grateful for such a name. Why, someone might have given it a mundane name. A workaday name. A name that implies an industrious occupation. The Cooperage, for example."

"A more pleasant name than Blackfern, I daresay."

Again, she could think of nothing to say. Nor could he, it seemed from his silence. The image of him standing by the river bank in a sweat-dampened shirt and fighting britches filled her head. "The afternoon has turned quite warm."

He nodded. Nothing more than polite. "Yes. Very warm. Shall I fetch you something to drink? Lemonade? Oh, but it's orangeade you prefer. Have I remembered aright?"

"Yes, thank you, but I don't recall telling you any such thing. How did you know?"

"You said so once to your sister."

"Which sister? Not recently I think."

"To Lady Aldreth. In London, last year. In the meantime, sit here where it's cooler." He released her shoulders and guided her to an oak tree where a table and chairs were in the shade. She watched the guests enjoying themselves as they always did at her father's entertainments. Even Mrs. Glynn. She rubbed the back of her neck, unable to erase her recollection of Lord Thrale so near to undressed. A too intimate vision. That broad chest. His strong thighs. He would not be a timid lover, she thought. He couldn't be. Not him.

"Ma'am." Thrale stood before her, a glass of orangeade extended.

"Thank you, my lord." She sipped the drink and fought to be someone besides a woman who admired a man in a sweat-soaked shirt. A woman of *Ton*. Not a serious woman at all. She swooped a hand toward one of the chairs. "Do sit."

He did, though he turned the chair so that he was facing partially away from her. Perhaps to have a view of the guests. Likely to put more space between them. He stretched out his legs. "Too many people here. Your lawn will be trampled to death."

She drank more of her orangeade and found she was glad of his company. "Will you live the rest of your life in the country, then? I don't know how else you'd avoid crowds."

"I would be very happy to do so." He tapped the arm of his chair. "Where has Captain Niall got to? Mr. Glynn engaged me to secure you and this seating whilst he brings his sister to join us. Niall, too."

"Ah." She sat forward. "I admire Miss Glynn exceedingly. Don't you?"

"She is an accomplished young lady." He tapped his fingers on the chair arm again.

Another silence descended. "Were you content in your solitude at Blackfern?"

"Hm?"

She waved to indicate he needn't reply, but he answered after all.

"The solitude of those years did not make me long for parties and entertainments, if that's what you mean."

"What? Never?"

"Never."

"I don't believe you." She took another sip of the orangeade.

"When I was young, I lived for parties. Lived for them. We all did. Even Anne."

"Ah, yes. Your assembly."

"The gentlemen who attended never looked as if they were unhappy to be there."

"With the Sinclair sisters in attendance?" His eyebrows rose. "I imagine not." He let out a breath. "As a young man, my days and evenings were occupied. I had little time for parties and no great love for them in the event."

"Did you attend no local gatherings? No dinners or teas? Were there no public dances like ours?" She set her gloved hands on the table. "Or did you retreat to your tower garret to drink cold tea and cast a gimlet eye upon the village below?"

"I dined out now and again."

"Did you?" The muscles of his thighs flexed when he moved his legs, and she thought of him pacing himself up that hill and back, ending, perhaps, at the Academy to spar, peeled off to his skin. "A yearly event for you?"

"Once a decade, more like." He let out a sharp and rueful laugh. "Blackfern is a solitary estate."

"High upon a hill with nothing but eagles and falcons for company?"

"Not quite." He shifted. The wrought-iron chair had been constructed for form more than comfort, and not for a man his size. He gave her a quick smile. "Not so far from that. At times, however, both in my youth and now, even I require gentler company than my own."

"I am trying to imagine you as a young man. I fear I cannot."

He made a gesture that included his person. "I have always looked like this. Just so."

"What about dancing. Do you like to dance?" She hastened to amend that sentence. "I mean, the young ladies are disappointed when you do not, so one would hope you enjoy dancing."

"I don't dislike it." He picked up his glass and frowned when he found it empty.

She pushed her orangeade across the table. "I am refreshed now."

"Thank you." He lifted her glass in a toast. "To your health, Mrs. Wilcott." He drank and said, glass still in his hand, "It is a gentleman's duty to engage young ladies to dance when he attends a ball."

"You make dancing sound tedious."

"Do I?" The cool gray of his eyes steadied her. God yes, let his eyes take her mind off his magnificent body. "I don't mean to."

"I wonder if you say that because you've done so little dancing," she said. "Did you have a dancing master as a boy? I can't imagine you being as clumsy as I was when I was learning to dance."

"I had no dancing master. My father failed to see to that."

She could not stop looking at his thighs, shaped by muscle, nor could she fail to recall the breadth of his chest. Magnificent in every respect. "How did you learn to dance, then?"

"My tutor saw I learned the basics."

"We Sinclair sisters had a dancing master for a time. Monsieur LeGrande. He told Papa he was French, but he had the most atrocious accent. Even I, who paid no attention to our lessons in French, could tell he did not speak the language well. I suspect he was German."

He plucked a dangling leaf from an overhead branch. "Shall I make myself a crown of oak leaves?"

"Dionysus?"

"Some woodland god."

"Dancing naked through the trees. Yes, please do."

His mouth curved. "Do you like dancing?"

She put her chin on her hand and recalled the days before she'd married, when she adored parties and being admired. "When I was young, yes."

"As if you're not young now."

"We are none of us as young as we once were."

He turned his torso toward her. The oak leaf fluttered to the ground. "That, Mrs. Wilcott, is not an answer. I did not ask if you liked dancing in the past. I asked if you like dancing now."

"I suppose I do."

"You danced in London."

"It was expected of me."

"Did you not enjoy yourself?"

"We grow out of our youthful pleasures."

"All young ladies like to dance. You, madam, are still in your youth." He waved a hand. "Therefore, you like to dance."

She gave him a sideways glance. "What other opinions will you declare for me? I shall make a list of them so as to have them constantly at hand."

"Several, as a matter of fact." He drained the last of her orange-ade.

"Do go on. I should like to know what I am to think."

He pushed her empty glass around the table, from one hand then to his other. "You have an opinion on poetry."

"Pray tell me what it is."

"That it is sublime."

"Are you certain of that?"

"Yes, madam."

"All poets or had you specific ones in mind? You named once, but I've forgotten."

"Milton." He held her gaze. "You feel Wordsworth shows prom-ise."

"If you say that's so, then it must be."

He leaned his forearms on the table. "Indeed."

A leaf floated from the tree and landed on his hat, then tumbled to the brim where it balanced. She reached for the leaf and tucked it into the silk band. "There. You are a proper god, now."

"And you a goddess?"

"No, sir."

"A nymph, then, as naked as the pursuing woodland gods."

"No nymph would run from a god such as you."

Again, he touched her, the side of his finger across her cheek, and her breath hitched at the contact, for no good reason that she could understand. He meant nothing by it, and she took nothing from it. "No?"

CHAPTER TWENTY-ONE

A hush fell like snow across a field when Mrs. Wilcott walked into the Glynn's parlor. Thrale schooled himself against any visible reaction. Niall was less circumspect. Like most of the men in the room, Thrale watched her. Breathtaking. Heartbreaking. Skin pale as cream contrasted with the inky black of her hair. A spray of tiny yellow rosebuds was affixed in her hair.

This could not be the woman with whom he had sparred. Eyes bright, focused, intent. Astonishingly fast. This remote beauty was not the sort of woman who would adore her late husband's mongrel dog nor demonstrate, convincingly, the weaknesses in his pugilistic technique.

It ought to be impossible for a woman to be that beautiful.

Full evening dress meant diamonds, paste or otherwise, what did it matter so long as there was bare skin to show them off? Predictably, she wore them to great effect. Her gown was violet and pale yellow, in the fashion for ballgowns that draped behind and had tassels and all that whatnot women wore.

It was no accident, he thought, that her gown was that precise shade of purple. Or that she'd kept her mantle close around her during the drive here. Or that she had disappeared to the retiring room upon their arrival. Her entrance was deliberate. Timed to make her the focus of all attention. He admired her statement to Mrs. Glynn and her ilk.

Someone nearby whispered, "Mercy."

His glimpse beneath that veneer of thoughtless perfection laid waste to his indifference to her. No longer could he see her and think, *yes, beautiful,* and be so little moved by that beauty.

Mrs. Wilcott moved easily through the crowd, or, rather, the crowd parted for her. He watched her with new eyes, and it occurred to him that at moments like this, there was never any sign of the clumsiness in evidence when she was among intimates. She was another woman altogether. She smiled at everyone and at nothing, and as Thrale watched, he saw a woman who'd turned her beauty into a fortress.

He studied her. Constructed and reconstructed everything he knew about her until his head swam, until his chest clenched with the enormity of the truth about Mrs. Jack Wilcott. She was among the enemy here, and she had come in the only armor she possessed. The crowd made way for her, and she moved unimpeded through the crush. Perfection in that purple.

Across the room, Miss Emily Sinclair stood with the so very pretty and interesting Miss Glynn. Thomas Sinclair stood beside her, a man of distinguished appearance, yet not well liked by the men who had so far married his daughters. One could not gainsay the results of his parental duty toward his daughters. Two of them married into the nobility despite their modest antecedents, one of them at the very highest levels.

Harry Glynn was not far away, one of the few men not entranced by Mrs. Wilcott. No, *he* was staring at Miss Sinclair. There were a number of young men near the two young ladies. He'd been shooting with many of them now and recognized several, including the vicar, who had never once missed a shot. Not once.

By now, Mrs. Wilcott had reached his side of the room. Nothing in her expression made a man think there was anything beneath the perfection of her exterior.

Though this was nothing like a party in London where there might be a hundred or more guests at someone's home, Withercomb Hall was nevertheless stuffed to the rafters with the local gentry from here and neighboring towns. A few of the guests were sporting men who had connections that got them *entre* here.

"Gar, she's walking this way. Is my neckcloth straight?"

"No better than she ought to be, I'll say."

"Venus come to life."

She stopped, and before his thoughts descended entirely into the unworthy, he thought her smile was not reflected in her eyes. That gown. He fought to start his brain functioning beyond his admiration of her appearance and managed only to stand there. Her smile dazzled, and it did so because she meant it to. It did so because she had locked away all her fear and vulnerability to become this creature of utter perfection.

"My lord."

Habit, not presence of mind, prompted him to extend a hand to her. She placed her gloved hand on his and he, determined to make at least half as good a show of this as she was doing, lifted her hand to his lips. He owed it to his pride to do better than stand here like a lump.

"Good evening, Mrs. Wilcott. I hope you are well."

She sighed, and that too was a thing of perfection. "I am, thank you. I hope you're having a delightful time."

"Thank you. Yes." He wasn't the sort who'd ever had difficulty speaking with women, even very beautiful ones. He did not know how to speak with this woman. More, half of him, more than half, did not wish to at all. He wanted the woman who boxed and told stories of battles and advised him how to train. He desired the woman who dared him to make her scream.

She moved into position at his side, and what was there to do but escort her to wherever it was she intended to go? "Shall I take you to your sister and Miss Glynn?"

She went oddly still. He did not like to see her suppress her spirit like that. She was too young to behave so solemnly. Whatever it had cost Mrs. Glynn to include Mrs. Wilcott among the guests, it had not been enough. He hoped the woman choked on her resentment. "Yes, please, do."

"Your every wish is my command."

"How flattering."

He leaned close and whispered. "There is no reason for you to be terrified of these people."

She said nothing, but he saw the flex of her throat, and, well, was she wrong? She was known here. The ruin brought down on her by her marriage was no secret to Mrs. Glynn and her confidantes. If Mrs. Glynn could not forget, how many others who had been in the same social circle at the time felt the same?

Guests made room for them as they proceeded. The phenomenon of escorting a woman like Mrs. Wilcott was not new to him. He'd done so before, with her or one of her sisters, but the sensation remained a heady one, and he disliked it a great deal. She wasn't a prize for him to show off. Nor did he become a different man because a beautiful woman was on his arm.

Mrs. Wilcott leaned against him, a necessity given the number of people in so small a room as this. Someone jostled them, and he brought her closer. Necessary, he told himself. But he felt guilty for doing so. There were unpleasant motives one could ascribe to a man who held a woman too close, and he did not wish for anyone to think that of him. In consequence, he set her back too soon.

Someone backed into her, and if he'd not reeled her back by the simple expedient of catching her wrist, she'd have fallen. He steered them away from the crowd, and when they were clear, they separated quite naturally. Mrs. Wilcott turned her head to his, and gazed into his face, and he, who understood what she was about, found himself thoroughly distracted. "Thank you, my lord."

Words fled his brain. His attention fixed on her face, the curve of her mouth, and then, when he tried not to be a besotted fool, he ended up staring at the strand of amber beads that followed the curve of her breasts, and all he could think was how much he'd like to have his mouth there. His hands, too.

Early in his youth, after his initial bumbling with women and sexual congress, he learned the acceptable boundaries of his preferences when he'd found himself in the arms of a woman who enjoyed what he did. He kept those urges under tight control. She threatened that control.

He breathed in and caught a whiff of her perfume. Violets. He forced himself to look away from her bosom and focus on her hair. That was no help, for he saw himself burying his fingers in raven tresses, pulling away the garland of lace and tiny silk blossoms.

A smile hovered on her mouth, and she touched his chest in a way that suggested more than might be entirely proper, which did very little for his self-possession. "You are resplendent tonight."

He blinked.

The inanity of her smile sliced into his soul. He had heard and seen her flirt like this in London. She was infamous in that regard. She put two fingers to his chest with enough pressure to end his mental lapse. A gentle reproof. Gad, just a glimpse of the real woman, and he was enthralled. He cleared his throat, far too aware of her. Her fingertips skimmed his lapel, but her focus was entirely on his coat, one of his best, as a matter of fact. She meant nothing by touching him. Nothing at all. This was for show, this was Mrs. Wilcott, the heartless flirt. Not the woman he'd come to know.

"The work of Cynssyr's tailor, if I'm not mistaken."

"Yes." Flint, upon being engaged by him, had insisted on a change in tailor and an immediate and wholesale update of his wardrobe. The man had permitted him, with great reluctance, to retain those items such as a gentleman wanted for private comfort. The battle had been hard fought.

"I prefer a less severe style for a gentleman of fashion, but this was an excellent choice."

"If I were not such a man?" He caught her hand and willed her to be that other woman. "What then?"

"Why, then, you would be a magnificent beast." Again, she ran a finger along his lapel. "This proclaims you to be what you are. Sober and upright. All that is admirable in a nobleman."

"Thank you." An ocean of ice floated between them, and he wanted to melt it away. He wanted her to be the delight she was when they talked of pugilism or maps or poetry. He wanted the woman who looked him up and down when he stood before her with fists raised.

"You're very welcome."

"Damn them all to hell, Mrs. Wilcott." He bent his head to her ear and whispered, "Damn them."

She left her palm on his chest. "I wish I could. I do. But there is Emily to think of." With her right hand she snapped open a yellow fan, and there was, once again, nothing in her eyes that mattered, only now he knew that for a lie. How could he not admire that sort of self-control? She placed her hand on his arm and again proceeded through the room.

Harry Glynn joined them when he and Mrs. Wilcott reached Miss Sinclair, Miss Glynn, her mother, and Niall. Her mouth curved, and she was entirely beyond reach. The picture she wanted others to see.

Into the silence, she said, "Mrs. Glynn. Good evening. Withercomb Hall is more stunning than I recall."

Mrs. Glynn's attention moved between Mrs. Wilcott and him and her son. "Lord Thrale." She dropped into a curtsy. "What an honor to have you here." She extended a hand to Miss Sinclair. "What happiness I feel to see my beloved children with a dear friend such as you."

"Thank you," Miss Sinclair said. "I am honored to be here."

Niall bowed. "Mrs. Wilcott."

"Captain Niall. I hope you are engaged for all the dancing tonight."

"I am." He adjusted one of his cuffs. "Though I confess myself devastated by your beauty no more by the thought that I might not dance with you."

"How charming, Captain. I'm quite sure it's not so. And you, Mr. Glynn. I hope you are well tonight."

He bowed. "As excellent as you are ravishing."

"What a charming thing to say."

She'd memorized those words. How could he not have understood that before? She'd arrived in London having in her head
dozens of meaningless phrases for situations such as this, and they
worked. Others saw what she intended for them to see; perfection.

Glynn bowed to Miss Sinclair. "And you, miss, you are an angel
come down from heaven to walk among mortal men."

"Goodness, Harry," said Miss Glynn. "I'd no idea you could be so
gallant. You're never gallant to me."

He tapped the side of his sister's head. "Why should I be gallant
to you? We both know you've not a single flaw, Clara."

Miss Sinclair rocked up on her toes. "Oh, excellent, sir. Well
done." She turned to him. "We've heard from Mr. Glynn and
Captain Niall. Now it's your turn, Lord Thrale. Or are you excusing
yourself from this contest?"

Thrale first bowed to Miss Sinclair. "My evening is complete,
Miss Sinclair, now that I have laid eyes on you." He turned to Miss
Glynn. "All is perfection here as well. No gentleman could find
himself in better company than yours."

Miss Glynn curtsied. "Astonishing, my lord. I was about to say
those same words to you."

"Most excellent," Miss Sinclair said. "You are silver-tongued."
She spread her hands wide. "We await your compliment of my
sister."

Thrale gazed at Mrs. Wilcott, and Glynn thumped him on the
shoulder. "He's stunned to silence by your beauty, Mrs. Wilcott."

"I was about to say that Mrs. Wilcott sets the stars in the sky."

"How enchanting, my lord."

Mrs. Glynn's expression had become increasingly sour as the
series of exchanges continued to ridiculous heights and soon
threatened to descend into giggles. "Harry, my dear boy, have you
said good evening to Mr. Leverton?"

"No, Mama, but I shall presently."

Mrs. Wilcott took a step back and then another. Subtly done,
until she was several feet distant from Harry Glynn and out of his

mother's line of sight. Someone called to Mrs. Glynn, and then from the ballroom, the musicians struck a chord, and there was rather a din as everyone spoke at once, and then spoke more loudly to be heard over the noise. Meanwhile, Miss Glynn whispered something in Miss Sinclair's ear that sent both young ladies into more laughter.

"There you are."

Mrs. Wilcott maintained her silence.

Miss Sinclair fiddled with the fan hanging from her wrist, and her focus went to something beyond her elder sister. "Hullo, Papa."

Thomas Sinclair was resplendent in evening clothes. A diamond stick pin glittered in the folds of his cravat and in the buckles of his shoes. He stood between Miss Sinclair and Mrs. Wilcott, a hand on either of their shoulders and shouted, "My two best girls. And here is Mr. Glynn. Good evening and thank you heartily for this hospitality. Everything perfect, exactly as I knew it would be." Sinclair left his daughters and clapped a hand on Thrale's shoulder. He was not steady on his legs. The man did like his hock, but even with several drinks in him, he could shoot and ride, and who would fault a man for enjoying himself at a party?

"Miss Glynn." Sinclair bowed. "There's a pretty girl."

"Mr. Sinclair." She curtsied. "You are kind to say so."

"Well, gentlemen, my lord." He clapped his hands. "Clancy against Granger, Thursday coming. And not a room to be had in Bartley Green or Little Merton. Not for love nor money."

Mrs. Wilcott coughed. "Papa. Please. Might we leave a discussion of sporting matters until a later time? I'm quite sure the gentlemen will want to find their partners for the first dance."

"Devil take you, Lucy. You lecture me often enough on how to judge if a man is a real prizefighter. Don't tell me this is not the time and place when it's all anyone can talk about, and here are three men in the thick of it."

"Papa."

"Do you see what I must endure?" Sinclair appealed to Niall and Glynn, and to him. "Do not hesitate to apply to my daughter, my lord and gentlemen, if you need to know how to elude the authorities at a match or judge a man's technique in the arena. She is expert."

Mrs. Wilcott gave Glynn a brilliant smile. He doubted there were many men who could resist a smile like that. He doubted, as equally, that she meant the smile.

"Oh, Papa," Miss Sinclair said. "Once, just once, Lucy said she thought pugilism seemed a thrilling sport, and now you believe she knows all there is to know on the subject."

"Seemed?" Sinclair leaned hard against Thrale's shoulder, drunker, he now realized, than was apparent to the eye. "Seemed a thrilling sport?"

"I'm sure I don't recall her exact words. Something much like that."

"Emily, my dear girl." He touched the side of his index finger to his nose until his eyes crossed. "My dear girl. Your sister knows more about battling than most of the men in this room."

Faint color appeared in Mrs. Wilcott's cheeks. Glynn and Niall had gone stone-cold silent.

"I think it's splendid if she troubled to learn a thing or two about a subject that interests so many men," said Glynn. "You are to be commended, Mrs. Wilcott."

Sinclair patted his coat pockets. "It was her advice to me that paid for this suit, which is a damned fair set of threads. Aikers against Fellows paid out at seven-to-one odds."

Niall cocked his head. "I lost money on that battle. Everyone was sure Fellows would prevail."

Mrs. Wilcott gave her father such a look it was a wonder he didn't wilt under that gaze. "Do not encourage him." She brought an arm forward to resettle her shawl—there was some particular name ladies had for that sort of lacy, gossamer thing, but damned if he knew what it was. A bit of the fringe tangled in Captain Niall's sleeve, unnoticed by anyone but Thrale, it seemed. She frowned when her shawl went crooked. She lifted her arm to catch the edges and made an inward motion.

"Not I," Sinclair said. "I put a hundred pounds on Aikers because Lucy swore it was a better bet."

Captain Niall frowned when the tangled edge of Mrs. Wilcott's shawl brought his arm forward. "What—"

Thrale stepped in and without comment disentangled the material from Niall's sleeve. Some kind of silk gauze woven into open patterns.

"Who do you like, Lucy," Sinclair asked. "Granger or Clancy?"

"Yes, do tell us your expert opinion, Mrs. Wilcott," Mrs. Glynn said. Thrale heard, and did not like, the nasty undertone of the question. "We await your advice."

"I fear I have none for any of you. I hope you will forgive me."

"Ma'am." Thrale put a hand to Mrs. Wilcott's back. "I have detained you here quite long enough." He surveyed the others. "Before we joined you," he said, "she told me she was parched, and I engaged to remedy that."

He walked her away from her father and the others.

CHAPTER TWENTY-TWO

Halfway to their destination, Mrs. Wilcott slowed. Thrale did not, much, mind their now glacial progress across the crowded room. She adjusted her gloves. "You've not said three words this five minutes. Does that mean you are sorry to have intervened? You needn't have. I am inured." She shrugged. "Mrs. Glynn will get in her digs. I was prepared for that. As for Papa, he's had more to drink than he ought. There is nothing new in that."

It was not safe for him to say anything in his current state, so he dissembled. Some. "Do not take silence as evidence of anything but my inability to enjoy myself at large gatherings."

She faced him, chin tilted, relieved, he fancied. "You don't care for parties. Yes, I recall you saying that."

"I had rather be at home than at a party. Give me a gathering of close friends or no gathering at all. I've no objection to solitude."

Some of the light returned to her eyes. "Yes, yes."

"What more does one need?"

"One day I will live in a cottage of my own. With a garden planted with damask roses and lavender."

"That sounds charming." He guided her away from the ballroom and into the less crowded connecting saloon.

"My cottage will have a mossy path lined with violets and a willow tree in the front. I shall sit in my garden and read Wordsworth, and Coleridge, and Shelly, and whoever else is a new and upcoming poet whose name we do not yet know, and I'll have all the novels I can carry from the subscription library."

"Paradise." He moved them aside again. "You will color maps, as well?"

"Every afternoon before tea. My sisters will call on me, and perhaps Miss Glynn, I hope she will, and I shall serve them hot tea, fresh butter, and clotted cream."

"Geneva wafers, I hope."

"Filled with strawberry jam from berries I've picked myself. Won't that be grand?"

He turned to ice. She was not speaking rhetorically. "You've found such a place? You intend to move from The Cooperage?"

She dipped her head once, and when she looked up her eyes sparkled with anticipation. She meant it. She meant to leave. "There is the loveliest cottage in Little Merton, and... Well. It mayn't come off. I haven't enough money set aside yet, though I won forty-three pounds on Aikers. In the meantime, here I am." She lifted her hands, and her gaze swept the room. "Comforted by dreams of moss and roses and delicious tea."

"I find it helps to think of anything but the crush of people."

"I find it helpful to know the exact number of guests." She gestured, a graceful motion, and yet one that ended with that exquisite silk sliding off her shoulder. "Did you know, my lord, there are eleven chevrons carved into the molding along this wall?"

"Eleven, you say?" He was bemused. He knew it and could do nothing about it.

"Yes. Eleven. I counted them as we walked." She put a hand on his arm. "But, my lord. You should not be here with me. You must ask at least some of these young ladies to dance."

"I do not care for dancing, as you well know."

"You must not disappoint them." There was a lull in the general level of conversation, and from the ballroom came the sound of the musicians warming up. Mrs. Wilcott gave him another look. He refused to acknowledge that one as well. "My sister, and Miss Glynn."

"Yes, though not immediately." He put a hand to his heart. "My word on it."

"Before you go do your duty, might I ask a favor?"

"Certainly."

"I heard only a few hours ago that there will be an impromptu exhibition tomorrow. Will you attend?"

"That would be imprudent of me." Guests streamed toward the ballroom now. He had no desire to join them. "To be present at an illegal gathering."

"Hardly illegal. But if it were, the constabulary here is lax in such matters." She extracted a banknote from the reticule dangling from her wrist and held it out to him. "I did not see Johnson in time. I meant to ask you before we left, but the time got away from me, and then in all the commotion of leaving..." She shrugged. "If you should find yourself so engaged tomorrow, purely by accident I'm sure, I would be grateful if you would put my ten pounds on Bellman to win. If and only if the exhibition between him and Fisk reaches the twentieth round."

He frowned at her hand. It was not a bad wager. With the odds firmly on Fisk, she could risk little for a large gain. But her request was quite specific. "What have you heard?"

"Nothing."

"Then why wager on Bellman? Fisk has lost but three battles in his last ten while Bellman is some unknown sprig fresh from America."

"If Bellman lasts to the twentieth, Fisk is unlikely to win."

This was Mrs. Wilcott, not some young man of the Fancy with more money in his pockets than sense. She was a student of the Art. "I repeat. What do you know?"

She pursed her lips and lowered her voice. "Bellman has been training with Johnson this past month. He takes a breather up Butterfly Hill three times in a week."

"Battery Fortress, you mean."

She lifted her chin. "I do not."

"You have two hats that say otherwise."

"I've not worn them." She smoothed the fall of her skirts. "Fisk relies on his strength."

"His considerable strength."

"You say he has not lost but three in ten battles, but he has fought twenty-five recorded battles. Bellman has a strong right and is fast to follow with his left. Fisk has lost eight matches, all but one of them after the twentieth round, and all his losses have been to men who are quick."

"You do know something."

"No more than anyone else who studies such matters."

"Are you for Granger or Clancy?" This must be the oddest conversation he had ever had at a ball. That icy perfection had fallen away, and he was entranced.

She cocked her head, and he saw a myriad of reactions in that pose; amusement, pride. Thoughtfulness. "Granger is the favorite by a considerable amount."

"That is no answer. What do you know about those two?"

"Not as much as I know about Fisk and Bellman. I have not yet completed my analysis of the records I have for the other two. Now, will you place my wager for me, or must I ask Mr. Glynn?"

"You ought to save your money. Put it toward your cottage."

"Is there any harm in a wager of ten pounds if I have the money to lose?"

He knew as if she had confessed all that she was funding her plan to remove to that dream cottage by wagering on battles. He knew her. He knew her resolve well enough to believe that if she meant to remove to a cottage, she would find a way. "You might live with Aldreth or Cynssyr, you know."

"I might." She went still in that way she had. "But I want to read poetry amid my roses and lavender. Not theirs."

He accepted the banknote. "Very well."

"If Bellman lasts to the twentieth."

"Should he last as long as that."

"He likely will."

"Your father has a wager on Fisk to win."

She stiffened. "That is his affair. I can do nothing to stop him."

He bowed in lieu of speaking then held out his arm again. "You are thirsty, yes?"

"I am."

They recommenced their stroll toward the refreshments and away from the ballroom. "I hope you will not hold it against me if Fisk wins."

"I'm sure I shan't, my lord." Not everyone was in the ballroom yet. A good many people remained here. The orchestra's warm-up became more vigorous.

"Now, ma'am. What is your opinion on the Clancy-Granger battle? What do you know thus far, absent your more thorough study to come?"

"Clancy has been training at the Academy these three months. You know this." He did, indeed. "His regimen is precise and unforgiving. He is six feet and four inches. Sixteen stone. Like you, he is quick for his size and brawn. His technique, which was good when he came here, has since become superior. His reach is unusually long."

"Granger is seventeen and a half stone. I've seen him lift his weight without difficulty."

"Yes, but he has a habit of milling, and though it has served him well, he favors his right."

"For good reason."

She lifted her hands. "I do not disagree. Granger is a fighter. Proven. But Clancy is strong, adept with his right and left, fast, with good wind and excellent bottom. He is a determined fighter. Canny." She tapped the side of her head. "Superior science wins over impetuous brawn. He is likely to come up to scratch in this battle."

"Granger, Mrs. Wilcott. The Ropemaker."

"Clancy was an observer at Granger's last two battles."

"Both of which Granger won. Handily."

"I have not said Granger is not an excellent fighter. He is. But he has not seen Clancy nor studied him."

"Granger cannot lose."

"Your passion for the man has nothing to do with his ability to fight." She leaned against his arm while she dug in her reticule again. This time she extracted a coin. "I will put this shilling against one of yours that Clancy will prevail in that battle."

"Is that all?"

"I am saving, sir. As you advised."

They were not far from the refreshments, and Thrale gestured in the direction of the footman standing at attention behind bowls of punch, orgeat, lemonade and orangeade. They moved closer. "Done, Mrs. Wilcott."

"Thank you."

Thrale reached the table and filled a glass with orangeade. Had he in his life ever had such conversations with a woman? No. No, he never had, except with her. They left the table and found a spot where there were fewer people, and she could consume the refreshment that had cost him his equanimity. He stood, hands clasped behind his back.

He ought to ask her to dance, but he didn't.

CHAPTER TWENTY-THREE

So many people. Too many. So many shoulders turned. Lucy left the Glynn's ballroom for the dark and increasing chill of a foggy night, in dire need of fresh air and a few moments of solitude before she returned to face more frowns and disapproval.

Lord Thrale continued to pierce the safety of her retreat behind her drawing room smile. He brought out the worst in her, all that Mrs. Glynn found objectionable; that dark part of her that embraced the lust she felt for him, the part of her that responded to his body. He was not interested, this she must remember. Or, if he was interested, he was determined to resist, and that was not a battle he would lose.

She walked farther into the darkness of the terrace. Inside the house, the orchestra struck a waltz. Harry had asked her to dance, and she had told him no. His mother would have flayed her alive if she'd done anything but decline him. She had not danced with anyone and did not intend to do so.

"There you are."

Her heart slammed in her chest, first, because she'd not expected anyone to come out here and second, because it was Harry. "Mr. Glynn. You should be inside dancing."

"As should you."

"As you can see, I am not."

"Mrs. Wilcott." He grimaced, but his frown was not directed at her. "Lucy. Can we not clear the air between us?"

"There is no need."

"There is." He kept his distance, and she was grateful for that.

"We are neighbors. You and your sisters are Clara's good friends. She feels the strain."

"I do regret that, for I adore your sister."

He jammed his hands into his coat pockets. It was easy, now, to look at him and see the boy he'd been. "I've told my mother she must treat you with more respect."

"Mr. Glynn."

"Harry."

"I wish you'd not done that."

He frowned. "I do not approve of her behavior toward you. It's not good *ton*, as she would say."

"She will resent me the more, I fear."

He gazed at her. Studied her and then shrugged. "It's true. I once fancied myself in love with you."

Lucy spent several long moments adjusting her gloves. She did not wish to answer him. Such a statement could lead nowhere comfortable when she had rather pretend all was well. Men had their pride. Though she did not want to put a dent in his, she did not see much choice. "I never knew. I'm sorry, but I was not observant as a girl. I was too young." Ruefully, she shook her head. "Far too young and silly."

"We were both too young." He pulled his hands from his pockets and gave her a grin. "I sometimes think that if Mama had not objected to you so thoroughly I'd have fallen out of love as quickly as I decided you were my destined lover."

"Oh, Harry. No." She laughed because he'd smiled when he said that.

He laughed, too, and he meant it, she was glad and relieved to see. "I've grown up. Seen the world a bit. Done a few things. Travel broadens the mind."

"Yes. It does."

"I didn't want you thinking I was still in love with you. I'm not."

"Thank you for that information."

"I know you did not return my ardor. I know. Mine was a

youthful infatuation is all."

She grinned back. "I was in love with the vicar."

He grinned, too. "Were you?"

"Quite desperately."

"Mr. Brown was a handsome fellow as I recall."

"Very."

"On to another living, alas, for the state of your heart."

"Before he made that terrible announcement, Emily had helped me plan our wedding."

"So efficient—"

"Harry."

At that sharp, hard, word, they both turned. Mrs. Glynn stood at the terrace door.

"Mama. Good evening to you."

"What are you doing here? With that woman?"

"Apologizing to her for your behavior."

"If that's what you think is going on between you, you're a fool. She's lured you out here to trap you into marriage."

Lucy's stomach sank to her toes. This was the confrontation she had hoped to avoid. Her only consolation was that the terrace offered a measure of privacy. "That is not so."

Harry remained unruffled. "She's not lured me anywhere. I followed her here."

"She meant to be followed. Do you not see that?"

"I must ask that you cease making that accusation."

Mrs. Glynn advanced on her son. "You will not speak to me so."

"I apologize. However, I will not have you speak so of her. That must stop. Mrs. Wilcott and I have been talking of old times and agreeing there is nothing between us but friendship." Still, he was calm, no anger in his words. "You will apologize, Mama."

The pit of Lucy's stomach hollowed out. "Please no. Do not argue because of me."

"I will not apologize, Harry, for looking out for you."

"Harry." Lucy came forward. "Please. Allow me to speak with

your mother in private."

"I don't think that's wise."

"Please. Go." She gave him a gentle push. "You'll make things worse if you stay. Your mother and I will soon come to an understanding." She gave him another push, less gentle this time. "Please, Harry. Go dance with some pretty girl."

"I had rather not."

"Go. I insist."

"Very well." He bowed and returned to the house.

When he was gone, Lucy faced the other woman. "I am no threat to your son."

"You've had your hopes pinned on him for years."

"No, ma'am, I have not."

"I knew I was right about you when you married that man."

"You have no notion of the circumstances of my marriage." She was a match for Mrs. Glynn. Whatever hatred the woman had for her was exceeded by Lucy's determination to withstand the vitriol.

"Were you with child, then?"

"No, and I will thank you, please, not to insult me or my late husband with such accusations."

"Fifty thousand pounds. That's all the circumstance you needed. You made yourself his whore."

Harry had managed to speak to his mother without anger. She could do the same. She could. "I was his wife."

"The wife of a man common as dirt."

"I confess it. Freely."

"You mustn't think that because you are now a widow that your fall is erased. You were a vain, empty-headed flirt deluded into thinking you could marry above yourself."

"I never wanted to marry your son."

"You disgraced yourself by marrying a prizefighter. All of us. And you came back here, where you are not wanted."

"By you, Mrs. Glynn. That does not mean the whole of Bartley Green feels as you do."

"You are not decent company." There was no longer even a veneer of politeness from her. The woman lifted her chin, so full of venom Lucy wondered that neither of them had yet died of the poison. "Bought and paid for by a baseborn man who wanted a lady in his bed. You demeaned yourself and your family with that marriage."

She would endure so much and no more. Her limit had been exceeded, and what a feeling that was, to be so angry she no longer cared to hold her tongue. "That is enough. You will not say even one more word to me."

"I want you gone from my house. Had you a shred of decency, you would leave Bartley Green."

"In that we are in accord." Lucy headed for the terrace door, appalled by the woman, appalled by the anger sweeping through her like fire. She stopped before Mrs. Glynn and held her gaze because she would rather die than have Mrs. Glynn think herself victorious. "I have suffered in your company and from your spite for the sake of my sisters and your son and daughter whom I hold in the highest esteem. No longer. No longer will I endure another word from you in silence."

She swept past the woman, head held high. She would walk home to The Cooperage if she had to. Behind her, she heard the terrace door close, and that was when the counter-reaction to her anger set in. She trembled, her breath shook, she could scarcely walk. She steadied herself with a hand to the wall. A count to twenty calmed her enough that she could walk away without fear of her knees betraying her. Slowly, at first, then faster. Faster yet, until her skirts whipped around her legs. She would have to pass by the ballroom, there was no hope for that, but she would collect her wrap and condemn her slippers to ruin.

She was at the top of the stairs and about to head down them and find a footman to retrieve her things when someone called to her. Thrale. She knew his voice and heard the curiosity in his query of her name. This was her fate, then, to encounter him at every turn.

She faced him, anger and despair whirling in her. She curtsied. "My lord."

"Your sister sent me to find you. You have been missed." He walked toward her, smiling, his arm extended for her to take. "Allow me to escort you to the ballroom."

The woman she pretended to be would say something silly. Words never touched her. *Whore. Bought and paid for.* She was untouched by emotion. Lucy smiled with the utter vapidity she'd perfected. She hated herself for that. "No," she said with feigned calm.

"Something to eat or drink, then?"

"No." The air in her lungs was trapped there. She could not breathe, and even after she got a breath, she did not dare speak for fear she'd betray herself. She opened her mouth to say something. Anything. She'd cracked. Wide open, and try as she might, she not could be what was needed of her.

His study of her stripped away her facade of control. "Mrs. Wilcott?"

"No. No." That was a sob. He was the only person who might understand. In all the world, only him, yet she could not impose on their friendship, if that's even what it was. "No, I must leave here. This moment. I cannot stay."

"What's happened?"

"I am not a whore," she said.

CHAPTER TWENTY-FOUR

Mrs. Wilcott's eyes filled with despair. This was worse than tears. Tears he could defend against. But this? She was wrecked. Lost in whatever private hell she lived in at such moments. If she had cried, he might have handed her his handkerchief and waited for the storm to pass. Irony of ironies, the collapse of her empty cheer tore at him worse than tears could have.

Someone, he would find out who, had dealt her an insult beyond endurance.

He cupped her elbow and walked her down the corridor, away from the stairs and the ballroom and curious eyes, away from the servants, and into an empty parlor. She was wooden. A doll without emotion, except he knew she wasn't. She'd buried her reactions.

"Don't," he said. He was aware that he, himself, struggled with strong emotion. He reached for her, pulled her into his embrace, and that proved disastrous to his equanimity. "All's well."

She threw her arms around him and clung to him, molded herself to him. His helplessness grew. He patted her upper shoulder, and when she began to tremble, he reached behind him and closed the door because God forbid anyone should find them like this, with her clinging to him, and his arms tight around her.

"Madam."

The word was stark. Too formal. Inadequate to the task of consoling her. Fury at whoever had insulted her warred with helplessness. He did not know how to deal with the collapse of his careful barriers where she was concerned. At a loss about what tack to take with her, he pressed his handkerchief on her.

She took it from him, but what good would that square of silk do when she had no tears to dry?

"Mrs. Wilcott." Hardly better than *madam.*

Until this visit of his to Bartley Green, they'd not spoken beyond what was polite. Now they had his nascent friendship, and that, and his respect and admiration of her, all that left him uncertain about what to do now. Action on his part threatened to take them into disaster, and yet, how could he do nothing? Frank lust—he could not deny he felt that—put them both in danger.

Her body molded to his. A new experience for him, consoling a woman. Women did not break down like this around him. He never behaved badly, and he did not associate with women prone to drama and high emotion. Though, in this case, he would allow that she appeared to have been provoked beyond tolerance.

"Hush." He rubbed her shoulders and spoke soft nonsense to her, aware, the entire time, that he should not be thinking about anything but consoling her. "You are safe now. You are safe."

Eventually, her grip on him loosened. At this first sign of a subsidence in her upset, he walked her to the fireplace and sat her on the sofa. Thankfully, she was recovering. He sat beside her. "Shall I call someone. A maid? One of your sisters?"

She lifted her face to him, and her despair was so deep and wide that when she grabbed his hand and shook her head, he remained with her against his better judgment. With her in this state, he did not see how he could do anything else.

And yet. A presentiment of disaster slid down his spine. They ought not be alone like this. Marriages had been the result of less indiscretion than this. That knowledge banged away at the inside of his head, yet no gentleman would abandon anyone in such a state. He could not leave her like this. Unthinkable. Not her. Not Lucy. And so, he stayed.

She continued to tremble. Any moment she might dissolve.

"Your vinaigrette?"

She shook her head.

"No woman of fashion ventures out without a vinaigrette." In London, he'd often seen her resort to the use of one to resolve some supposed excess of emotion. Others found the affectation charming. He'd always thought it tedious. Tonight for some reason, she did not have one. No ring, nothing on a chain around her neck.

"Perhaps your reticule?"

"Useless." The response was throaty, and his mind hared off in dangerous directions. Would she sound like that after sex? He was a man, and men had such thoughts and reactions to women. That did not, however, mean he would act on disreputable impulses.

He opened the reticule hanging from her wrist and fished out a hinged gold container in the shape of a seashell. He opened it, but she pushed his hand away. Forcefully.

"No."

"You are overwrought."

She waved a hand. "Vinaigrette. Useless bother."

He closed his fingers over the damned bit of gold. Now what? Must he resort to words of sympathy? More consoling pats? "Then why do you have it?"

"A diversion." She sniffed and returned his handkerchief.

That was a universe away from the sort of answer he'd expected. "From?"

"Idiots, for one."

He frowned.

"Not you." Her eyes got big, and he would have given most anything to be able to pull her into an embrace and assure her he had not taken offense. "Oh, no, no. You think I mean you."

He'd need the damn vinaigrette himself if she shed actual tears. "Madam. I do not."

"You do."

"I assure you, that is not the case." He looked around, desperate for a distraction that did not involve a vinaigrette. And found one. Behind the glass doors of a tall cabinet was a decanter of some liquor or other and tumblers. A drink would steady her nerves, if it was anything acceptable for ladies. If not her nerves, then his. Part of him didn't care if the stuff was Blue Ruin so long as she stopped looking as if her world had ended.

"My lord." She swallowed. "I apologize."

"No apology required or accepted." He strode to the cabinet and found it unlocked. Port. He splashed some in a glass and brought it back to her. She sat too quiet. Too remote. He crouched before her. She drew several quaking breaths and, eyes briefly closed, covered her mouth with her free hand.

"Do I need to kill someone for you?"

Her eyes opened wide. How the hell could she be so beautiful it hurt? He was not proud of the flash of possessiveness that followed. As if she were nothing to him but an object to be obtained. As if by winning her attention, he laid claim to prestige and respect from other men.

"Be serious," she said.

"I am. Completely. I will if it's necessary."

Three more breaths. She pulled her hand free of his to dig her own handkerchief from a pocket, but she crushed it in one hand rather than dab at her eyes with it. "You're kind to offer. But I won't have you killing anyone." Her breath shook. "It's not polite. Killing people."

With a measure of relief at any sign of improvement, he pressed the glass into her hand. "Drink."

She stared downward and sniffled.

"It's port."

"I realize that." She gave him a stern look. "Port is not a drink for ladies."

"Choose your distraction, ma'am. The port or the vinaigrette."

"Martinet."

He allowed himself a smile. "As a matter of fact, yes."

"That was no compliment, sir."

"Yet, I am flattered."

"Don't be." She gave him a tremulous smile that tugged at him in an unwelcome manner. Alluring.

"Now, will it be pistols or the saber?" Rather surprisingly, she understood him immediately. "Or shall I thrash the man?"

"None of them." Her voice was hoarse, and he ought not to find that half so appealing as he did.

"It's no great trouble."

She took a sip of the port and shuddered. "You must think I'm the greatest fool you've ever known."

"You've spent the last year convincing me of that." Good. Good. They were slipping back to that more comfortable distance that acknowledged nothing between them but respect and a love of pugilism.

Her eyes fixed on him with disturbing clarity. Sapphire blue and fathomless. "I did not mean to fail with you. And so badly. You are too observant by half."

"It might have happened to any woman." He winked at her. "It is my charm, ma'am. Few can resist."

"Yes. Your charm. Of course."

"Have more than a drop of that. You'll feel better."

She took another sip, shuddered again, and pushed the glass back into his hands. "Gah."

Thrale tossed back the contents, then considered the empty glass. "That's decent drink."

"I'm sure that's so since I dislike it a decent amount."

He laughed and, stupid man that he was, thought himself safe. His gaze flicked over her, taking in her figure and the way full evening dress flattered her and gratified less admirable instincts of his. "Now, Mrs. Wilcott. Who insulted you?"

Her expression shuttered. The effect was subtle, but the before and after were too stark to ignore. Her blank expression was in place, as effective as a ten-foot thick wall at keeping him at a distance. He found it maddening, that wall. Undeserved, too. They had moved far past that.

"What was said to you. That is not an insult to be borne."

"But I am not a lady. Not since the day I married The Devil Himself."

Not a lady. "Even if that were true, and it is not, your marriage does not make you a whore."

She touched his cheek with her gloved hand, leaning forward, and for several long moments all he could think was that there was no safe reason for his gut to tighten or to feel the air vanish. There was a difference between acknowledging a woman's effect on him and having the intention of acting on that. Different worlds.

"Give me his name, and I'll kill him. Happily."

"No." She smiled grimly. "You shan't."

"I don't see there's anything you can do about it."

"Will you challenge Mrs. Glynn to a duel?" She gazed into his face, so sad, he was ready to fetch his dueling pistols this moment.

He ought to have guessed Mrs. Glynn would be at the center of this. "Sabers at dawn."

"How gallant you are, my lord." Her voice became a siren call to his baser urges. She knew what she was doing, and he knew why. Thrale resented that he was not immune. He'd heard that silky voice from her before. Soft words spoken with an intimacy that made a man forget his own name.

"Too late," he said softly, because he knew the real woman. "I've sparred with you. Traded jabs with you. We know each other now. Better than most."

She smiled. Such innocence and wonder, a pattern so perfect he felt the edges of doubt again. But he hadn't imagined there was more. He hadn't, and he resented that she would behave as if he didn't know the truth, as if he were as easily deceived as any other man. The insult of that cut deep. She lay a hand on his arm, and there was again that glimpse of the real woman, and he wanted that woman with irrational desire. "My lord. Don't misunderstand me."

"I don't. Not at all." He considered getting himself another glass of port. "Am I to have no explanation of what led her to say such a thing to you?"

"I should not have come here."

"I'll have a word with Glynn." He brushed a finger across her cheek.

"No." Color spread along her skin, the faintest pink. She shook her head, but it wasn't a denial of his request. "I was stupid. Stupid to come here and think she would not mind."

"Did she confront you because of our compliments to you? To all of you, but to you?"

"I don't know. Perhaps. Men say such things to me often, they always have, since I was old enough to be out. They flirt. They tell me how beautiful I am and how they cannot live without my love." She made fists of her hands. "I have always observed that to a man, they survive without it."

"Indeed."

"They say such things, knowing nothing of who I am. I never believe them. I don't know why anyone else would either. I didn't believe any of you. Why would I when it was all in fun?" She lifted her shoulders. "She was right, though. Devil married me for my face. For what men do and think when I walk into a room. Because my father is a gentleman. He did not know me at all, yet he was mad to possess all that."

Thrale took her hand and pressed it, and that was unintended, touching her at all. "You do not need to convince me of anything."

She turned her head to him, eyes big, and he was lost there. "No?"

This time there was no life in the wondering tone she adopted, and they both knew it. He couldn't help a twitch of his lips. "You know you do not."

He leaned over her, one arm stretched out on the top of the sofa. His mouth hovered near her ear. With his other hand, he brushed a finger along the line of her throat, from her jaw to the upper curve of her bosom. Because he was a bloody damn fool.

Even before he touched her he knew he'd made a mistake. A mistake so vast there was no retreat from it. They were vulnerable, both of them. Her gaze connected with his, steady at first, and he thought, *she did not notice*, and then her eyes turned curious. Then aware, and that did him in. That change lanced through him.

She continued to look at him, as fascinated by the tension between them, so he fancied, as he was. He could not look away. Not for his soul. He slid his fingertip upward, along her cheek to her mouth, over her lower lip. His body roared to life.

She went utterly still.

He ought to say something to break the tension. He ought to lean back. Stand up. He should not be touching her or wanting to kiss her. More. More than that.

"Oh." She whispered the word, soft and sweet, with such longing that yet another shiver of arousal went through him.

To hell with mistakes. To hell with judgment. Or decency or circumspection.

In his imagination, he stood, as calm and collected as ever he was, bowed to her and took his leave. He did none of those things. In his mind, he walked away. In reality, he moved closer.

"Nothing can come of us," she said with more calm than he possessed. This woman, the one before him now, stripped to her essence, drew him, the light behind her eyes, the allure of intelligence and wit. "Nothing that will last."

"I confess myself unable to think of anything but what comes in the next five minutes."

"Five minutes?" She smiled, and that curve of her mouth turned his thoughts to mist. "Is that all?"

"No."

"You don't like vain women, my lord. Silly ones even less, and you once thought me both those things." She was giving him an out, and he was too pole-axed by the tension between them to take what she offered.

"I don't think that now. As well you know." From somewhere in the barely functioning portion of his brain, he dredged up words to stop this, but the words were wrong. Inadequate. Untrue. He cupped the side of her face. "You are nothing like I thought."

"I'm not myself just now."

"On the contrary." He let his hand fall to her shoulder.

"Do you mean to confuse me?" Her smile seared him, and such was the impact on him that he ignored—deliberately—the danger he was in.

"At the moment, you are very much yourself." His fingertip made a circle in the hollow above her collar bone. "If you weren't, I'd be on the other side of the room, as far away as I could be."

She drew back. Not much. Not enough. "You should. One of us ought to."

He brushed his lips over hers.

She did not, he noted, draw away from him. Not at all.

Her mouth parted, and she sighed, and her arm draped lazily around his neck, and for a time he consoled his sense of propriety with the belief that this was all that would happen between them. Soft, so soft. A kiss only. No harm done.

She relaxed against him and sighed again, with such pleasure he could not help continuing. When, at last, he pulled back, more or less in control of himself, he saw her anew. Newer eyes than even five minutes ago. This woman—this one—was worth his soul.

"No," he said. "I shan't do that."

He kissed her again, with less restraint this time, and she answered that passion. His mind spun away from anything but the physical.

CHAPTER TWENTY-FIVE

Their embrace turned as carnal as his thoughts. His kiss. His kiss turned carnal, and she answered that, and his body responded with arousal that consumed. She wasn't passive. Nor resisting him. She was kissing him back as if they'd always been lovers.

It seemed to him they had been.

Her arms tightened around his shoulders—miraculous, intoxicating—then slid up to twine in his hair, and all he could think was how good it felt to have a woman in his arms who kissed him as if he were the only man in the world who mattered.

He slid his hand down her side, then back to pause at the curve of her breast. He'd gone too long between lovers not to react to touching a woman like this. A woman's curves. Soft skin. A mouth that met his. He wanted her naked. He wanted between her thighs. He wanted her eyes on him, soft and dazzled with pleasure. His palm molded the curve of her bosom, slid upward to the skin above her neckline.

She gasped into his mouth, a sound replete with such pleasure that he brought her closer, unmindful of anything but the desire raging between them and the fact that the woman in his arms was considered unobtainable. She flirted. She danced, and enjoyed being in company, and there was not one man who could lay claim to her affection over any other. He gathered handfuls of her skirts, and the moment his searching fingers curved over the bare skin above her knee, she parted her legs. There was no denying that invitation.

She'd been married. She knew what men and women did. His

fingers glided to her sex and found heat and slick damp, and she gasped again, an abandoned, wanton intake of air. Her arms tightened again, brought him closer, and before he could anticipate her or himself, she found the fall of his trousers. One stroke upward was enough to push any thought from his head but those involving sexual congress.

Her eyes fluttered open and met his as she gripped him, and he fell deeper into the moment, into her. "Oh." The word hung on a breath. "Oh, so lovely."

She found the first button and the second, and he unfastened the rest. She shifted onto her back, Lord, yes, yes, yes. He needed her, burned for her. That was her, saying those words. *Yes, yes yes.*

He came over her, one hand on the sofa above her shoulder, the other moving aside her skirts and petticoats, and he met her gaze head on, searched for reluctance or fear or the formation of a denial, but she said, "Please, oh, please."

He shifted and stroked once. Inside. Inside the softness of her. "God in heaven, yes."

This. This. The silence took them both. No words. Nothing but sensation, the taut peaking of desire. He was inside her, his cock snug, and he did not give the slightest damn who she was or who he was, or the fact that she had connections to powerful men or whether she'd married suitably or not. He didn't care about anything but the sound of pure satisfaction she made when he came into her. He thrust again. Harder than was polite, but then he never had been a polite lover. She didn't seem to mind.

She drew breath and strained toward him. "I'm going to come."

"Not yet." The words came from miles deep in his soul. He had to grab onto the meaning and even so the words came out, useless. How was it possible they could do this without the awkwardness of lovers who had yet to learn each other?

She brought one hand above her head and braced her palm on the arm of the sofa and arched to him, and he went mindless, moving in her, feeling the slide of his prick in her. "Harder." She made another sound, a greedy groan. "Please. Harder."

Thrale dipped his head and captured her mouth. His prick was inside her, surrounded by her, so soft. So soft. He stopped being gentle because she'd asked for that, but all the same he was careful of her. He was larger and stronger than she was, and what he liked, what turned him inside out as a woman's lover, was unlikely to be what she meant by *Please. Harder.*

Every thrust exposed the head of his cock, and she answered the thrust forward, and he was going to lose his mind again. Lose control. He restrained himself, timing his thrusts, but his thoughts spun out ahead of him to the possibility of *Please. Harder.* Just thinking about that aroused him.

She turned her head away and then back to him. She stared into his eyes, and he had never in his life been so filled with a sense that he had won. He was the victor because this aloof, remote woman was fucking him. Letting him fuck her. No delicacy, just this rawness of sex and carnal need between them and reflected back in her eyes and her breath.

"Please." She bit her lower lip. "Harder."

He shoved forward, not as hard as he wanted to, but more than he'd dared before, and the ripple of her response made him groan.

"More. Damn you. More, more." She kept one hand jammed against the side of the sofa arm. With the other, she gripped his shoulder.

Thrale pushed forward again, rougher this time. His heart beat fast. Faster. Anticipation built. "This?"

"Yes. God, yes."

For several moments, there was nothing for them but his brutal sharing of his body, and his awareness stretching out along a shiver of incipient orgasm. One of her legs was up high, nearly around his waist, giving him an angle that allowed him deeper penetration. This wasn't a woman of delicate senses, for all that he'd never known one more delicately formed. The connection between them sharpened. Became richer. Fraught with possibility.

The hell with restraint. The hell with it. Her passage contracted around him, and he pulled out of her. A close thing, any longer, and he'd have come, and he wasn't ready to be done.

"No!" The word came from her in a sob. Her fist pressed against the back of his shoulder. "Fiend."

He sat back, his prick hard, and he waited for the flush in her cheeks to fade to pale pink. He put a hand over her sex, sliding a finger along her slick folds, finding the spot that made her groan. Want ached in him. His needs, his, pray God, would match hers. "How rough do you want me to be? Beautiful Lucy, tell me. I need to know so you have what you need from me."

She gripped the sofa with both hands and locked gazes with him, and he believed to his core that he was seeing her without pretense, and there was fire there, in her heart, in herself, that she did not let anyone see. But for him. She was letting him see.

"Tell me," he said, "and I will oblige you."

"I don't know." She glared at him, and that petulant frown filled him with smug satisfaction. "Until I tell you it's too hard."

He smiled, savoring the view of her, the feel of her sex, his arousal and the fact that she was a match for his tastes. "Are you easily offended?"

"I'm offended that you've stopped."

He studied the flush that pinked up her cheeks. "If I fucked you from behind?"

At his obscenity, she drew in a breath, but that was lust there. Desire.

"Beautiful Lucy, magnificent Lucy, would you be offended by that?" Arousal roared through him. "As hard as you like, madam. As long as you tell me when…if it's too much."

"I won't take offense."

"Shall we have your vinaigrette to hand?"

"Oh, you beast." But she laughed, and so did he, and then he turned her over, or she did herself. A mutual adjustment of their bodies. He pushed her skirts out of the way and settled his hands on the curve of her bottom, fingers downward, and the moment before he penetrated her, a finger along her sex.

He went in hard, and though she let out a sharp breath, she pushed back. Again. Again. And she adjusted to him, to this new rhythm. He circled an arm around her waist and pumped, and he heard the air leave her lungs and the intake of air, and he felt the silk of her, and he went harder again, holding her body immobile.

His heart raced, and his world narrowed to her. Just her. Taking him higher. He propped one hand on top of the sofa arm, and holding her tight, changed the rhythm, a slow withdrawal now, lazy even. His entire body clenched. When he thrust, though, his penetration was fast and hard. On the edge of brutal. Almost more than he could take.

He gathered enough of his wits about him to be sure he'd not gone too far. "Is aught well?"

"No. Damn you." She arched into the curve and shape of his body. "You said you would oblige me."

"I shall." He slowed. Deliberately. "In due time. I promise."

"Damn... you."

Brutal this time. This was beyond anything he'd imagined about her. He worked his body hard, and it was for this. For fucking a woman so perfectly beautiful, willing, and passionate, with a body he'd honed for the purpose. His control spun away, not yet out of reach but not in reach either.

They ended up on the floor, face to face now, and he fucked her long and hard, and she clung to him, she met each thrust of his hips with hers. A desperate coupling that built between them. He pinned her arms over her head, words coming from him, spilling from him, murmured endearments, for pity's sake, crude words.

He settled into a motion that had him hurtling toward climax. Soon. Too soon. He changed his angle to take the edge off, and whatever he did, that roll of his hips to give her a moment before he slammed into her again, broke her apart, and she was beyond lovely, beyond arousing. He dissolved into the moment, and his life peaked.

Here. That sense that he would spend.

So close. Too close to his climax.

Every instinct in him wanted deeper in her, to come while he was surrounded by her. But he withdrew, barely in time. Anything else risked compromising them both. He could not possibly. And still his climax shattered him, pulsing through him.

He came back to himself slowly, languorously. Beauty, disheveled in his arms. He kissed her once. Then again, softer. Tender, even. Her arms were around him, their clothes a mess, and she still broke him. Guilt stole over him now. Not regret, but he should not have been so rough with her. At some point, he'd kissed her hard enough that he'd left a mark on her shoulder. A tiny, strawberry bruise.

She watched him, though, with a soft, private smile of repletion. "No," she said. "Don't be like that. It was lovely." She sat up, him, too, as must needs be, and he had to accept this change between them. Fastidiously, she assisted him with putting his clothes to rights, already retreating from him. Returning to untouchable beauty. "We'll be missed," she said.

"This won't be enough for me," he said.

She leaned forward, composed and far, far away. "But it must be."

CHAPTER TWENTY-SIX

L ucy and Emily arrived at Rosefeld shortly before eleven o'clock in the morning. The house was every bit as intimidating as Aldreth's London home; more actually. His Portman Square townhouse was smaller than Rosefeld, more intimate. She should not be so unnerved by the size and opulence, but she was. She always had been.

Mary and Aldreth had arrived this morning, and the moment the news arrived at The Cooperage, she and her sister had headed for Rosefeld. Emily marched up the stairs without a thought, but Lucy stood before the gleaming front door and traced a finger over the letters carved into the marble at the side.

Rosefeld. So many memories. As a girl she'd dreamed of being invited to visit, a proper visit, involving one's best gowns, tea, and dancing, if fortune smiled. She'd meet and fall madly in love with various noblemen, including, naturally, the then quite young heir to Rosefeld. Indeed, this was a house that had been the scene of oft-imagined drama.

She counted to twenty and went in. Emily was halfway up the stairs, facing the open front door, waiting.

"There you are, Lucy. I thought you'd decided to go home."

"No." She slipped out of her cloak and handed over her umbrella.

"Good news. Mary says Aldreth went out. That means there'll be something left for us to eat."

Aldreth's butler took her things and bowed. "Good morning, Mrs. Wilcott."

"Good morning to you."

Emily called again, from the top of the stairs this time. Lucy hurried up the stairs and followed her sister into the front parlor. Mary met them halfway and hugged them in turn. This was Lucy's favorite room at Rosefeld. The walls were orange-red, the ceiling and molding white as summer clouds. Two chandeliers dripping with crystal-drops hung at either end of the rectangle. The curtains were open to the view of fields falling away to the river, and there, at the edge of the panorama, was Butterfly Hill. Like Emily, she sat near the carved marble fireplace. There were one hundred and twelve rosettes carved in the ceiling above.

"We weren't going to come here so soon." Mary passed Emily a bowl of sugared almonds. "Aldreth insisted."

"Thank you. Will you have some, Lucy?" Emily extended the bowl half an inch. "No? Then I'll finish them myself."

"You know Aldreth and boxing. He's mad about it."

"Oh, that." Emily chose an almond. "If I hear another word about Granger or Clancy or Bob Mabobbie, I'll scream. It's all anyone can talk about. I wish they'd stage their match and have it done with."

"Aldreth was beside himself at the thought he'd arrive too late."

"I've heard the battle is scheduled for Thursday morning," Lucy said. "If he means to attend, he's come just in time."

"Not 'til Thursday?" Mary reached for the almonds, but Emily moved the bowl away. "We might have remained a day or two longer in Town instead of upending the entire household. I blame Bracebridge."

"Bracebridge?" Emily set the bowl on her lap. "What has he to do with anything?"

"He told Aldreth we had to leave immediately or miss the deba-cle." Mary rolled her eyes.

"Battle," Lucy said. "It's called a battle."

"Is it? I pay no attention. Bracebridge got wind of it somehow, and ever since all Aldreth could do was insist we leave immediately."

"He is here, as well?" Emily said. "Bracebridge, I mean."

"Yes."

"Here?"

"Not at this moment. He and Aldreth left before the children were settled, off to fetch Thrale for some misadventure or other. Did you walk here? I wonder you didn't pass them on your way."

Lucy leaned in and took several almonds from the bowl on Emily's lap. She was relaxed now. Aldreth was out, and he'd taken up Thrale, so they would have an uninterrupted visit. Conversation moved to Anne and her young son, the future duke of Cynssyr, one day in the distant future, one hoped. They were doing well, thriving both of them, with the duke as proud as any papa of his progeny.

The double doors on the opposite side of the room opened. Lucy, who had the best view, expected a servant with more tea and food. Instead, she connected with Lord Thrale's iron-grey eyes. The breath left her. Behind him was Aldreth and behind him was Bracebridge, and behind him, Captain Niall and Harry.

Thrale bowed smoothly. "Lady Aldreth. Miss Sinclair."

Emily waved.

Aldreth breezed in. "I told you the company here would be far prettier than anywhere else in Bartley Green. Lucy. Emily." He swooped down and snatched the almonds from Emily's lap.

"See here, Aldreth."

Aldreth scooped up a handful. "You know they're my favorite."

The others came in. Lucy hardly knew where to look between Bracebridge's scowl and Emily's brittle smiles, and Harry's too careful demeanor. And Thrale. There would be heartbreak here, that was certain. There were greetings and then an unseemly descent on the tea. The butler had anticipated the consequences of so many gentlemen arriving, for more tea and food arrived on their heels.

Lord Thrale took his tea from Mary and walked to the window to stare at the view. Lucy did her best to emulate his coolness.

Captain Niall sat near her. "Mrs. Wilcott. Good morning to you."

Aldreth, Bracebridge, and Harry plunged into a heated debate of the upcoming battle and whether to take the odds on Clancy. She raised her voice to be heard over the general noise. "Likewise, Captain. I wish Miss Glynn had come. It would have been delightful to see her."

"It was coincidence we met with Mr. Glynn on our way here."

Thrale continued to stare out the window. What was he thinking? Did he regret what they had done? She did not. Bracebridge called to him, and Thrale turned. He did not look at her, which was what she had asked of him. And not what she wanted. She wanted to be alone with him again. She wanted to kiss him everywhere, she wanted to stare at him, stroke him, explore his body in detail, to drink in the sight of him.

"Excuse me, Captain Niall." She set down her tea. "Mary, I'll only be a moment."

Her sister nodded and returned to her conversation with Emily.

She left the parlor, down the corridor to anywhere, really. Anywhere but here. She wanted to go home. She wanted to be far away from Rosefeld and Lord Thrale, even though she knew she ought to do as she always did and disappear behind a wall of good cheer. Thrale made that impossible.

She opened a door and went in whatever room this was. Her breath rattled. She sat on a sofa. The room, a parlor, was dimly lit because the curtains were drawn, and the air had more than a touch of cold since the fire had not been brought up yet. She concentrated on composing herself. She would have to return to the others, and if she did with the slightest sign of upset, she would never hear the end of it from Mary or Emily. Or anyone else.

Her body could not forget Thrale. The sensation of him. The unforgiving hardness of muscle, the sound of his breath, his moans, the way he stretched her, thrust into her, the taste of him. Lust, pure lust, and what lady wanted a man to make love to her without delicacy, with rude words in her ear, with hands and fingers and lips in private places? What lady welcomed a grip that set her at the very edge of pain?

Sitting was no good. He'd reduced her to a mass of unseemly desire and feelings she'd not had since Devil. She stood and paced from the sofa to a mahogany sideboard at one side of this small parlor. What had become of her that she was losing sight of the difference between the woman she'd been and the woman she was expected to be now? True, she missed her life with Devil, his frank ways with her, how they'd learned to enjoy each other, his love of the physical. And hers. Hers, too.

She wanted Thrale with an ache. She wanted sexual repletion.

The door opened, and she looked up, already knowing before she heard a word or saw who was there, that Thrale had opened the door. Her heart stopped beating, and then it beat too fast, and her stomach fell away, because, he was here. And why, why, would she feel such anticipation?

"Madam." His stern address slid through her like a knife, but that was his nature. Reserved. Steady. His eyes, the way he looked at her, told her why he was here.

Without her quite realizing it, she'd moved toward him, breathless, foolishly breathless, because he had proved himself exactly the sort of lover she wanted. Exactly the sort of lover a lady should not want.

"My lord." She called on all the serenity at her command. She could be dignified. She could be. Her shawl did not drape evenly on her shoulder, but she didn't dare look or move for fear it would fall, or she'd drop it, or catch a button in the fringe, or make herself ridiculous as so often happened when she was pretending to be a proper lady.

He looked at the floor for several seconds before he spoke. When at last he met her gaze, he coughed once. "I was hoping for a moment of your time. If I may."

"You may." She curtsied as a lady ought to when in the presence of a nobleman.

Thrale walked to her, and the back of her knees went shivery.

He came close enough that, if he'd wished, and if she held out a hand, they could touch. What would it be like if he kissed her? Would she let him? Would she feel that same longing?

A noise in the corridor, a door closing, startled them both. But there was nothing more after that. His gaze flicked to the doorway then back to her. He tilted his head. "Did you leave because of me?"

The sofa was too far away so she reached to one side and touched the table there, to ground herself. She did not want him to see yet how much she adored his body. Admired it. Lusted for him. "Yes."

For some time, an eternity, he said nothing. She as well. She kept a smile on her face. Or hoped she did. The muscles of her face moved, but what that twitch of her mouth and cheeks might look like to anyone, she did not know. A grimace?

"Because," she said. "Because I could not stop staring at you and thinking of you. Mary was bound to notice."

He walked to the door, and she expected him to leave, but he didn't. He pushed it closed. She heard the soft clack of wood against wood. He turned the key that had been left in the lock.

She rested her hand flat on the table beside her and stared at her glove. No lady, then. Despite appearances.

Thrale returned to her.

"I cannot think when you are near, my lord." Yellow kid, with a row of sixteen tiny pearl buttons. She walked away, toward the sideboard. He followed and stopped behind her.

She was blithe. A woman of no substance. Until he curled a hand around her throat, resting his palm there. There was incipient violence in the way he held her, though he was nowhere near hurting her. He must have stripped off his gloves when he crossed the room, for his hands were bare now. The first time Devil held her, she'd been shocked by the hardness of his body. Warm skin over unforgiving muscle, and she'd been innocent enough at the time to think it was because he was not a gentleman. That a gentleman was soft, and other men were not.

His fingers angled up until they were resting on her throat and the underside of her chin. The muscles of his arm pressed against her shoulder, his forearm lay across her upper chest. His other hand traced over her bosom, at first over the bodice of her gown, then along her skin. He put his mouth by her ear, one finger, then two, three, delving beneath her neckline. He whispered, "Lucy. I want you. Now."

His words turned her liquid inside. She was nothing but the shiver of longing turning her boneless.

"Hard, and fast, and then I want us back in that parlor with no one the wiser about what we've done."

"My lord." The words came out a whisper.

He gathered a handful of her skirt, slowly at first, because his other hand was wandering down her throat, holding her with enough pressure that she felt his strength, leaning close enough that she felt the power of his torso. "Short stays. Good. That's excellent."

Breath caught in her throat. He was not touching her gently or with reverence. He held tighter, and then her skirts were up enough that he could trap them around her waist, which he did. She was wet, trembling, quivering, so needy she forgot she ought to be delicate. "I need your prick inside me."

His hands settled on her backside. "Here, then?"

"Now."

He shifted them both, bringing her along with him until they were at the right of the sideboard. He slid a hand between her thighs and lifted one of her legs until she had no choice but to lean forward. Then more. More. He lifted her leg until her thigh rested on the sideboard.

"Like so. Yes. Not too much?"

She was completely open to him, and the fingers of one hand delved, stroked, deft fingers, clever fingers. He pressed a hand to the middle of her back, and she felt his body shift again, the move away of his hips to give him the space to unfasten his trousers. One of his arms circled her waist. His torso touched her back, pinned her in place.

"Like before?" he said. Gruff.

"Please."

"Tell me if it's too much."

"It's not enough now."

He laughed, low, so low and sure. And then he shoved into her. Hard. Fast, holding her waist tight, his other hand on her thigh, holding her leg, and she let out a hard breath. He found a rhythm, and that took her away from everything but their bodies. She felt his strength, and his restraint, and the way he angled himself in response to her. Her body hurtled toward orgasm, out of control.

He banged into her. He was strong and hard with muscle, an unforgiving body, and she went over, falling, tumbling, soaring into ruinous pleasure. He followed, but pulled out just when she needed that last lovely thrust a man made when he'd come. But, Lord, he must. He must do so if they were to be safe. If she was to be safe.

He stepped back, fastened his trousers, and she could not move. She was boneless with pleasure. He came back to help her put her clothes to rights. When they faced each other, he kissed her hard and deep, his hand back to resting around the front of her throat, stroking. His mouth gentled, and that melted her, too. How strange that he could kiss her with such tenderness.

They parted, and he said, "We go back, you first. No one is to guess what we've done, yes?"

She had no true gentility. None at all. She drew a finger down his chest and gave in to the joy of his wanting her. "I'll be thinking of your cock in me."

He leaned in and took another kiss. "Do."

CHAPTER TWENTY-SEVEN

I n a private room at the Crown & Pig, Thrale sat exactly the right distance from the fire. He'd eaten an excellent dinner, in excellent company consisting of Niall and Glynn. Sinclair, who had gone with them to the Academy, along with Aldreth and Bracebridge, to watch the exhibitions, had declined Thrale's invitation with a rather well done insistence that the younger set must enjoy themselves. He'd business with Aldreth, he'd said.

The three of them were now pleasantly exhausted from their afternoon spent fists raised and toe to the line and were finishing off an excellent Italian red that Glynn had kept in the inn's cellar against such dinners as this. A better than decent way to pass an evening. Niall was slouched on the chair at the other side of the fireplace, legs stretched toward the fire. Glynn was seated likewise on the other side.

Niall was a good opponent in the ring, but a known one, as they often sparred when they were in London. Glynn was another matter. Mrs. Wilcott's assessment of him as a fighter had been spot on. He'd have been cautious in any event, for a stripped down Glynn showed a muscular physique. Nevertheless, he'd gone into his bout with Glynn with her information about the man's left floating in his thoughts. He might otherwise have been taken unawares by the viciousness of the punch that followed his right.

For his own fighting, he felt the difference that was a result of his newly gained control over his technique. Johnson had noticed it, too. He'd sparred again with one of the fighters Johnson was training. He took fewer punches and landed more of his own, and once the young man understood this was no accident, he'd nodded, and Thrale had found himself battling at a level that threatened to put him on his heels. He'd held his own.

"Life," Thrale said, "could be worse than this."

"True words," Glynn said. "True words."

If nothing else came of his visit to Bartley Green, his friendship with Glynn was worth savoring. Aside from his pugilistic skills, the man was astonishingly well read. Like Niall, Glynn knew when quiet was called for and when it was not, but what he liked best was Glynn's willingness to be unabashedly crude.

"Indeed, milord, it could be worse." Glynn shifted on his chair and winced. Sore ribs, and may he feel the ache at least as long as Thrale would feel his own bruises. "You could have hit me harder than you did. I thank you for your restraint."

"You're welcome, sir. Very welcome." He lifted his glass. "I hope you two will visit me at Blackfern when I am there, and in Town whenever you happen to find yourselves at loose ends in London."

Niall hefted his mostly empty glass. "I'll drink to that."

"I as well." Glynn met the toast.

"You had better take me up on my invitation."

"Hear, hear." Glynn touched his side. "Damn you, Thrale. I take back every word I said about your restraint. Need you have hit me quite that hard?"

"I ask the same of you."

"I was fighting for my dignity."

Thrale snorted.

"I was. Damn me, man, you'd take Granger himself."

"If he had one hand tied behind his back."

Niall laughed. "I'm not so sure of that. I own, I am relieved that I did not allow you to pummel me the way you did that poor fool."

Glynn acknowledged that with a wry grin. "I'll make a better account of myself next time, my word on it, my lord."

"I shudder to think of that."

"A question for you, my battling friend." Glynn leaned forward, gingerly rubbing his side. "You are given a choice between two events. Neither will ever happen again, and you may choose only one. An epic battle between"—he waved a hand—"name your fighters."

"Granger and Clancy?"

"That." He nodded as soberly as was possible for a man half drunk. "Or the perfect fuck. Which will you choose?"

"Is there a choice?" Niall said. "That's not something you ask a man."

Glynn lifted a hand. "It's a serious question, Niall, and I have asked him. You'll answer the question next, my friend."

Niall shook his head, disgusted. "Who'd choose anything but a woman?"

He gave a low laugh. "My lord? Your answer? The perfect fuck or an epic battle?"

"The fuck." Thoughts of Lucy—Mrs. Wilcott—filled his head. Gad. He knew just the woman to give him that fuck.

"What's this? Not even a moment to reflect?"

"Did you think I'd choose the battle?"

Glynn cocked an eyebrow. "With a certain woman, then?"

He smiled slowly. With great satisfaction.

"Oh, oh! You have. Who was she?"

Although he trusted both men's discretion, the fact was, he was not about to compromise himself or Mrs. Wilcott. "A man needs encounters like that. Moments with his pulse racing because he's about to die in the arms of a beautiful woman."

"I'll second that."

He doubted either man had any trouble attracting willing partners to his bed, though he suspected Niall more frequently did so, simply because in London one had more opportunities. He was going to have to get Glynn to Town for a session at Gentleman Jack's and a night or two or three, among the *demimonde*.

Glynn gave him a knowing look. "Whoever she is, may you soon fuck her again."

He laughed. "I'll say, hear, hear, and leave it at that."

Silence fell again. Comfortable. Then, he and Niall spoke at the same time.

"Speaking of ladies," Niall said.

"Since you mentioned battles—Please, Captain, you first."

"I meant to say that as the subject of lovers has come up, I heard the most astonishing rumor about a certain beauty."

Glynn said, "Oh? Do tell."

Niall picked up the bottle they'd nearly emptied and poured the remainder into their glasses.

"A certain milady most notorious, who would have us believe she is unobtainable, is, in fact, engaged in an affair."

Thrale's chest tightened, but he maintained his composure. "Someone we knew in London?"

"Yes." Niall laughed. "Oh, yes. A widow, it happens, whose paramour is a married man."

A married man. And so his worry that Niall could have discovered him and Lucy was put to rest. He relaxed on his chair.

"Is that so unusual?" Glynn lifted his glass and examined the contents by the light reflected from the chimney glass. The muted sounds of song from the tavern downstairs carried in the silence. "A gentleman may have his mistress, after all."

"None, I daresay. But as I said, the woman pretends she cannot be had for love nor money." Niall leaned forward. "The man in question let it slip, or I'd have suspected nothing. She'd have us believe she dislikes him when nothing could be farther from the truth."

Glynn sighed. "That's what comes of all you Londoners and Flash men showing up in Bartley Green. I'll be damned glad when the lot of you are gone. Present company and pretty whores excepted."

"You won't like London much, then," Thrale said.

Niall said, "There are pretty whores in Town, I grant you that, but none as pretty as your local beauties."

"They are here in Bartley Green? This woman and her married lover? Do I know her?" Glynn sat forward. "Or her paramour?"

Niall looked at the ceiling. "They could be here right now, in this very inn. She might this very moment be giving him the perfect fuck."

Glynn tipped his glass in Niall's direction. "May we all find that perfect fuck."

They drank a toast to that, and Thrale rested his head against the back of his chair. There was an edge of resentment to Niall's amusement that bothered him.

"At least she's come up from amusing herself with lowborn men and will give time in her bed to a gentleman."

"When the lights are down," Glynn said, "there's no woman can tell the difference between noble cock and common cock. It's how you use what you've got between your legs that matters."

Thrale kept silent.

"Maybe so," Niall said, "but I daresay the one with the noble cock can put a sparkle in her eye and around her neck. If you're going to fuck a man, as well have one who can do both."

"Point, Captain Niall. Point."

"I fancy this woman even more now I know I needn't come up to snuff. If she'll take common, then she ought to take my gentle one at no expense to me."

Glynn pointed at him. "It does not pay to stint the woman you hope will keep you amused in bed. That's been my experience."

"God love a randy widow." Niall let out a breath. "You'd never think it to look at her."

Thrale stomach twisted into a painful knot. He did not like this conversation. Surely, Niall did not mean Mrs. Wilcott? He'd said her lover was a married man.

"Who is she?" Glynn asked. "I could use a woman just now. It's a poxy risk going with one of the commodities in town for the fight."

"As if I'd tell you who she is when I'm after her myself."

"Someone in Bartley Green for the duration? Good Lord, man,

have pity, I've enough to deal with now I am home. If, as you say, she'll take a gentleman's equipment, I'd like to try my luck."

"I'll win her from her current lover. I promise you." Niall finished his wine. "Then we shall see. I'll put a sparkle in her eyes and set her up in London."

CHAPTER TWENTY-EIGHT

Praise every star in the heavens, she was home. All the way from Bartley Green she'd alternated between outrage and soul-shattering despair, between fists clenched and ready to fight and blinking away tears. Yes, she was home, and she raced up the front stairs and burst inside and there stood the footman, eyes wide at the heat of her entrance.

It was all she could do to greet him with any degree of calm. She let go of her mantle too soon, and the servant had to make a hasty grab to prevent the garment from falling to the floor. "Oh," she said. "Clumsy of me. I'm so sorry."

"Ma'am," the footman said.

She stood there, a stone, a wall, a fortress while inside she died at the horrible possibility that he'd heard the talk, too. Servants heard all the gossip.

He gave her a half bow, and he was so guileless. Surely. Surely, he had not heard what they were saying? Not so soon. The strain of feigning serenity near broke her in half. The stairs were a thousand miles away, but she managed to cross the distance without tears or worse. She climbed the stairs, and before she'd reached the first landing, the toe of her slipper caught in her gown and she heard a ripping noise.

She caught herself from a fall and then stared in dismay at the hem of her gown. Four inches of lace dangled from her hem. Thank goodness this had happened at home, in relative private, for her luck in such matters guaranteed that despite any care she took, she would trip on that strip of lace at the moment most likely to do some innocent soul a public harm and humiliation.

She bent down, grabbed the lace, and yanked. The edge of the strip of lace cut into the side of her hand. She adjusted her grip and realized that if she stayed crouched as she was, anyone who came along would trip over her. She bent to get a firm grip on the bit of lace.

There was a satisfying tearing sound when she yanked, but, unfortunately, the result was an even longer strip of dangling lace still attached to her hem. She fisted her skirt near the point where she wanted the lace to rip, got a firmer grip on the material and yanked. Another tearing sound floated to her, but that was the actual hem of her skirt tearing, not the lace coming free.

"Blast and may the devil take you!" Too much lace dangled to think even a dozen cleverly bent hairpins could hide the defect. While she wished the dratted lace would simply vanish, the light changed. Because, she realized, someone had come up the stairs.

Captain Niall gazed down at her, half bemused, she rather thought. Let him think she did not matter at all. "Oh. It's you," she said.

"Yes. It is I."

Lucy smoothed out her expression. She knew better than to let any man see enough to guess her thoughts. She released the lace and her skirts and stood. Aware of the now lengthy strip of lace still attached to her gown, she curtsied. "Captain."

"Mrs. Wilcott." Thrale thought highly of him, and that was something. Lord Thrale did not give his good opinion easily. She did not dare move any more than was absolutely necessary.

"What, may I ask," he said with a crooked smile full of charm, "are you attempting to do? Murder your skirt?"

"I wish I could." She was no stranger to finding herself in an awkward place, and she was safe behind the facade she'd perfected. He could no more know her thoughts than the man in the moon.

He stared at the floor and that long strip of lace, and, no doubt, the place where her hem was torn. "I'm happy to murder it for you.

Shall I?"

"Yes, thank you."

"Let's go in here, shall we?"

He meant a closet used by the staff to store trays and glasses and other detritus was five feet to her right. She headed for the room. Half a step inside, she trod on the lace and pitched forward. He caught her before she crashed into the sideboard that took up most of the room. The surface was cluttered with empty and half-empty crystal, the china cleared from the luncheon she'd missed, silverplate, and the remains of plates of food. A tray of mostly empty goblets and champagne flutes projected far enough off the edge that she was fortunate her clumsy entrance hadn't knocked them over entirely.

He went down on one knee and drew a penknife from an inside pocket of his coat. Her gaze followed him, and she mentally retreated from the moment. She focused on the sideboard across from her and counted goblets. The distraction sufficed.

"Mrs. Wilcott," he said in a droll voice.

"Mm?"

"Lift your foot? You've trod on this bit here, too close."

"Yes, of course." She lifted her foot. Her skirts moved when Captain Niall took hold of the trailing lace, and Lucy lifted her foot at the same time Captain Niall applied pressure with his penknife, and she lost her balance. For half a second, all was well. And then it was not.

Disaster came too fast to recognize. All she knew was that she was falling.

His hand shot up and captured her upper arm and though she tilted horribly to that side, she momentarily stopped falling, and she believed the danger was over.

Gravity continued to pull at her, and her balance vanished, and then his grip shifted and so did her balance and she was falling again, all so unexpectedly, and he brought up his other hand.

"Have a care!"

"Oh!" She landed on her side, and hit her head on the side of a chair stacked with plates. The chair shot across the floor toward the sideboard. The collision rattled the goblets. She attempted to right herself to no avail.

Captain Niall's fingers tightened on her arm, painfully, but he laughed as he caught her. "There's a love."

She froze at the tone of his words. The way he spoke was not mere flirtation. They were replete with expectation.

There's a love.

He did not move. He ought to have. He ought to be asking if she was injured, if he ought to call a servant. He ought to have already brought them to their feet. His arm shifted around her.

"You've not injured yourself have you?" he asked.

She meant to say, *yes, I am quite all right* because, miraculously, this was true. She'd not been injured in her fall.

But Captain Niall looked at her, and his gaze held hers, and his arms tightened around her, and he said, "Shall we, then?"

She pushed at his shoulders, hard enough. More than hard enough, thank you, to give him his reply.

He stood, and that relieved her anxiety. He brushed at his trousers and then held out a hand to help her to her feet. He did not release her. "Later?"

"Forgive me, I'm not sure I understand what you mean." She gave him her brightest smile.

"You *are* a beauty, there's no one can deny that." He looked her up and down. "I could drown in your eyes. Die over your sweet lips."

"That is absurd. Please do not say such things." She moved away, and he followed.

"I watched men lose their heads over you last season. You were cold, so cold, despite your smiles, and I saw them and watched their fates, and thought there's a woman no man will have however hard he tries. I did not, you may have noticed."

"I thank you for that."

"Patience, they say, is its own reward." He took something from his trousers' pocket and pressed it into her hand and folded her fingers over the object. "Tonight, then. I await you with baited breath."

Lucy opened her hand.

A key.

There's a love.

What safety she'd found at home crashed around her, became dust in her mouth, ashes in her throat. She lifted her head. "You are mistaken."

Captain Niall returned her look. "We're dining here tonight, is that not correct?"

"What has that to do with anything?"

"I'll retire early. Midnight?"

"Whatever you've been told..." Her voice shook. "Whatever you heard, sir, you were wrong to believe it."

"Jack Wilcott says different, doesn't he?"

Mrs. Glynn was right about her. Once ruined, always ruined.

She dropped the key on the floor and walked away.

CHAPTER TWENTY-NINE

Lucy sat in her usual place at the river, aware that this was a morning when Thrale took a breather. Roger lay at her feet. She had not come here in order to waylay him. A lady, a true lady, would never permit the slightest appearance of impropriety. A lady would change her habit of the past three years and find another place to walk her hound in the morning. She had tried valiantly to live a well-regulated life, safe from gossip and rumor. For what?

During her time in London, she had observed the ways in which couples met and, often, paired off. One went where the object of one's desires would be. And here she was, where Thrale would be when she might have walked to a different spot to avoid him. As he might do. Thrale had adopted a routine that intersected with hers, and neither had he changed his habit.

She peered into the water and watched the eddies and whorls. The ripples carried a leaf in circles and there was the flash of a fin. Birds called and chirped and sang. If she were to watch the field, she would sooner or later see a hare or a deer, and she would hope that Roger slept through the appearance. He'd be after a rabbit in a flash, and there'd be no stopping him until he had exhausted himself.

Thrale made his appearance, and her heart leapt because she had time, before he saw her, to study him unabashedly. He kept an even pace as he approached her section of the river. He was stripped off to his shirt, with a sash run under the flap of his breeches and tied off at the side.

He walked to her and gave Roger a pat on the head when the dog sat up. "I am not fit for company."

"No," she said in a low voice. She reached for the sash at his waist. "You are not."

He smiled, and that smile darkened when she loosened the knot. He covered her hand with one of his. "Not here in the open."

"Where, then?" She cupped him, pressed her palm against him, savoring the hard length of him.

"My room."

She kept a hand on him, and part of her was astonished that he wanted her, a man like him. They could be lovers. She could be the perfect lover, and once she'd removed from Bartley Green, well, they would see. "Very well then."

Twice on the way back to The Cooperage, he stopped to kiss her; short, crude kisses, and both times she worked her hand between them. What a heady sensation, to have him kiss her like that, to put her hand on his parts and hear him groan. They got to his quarters via the rear stairs. She stayed in the back corridor long enough for him to put Roger into the care of his valet and dismiss the man until such time as Thrale called for him. Only then did she come in.

He closed the door and pushed her back against the wall there and kissed her the way he had outside, a rough, lingering invasion of her mouth with his tongue. She drew away and got a hand on the knot of the sash that held up his breeches, and he said, "Hell, Lucy."

"Sit." She pushed him toward a chair and he, one hand holding up his breeches, backed up.

"I'm not decent."

She put a hand on his shoulder and pressed down. "Thank goodness."

He laughed as he sat, almost a growl. "I need a bathe."

"You do." She studied him. He was magnificent with his clothes in disarray, and his hair unruly, and his breeches threatening to fall away from him. "Well. My lord. I'll bathe you, then."

"Will you now?" His voice stayed low and rough.

"Best take off your shoes and stockings."

"I shall, ma'am." He did, with fair speed, too. She took a sharp breath and walked to the basin. "Should I come over there?"

She splashed water into the bowl. She didn't care about being proper or being a lady, she wanted his arms around her, his mouth, his body, she wanted to feel that shiver of arousal at the sight of his face when he moved in her. "Perhaps you ought to."

With a hand holding up his breeches, he joined her.

She eyed him. "Peel off your shirt, too."

He obeyed instantly, and she stared. Devil had been a bigger man, but Thrale's torso was no less a living anatomy lesson. She drank him in and gave in to all her wicked, ruinous inclinations. She wanted to touch him. Kiss him. Run her hands over him. She touched the middle of his chest.

He went still.

"Dear God," she whispered. His skin beneath her fingers was warm and damp. "You are flawless."

His gaze on her darkened, and he dipped his head for a kiss. She rested a palm on his chest. Hot skin. Damp. Lord, the muscle there, the breadth and heft of him. Hard muscle under his skin, a man who could easily overpower her and do her harm. If he wished.

He retreated when she gave him a push.

At the basin, she dampened one of the cloths and wrung it out, then went to him. The former Miss Lucy Sinclair, innocent, silly, and vain, might never have existed. She was Mrs. Devil Wilcott, and a ruined woman, and as such, there was no reason not to surrender to base urges.

She started with his face, and he turned his head to one side and then the other. Slowly, she worked her way down his torso to the top of his breeches, then moved behind him to do the same to his back. "You have a new bruise."

"One of Johnson's young men gave me a proper ribber yesterday."

"You returned the favor, I hope."

"The claret flew. His not mine." He meant he'd hit the other man hard enough to draw blood. He turned enough to see her. "I told him if he went easy on me, I'd show him I meant business. They do, those fighters who need the prize money; they're afraid to hit a gentleman hard enough to bruise. But Johnson was there and made it clear I was his student."

"He's an excellent instructor."

"I'm better now, with what you taught me. They take me more seriously. Even Johnson."

"As they must." She tapped his upper torso. "Turn, my lord."

He didn't though. His eyes turned to steel. "At first, he thought I was soft. I let him have a punch or two, let him think I thought he'd hit me hard. Then here." He feinted an uppercut that touched beneath her arm pit. "Hard. And then again, and again. Johnson mocked him for being afraid to hit like a man, and then we had a proper go. You should have been there, Lucy."

"I wish I had been." She ran the cloth down the length of his spine, and he turned his back to her while she dawdled and admired that broad expanse of muscle and sinew.

"There's a battle tomorrow, more an exhibition, I suppose. Private, but there will be prize money offered for those who need the enticement."

"At the Academy?"

"No."

There was something in the way he made the denial that piqued her interest. "Where, then?"

"Emmer's Field."

"That's nowhere near town." She rested a hand on his back. Emmer's Field was between two woods. Not a large clearing, but one that afforded a measure of privacy. "Will you be fighting?"

He torqued his upper body to look at her. "Eight in the morning. Keep Roger at The Cooperage, and you might contrive not to be seen."

She kissed the center of his back. His skin, damp from her washing of him, was warm. Her mouth followed the flare of his shoulder muscle. "I'd like to see you."

"Would you?"

She nipped his shoulder. "Very much, my lord."

"Then, madam, you shall." He dropped his breeches and stripped off his small clothes. "At Emmer's Field."

She touched him with reverence, that spot above the curve of his behind. Fighting had shaped him, those morning breathers up the hill had made him hard and lean, and her body responded to that. Her hand slid along the curve of his backside. She ran the cloth over the rest of him and with much admiration of the backs of his thighs.

She walked in front of him and did the same, and the silence between them turned thick with anticipation. She sank to her knees before him and washed his stones, gentle. Her insides turned to jelly, and she'd not felt this way since before Devil died, this soaring, hungry need to touch a man's body, to have him surrender to her.

Once more she dipped the cloth in water and wrung out it. He was hard, and the shape and heft of him was so perfectly, wonderfully male. She washed his privy member, careful, so careful to avoid the tip no longer covered by his foreskin. When she was done, she dropped the cloth in the basin.

He extended a hand to help her up, but she ignored the offer and stayed as she was. She curled a firm hand around him and moved her fingers upward. He sucked in a breath.

"I have decided, my lord, that I do not care what you think of me. I want to adore your cock."

"I exist for your pleasure alone, I assure you."

"You do. Just now, you do." She looked up and into eyes the color of fog. He was without a stitch of clothing. She ran her fingers from his sternum, which was as high as she could reach from her knees, to beneath his navel, then around to the edge of his hip. "You are the loveliest thing I've seen in some time."

"For you. I am for you now."

"A most beautiful prick."

"For you," he said. He took half a step forward. "To do with what you will."

He was different from Devil, she already knew that. A different man, a different soul. They met differently, and that changed the pleasure. The thought of making him come apart put a sharper edge on her arousal. She bent, breathed in and kissed the crown of him. A lick, then another, and with that the deep satisfaction of feeling the clench of his thighs as he steadied himself.

She drew away, still holding him with a hand and stretched for a chair with the other. He understood her intent, for he reached and brought it close. He sat, legs spread. She fellated him, and learned him, and there was nothing much better than that moment when she felt his release, the pulse of his climax, the shudder that went through him, the hiss of his breath, the way he gave in to pleasure.

She turned her head to one side and kissed his thigh, and then he wrapped an arm around her, leaning forward, bringing her hard against him, steadying them both. He took possession of her mouth, and while he did that, he drew up her skirts. She adjusted to give him the access he sought.

His fingers slipped in wet. "Did you like that?" His voice was low and crude, and that set butterflies soaring in her stomach. "Your mouth on me?"

"Yes." She grabbed his head and, muscles tight with the effort of keeping her balance, said, "I adored that."

"All of it?" He grinned at her.

"Every inch, my lord."

"Do you like this?" He slid his fingers through the slickness of her.

"Yes."

"I'll not stop then."

"Oh, don't. Please."

He knew what he was doing, fingers slipping in her, between, then in. His fingers sought, and moved, and reacted to her, and once she'd clutched the arm of the chair, he held the nape of her neck, harder than he had been doing until now. His eyes were steel now, steady, fixed on her.

The way he watched her face felt too private, too fraught with a future in which he broke her heart, and she could not bear to look. She wanted the pleasure, only that. Nothing between them but that, and she closed her eyes and chased the peak.

"Stay," he whispered. His fingers stroked the back of her neck. "Stay with me. I want to see you with me when I've fetched you."

She couldn't. She couldn't. Her heart was already broken. What was left to her, she needed for herself. Safe for herself, for the life she had planned. He drew an orgasm from her, hard, unforgiving, and she gave in to herself, to his fingers, to him, and she did open her eyes, and met his, and she went under.

After a moment, Thrale put his mouth by her ear, holding her steady with one unyielding arm. He took her face in his hands, cupped her cheeks. "Is it possible?" he whispered.

"What?"

"Us."

"No." She touched a hand to his. "You know it's not."

CHAPTER THIRTY

At twenty before eight in the morning, Lucy turned from the window of her bedroom. As she did, she caught a flash of white from the corner of her eye; a woman, she realized, walking away from the house, not back to the house. Despite the early hour, not one of the servants.

That was Emily striding toward the field behind The Cooperage. Without her maid. Without a footman. If she meant to go to Rosefeld, well, it was too early to call, even on family. She watched Emily and knew, simply knew, that her sister was not going to Rosefeld or to Bartley Green. She was heading for Emmer's Field.

How she'd found out about this morning's happenings, Lucy did not know. But she had, and there was no way in which Emily's presence there could be anything but inappropriate. Not even Lucy knew for sure how many men would be there. Thrale had said this was a private gathering, but there were so many of the Flash here, a private gathering might be quite large.

Lucy put Roger into the housekeeper's care with strict instructions that he was to be kept inside. She did not know where she would end up or how long she would be away, not with Emily to take in hand, and Roger was more than capable of finding her if he got out and followed her.

Dressed in her plainest, drabbest cloak, she hurried in the direction she'd seen Emily walking. When she broke onto the path that led to Rosefeld, she did not see Emily, and her hope that Emily was not taking a terrible, foolish risk evaporated. She walked faster, through the trees, dense in places. Once, she saw the shadow of a deer, but she paid it no mind. Emmer's Field was close. Presently, she heard voices, enough to be worrisome.

Lucy came around a turn the path that would take her to the very edge of Emmer's field, and there was Emily. She'd stopped walking but was not standing in the open. Foolish, yes. Stupid, never. Her sister lurked in the trees, looking at the clearing twenty feet distant where a crowd watched two men who faced each other, fists raised. Both were peeled off to bare chests, both with neckcloths used as sashes to hold up their breeches. Magnificent specimens both of them.

Lucy blinked. One of the two was Thrale. This was no surprise, but the other? Heavens, that giant of a man with his dark curls blown about by the breeze, that was Lord Bracebridge, and he might be the rival of any prizefighter's physique. He'd fought for money in the days when no one dreamed he would ever inherit, not with so many brothers before him. She'd found the records of his battles. He'd done well and earned a reputation as a vicious, relentless fighter whose strength covered a multitude of technical deficiencies.

At the perimeter of the ring Aldreth stood in his shirtsleeves, neckcloth unfastened. The breeze was strong enough to mold the front of his shirt to his body, giving her a full on view of his elegant, athletic build. Aldreth was holding his watch because he was keeping the time. She did not recognize the men acting as referees. Harry was Bracebridge's bottleman. Captain Niall appeared to be fulfilling that function for Thrale. Flint stood to one side with an armful of coats and neckcloths.

Thrale and Bracebridge were toe-to-the-line, waiting for the signal to recommence, for neither man was fresh. There was a great deal of shouting of advice to the combatants and wagers between the observers. Some of the men looked to be lively indeed. One of them lifted a flask to his lips and drank, then passed it to a compatriot who did the same. Behind them, a wager was made and money passed to Arthur Marsey.

A shout went up, and the round began.

Lucy joined Emily in the protected spot she'd found and took a firm grip on her sister's wrist. The location of the ring was no accident. Thrale had very likely arranged its placement so close to this area. Thank goodness, else Emily would have already been discovered. In a low voice, she said, "This is not right. Go home. This moment."

Her sister turned to her, determination etched into her face. "What are *you* doing here?"

"Preventing you from making a fool of yourself."

"Is that so?"

"Keep your voice down, Emily." She recognized her sister's stubborn look, and panic lapped at her. When Emily made up her mind about something, that was often that. But, this was no fit scene for a young lady. Thrale and Bracebridge were peeled off and several of the others had removed their coats. "We don't need another Sinclair sister put beyond the pale."

"You exaggerate."

"It is enough that I am unforgiven."

"That's not so."

"It is. Go back to the house. Whatever you have planned, it's foolish. It will backfire. Not here. And not now." She looked toward the field and saw Thrale take a ribber and counter with two of his own. This was a fight she would dearly love to watch. "What if someone sees you?" If one of those men glanced their way and saw them, that would be a disaster. "He will not think better of you if he finds you spying on him, I promise you."

"I'm sure I don't know what you mean."

A shout went up from the spectators, and Lucy gave a mental curse that she'd missed the cause. "I'm sure you do. Let's go back to the house now."

"Can you tell who's winning?"

"Bracebridge has decent technique." Better than what had been said of him in earlier days. She watched them, studied the shifting tableau. "He's fast."

"Oh. Ouch."

"And strong." He'd been a brawler by reputation. Ruthless and strong enough to overpower fighters with better technique. "Physically, they are well matched, those two." She tried to watch the fight without bias. The truth was, Thrale had better art. Better science too, no less than she'd expected. His expression of the art, with all that implied for knowing one's opponent, observing him, adapting, all that Thrale had. They seemed to have agreed there would be no blows above the shoulder, but he punched without mercy.

No mercy at all.

"Is Bracebridge winning?"

"I cannot say."

"He's hitting Thrale more. Why do you not say he's winning?"

"Oy, there!" A deep, male voice boomed over them. Emily blanched, and Lucy felt quite sure she'd done the same. Her heart thudded. "Oy, there, in the trees!"

"Go. Now." She grabbed Emily's arm, turned her around and pushed her in the direction of The Cooperage. Emily jerked away, but she had the sense to hurry toward the house.

"Who's there?" The voice was closer, and whichever of the men had seen them was now tromping through the trees, heading in their direction.

Lucy caught up and pushed Emily ahead of her. "Faster," she said in a low, hard voice. "Run, and I won't tell anyone what you've done."

The threat was enough. Lucy would have been close behind Emily—she had no desire to be caught here either—but the hem of her gown caught on a bramble. Not even a yank freed her gown. She backtracked her steps in case that solved the problem, but her skirt was more entangled than before.

The man after them was closer yet. She prayed it was Aldreth. He might at least think it was amusing, and if she told him she'd followed Emily and managed to send her home, well, he'd be on her side in the matter.

"Mrs. Wilcott."

She stood stock still.

"Are you lost?"

Emily was well away at least, she so she turned, and with one arm behind her, yanked on her skirt again. Miraculously, the fabric came free, albeit with a ripping sound.

Thrale stood not an arm's length away, naked from the waist up. Good heavens. She opened her mouth to say something that would have been unwise, but sweat trickled down his forehead and temples, and when he used the crook of his elbow to rub away the drops, muscle moved everywhere. She was absolutely unable to think. He had a raw bruise on his shoulder.

He put his hands on his hips, and the only thought in her brain was that she'd never in her life been more aroused than right now. Not like this. Not with her so unable to think. Not with a man so perfectly formed. A series of physical reactions flooded through her, pushing away her good sense as a threat to what she wanted right now. Thrale. She wanted him. Longed for him.

He didn't speak. Or move, and it seemed that whatever was wrong with her, why, the same thing was wrong with him. Her breath caught in her throat, and it didn't even matter that she'd dropped her pretenses. They were both stupid with lust. She slid her fingers over his skin. That was muscle. Firm and so sleek. She stroked up, over the ridges of his belly.

Thrale tipped his head, one eyebrow arched. He grabbed her hand and walked them farther into the trees and away from the men and from the Cooperage. They ended up close, so close. His lips parted, and after a moment, he said, "Like what you see?"

Her fingers trailed up, and she diverted her upward direction enough to the right to reach his nipple. "I want to lick you. Here."

He looked over his shoulder and then back at her, and his gray eyes, usually so cold where she was concerned, were considerably not. "Please."

No doubt he expected she wouldn't. Well. She had something of Emily's defiance in her after all. She leaned forward and pressed her lips to his skin. Not to his nipple but to the swell of his upper arm. He tasted warm, salty. Like the sunlight he'd been standing in before he came haring after her.

He gripped her arm. "Not here. Not so close."

With him still holding her arm, they walked deeper into the trees, away from Emmer's Field, away from the noise. Off the path. They reached a place where there was less space between trees. Older oaks with thick trunks and branches and dense, green foliage. "Here will do."

She faced him, put her hands on his chest. "Did he hurt you?"

"What?"

She looked into his eyes. She knew the effect she had on most men, and she watched his pupils react, the way he assessed and then that slow, liquid smile on his mouth, as wicked as any man could be. "Bracebridge. Does he hit as hard as I suspect?"

"Harder." He put a palm on the back of her neck and pushed her back until her spine was pressed against the trunk of one of the oaks. He closed the distance between them. The contact sent her stomach off the edge of the world. "He's still too much of a brawler, though."

She put both her palms on his chest, filled with such dizzying arousal that when his mouth touched hers, not gently, she had no defense. What's more, she didn't want any. She wanted him to shake her to her core.

He could do that to her. Shake her free. He could make her long for his cock inside her, taking her hard, right at the edge of more than she could bear. His lips opened over hers, and she reciprocated. His tongue moved into her mouth at the same time his hand tightened on the back of her neck. Eyes mostly closed now, she moved her last two fingers and felt the peak of his nipple underneath. He made a noise that sounded like deep appreciation, and what woman didn't long to hear such a sound from her lover?

Kissing like this was—oh, God, she thought she'd never do this again, and the thought that Lord Thrale, of all people, was the man with his mouth on hers, sent her out of her mind. She leaned into him, returned his open-mouthed kiss, touched his tongue with hers. He was hot and damp from his exertions, and she didn't give a fig. His hands wandered below her waist, tentatively at first and then not at all, when she threw her arms around his shoulders.

The sound he made when he realized she'd capitulated everything to him went straight through her. Part growl, part grunt, it was like being given a window onto the ocean after being locked away for years. She embraced the moment when he gave in to whatever he was feeling, when it was more than mere contact. His hand landed on her hip—how convenient that she was wearing short stays again—and curved around to her bottom where he pressed her forward.

Her hand moved down to the waist of his breeches and then along the flap, and his fingers closed around her wrist and pushed downward. He let go of her bottom and covered her hand so that she cupped him, and another shiver went through her.

This time she was the one to make a sound, a moan of longing and desire because his delicate parts did not currently feel delicate at all. He was holding her like a man who knew what to do with his body, who thought of his partner. She let herself drop deeper into this madness, stirred past reasoning, astonished that she could react this way to anyone. She knew the path they were on, none of the particulars were new to her. Or to him.

He grabbed a handful of her skirts and pulled up.

CHAPTER THIRTY-ONE

Thrale groaned because, Jesus Lord on high. The woman had a hand on his cock, and now she drew a finger along the length of him, and he would be mad with lust soon. Stark mad. This was not the place to ravish a woman or to allow a woman to ravish him. The rest of him was engaged with his erection, her hands on him, and the imperatives involved in that.

Mrs. Wilcott drew away. Not much, but enough for disappointment to roar through him. Her hand stayed on his prick, though her fingers were still. He looked into her eyes, hoping to see her as ruled by lust as he was. Was she?

"My lord," she said, breathless, the words trembling.

He held her gaze, and managed to summon words. Crude words that reflected his mood. "I want to fuck you now. This minute. I hope to bloody hell you are in charity with that sentiment."

The woman in his arms, and who still had her hand on his privity, mirrored the lust roaring through him. She slid a finger across his chest and removed her hand from his parts. He ought to object to that. She focused on his torso, and despite the dreamy cast to her eyes, she was a thousand times more vibrant than he'd seen her before. "So lovely."

A voice from the meadow rang out. Distant. Heading away from where they'd gone. "Hullo there, Thrale! Are you lost?"

Damn him, all he could think was that if he'd not wasted time talking, he might be just finishing.

"Do you want to answer whoever that is?" she asked.

He gathered a handful of her skirts and pulled up. He was a

randy sod. A greedy one. A glutton. "I'd rather fuck than fight, and that's the truth. So, no. I do not care to answer anyone but you."

The smile that broke across her face killed him, sent what decorum was left him to southern regions where it died a merciful death in lust. She said, "Good."

That was all it took for him to put action to desire. His fingers brushed her naked skin, well above her stocking, and it was the work of half a second to have his hand around the back of her thigh, pulling up. He bent his knees, and she adjusted, and the sound she made when he thrust home brought an answering growl from him.

His blood raced through him, hot, needful. This was the kind of sex he craved. Out of bounds. Rough. Not the least proper, and with a woman who wanted the same. She threw her arms around him, held tight, and met his strokes as best she could with them like this. He buried his prick deep in the softness of her, withdrew, and returned to that soft, slick, heat. His arms and shoulders strained with the effort of holding her, and that felt good, too. The effort sped him onward, that fact that his strength was required pushed him harder.

There was nothing better than fucking a woman who enjoyed the act and who knew how to fuck back. Who she was only added to his arousal. Mrs. Wilcott, whom he should not be touching. Should not. Lucy, who deserved better from life than had been her lot. He should not do this, but he was no more capable of not finishing this encounter than he was capable of breathing underwater.

"Thrale?"

Niall, he thought, and not from as far away as before, but not near. Not near enough that he had to worry.

"Hurry." The word was half-moan, half-whisper. She clutched his shoulders, but her fingers slid in sweat and glanced over a bruise that made him flinch from the contact.

He pinned her, pushing hard against her, holding her tighter than he would have another woman. Her natural reaction was what he wanted, what he dreamed of. She allowed him to master her and at the same time demand that he pleasure her.

Holding her like this, he could thrust harder with her being unable to adjust. Not fair. Not well done of him. He shoved himself forward. Yes. Yes. Again, yes. She reacted to that last with a hitch of her breath that told him the boundary of acceptable was too close. If she knew how he craved that vicious twist in him when she cried out like that, half surprise, a groan, would she be appalled?

She got a hand loose, and he let that happen, and she wrapped her palm around the back of his neck and brought him closer. "Again," she said, with her breath coming hard and a light in her eyes that made her look drugged. "Again. Like that."

He did. The fires of hell beckoned and whispered that here he would find all that he needed. He adjusted his hold on her, pinned her again and this time let his fingers sink deeper until she made that sound again, pain and pleasure at one and the same time, and that twist of need in him blossomed out. He had to be hurting her. He was, he knew he was.

His body wound tight, heading for a climax that would shatter him. But she broke first, and that astonished him. She stifled her cry, and her body clenched around him. A flush deepened in her cheeks, and she sobbed through the pleasure. *Thrale. This. God.*

Tension moved from the base of his spine through his balls with that world-ending peak—one more thrust. Another brutal shove into her. The sound she made in response lanced through him. Another thrust while she kissed the side of his mouth. He kissed her, deep, deep, one more push into her, and then it was nearly too late.

She clasped her hand around him and worked the final peak of his orgasm, and he went away. He opened his mouth, and she covered his lips with her palm, reminding him where he was, with whom.

His mind cleared, and he stepped away, his breath roaring through him. Insanity, this. Taking her like that, letting himself come too near to chaos. Wanting her, Mrs. Wilcott, Lucy, like this.

He thought about apologizing but didn't. He wasn't sorry and frankly, she didn't look sorry either. She looked well-fucked. He bent to her and whispered, "I'd fuck you again in a minute."

She leaned against the tree trunk. "If only you could."

"If we had five minutes, I'd prove it to you."

"And here I thought I'd wrung you out."

"You did."

He helped her put her clothes to rights, her hair, and while he did that, he leaned down and brushed his mouth over hers. So sweet. He drew away, and kept her in his arms. She took his hand in hers and examined his knuckles. They were red and raw. The cloth he'd wrapped around them hadn't done much to protect him. "Hitting him is like hitting a boulder."

"My poor Thrale."

"I was making a good account of myself, though."

"You were. I think you would have won. He's strong and fast—"

"Yes."

"—but not as disciplined as you. He might have gotten lucky, though. I have records for three of his battles, and that was his reputation. A miller with strength, luck, and a refusal to give up."

"Praise God he did not have luck."

"I wish I'd seen more."

He fingered her mantle. "It wasn't you we saw."

"No."

"Your sister, I take it."

She pressed her lips together.

He lifted a hand to her mouth. "I won't say a word."

"I sent her back to the house." A crease appeared between her eyebrows, and he had to stop himself from running a finger along that sable arch. "I don't know why she's developed this interest in boxing."

"With all the talk about Clancy and Granger? It's no wonder. It's all anyone talks about."

"Johnson says Thursday."

He nodded. He'd heard the same thing. "Yes."

"Thrale."

This time, whoever was calling for him was closer.

"Where the devil have you got to? Bracebridge says you forfeit."

"Go," she said. She picked up her skirts and walked away from him as if nothing had happened.

He watched the sway of her hips for half a second and caught her arm before she was out of his reach. She looked at him, and he said, "Whatever this is between us, it's not impossible."

"It is. You know it is."

"Why?" He released her.

"There's more than that involved. With all this."

"Not much more." Jesus, he'd left a mark on the back of her neck. He knew there were others on her body. Near the tender skin of her thighs, her bottom. He touched the mark on her nape and adjusted the collar of her dress to hide it. "It doesn't have to be like that. I don't need that."

Under different circumstances, her confusion would have amused him. "Need." She tested the word and then set a palm to the side of his face. "You held back. I could feel it in you."

"Yes. I did."

She smiled, slowly, sadly, even. "I wish you hadn't."

CHAPTER THIRTY-TWO

C lancy versus Granger.

The battle had taken place. The hubbub in Bartley Green was unnerving, exhilarating. Electric. Everywhere, conversation flew about the great confrontation. In the street outside the Academy, Roger whined, unhappy with the noise. Lucy rubbed his shoulder.

The tumult was on the scale of Molineaux versus Cribb. Her husband had been ringside at that great battle while Lucy had been in the village. Devil had found her afterward, full of tales, descriptions to write, and with hastily penned notes of his recollections of the encounter for her to transcribe. She could hear him in her head.

Lucy, you should have been there. He brought out the claret with a tremendous blow, and all the men who'd put money on their lad, why, they groaned, not knowing that in the very next moment the world would turn on end.

As with that previous fight, Flash men swarmed the streets, some celebrating, others not. The din was remarkable. She'd already been past the Crown & Pig, overflowing with men either jubilant or in despair, spilling into the street with a pint mug in hand. Singing, shouting, reliving or reenacting key moments from the battle. It was absurd to think she would come across Thrale here; it wasn't why she'd come, but now she was here, she wanted to see him.

Someone had propped open the front door of the Academy with a brick. What she could see of the vestibule was much like the Crown & Pig; packed with men. She saw Flint, grinning, an elbow leaning on the shoulder of another man. Her pulse leapt. If Flint was here, then surely so was Thrale?

He must be. There was Bracebridge and, yes, Cynssyr; he'd made it from London in time, then. Aldreth must be somewhere in there, too. She shifted position, fingers clenched around Roger's collar. There. There he was. Thrale. His gaze swept her, moved on, then came back to her, and, yes.

Her heart pounded. Leapt, and her blood raced through her.

He pushed through the crowd, disappeared from sight, then reappeared in the doorway. His eyes went wide when he stepped onto the walkway. Lucy could not have moved had her life depended on it. He pushed past the last revelers between them, and Roger whined when he reached her. He took her elbow.

"I won't ask what you're doing here. Foolish though it is. Cover your head." He helped her arrange her shawl over her head so it draped her face in shadows. "Come along then. Bring Roger. Anyone who sees him will know you're somewhere near."

He led her to the Academy's private door, the one that entered onto the corridor to the upstairs private viewing rooms. The noise receded. He opened two doors before he found one that suited him. He closed the door after them and spun her into his arms, moving in a circle as if they were dancing. "It was a battle, Lucy. The greatest, grandest, most magnificent battle ever fought."

She let her shawl float away. Roger lay down with a canine sigh. "Is it true, then? Clancy won?"

"He did." He could not help grinning back. "As you predicted."

She stopped moving, and they stood so, with Thrale's arms around her. Reality sank in, and she whispered, "Nine hundred pounds. I've won nearly nine hundred pounds."

"You played deep."

"I don't approve of risks like that." She took a few steps away. "I could afford the loss, if he'd not won." She held out her hands. "Look at me. I'm trembling. I ought not have done it. But the numbers were there."

"You understood the risk."

She faced him, her smile wide. "There's a house on the other side of Bartley Green, in Little Merton, with a garden and two parlors, and room for Roger." She beamed at him as her change in fortunes sank in. "I shall have my maid, and a cook, and a footman to come in days. My own home. Where I may do as I like, when I like. My sisters may call on me whenever they are here, and I shall serve them tea and Geneva wafers."

"I will be sure to call on you."

She laughed, still trembling because her life had just been transformed completely. "My little cottage shall have the noblest visitors. A duke, a marquess—if you keep your promise. If Bracebridge calls, an earl. Why, I shall only miss a viscount if Aldreth comes, and he will, I know he will. Anne and Mary and Emily need never worry about Papa, for I shall be near enough to look after him well enough."

"Will you keep a carriage?"

She turned in a circle, one hand lifting the hem of her skirt. "A carriage? Yes, Yes, I shall have a carriage, and a matched pair. With room for Roger."

"You may drive to Town whenever you like."

"Do you mean London?"

"Yes. London."

She snapped her fingers. "I care *that* for London."

"It's not far." Thrale went to her. Roger opened one eye, but he and Thrale were fast friends, and the hound returned to his rest.

"Tell me about the battle, Thrale. Tell me everything."

"By the end, a decisive win for your man." He put his hands on his hips. Jubilant conversation floated up from below stairs.

"Fifty rounds, I heard."

"Fifty-three."

"How much did you have on Granger?"

"It happens I laid down a certain sum on Clancy as well." His eyes sparkled, and she could not help smiling back at him. "My losses on Granger were mitigated. I thank you for your information and expertise."

She shuddered. "Imagine what you'd think of me if Clancy had lost."

"Do you think I would be dunning you for my losses?" He touched the tip of her nose. "Lucy, my love, I understood you were not making a guarantee. Only a reasoned analysis."

"Was there a crush? A thousand men, I heard."

"There might have been. The crowd in Granger's colors far outnumbered those in black and scarlet. I never saw so many men in green in my life."

"What was the battle like? Will you tell me? Oh, please, do tell me."

"Aldreth and Bracebridge were chosen as umpires."

"Were they? I'm not astonished, though. Tell me all that you recall. Was Granger in fighting shape? How did Clancy compare?"

"Granger's arms were like tree limbs." He demonstrated with two hands. "Legs like trunks. Seventeen stone, ten pounds. Clancy weighed in at sixteen stone exactly. They were a sight when they stripped off. Two big men."

"And the battle itself? You wouldn't be so cruel as to refuse to tell me, would you?"

He laughed, and so did she, and then he proceeded to tell her about the fight, several times demonstrating the key moments in the battle. "By the fiftieth round, Granger was reeling badly, though he'd got in more than one tremendous blow of his own. Clancy withstood them all.

"By the fifty-third, your man was hitting has hard as he had in the first. And then, the penultimate blow." He demonstrated the strike. "Granger swayed and fell against the ropes. Clancy could have finished him off, but Granger was in no condition. Granger pushed off the ropes, and I tell you I am not convinced his brain was engaged. One more blow—like so—took Granger to his knees."

"That was it, then?"

He nodded. "Not a sound could be heard for several seconds

after he hit the ground, and then, there was an explosion from his supporters, 'rise up, rise up.' He tried. He did. But his knees were jelly, I could see them shake from where I stood. He toppled like a felled tree. Time expired without so much as a twitch from him, and again there was silence. His second went to him, and then the surgeon, and Clancy crossed himself, and there were whispers Clancy's previous blow had killed Granger."

"No, oh, no." She knew Granger hadn't been killed, but the thought brought back terrible memories.

"Presently, Granger stirred, and when he'd been hauled to his feet, he extended his arm to Clancy and they clasped hands."

"Devil would have loved to be there."

"I don't doubt that he would have." He took her hand in his and drew her near.

"He would have." She was over the moon. Nine hundred pounds, and a great battle that made her feel Devil was near. "He would have."

"Lucy."

"My lord?"

He stared at her so intensely she did not know what to think. "I've told Captain Niall he has made himself unwelcome in my company." He tensed. "He will be gone from The Cooperage before day's end."

"But, why?" Some of her joy shrank away. "Why, Thrale?"

"I have observed his behavior toward you."

"You dismissed him on my account?"

"That, too."

"He is your friend."

"No longer a friend. I should have spoken to him sooner. My apologies if I've overstepped, but I could not countenance his behavior toward you. Nor"—he pressed his mouth together—"certain statements made in my presence. He made himself abhorrent to me."

She closed her eyes. "Not because of me. Please, not."

"Lucy. You have a right to a better life. A right to better treatment. From your father. From men like Niall." Thrale took her head between his hands and kissed her. She softened against him, giddy, and then a deeper kiss, and she fell, his, in this moment.

He kissed her tenderly, gently, and his arms slid around her, and when they parted at last, he clasped a hand to the back of her head and drew her to him.

"Lucy," he whispered. "Lucy, what am I to do with you?"

"Come visit me at my cottage." She twined her fingers in his hair, and her heart settled into the right place now. Thrale would call on her. And if he spent the night, then he would, and they would be friends and lovers. "Come as often as you like."

CHAPTER THIRTY-THREE

Lucy told herself she *would* do this. No matter the consequences. She was determined. From her place in the doorway where she'd stopped to get her nerves in order, she saw her sister working industriously in the small parlor at Rosefeld. Mary sat at the desk where she wrote letters and checked the household accounts. That last was a skill they'd both learned from their meticulous elder sister.

Lucy wanted nothing more in the world than to turn away from the door and avoid this discussion. Not a discussion, no. She would lose her will if she had to debate her decision. She was not asking for an opinion or for permission. Not at all. She was delivering news.

This must be done. Must be, or she would never be able to start her new life.

Her aversion to conflict of any sort was a crack in her foundation. One might not see the flaw in the clay that formed her, but it was there, compromising the very structure of her character. Well, no more. She squeezed the edge of the door. No more floating through life, never resisting the direction the winds might send her in. Her stomach tied itself in a knot, but she knocked on the side of the doorframe anyway.

Mary turned sideways on her chair and smiled. "Lucy. Good morning."

"May I come in?"

"Yes, of course." Mary pushed aside her ledger and the papers before her. "Please. This is a welcome break."

Lucy went in, and was that not a triumph that she shut away the dozen excuses for putting this off? What difference would it make if she announced her decision tomorrow or the next day? Over the course of a month, say, a delay of three days was nothing. Why, another week would hardly matter.

When she reached her sister, Lucy adjusted her shawl around her shoulders and sidled closer to the fire. Mary never seemed to feel the cold the way she did. Her nerves continued to fracture her determination. "I'm not interrupting, I hope."

"No, never." Of all her sisters, Mary's features were most a meld between their parents. Their mother's eyes, their father's mouth. Anne and Emily most resembled their mother; blonde and delicate. Lucy looked like their father, with his dark hair. Mary's hair was a brown that was surely the result of a precise mix of black and blonde.

She inched toward the fender and wondered what Mary would say if she added more coal without asking permission. One never wished to offend. This was Mary's home, not hers. Soon, Lucy would have a home that belonged to her. With everything ordered and arranged exactly as she liked.

Mary folded her hands on the desktop. "You look as though you brought the world in here with you. I take it you have heard the news."

"What news?"

"I had it from Aldreth. There was a match the other day—"

She could not restrain a grin. "Was there?"

"You know there was. But this morning Aldreth told me someone made off with the prize money, and a considerable additional amount being held for others. Eight thousand pounds, all told."

Lucy put a hand to her upper chest. "No. Oh, dear, no." This was news. Terrible news. Prizefighters risked jail and fines for stepping into the ring. While it wasn't unheard of to have someone abscond with the money, it wasn't done. It wasn't. "Say it isn't so."

"It is so. Aldreth said your guest, Captain Niall, gave someone a considerable sum to hold for him. Money he could ill-afford to lose, I'm told."

"Have they got it back?"

Mary made a face. "No, they have not."

"The fighters must be paid. They must be."

"Cynssyr has made the prize money good. Along with Aldreth, Bracebridge, and Thrale."

Someone would have had to. No gentleman would allow fighters to go without prize money duly fought for. Not with the risks they took and the enjoyment everyone found. It simply wasn't done. "Do they know who was responsible?"

"One Arthur Marsey was holding the money, and at the moment he's not to be found. Aldreth and Bracebridge are searching for him now. They fear foul play."

"Mr. Marsey?"

"Yes."

She'd done her best. She'd tried to warn Captain Niall, and now she could only hope Marsey was found and the missing money recovered. "Terrible news."

"But enough of that. I was tired of hearing of it five minutes after Aldreth told me. Now, you came here to tell me something. What is it?"

Lucy gave a wry smile, and then, to her surprise, the words she'd rehearsed slipped out, cool as water in the morning. "I have decided," she said, "to move out of The Cooperage."

"Oh."

"If all goes well, I shall do so by the end of the week."

"To?" Mary rearranged several of the papers on the desk.

"Little Merton." She loved all her sisters, but she and Mary were the least alike, and when they were children, the most often at loggerheads. Mary had all the determination Lucy had lost over the years, as if her sister had gathered the will and nerve that had deserted Lucy. If her sister thought for even a moment that Lucy was persuadable on this, her cause was lost.

Mary stretched out a hand for hers. "Lucy. Darling. Why?"

"Can you really ask that? I only tell you now to be sure you can take in Emily in time. You know why. You know that if I am not there you must look out for Emily."

"Of course we can. Of course. But come live here. With us." Mary took her hand. "I was planning to ask you in any event. Aldreth and I should be so pleased if you did. Both of you. You ought to. There's no one for you here in Bartley Green, but in London? So many gentlemen approached Aldreth about you. Despite every-thing."

"Yes, that. Despite that." She frowned. "Do you think any of them would have continued in their interest once they learned about my marriage?"

"It would not matter. Not to a man who loved you."

She laughed. "It would, Mary. You know it would. It does matter."

"With Aldreth and Cynssyr as your relations? I think a gentle-man would overlook quite a lot for that, even without his emotions engaged."

Lucy returned her sister's level gaze. This was something, look-ing at Mary despite the sag in her stomach, her dry throat, and the thud of her heart against her ribs. "Thank you, Mary, for your kind words. But my mind is made up."

Mary gave her hand another squeeze. "There's no reason you can't find happiness, too."

She'd memorized the points she needed to make. "No one will think it odd that a widow does not remarry."

"Please, please." Mary's lips thinned. "An unhappy marriage does not mean you can never be happy. Don't shut off the possibility because you were unhappy once."

From within her she found more words, and it was astonishing that the house did not come crashing down around her shoulders when she broke her years of silence with the sister whose opinion she feared the most. "You and Anne are so certain my marriage was a disaster, but it wasn't."

"You did not have to marry him." Mary stood too quickly. "If only you'd waited, Aldreth would have put everything right. Instead, you went off on your own. Without a word to anyone until it was too late."

"I loved him, Mary."

"No. No, I know you did not."

"Not at the start. You owe a debt to Devil—"

Mary's eyes widened. "A debt. For stealing away with my sister? I refuse to pay that debt."

"Whether I loved him at the start or not, my husband paid for your wedding."

"He did not."

"He did. Papa sent him the bills for your wedding party, and he paid them without a word of complaint. A stack of them an inch thick, Mary. From the stationer, the milliner, the confectioner, the butcher. He paid for the roses, the ribbons, and all the decorations."

"Aldreth paid Papa's debts."

"If he did, he paid new ones or perhaps the ones for which there was no paper. Devil paid the mortgages and everything for which Papa had a dunning letter. Mary, please. I do not wish to argue."

"You ran away. You ran away and married that man when you did not have to."

"It was Papa's idea. All of it. Because Devil was rich."

"No." She closed her eyes. "I cannot believe it. I cannot."

"I am moving to Little Merton, not Timbuktu. I came here to tell you good-bye and to make certain you and Anne would step in to look after Emily. You know Papa shan't, and I will not leave her there with him. We cannot leave her alone."

Mary walked away from the desk. "Has it been that awful at home?"

"It's been worse, you know that."

"You should have said something."

"Why?"

"My heart breaks to think you've been unhappy and never said a word to any of us. We know what Papa is like. Anne or I both expected you would tell us if you needed help."

"You underestimate Papa. Aldreth and Cynssyr keep him on a short leash, Mary. It's better than it was before they stepped in. Of course. But he's found ways to avoid their management of him, and they cannot stop him from spending money meant for bills on something else. Or taking the money they mean to be for Emily and me."

Her sister took a step toward her, then stopped. "Oh, Lucy, poor Lucy. You should have told us."

"Even so, how could I be happy at The Cooperage after what Papa did? You know my meaning. Could you live with him again with any hope of happiness?"

"No." Mary licked her lower lip. "No. No, I could not."

"I want to be away from there, and I am asking now for your help. Take care of Emily."

Mary came close enough to take her hand. "Aldreth and I would be glad to have you with us. You know that."

"I do. I do know that. But I had rather live on my own. A little cottage away from Bartley Green. You'll look after Emily, won't you?"

"You know we shall."

She smiled, and it felt like the first true smile since she'd come back. She'd done it. Saved enough to live on her own. Her new life would begin, and she hoped it would not be too much to think that Thrale would be a regular caller.

CHAPTER THIRTY-FOUR

Thrale stood in the driveway with Sinclair, Aldreth, and Bracebridge, admiring the gleaming phaeton that Sinclair's young groom had just driven from the carriagemakers to The Cooperage. The lad sat with one foot propped high on the floorboard, a hand draped over his knee, grinning ear to ear.

"They're a fine pair. Finest I've ever handled. And the phaeton? Smooth running. Nary a bump all the way here."

"Did you pace them?" Aldreth smoothed a palm over the right-hand horse's sleek hide. "How fast?"

"If I had, milord, I wouldn't confess it."

"A guess," Thrale asked. The pair were beauties. And the phaeton. A sweet conveyance, no question.

"Well, milord, my guess is they'd do a mile in four minutes. Maybe less. Post to post."

Sinclair walked around the phaeton, examining the work, running a hand over the crimson lacquer. He inspected the horses, grinning as broadly as his groom. A new phaeton required new horses, and yes, Sinclair had bought a matched pair the color of ink and had them delivered to the carriagemaker's.

"Excellent work." Bracebridge smoothed a hand over the boot. "Who did you say made this?"

"A fellow in Little Merton." Sinclair continued his circuit around the phaeton. "As good as any a man can get in London."

Bracebridge nodded. "I daresay."

Sinclair came around and clapped Bracebridge on the shoulder. "Take them down the road and back, why don't you?"

The other man shook a curl off his forehead. "You needn't ask me a second time."

The groom hopped down, and Bracebridge jumped up. He took the reins in one hand and curled the other on the whip, though he left it seated for now. The groom shaded his eyes from the sun. "They want an easy hand, milord."

"I'm gentle as a lamb." He pointed at the groom. "Don't you forget it."

Sinclair clapped his hands. "Wait until His Grace sees them. Ten to one, he'll want to buy them off me."

The front door of The Cooperage opened, and Lucy and Miss Sinclair came out. Thrale couldn't look anywhere but at Lucy. Ever since the outcome of the battle she'd been radiant. There'd not been time to see her alone yet, but soon, he hoped. Pray it was soon.

Miss Sinclair fairly skipped straight to the horses. "Oh. Oh, aren't you handsome?"

"Girls, my girls," Sinclair said. "Have you heard the news? Lord Thrale has invited us to Blackfern."

Miss Sinclair glanced at Thrale but kept a firm hand on the bridle. "That sounds lovely. Thank you, my lord, for the invitation."

"We're to leave straight away. Did you hear, Lucy? Warn the servants you'll be needing all your finery."

Thrale recognized Lucy's blank reaction. What's more, he knew that underneath that serene beauty, she felt the barb. He understood better now why Cynssyr and Aldreth were so cool toward the man.

"Yes, Papa. Fair warning shall be given."

From the phaeton, Bracebridge glowered. "I mean to give my valet the same warning."

Miss Sinclair shot the earl a grateful look, but Bracebridge paid no attention. She devoted herself to stroking the nose of the lead horse, not looking at anyone.

"Does that not sound a most excellent plan, Lucy?" Sinclair said. "A month or two at Blackfern?"

She met Thrale's eyes then glanced away. "I'm told the black ferns are a rare sight, is that not so, my lord?"

"Exceedingly rare, ma'am."

Miss Sinclair addressed the horse. "I wish I'd brought sugar for you, you beautiful creature. Do you mind, my lord? I can fetch sugar from the kitchen and be back before you know it. May I?"

"Don't ask me," Bracebridge replied. "Ask your father. They're his cattle."

"Papa?"

"As you like, my dear."

Miss Sinclair grabbed her skirts in preparation for a dash back to the house, but the groom pulled two lumps of sugar from his pocket and held out a hand for Emily to take them. She did, with a thank you.

Meanwhile, Lucy had gone still. Thrale's heart followed suit. "What do you mean, Lord Bracebridge? The horses are his. Are they not yours? The phaeton, as well."

"No, Mrs. Wilcott." Bracebridge tipped his hat at Lucy. "Don't be thinking I'm more fashionable than I am. The cattle are his and the phaeton, too."

Lucy turned to her father, and Thrale knew this moment was headed nowhere pleasant. "Papa?"

"My lord," Sinclair said to Bracebridge, with no acknowledgment of his elder daughter's distress. "Why don't you take Emily for a drive? Go along, my dear." He gave a too-hearty laugh. "Up you go, there."

"I should like that very much."

"Don't drive too fast, my lord."

"Wouldn't dream of it." Though he looked none too happy, Bracebridge extended a hand to assist Miss Sinclair up. No one said anything as the earl directed the phaeton to the road, Miss Sinclair at his side.

"Papa." Lucy turned to her father. "A new phaeton?"

"As you see." He pointed at the driveway.

"Did you pay for it, Aldreth?"

"No."

"My girl." Sinclair flushed. "An it happen, I paid in full. Not a penny in arrears. No need to ask others to see to furnishing my stables."

"In full?" She rested a hand on her upper chest. "How?"

Thrale's foreboding increased. "I assume he put money on Clancy, Mrs. Wilcott. I know Cynssyr did. He won enough to buy himself ten new phaetons."

"Did you, Papa? I thought you wagered on Granger. What changed your mind?"

"Now, never you mind. I never said I only took odds on Granger."

"Crafty man," Aldreth said, slowly.

"Yes." Lucy examined the tips of her shoes. "That is happy news, Papa." She gave them a smile of fragile perfection. "While we wait for Bracebridge to return with Emily, you'll come in for tea, I hope?"

"Of course." Aldreth gave Lucy a kiss on the cheek. "But you'll find we all wish our maiden voyage in your father's fine new rig."

"Yes." She bobbed her head and returned to the house. "Yes, of course."

At his first decent opportunity, which did not come until after Bracebridge brought Miss Sinclair back to the house, Thrale went inside. He found Lucy in her room, on the floor beside an open wardrobe. Her head was bowed, and she had one arm around Roger's neck. A lock box was beside her. Empty.

She shoved the box away from her, hard enough to break one of the hinges when it rolled. "Every penny. Gone."

CHAPTER THIRTY-FIVE

W as disaster too strong a word for the tea that had been served to his guests? No. It was not. Which was why Thrale was waiting in his office for his butler to make an appearance.

He and his guests had gathered for tea after their walk to the waterfall. The scenery there had impressed everyone, and he had basked in their appreciation. God knows there was nothing much beautiful about the house. His father had left the waterfall alone, and its beauty made up in some small measure for all that was uncomfortable and drear in the house.

Nothing could compensate for the tea. Debacle was too kind a word. The service was slow in coming, the water was not hot enough. The tea was weak. Edible was the kindest word to describe the food.

He hoped Flint could save him from worse disasters looming. If he had not sent his valet on ahead with the the luggage, what worse conditions might have awaited them? The house might not have been habitable.

During tea, Cynssyr had politely wondered if he might send for his chef, who must be bored in London, with no one to cook for. At the time, Thrale had been standing by the window staring at the dust clinging to the window glass. He'd been remiss. Not just that, but a deliberate miser. He'd resented his father so thoroughly he'd starved Blackfern.

He thought of The Cooperage and Rosefeld and saw with clear eyes that his home had gone too many years neglected. Everywhere he looked, he saw evidence that in refusing to follow his father's path, he'd done an equal wrong. He'd accepted the duke's offer of bringing Jubert from Town, and the duke, bless his soul, had gone immediately to a desk to write the instructions.

During the painful years of retrenchment after his father's death, he'd been forced to reduce the staff to numbers his income could tolerate, but he had never, with the improvement in his fortunes, allotted more resources to the house and grounds.

While Thrale waited for his butler to make an appearance, in vain it began to seem, he felt the oppression of what he'd let happen here. He never entertained when he was in residence at Blackfern. He refused to because that was all his father had ever done. And here he was, breaking that resolve and finding himself paying double for his sins.

Now, he saw not the restraint and economy required to repair the title, but a monument to resentment. His father's excesses were gone, that dreadful mix of the Byzantine, the Rococo, and Chinoiserie, and where the expense had not been funded from the entailments, he'd sold what he could wherever he'd documented his right to do so. He'd replaced all that with the opposite. Every painting his father had acquired had either been sold or packed up and stowed in the attic. Carpets had been rolled up, statues, busts, all the artifacts from his father's tour of Arabia discarded, auctioned off, or boxed up.

He stared out the window of his office long enough to come to terms with his failings. He had much to remedy here. A great deal to atone for. His butler appeared at last, and when the man stood stone-silent, Thrale understood the man expected to be let go, like as not without a character.

"My lord."

"You and the rest of the staff have done what you can with inadequate resources. Please let them know I appreciate their hard work." He gave a curt nod. "Their efforts and yours will be amply reflected in the upcoming quarter's wages."

The man's astonishment cut to the bone. "Thank you, milord."

"Is the kitchen fit for supper or ought we to dine out?"

"You may dine in, my lord. We've laid in provisions sufficient for your visit."

"Pray God, the duke's chef will come from Town as soon as travel conditions permit. His name is Jubert. Let the cook, whoever that might be, know Jubert will run the kitchen once he is here. Ask him, please, to learn what he can from the man."

"My lord."

"Hire whomever else you need. Bring down anything in the attic that will give this hulk some soul."

"Milord."

"I maintain that an excess of gilt is never in good taste."

"No, milord."

Thrale nodded. "Good day, then."

With that, he was alone in his office, once his father's. The space was as dreary as the rest of the house. In here, he'd had the walls stripped to the plaster and all his father's personal possessions taken away. A single lamp sat on the desk. The blotter was unused. There was nothing of his father in here, and nothing of him, either.

With a grunt, he left the room, and then the house, and even outside he saw nothing bright. Nothing to catch the eye and make one think *here is something of good taste.*

He strode down the driveway, and what he saw told the tale of his failings. The gravel was sparse and the road rutted. By some miracle of oversight, he'd not ordered the destruction of the lime trees that lined the drive. His father had put those in, too. Well. He would leave them be. The trees never did anyone any harm.

When he reached the first curve of the drive, he faced the house. He set aside his resentment of his father and his years of sacrifice in order to save the estate from excesses that had not been his. He studied Blackfern. The bones were good, but there was no sense of welcome. No window boxes of flowers, no color anywhere. The house looked as cold and forbidding as his reputation.

What Blackfern needed was what it had lacked these last thirty years, which was all the charm and warmth his father had stripped from the place, and everything he, himself, had denied the property since the titles came into his management. There was no love here. No wife to gentle his hard edges. No laughter from children. No son or daughter about whom he might say, *Isn't he just.*

Thrale walked a deliberate circle around the immediate grounds. Wherever he looked, he was confronted with his crimes. His father had bled the place dry; packed it with gilt and useless, ruinously expensive *things.* As for him? He'd starved Blackfern. His responsibility was to be certain the estate thrived, and he had not done that.

The scene was no different at the rear of the house. His boots kicked up dust because the path needed new gravel. The fences around the paddocks were neat, but patched, not replaced. The stable block looked barely up to the task of housing horses and gear and grooms. Not a single marigold was to be seen when there had once been an entire bed of them. Had he not told Mrs. Wilcott that he grew them here in his mother's remembrance?

His path took him near one of the smaller gardens, a corner meant to be private. A favorite spot of his mother's. A flash of cardinal red caught his eye as he passed. Color in a landscape he'd stripped of vitality. What he found when he stood at the entrance to the garden, were Lucy and Roger, for of course she had brought Roger with her, and the dog was more than welcome. One of the groundsmen—his only groundsman, stood by with a spade and a bucket while Lucy, on her knees, dug about in a bed of wilted greens.

Roger trotted to him to have his ears rubbed, and Thrale obliged. The groundsman looked as worn and tired as Blackfern. He snatched off his cap and bowed. "Milord."

Thrale answered with a nod. Lucy turned and pushed back the brim of her wide hat. The bodice of her gown was red. A red-and-gold shawl lay on the marble bench. "Good afternoon, my lord. I am rescuing your marigolds."

"I see you doing something." She'd retreated behind the walls of her private fortress. Not as high or as thick as before, but there. He meant to convince her to let him through.

"I commandeered your servant to assist me." She pulled off her thick gloves and addressed his groundsman. "I think we are done here for now. You'll watch over this, won't you? In the coming days."

"Yes, ma'am." He bowed and left, spade and bucket in hand.

"Such a picaresque spot." She extended her hand to him, and he assisted her to her feet. She curtsied when she was up and had shaken the dirt from her skirts. "I came here to read, and what should I find but marigolds in distress. I said to myself, this must not be."

He could not look away from her. What a journey she had endured from Bartley Green to Blackfern. A day and a half of travel north, one night at an inn, and a perfect picture of serenity every mile they traveled. She had been pleasant even in the presence of her father whom Thrale could not forgive. Not in a thousand years could he forgive the man for what he'd done. She had retreated from them all. Even him.

"Thank you," he said. He wanted to tell Aldreth and Cynssyr what Sinclair had done. It killed him that he could not, but he could not betray the confidences she had made to him. She would never forgive him if he did, not even if his intentions were good. The best he could do was make the two men aware something had happened, which he had done with all the delicacy required. Without the details, Lucy could not be made whole.

She went to the bench where she'd left her shawl and, he now saw, a book. "I hope you do not mind."

"Not at all." He grasped her hand when she picked up her shawl. "Stay a while?"

She settled her shawl around her shoulders and sat on the bench. "Yes, surely."

"What do you think of Blackfern? Your unsparing opinion, if you please."

"I find it much like you." Roger lay at her feet, and she bent to pat his shoulder.

"That is no compliment."

"I like the severity." She peeked at him, hiding a smile. "Some of it."

"My father lived in the moment. Decisions made on a whim, fancies pursued without a thought to the expense." He pointed to his left. "I had to tear down an entire wing my father added when I was ten. Thousands of pounds spent on that foolishness, and by the time I was twenty, it was worth one's life to venture in."

"Oh, my."

"I sold thirty horses after I inherited, across three stables. Ten carriages. A property in Ireland. I dismissed most of the staff. I cleared out the attics in two houses and sold a tin mine to pay the immediate debts. Tax bills to be paid. Five properties in disparate Counties never visited by me or any of my predecessors in the last fifty years. To let, now. A hundred years' lease of an entire row of London townhouses had expired. Vacant for a decade, not a penny of income from them since the new leases were never signed despite a dozen letters from our solicitor begging that they be executed. I was required to make a not insignificant outlay to put them to let again, and I am only now recouping those losses."

He concentrated on the rose behind her, a thick vine grown out of control, a riot of deep green leaves and white blooms. "He loved all that was opulent, and I have removed every sign of his indulgence. You have seen the house. Anyone with half a measure of observation can distinguish his mark from mine."

"Your tastes are spare, indeed."

"No." He shook his head. "Therein lies the problem. I've no notion what my tastes might be. My criteria has been to remove all signs of his taste."

She made room for him on the bench, and he, navigating the inert Roger, sat beside her. "I do not dislike Blackfern. You retrenched, my lord. From what you've said, it was necessary."

"It was."

"And now, perhaps less so, yes?"

"I find I cannot give up my habits of economy."

"Consider, though, what mark you will put on Blackfern."

He gave a rueful laugh. "My mark is the obliteration of my father's."

"That was your reaction to the situation in which you found yourself. You have not looked for the soul of Blackfern yet. But it's here."

"Where?"

She gestured. "Here, in these marigolds. In this secret retreat."

"I've neglected them, as well."

"I'll look after them while I'm here."

"Please. Please. I'll tell the groundsman he's to follow your advice."

"You won't object to flowers?"

"As many as you think will save the place." He took her hand in his and wrapped his fingers around hers. He had not, the few times an opportunity arose on their way here, broached the subject of her father. Such a discussion, if she wished to have one, required privacy, and they had not had any until now. "Lucy."

"My lord."

"Thrale. At least that."

She shrugged one shoulder.

"I have not known what to say to you these past days."

"Nothing need be said."

"I have been strangled with the effort it takes to speak charitably to your father."

"There is nothing to be done about that."

"That does not mean I cannot be outraged as well."

She glanced away, lips thin. Her expression relaxed when she looked back. "I live in his household. Most would say that whatever I possess, is his."

"Not so."

"That I was able to set aside money at all is due to my living under his roof. He provided all that I needed."

"How many bills did you pay from your pocket?"

She did not answer.

"What will you do?" He wanted to buy her the damned cottage himself. Lease it for her if he must. And he could not. How could he? Nothing could be more inappropriate. Nothing less damaging to them both if it were discovered. Nothing less welcome by her.

"A retrenchment of my own." She bowed her head for some time. "I cannot stay with him. I cannot."

"No. I should think you would not wish to."

"I'll live with Anne and Cynssyr, I expect, unless Emily would rather live with Aldreth. She might. She and Mary have always gotten on well." She made a face. "I shan't be able to save as much. Not without the wagers, and I don't see how I can continue if I leave Bartley Green."

"I will place your wagers for you." He sat straighter. This, he could do. "Whatever system you like, I will act as your go-between, when and wherever necessary."

"It's kind of you to offer. But without Johnson..."

"I will assist you, and in return—"

She looked down her nose at him. "A tit-for-tat?"

"But of course. I shall want your compilations of data. For my personal use only. I'll have my secretary make the copy, if you agree."

"Is that all? And here I thought you wanted blood and tears, not the contents of my head."

He was pleased to hear her laugh. "A fair exchange, I say." He lifted a hand. "On my honor, I will not share it or have your name connected with it in any way." He picked up her book. "There is no need to answer yet. Consider my offer and decide at your leisure."

"Thank you. That's kind of you."

He tapped the cover of her book, and gathered his nerve. "At the risk of offending you, I have another proposal to put before you."

"What, my lord?"

He gripped the book hard. "I will advance you the money required to lease that cottage. If it happens that I hold the funds from your wagers, I can apply a portion to your debt. I would, of course, provide you a quarterly accounting." He turned his head enough to see her. She sat motionless. He could not tell what she thought. "Take this under advisement as well. Silence from you is a proper decline. If you agree, however, then I will have the legal documents in your hands before you return to Bartley Green. Given your situation, I will engage my banker to disburse those funds directly to your lessor."

"Sir."

"Please, take your time. Nothing more on the subject need be said." There. He had done all that he could, though none of it was what he'd wanted to do. He would have bought her a house, happily. He would have put her winnings back into her hands. Both were unthinkable. "He opened to the frontispiece of the book she'd brought here. "The Works of Charles Lamb."

"I did not see that you have a copy of Milton in your library."

"I'm sure I have. But no matter. I've still got the one I found at The Cooperage."

"You brought it with you?"

"I did." He met her gaze. "When I read the pages, I am reminded of the intellect of whoever wrote those notes. He was a clever man, whoever did that."

"Very clever." She took the Lamb from him. "I hope you don't mind that I've brought this out here."

"Not at all."

She riffled the pages. "The pages are cut. I presume this is a book of yours, not your father's."

"Quite so." He took back the book.

"That is a bad habit of yours, sir. Taking books that someone else has been studying."

He opened to the page she'd marked and began to read. "Hypochondriacus."

By myself walking,

To myself talking,

When as I ruminate

On my untoward fate.

She listened to him in silence, and when he was done, she re-
peated the lines, "*In my heart festering, In my ears whispering.* You read
that beautifully. Will you read it to me again?"

And so he did, and it was pleasant to sit here with her, with
marigolds freshly watered and Roger at their feet, and him having
done what he could to assist her. When he finished reading the
poem and two others, he returned the book to her. "Now you must
do me the same favor." So saying, he turned lengthwise to rest his
head on her lap. "Go on."

She cleared her throat, and he folded his arms across his chest.
He'd startled her, he saw. But then she turned the page. "The clouds
are blackening, The storms threatening."

She read very well, and while she read, she rested a hand on the
side of his head. Who would have thought an afternoon at Blackfern
would be idyllic?

CHAPTER THIRTY-SIX

Thrale stood at the edge of the lawn with a stick in one hand and Roger staring at him with hope and longing. He threw the stick, not hard and so not far, and the dog loped after it. As he watched, he came to the unhappy conclusion that he no longer controlled the state of his heart. How this had happened to him—of all people—baffled him.

He watched Roger return with the stick, but his mind was on the four sisters sitting on a blanket at the edge of the lawn. Lucy might never want him as he wanted her. He bottomed out at the thought that he might not win the woman who mattered to him more than his own life. If he did not? He would have to live with her choice and his loss.

Bracebridge, who happened to be standing beside him, said, "What do you think?"

"About?"

The earl gave him a sideways look because, yes, Thrale bloody well knew about what. "My left arse cheek."

He leaned back to look. "Still there."

"Still pretty enough for you?"

Thrale looked again. Bracebridge reached back with both hands and flipped up his coattails. Thrale shrugged. "Eh."

"Milord, you know 'tis the prettiest arse cheek you'll ever see in a pair of breeches."

"Certainly true."

"Then why the devil do you look like you've seen the ghost of your dear departed father?"

His chest pinched. "I see him everywhere in this damned place."

"Lacks a woman's touch, I'd say."

"It does." He tossed the stick again. "As do I."

"Pick a woman you fancy and who won't drive you mad. Court her. Marry her. Done."

"Yes, of course. I ought to have thought of that on my own." The woman he wanted would never tell him yes, or if she did, it might be from desperation or some misguided, in his opinion, loyalty to her father, or to keep her sisters from worrying about her.

If he asked, she might tell him no, and that would be worse than uncertainty. He couldn't. It was too soon, her recent setbacks too raw for him to interfere in order to have what he desired. She wanted her independence. Needed it. He needed to let her be until she believed *yes* would not take from her what freedom she'd gained; despite the truth that he offered security for her future.

Roger reached the stick he'd thrown. Rather than bring it back to him, he trotted to Lucy. She accepted his tribute and put her arms around him. The dog sank down and lay his head on her lap.

"Interesting woman, Mrs. Wilcott."

"Agreed."

"I met her husband once."

That got his attention. "Did you? When?"

"In my less reputable days. When I was Mr. Devon Carlisle, and not welcome at home." Bracebridge had been the youngest of several sons and, upon refusing a commission, had effectively thumbed his nose at his father and found himself unwelcome among his family. He'd made his way in life through means not entirely legal. One heard, for example, that he still owned a brothel. "I made an appearance or two in the ring. To make ends meet."

"You battled Devil Wilcott?"

Bracebridge touched the bridge of his once broken nose. "Do you see this face?"

"The Devil Himself did that to you?"

"He did."

Miss Emily Sinclair left the blanket she was sitting on with her sisters to race with the eldest of Lady Aldreth's children. Bracebridge followed the progress of their contest. The earl of Bracebridge was not the sort of man one would call handsome. He was prepossessing, and there were women who liked that. "I lasted twenty-two rounds. This was before he married her."

"What was he like?"

He laughed. "Jesus, he could hit." He shrugged. "That's no secret. I was lucky to last twenty. But I took my third of the purse and that got me through a rough patch or two. At the time, it was worth this nose."

Miss Sinclair and the future Baron Aldreth were racing the perimeter of the lawn with her pretending to be about to catch the boy at any moment. Her bonnet was long gone, and she had her skirts pulled up nearly to her knees. The entire parade came their way and young Mr. Dunbartin hid behind Bracebridge, arms around his legs, head poking out from one side of him.

"You shan't catch me, Em."

There was a reason Miss Sinclair was called The Divine Sinclair. She was, in her way, as beautiful as Lucy. She crouched down, eye level. "Oh, but I can. I shall, you little imp."

"Someone ought to do something about you." Bracebridge reached behind him and swung the boy up and set him on his shoulders. He shrieked with joy. "Fear not, lad. I won't let her have you."

Miss Sinclair stood, hands on her hips. She was breathing hard from her run. "Oh? Is that so?"

Bracebridge gave her a long look and her cheeks turned pink. "Take her in hand, Thrale."

"Thrale?" she said. "Not you? Coward."

"No. And now, Mr. Dunbartin, shall I take you to see the horses?"

"Yes, yes, please!"

Bracebridge strode away with the boy waving his arms and calling out for everyone to look at him.

"I'm quite sure," Thrale said, "that he did not mean to be rude."

"Yes, he did."

"I apologize on his behalf."

"He doesn't deserve it."

"You do."

Miss Sinclair considered him in silence for some minutes. "Are you going to offer for Lucy?"

"That's a bold question."

"Are you?"

CHAPTER THIRTY-SEVEN

At half past one in the afternoon, Lucy stood before the door to Lord Thrale's room listening to the silence of the upstairs. For the last half-hour of this rainy afternoon, the gentlemen had been in the billiards room. In fact, as she passed, she'd heard Cynssyr claim a victory, to much dissent. The gentlemen were fully occupied. She felt confident she would not be interrupted.

Five or ten minutes was all she needed. Less. In. Find her Milton. Leave a vase of marigolds in its place, and with it a note declining his offer of assistance. Out.

She appreciated Thrale's offer. She did. But accepting his help was too risky. Someone would find out who had funded her venture, and all it would take after that was a word in the wrong eager ear, and she would be ruined again. There would be hell to pay for that. For her and Thrale.

His door was unlocked, the rooms silent and darkened. Nothing could be safer when one wished to enter a room unobserved. As she wished to do. In she went, the note and her vase of marigolds in hand.

Thrale's rooms were rear-facing with an anteroom comprising the first chamber and in which she now stood. Doubtless, Thrale had been even more diligent about removing signs of his father's excesses here than elsewhere in the house. This room, perhaps alone among all the rooms at Blackfern, bore the imprint of the present Marquess.

The curtains were open, and tiny drops of rain dotted the window-glass. The view was much same as from her room; a portion of the rear gardens, the pines to the north, and fields beyond that. Several issues of *The Sporting Gentleman* lay on a table, beside them, a pair of gloves. A mahogany box on a desk was carved with the Thrale crest. Next to that, was a stack of letters. A coin, a cloth-bound ledger book. Pen, ink, sealing wax.

None of the books on the desk and tables were her Milton. She'd known upon coming here that it was a risk she'd not find her book. He might have it with him, or he might not have brought the book to Blackfern at all, despite what he'd said. Both volumes of Lamb were here, though, along with the third volume of *The Mad Man of the Mountains*. She had half a mind to take that as well. Thrale needed a proper bookmark. Several of them. A folded sheet of paper marked his place in this volume; he was reading ahead, the rogue.

Lucy turned in a slow circle. If not here, then where would he have put the Milton? The bedchamber door was ajar, darkened and as silent as the anteroom. She made a more thorough sweep of the desk, taking care not to disturb anything. Everything so severe. Even if she did not find her book, she intended to leave the flowers where he would not fail to see them.

He might well have left the book in the bedchamber. Likely he had. She pushed open the door and went in. The air smelled like him, and it made her think of his mouth and the way he touched her, and she could not think of that. She placed the marigolds and the paper on the mantle.

On a round table next to the fire was a book of the right size. Her Milton, she was sure of it. She crossed the room, and yes, indeed. Triumph was hers.

Another sheet of folded paper marked his place in the Milton. His place. In *her* book. She yanked out the sheet with the satisfying sound of paper against paper. He'd used a letter to mark his place. His correspondence was none of her affair. She placed the letter, written small and crossways, in the center of the table and tucked the Milton under her arm. Neat and tidy. When she turned, her heart stopped.

Thrale stood at the side of the bed near the foot of his massive four-poster. He wore breeches, his braces, and a shirt, and nothing else. His hair stuck up on one side. Even when he'd dragged his fingers through the thick mass, the unevenness remained.

He was not wearing a coat.

"Lucy?"

Nor a waistcoat.

"My lord."

Nor a neckcloth. Nor shoes nor stockings.

His untidiness made her want to smooth his hair and straighten his shirt, when she had no right to such fond and familiar contact. He'd been so kind to her. Considerate. Tolerant. He'd been her lover. That was true. Her lover. To tell herself anything else was dishonest.

She gave him her most exquisitely empty smile. He would not be fooled, but that was no longer the point.

He ran a hand over his face and managed to look adorably sleepy. "Are you lost, madam?"

"Not at all."

His eyebrows shot up, and when his astonishment faded, there was a different reaction from him. "You are here by design?"

She kept smiling. She smiled beyond the whirl of challenge between them. She was prepared, of course, with the excuse of the marigolds, but she abandoned that for a far more dangerous path. "I ought not tell you."

"I think the opposite." He made no move to adjust his clothing. "Neither of us wish to misunderstand this encounter, I'm quite sure."

He was in his shirt sleeves. The center of her stomach turned to jelly. He'd kept his training regimen here at Blackfern. She managed to bring her attention to his face. "If I do, you must never, ever tell anyone that you know."

"Why?"

"Promise you won't."

"Certainly not."

"It's nothing nefarious."

"Then there is no need for secrecy."

"Do you, sir, tell strangers your secrets? Or do you suggest none of us have a need for privacy?"

"If you have a secret to divulge, then, provided I am satisfied with your motives, I will not betray your confidence."

"My sisters and I have long played a private scavenger hunt." Inspiration struck, and it was all she could do to keep from breaking into a grin. "Between the four of us, you understand."

"Go on." He walked to the basin and poured water into it. He washed his hands and face while she spoke.

"We must remove an item from a room, an innocuous item, such as a candlestick from a parlor, or a book from the library, and replace it with something else—the following day, you see."

He turned. His open shirt exposed a portion of muscled shoulder. He returned her smile, thoroughly entertained, it seemed. "You do this why?"

She lifted a hand. "It is a game we made up when we were girls. Anne thought of it. To distract us. After our mother passed, and Papa was so—unhappy."

"I see."

"We've played ever since. With refinements, of course, over the years. And we are playing today. Emily, I've no doubt, has snuck into Aldreth's room and taken his braces."

"Braces."

"Yes. It's a private joke amongst us now, the way Aldreth's braces appear in the oddest places. A chandelier, once." Her story was spinning away from her, and she forced herself to take a breath. To slow down before she invented details so absurd the paper thin excuse between them would tear away. "And so, I came in here, thinking you were playing billiards with Aldreth and the others."

"No." He returned to the bed. Near it. The other side, though. Closer to her.

"So I have discerned."

"As any clever woman would."

"In the event, my lord, I have settled on my common item." She lifted the book. Perfectly within the rules, as you can see. A volume of no importance—"

"To you."

"—which tomorrow, I must place elsewhere in the house to be found in an unexpected location."

"Where might that be?"

"I've not decided. Such things require the proper consideration, you know." She was beyond delighted that he continued to play along with this game. "A hint of the absurd."

"I feel you have achieved that."

"You say so because you've never played."

He propped one hand high on the bed post and leaned toward her. The open placket of his shirt gaped wider. "Is there a winner?"

"Yes, of course. There must always be a winner." She curtsied. "My lord."

"To much private hilarity, I expect."

"As you may well imagine."

"I do. Indeed, I do." The way he was looking at her, with such hunger when they weren't lovers anymore, they hadn't been since coming here, sent a secret thrill through her. She wanted them to be. She wanted him.

"The prize, sir, is in the winning. In having been the cleverest. Mary once secreted a quill in my serving of soup. It was devious of her."

"Was she declared the winner?"

"Yes, she was. But we are sworn to secrecy, my sisters and I. If you were to ask them, they would deny everything."

"Yet you risk all by revealing your secret to me. Why?"

"I am discovered." She waved the book in the air. "Mercy, sir."

"Have you not, in being discovered, lost the game?"

"Not yet."

He ran the side of his thumb across his lips and looked her up and down. Slowly. In a way that made her decidedly warm. "Are you asking for my assistance in cheating?"

"Never." She looked him up and down, too. "I am explaining why my presence in your bedchamber is innocent and proper."

Thrale leaned against the end of the mattress. She could not stop looking at his chest. That portion of skin exposed. "Innocent, to be sure. But proper? Never. Suppose Aldreth came in here and found us like this? Or Bracebridge? Or, God forbid, Cynssyr?"

"They're downstairs."

"Do you know that for a fact?"

"I do."

"You thought I was downstairs, and you were wrong about that."

"But not the others." She curtsied. "I'll be on my way now."

"I should hate," he said, as grave as anyone could ever be, "to be obliged to marry you. Just as you would not care to find yourself obliged to marry me."

Her mouth went dry as dust.

"Does anyone know you planned to come here?"

She shook her head.

"Well then," he said, softly, "You might stay."

The words were miles from what she expected he would say. Her silence overtook them both, and was that not delicious?

CHAPTER THIRTY-EIGHT

H e glanced behind him. After these days, weeks of seeing her and having no good opportunity to find her alone—with all four of her sisters here, her father and brothers-in-law, and all her nieces and nephews, she was never alone. They were alone now.

"There's a bed here," he said.

"Yes. I see that." In the semi-dark of his room, her voice was low and silky and full of knowing, and his soul answered that.

"Think what might be done there."

"I can't imagine since, alas, my lord, I am not the least tired." She was wearing a blue frock with lace and ribbon and what not. He wondered how long it would take to get her out of that pretty confection. "Have you something in mind?"

"Words."

"Will you find better ones in that bed?" she asked.

During his time in Bartley Green, he had learned to bring to-gether his admiration of her, the delight he found in their banter, the glimpses into her intellect, with his reaction to her beauty. Aspects of the same person. The whole of Lucy.

"No. In fact, I hope to lose them." He reached for her hand. He'd been in love once before, but he could not recall wondering whether she might return his feelings. They had fallen in love at the same time, and out of love at nearly the same time. He had no such certainty about Lucy's feelings for him. He'd never been so afraid of taking a wrong step.

"That's careless of you." The curve of her mouth sent him wild with lust. "Fortunately, I have a good store of them. What else?"

"Kisses. Like this, perhaps." He drew her near and kissed the tips of each of her fingers. He would not think of anything but this. Not of her leaving him, nor her preferring to live alone. Not the gut-wrenching fear that she would meet another man. "In interesting places I might otherwise not reach."

"I confess myself intrigued. Is there more?"

"Caresses." He drew a finger along the top of her shoulder. Such soft skin. Delicate. Bruises showed easily on skin like hers.

"That sounds...pleasant."

He tugged on her hand, and she came closer. "Pleasant. You sound as if you think I'll bore you."

"Would you? Please?"

His pulse doubled. Tripled. "Bore you?"

"Will you?" Her eyes danced with amusement.

"If you insist, yes. I'll use you well. Both of us. I promise that." With but inches between them, he touched her cheek with one finger. His world, his very existence, condensed and intensified. He led them away from his bed. She had the Milton clutched in one hand. So complete was her control over herself, and so deft was she in the way she intended others to see her, that he had for too long dismissed the possibility that the marginalia in the pages of that book was hers. They were hers. Her words. Her passion and wit.

At the fireplace, he took the volume from her and placed it on the mantle. Next to a vase of marigolds that had not been there when he went to sleep. And a note. He walked away from the fire, away from the mantle-to-ceiling chimney glass. At the window, he read the note. She had signed it with the letter L.

"I can't," she said. "I can't accept your kind and generous offer."

He put her note into one of the drawers of a chest of drawers. "Will you move in with Aldreth or Cynssyr?"

"The duke, I suppose. I get on better with Anne than Mary."

He returned to her.

"The Milton is mine," she said. "I want it back."

He traced a finger along the neckline of her gown and was gratified to hear the intake of her breath. "I am aware."

"Why did you take it, then?"

"I can think of more interesting uses for your hands than holding a book." He slid his finger along her neckline once again. If it took him half an hour to get her naked, he would enjoy every minute. "I shall return the book by and by."

"Unfair."

"What?"

"We are nowhere near the bed now."

"Forgive me. You said you were not tired." He dipped his head and kissed her, and she kissed him back. They were in his room. His bedchamber, and he was not dressed, and she was still kissing him, and there was a danger in that, in assuming she would want more from him than a kiss.

For once, though, their interlude here would not be foreshortened by the danger of being interrupted. Flint could be counted on to be discreet, if it came to that. He could kiss her as long and as often as she would tolerate from him. His body's response made him selfish and impatient even when he knew both those things tended not to provide the outcome he wanted here. If this went on much longer, he'd lose his mind.

He drew back and rested his hands on her shoulders. If he had learned anything from his youth and young manhood it was how to control his impulses. He did so now. His cock remained full staff, but he set the sensations at a distance because he was no more defined by his erection than she was an object to be acquired and possessed. "Join me in that bed?"

She knew what he meant. No pretenses this time. Deliberate decision, not passion run away with them. Not madness shared, but open agreement between them. Not capitulation but a grant of herself to him. She pressed against him, ran her palms along his back and shoulders, her hands warm through his shirt. "I cannot think when you are so near."

"If we're to be lovers in that bed, there are things you must understand about me, and that I ought to understand about you." She might tell him no, more disappointing than any other *no* she might give him, but he did not think so.

Her arms stayed around his shoulders, and they were close enough for him to recognize her retreat into herself. So familiar now. Dangerous to them both. "What do I need to know besides you have invited me there?"

She smiled when she spoke, but her voice held a note of cynicism. He returned the smile, though not the false emotion.

"We've given in. To each other. We've played, the two of us, and I hope to God you have enjoyed that as much as I have. The words, the pretense." He put his mouth by her ear and whispered, "The fucking."

Her fingers toyed with the hair at the back of his head. "You have not yet shocked me."

"I hope to soon."

"Is it possible you don't know how very like the rest of your sex that is?" Her voice went lower yet. "To want your cock in a woman. You can't shock me with that information."

She was playing with him, and he loved it. He adored her for it. "I want my cock in *you*, Lucy. But you must know by now I want more. You know my inclinations in that regard." He cupped her shoulders. "I am wrong to think you share them to a degree? Or at least do not despise them?"

She licked her lower lip, and he bent his head and licked there, too. She pulled back slightly, and then relaxed. He kept a hand on her shoulder. "I do not want a misunderstanding between us in this regard."

"I am here, sir. In your bedchamber. Not elsewhere in your house."

"Yes, but have you merely submitted to my desire? Or have you given in to yours?"

She lifted her chin. Her lower lip glistened with damp. "Is there a difference?"

"Yes."

"So you say, but as a practical matter, I think not."

"Yes. Yes, there's a difference."

"A nice distinction, I suspect."

"Very nice." With his thumb he traced her lower lip. "It's the difference between eating your favorite meal when you are hungry and eating because food is put before you."

"I won't apologize for what I like."

He managed not to smile his triumph too soon. "Don't ever."

"Nor for what I did with Devil." She lost some of her control, for her eyes were desolate. "Nor how I felt with him. Or with you."

He kept his arms around her, brought her close. "I can restrain myself, be tender, if you prefer that. Gentle."

She leaned toward him. "Never the other? Is that what you mean to say? Never so hard I'll count my bruises later?"

"Yes. I do mean that." Could he endure this? He must. There must be no mistake. Not with her. "If that's what you prefer."

"My lord." She stroked the outside of his ear. "My lord, that would bore me to tears."

He hardly dared breathe. "Would it?"

"It would."

"If I say I'd like to strip you naked, then you won't agree until you believe the world can't be right until I do." He leaned closer, slid his hands to her hips. "I promise you, I will do everything in my power make you feel you must be in your bare skin."

She drew in a breath. "Such a promising man you are."

"I don't like delicacy in bed, you know that by now."

"I do know."

"I have no patience with women who prefer the act to be neat and quick and incessantly tender." He brushed his thumbs along the side of her throat. "I want your hands and your mouth on me. In places that might shock you."

"You assume I am easily shocked. Why?"

"You." He drew in a long breath and considered all the ways in which she deflected attention from herself. "You. So young. Yes, young, for all that you're some years widowed. I look at you and see your delicacy and that empty-headed smile, and though I know it for a lie, I still fall into the trap."

"Careful, my lord, of ladies and their traps."

He laughed. He could not help himself. "And you, madam, must be careful of a gentleman who hopes your world will not be right until he's made you a mass of need."

"A promising, dangerous man."

"Promise me." He was half mad with lust, and she knew it. She did. He grabbed a handful of her skirt and pulled up, and up, and up until his hand was on her bare thigh. He slid a hand to her mons, and when his fingers sought entrance, and their eyes locked, she shifted her stance to give him the access he wanted. Needed. Desired. She was wet, so warm, and he was tender. For now. "Promise me when we are in that bed that you will do nothing unless you can't live in your skin without action."

"You'll give me back my Milton, then?"

He forced himself to take a breath before he answered, sliding his fingers into her, and back, into her, then back. But he stopped, and her eyes popped open. "That is not the condition I've put before you. The Milton is yours. Whether you leave now, or if you never want more than this, the book is yours."

"Very well, then."

"And you, for now, are mine." He turned them so the dying fire was to her back because, of course, of course, she would not face the chimney glass. He could see the back of her head and the slope of her shoulders. He moved behind her and pressed his lips to the nape of her neck. "I like sex dirty and loud, and I want a lover who'll at least consider indulging in the occasional perversion. It's no good if you imagine something else when you're in bed with me."

She stayed motionless.

"You heard the talk about me. In London last year." He pushed aside the few curls that dangled along the side of her throat, and let his fingertips glide over the tender skin there. "The reason so many believed I could have done something like that."

"You'd never hurt someone. Not deliberately."

He shifted so he stood in front of her again, but he did not speak until she was looking at him. "I would if I were asked. If I were begged. If I knew you agreed."

Her eyes went wide.

"If that frightens you, you ought to go now."

"I'm not afraid of you."

"That's no answer."

"I don't want to go." She grabbed his forearm. "But that is no guarantee of yes. My lord."

"Understood." He moved behind her again, and he continued unfastening her gown. Half way through it burst into his head that his bedroom door was not only unlocked, but open. Flint would know to retreat, but he was well aware that Cynssyr had found himself married against his inclinations on account of a door left unlocked. He did not wish Lucy to find herself in that position.

"A moment." He strode to the door and locked it and crossed back to her to find her lapsed into quiet. She stood with her back to the fire, her gown in disarray, her lips firmly together. The edges of his lust crumbled. "You've changed your mind." Behind her once again, he straightened her gown. He'd just re-fastened the top hooks when she turned.

But she didn't pull away as he expected. Feared. Instead she slid her arms around his neck and brought his head to hers. "Thrale." Her breath warmed his cheek. "Beautiful, dangerous man, I am not afraid of you. I never could be."

"You should be." His fingertips danced down her arms. "You should be."

"If you want me, however you want me, I am yours."

She did not mean that as he wanted. "However you want me, I am yours, Lucy. Never doubt that."

She kissed him. God, she did, and if he'd ever thought a kiss was nothing serious, this moment proved him wrong. From the very moment her mouth touched his, his world shifted. He wasn't pursuing her, no words, no games behind meaning. He was not in control of this encounter. She was. She was seducing him. Had seduced him, and he'd fallen.

If she left him afterward, so be it.

Her upper torso rested against him. He wasn't wearing a waist-coat or coat, and he was in his bare feet, and she melted against him with languid grace and took his mouth. One of her hands cupped the back of his head, sliding into his hair. There was this moment of unbearable tension that contained all his doubts and worries and fears that she was not the sort of woman he could show himself to, and that he had already gone too far with her and might now be too far gone to care about the consequences.

Her body was soft where she was not laced up and corseted, and the hunger in the way she kissed him pushed him to the edge of complete capitulation. Words said at the wrong time would send him to ruin. Her arms stayed around his shoulders, their bodies close together, closer, not close enough. He tightened his arms around her, and he kissed her back, and she was just about the perfect height for him.

As this kiss ended, he caught at her mouth again. A nip, and then she sighed, and he thought he might never have this chance again so he bent his head to hers again and kissed her. Again. Drawn in. Lost to her, his control unraveling.

He knew his way around women. He did.

He opened his mouth, and hers parted in answer, and their kiss turned him into a roaring mass of want. There was no room in him for anything but this. The two of them. His campaign of control and calm unraveled when faced with his hunger, and the way she kissed him. The way she kissed him back.

All this time, his hands had been wandering, and he knew he shouldn't. Not when he was too close to the edges of everything, but, hell, oh hell, he loved sex. He loved the way his prick lead his body into sex. He loved the way a woman felt in his arms and against him. He loved when he made a woman come apart. He loved most when the woman was Lucy.

Her hands slid down to his chest and pushed, and he steadied himself and took a step back.

"My lord."

He gazed into her eyes, dazed eyes, eyes that mirrored his state. He reached for coherent thought and found none.

Her hand stayed on his torso, and she pushed him backward— this was her no, then. He put the length of another step between them, but she followed, and he thought he'd not given her enough room and backed up again, and again they were too close. It was his prick that got the message through to his befuddled mind that she was pushing him in the direction of his bed.

"Are you sure?" he managed.

"Yes."

The backs of his legs hit the mattress, and he caught her around the waist and kept her close. "You can't begin to guess how badly I want you. The things I want from you."

She put her hands on either side of his face, and for a moment he was stupefied by the perfection of her features. "Since I came home...I never wanted anyone to touch me. I never wanted anyone, not even you last season."

"You slay me."

"Good."

His hands wandered. "You have on too many clothes. Too many."

"And now you're here, and you come along with this..." Her attention slid down his chest, and while she did that, she pushed his braces off his shoulders. "I want to feel like this. Please. Just like this. Make me feel like I'm about to fall off the edge of the world."

CHAPTER THIRTY-NINE

"Lucy." The sound of her name whispered in that longing tone tugged at her marrow. Sensation pulled her down, down, far away from herself to the very core of her body's reaction to Thrale. Her lips retained the imprint of their kiss, the taste of him was on her tongue, where he'd touched her, her skin tingled.

They fell, in a tangle of limbs, onto his bed, and Thrale spread himself over her, the weight of his hips pressing against her body. Desire hollowed her out and anticipation became longing became need.

He bent to take her mouth, without restraint this time. While he kissed her, their mouths open, tongues meeting, and, oh, the warmth of his body, the heat of him, the scent and the plain fact that they were in his room, his personal private rooms where they would not be disturbed, dizzied her. She melted, melted away into the moment of his touch.

Thrale moved to his side and pressed a hand to the outside of her thigh, just above her knee, and as their kiss continued, his hand moved higher. His body was solid and where she touched his arms or shoulders she encountered hard muscle. But then, she knew how he used his body, trained it, honed to a purpose.

Clever fingers. His bare hand was on her bare thigh, sliding around to the inside curve. She bit her lower lip to stop a moan.

"Do you want to be naked yet? Or are you content like this?"

She pushed up on an elbow, her mouth damp with his kisses. "I'd like you to be naked."

He sat on his haunches, his shirt askew and showing more of

one side of his upper chest. He grinned at her, a lopsided curve of his mouth, while he grabbed handfuls of his shirt and pulled it forward over his head.

This was no gentle man. Not with a body like this. She recognized the bruises, some of them more faded than others, the mark of his training. More than a gentleman fighter usually incurred. She leaned forward and pressed a palm along the curves and slopes of his upper chest. Warm skin fit tight to bone, sinew and muscle. Taut. She traced a finger downward, toward his nipple and pressed there. He sucked in a breath.

"My lord."

"Mm?"

"You are not naked yet."

"Allow me to remedy that." He pushed back, sliding off the bed long enough to shuck breeches and small clothes. He knew he was beautiful, that was plain from the way he stood, waiting while she drank him in. Well. He was entitled to be proud, with a body like his and a cock like that.

A cock such as his demanded adoration. She moved to the edge of the mattress, close enough to touch him. He was erect, and when she touched him, he sucked in a breath. Her other hand wandered to his hip, then around to the roundness of his backside. Muscle flexed under her touch, but her attention now was on his sex. Thrale's hands settled on her shoulders. A light touch.

Lucy leaned forward, and his fingers flexed over her shoulders. "Am I wicked to think you are magnificent?"

"Not at all." The words came out clipped.

She held him, lightly. "I do want this inside me."

There was suppressed laughter in his reply. "I would be happy to oblige you. Will you let me? Do you desire that beyond reason?"

She curled her fingers around him. "I'm fascinated by what you say are your perversions."

"Oh?" The word came with a soft and deceptive neutrality.

"Tell me one of them."

"Something I've done? Something I hope to enjoy in the near future?"

"Mm. Yes. Both, I think." She lowered her head to him and kissed the top of his penis. There was no filling the hollowness of her need, nothing but him.

"I don't know what to tell you. What's safe." He touched her head, and she glanced up to see him serious beyond the involvement of passion. "Yes is not enough for me, you must understand that. God knows there are women who agree because they've no idea how to say no, and I will not have that from you. It can't be like that."

"Are you suggesting I don't know my own mind?"

He put his hands on either side of her head. "I need to believe in any yes you give me, and that can't happen in one afternoon." He tilted his pelvis toward her. "If you want to use your mouth on me, please, I beg you, do." He sucked in a breath when she kissed his cock again. "Lucy. Lucy...God, yes."

She slid her fingers around him.

"Before I'm too far gone, please. Use your mouth as you see fit. But if I want to take your mouth later? In a while, that's something else entirely. Do you understand me?"

"I'll oblige myself, then, sir. For now."

"Please."

She did, and he tasted like desire. The shape of him, the texture, the sound he made as she learned what he liked, as she took her pleasure in his prick in her mouth. More than his sex. Every part of him sank into her awareness and transformed her into a creature who needed. She lost herself to the taste and texture of his sex, and his deep groan became her pleasure, too. Somehow they ended up on the bed, Thrale in his bare skin and her sliding her hands over his body, not sleek by any means. Unforgiving. The power. Yes, he was strong, and she knew because they'd boxed, even if only in jest, that he was fast, too. She could not stop touching him.

He lay on his back, one knee raised, and she pressed her mouth to him and discovered what made him react even while she explored and touched him where she pleased, and that was lovely beyond anything she would have guessed. Her wandering hands and mouth arrived again at his sex, and he made a sound in the back of his throat that emptied her out.

She sat up, a hand resting on his belly. His cool grey eyes settled on her face, questioning. Words rasped from her throat, heavy with need. "Lovely, lovely man."

He lifted a hand to her arm, sliding a finger along her forearm. "Thank you, ma'am."

Lucy leaned over as if she intended to kiss him again, and he lifted his head in acceptance. "Lord Thrale. At last you are naked."

His fingers tightened on her arm, and then released her, and he was tracing a line across her bosom, along the top of her shoulder.

She bent closer. "I want to be naked, too."

"I should like it very well if you were. Even more if you felt you must be."

"I must. I truly must be." She turned her back to him so he could unfasten the hooks of her gown, and while he did that, his fingers brushed her skin. It was an awkward business, getting her clothes off, but they managed it. He had the presence of mind to fold her clothing over a chair. She would have tossed them wherever they might go.

At last, she stood facing the bed, between his thighs, down to nothing but her linens. She lifted her arms when he pulled up her shift, and that he let drop to the floor. Trepidation edged her state of arousal, but she held his gaze, and though his arousal was obvious, she felt, for the first time in her life, that he desired her for more than her face and her body, and it brought a lump to her throat.

He reached for her hands and brought her close, and he kissed her, sweetly, so sweetly, as if he cared for her, and then he released one of her hands to set his palm to her lower back. A stroke of his hand, trailing fingertips along the valley of her spine. Their skin touched, her breasts pressed against him, against the hard planes of his torso, he continued the kiss, continued the sweep of his fingers along her spine.

He stopped kissing her, but his mouth hovered over hers. She was not coherent, could not think beyond her need. "Do you think you can live now?"

Lucy brought up her hands and shoved him back on the bed, and she followed, sliding her bare skin over his, and he groaned, a sound that made her want to cry out with the same need. He rolled, with her in his arms so he was on top, and she had never been this ready in her life. She bent her knees to give him access. "No, no, I can't live. Please, save me."

He laughed, and so did she. His lips touched hers, then her chin, then the base of her throat, and he continued down, hands and mouth sweeping away all but their bodies. Her body. His mouth slid along her breast, his tongue flicked over her nipple, and she called his name. He slid a finger along her sex and she was wet, slick, and, too close to the edge. Too close to falling and she fell, fell, fell, and all the while he moved his fingers in her, and she died away.

When she came back to her body and opened her eyes, he was watching her, and her hunger for him flared as sharp as ever. She threw a leg over his upper thigh and arched, and he shifted, too.

The slide of his sex into her threatened to send her over the edge again, and it was perfect, sublime, that push of him into her, and the lump that had been in her throat came back and emotion burst through her, overwhelmed her. She tried to memorize every moment, every sensation, afraid she might never feel this way again.

He stroked in her, and she met him, matched him. The silence between them was profound, yet it bound them, too. She squeezed shut her eyes and let her senses concentrate. His thrusts quickened, and she matched that too, and when she opened her eyes, she saw him as lost as she was, and she had never in her life seen a man so fierce.

Except.

Except he pulled out of her too soon. She wasn't ready for that, and she hissed in a breath. He stayed over her, breathing hard, still fiercely concentrating. He had not spent himself, and when his eyes came back and met hers, he smiled.

"A near thing," he said, and then he had her in his arms again, and he rolled onto his back, bringing her over him, and their gazes met again, he held his breath a moment, during which she understood the intent behind the maneuver. "Yes?"

She straddled him, and sank onto him, that unbearable edge had dulled just enough. He held her hips, fingers gripping, and when she'd adjusted and they'd found a gentler rhythm, he slid his hands along her thighs and then upward to cup a breast, and that edge came back, more intense this time. She bowed into his palms, and he spread his fingers wide over her. He slid a finger over her nipples, then another, then a tug on her, and she nearly came apart.

Thrale sat up, holding her, and bent his head to her breast. She threw her arms around his shoulders and held on and against the backdrop of arousal that came with his mouth on her breast, she thrust her pelvis against his, needing him deeper, and he responded to that.

"More?" he asked. A feral light snapped into his eyes, and he held her tighter, tight enough that he controlled the pace. "What is it you want?" She held him, kissed his shoulder. Nipped his skin. "I need you to tell me. Don't make me guess." He slowed his pace, going back to that lovely, tender coupling from earlier, and it was not what she wanted. She wanted that look in his eyes again.

"Don't." Her fingers gripped his shoulders. "I want you here. With me. Hearing me tell you I want more. More, Thrale. More of your cock in me. I'll die if I don't have that."

"I'd rather you died if you did."

"Beast. Yes. Please. That sort of death. I'll tell you if it's too much. I swear it."

He grabbed her head between his hands and kissed her, a brutal taking of her mouth, and she reveled in his possession. While he kissed her like that he reached between them and pushed her thigh until there was room for him to settle.

"I want you inside me."

He kissed her stomach, then her belly and then his mouth was between her legs and she could scarcely believe he would—he set about destroying what chance there had ever been of her not giving in to pleasure. He made her come with his mouth and fingers and his hands on her body, and they tumbled back to the mattress with him over her, stroking into her hard, and it was breathtaking the way he did that, the look on his face, the concentration, the way his mouth tensed and relaxed; the flex of his muscles.

She reached upward, looked to brace herself, and he saw that and shoved her upward until she had her palms pressed to the headboard, elbows straight, and she rocked her pelvis toward him. Her mind emptied out of everything but his male body, and her use of him. He pulled out of her, and she turned onto her stomach and he grabbed her hips and rammed himself into her, and she shouted his name.

Tomorrow she would have bruises, she was sure of it, but he was careful, so careful not to grasp where tomorrow others would see. He was hard inside her, hard against her. His fingers snaked in her hair, curving around the back of her skull, holding her, and with his other around her waist, he fucked her. Hard. At the edge of too hard. She could never get enough of his relentless body. She came just from that, from thinking about him doing this to her, and his actually doing it.

They ended up with him over her again, and she held tight and whispered his name, groaned it, gave into the sounds coming from her and the delirious joy of his body, hers to accept.

He withdrew before she was ready, just when she was on the edge of coming again and if she'd not realized at the last seconds that he was at his crisis, she would have clung to him. As it was, his cry drowned out her moan that was really objection at being left at the peak like that.

"Madam." He got his breath back.

She touched the side of his face. "Lucy."

CHAPTER FORTY

"Lucy isn't like Anne." Emily put her hands on her hips and craned her neck to look Bracebridge in the eye. Always an effort, since he was tall, and she was not. Of all her sisters, she was the shortest, and she hated it. She hated being the dainty one. She never felt dainty, but she was. There was nothing she could do to change that fact. Men built on the scale of Bracebridge were always a reminder of why she wanted to be taller than she was; because so many men thought she was helpless.

Bracebridge thought she was annoying, she knew that. Therefore, she did her utmost to disguise her physical reaction to him; the butterflies that swarmed in her stomach, the quiver at the back of her knees, the memory of what she'd felt when he kissed her, the way she'd instantly surrendered to that heady desire.

He scowled at her. "Do you think I'm that daft, that I don't know that?"

There was nothing worse than being hopelessly in love with someone who disliked you. No matter how hard she tried, her reaction to the man could not be unfelt. She admired his loyalty and his wit. She admired the way he moved, and the way he was vital even at rest. His confidence drew her, and no matter what anyone said about his looks, she found him unbearably attractive.

Worst of all, she'd seen him naked under circumstances both improper and impossible to forget. She hated that she could not set aside those memories, nor the images. Bracebridge. Naked. Glaring at her with his black eyes. While she could pretend it hadn't happened, privately, she was unable to forget. She had charged into his bedroom, ready to do battle. She'd had no choice, and he had not been alone. Sometimes she was convinced he'd gotten out of bed for the sole purpose of taunting her. If he did not care that she'd seen him nude and in the midst of intimacy with another woman, why would he care about any other feelings she had?

Fact: he did not. He did not care for her, and never had. He was too old for her, or she was too young. She was too happy or not happy enough, too much of everything and not enough of anything. She had long ago given up hope that he'd consider her an equal the way he did Anne. Or Mary. Or Lucy.

"Well, she's not like Anne, and if it's true you're aware, I'd like to know why you treat her as if she is."

He crossed his arms over his chest and gave her one of those dark looks that would have made a sensible woman run for her life. She had months ago reconciled herself to his contempt of her. Sometimes for two or three weeks at a time, she forgot the unfortunate state of her heart, and then she would catch sight of him, and she turned into to a heap of romantic despair.

"Is that so?"

"Yes. It is so."

"That you want to know why I do anything."

She drew a breath. He was being deliberately infuriating, and it was working. "Lucy has always been the quiet one of we Sinclair women."

"God knows it isn't you who's the quiet one."

She smiled as brilliantly as she knew how. This was not the sort of man she'd ever imagined tugging at her feelings. He wasn't elegant or devastatingly handsome, and his manners left something to be desired. For heaven's sake, she'd found him in bed with a married woman, and that was a sin. "You must be patient with Lucy."

"Why? I'm not the one courting her."

"Stop being difficult. You and Lucy are perfect for each other. If only you'd stop behaving toward her as you do Anne or Mary."

"I don't need lessons in how to behave to a lady."

She sniffed. "I beg to differ."

"Beg all you want."

Just like that, everything went off kilter. His voice slid through her like warm silk, and it didn't matter how much she resented her attraction to him or how thoroughly she understood they did not suit, she could not stop her visceral response to him. She grabbed fistfuls of her skirts, then realized the picture that must make and released the fabric. She forced herself not to move. "It is not, my lord, as if I think you are not charming. Why, I recall quite well an occasion when you had no trouble at all seducing a lady."

"I didn't seduce you."

She tipped her shoulders back. "I beg your pardon?" Then she realized that what he'd meant, and what she'd meant were not the same thing at all. "No. You did not. No one could call *that* seduction."

He held her gaze. "My point, Miss Sinclair. My point."

"*I* meant a woman I met at a certain London townhouse. You were both so charming in your utter lack of appropriate dress." She'd taken a risk confronting him like this, but he always made her feel out of control and off-balance. Lord knows it was dangerous to directly and deliberately recall her encounter with a very naked Earl of Bracebridge.

"Someone ought to take you in hand."

She made a face at him. "Alas, Lord Thrale declined that honor."

"Lucky man, then."

Something in the sound of his voice tugged at her. She took a step forward and put a hand on his upper arm. He wouldn't have her, and that was her heartache. He'd already lost the woman he loved, and she could not bear the thought of him bearing another loss like that.

"You and Lucy would suit."

He gave her a look of such deep scorn that she did not know whether to laugh, be offended, or come to tears.

"I mean it. I'll help you, Bracebridge. Lucy deserves to be happy."

"Do you think I don't know that? Or don't want that for her?

Don't insult me."

"If you knew her, you would fall in love with her. You could not help loving her. She's a secret fondness for bad poetry. She reads that drivel by Coleridge, for pity's sake. She's been reading Milton, so that would be a fruitful direction for conversation that will engage her. Oh, and she adores marzipan and prefers orangeade over lemonade."

"You don't care for Coleridge?"

She waved a hand. "He can put together a clever rhyme or two, I suppose."

"He can bloody well do more than that."

"There's no need to curse just because you have execrable taste in poetry. I hope you don't intend to curse at Lucy."

"No, Sinclair, I do not."

"At any rate, if you both like Coleridge, then it proves you and Lucy are an excellent match."

"Do you like marzipan?"

"Not much."

He put a palm on the wall and leaned his weight on it. "Lemonade or orangeade?"

"Neither. Stop trying to intimidate me when I'm trying to help you."

"Is it working?" He leaned closer and gave her one of those black glares that were so effective in keeping others away, and that had the opposite effect on her.

"Not at all, my lord."

"Cakes?"

"Do I like them? Yes. Do you?"

"Not a bit. Mozart?"

"Only a buffoon wouldn't like Herr Mozart."

"Can't abide the man's music."

The more he tried to lower over her, the more determined she became not to let him think for a moment that he would succeed. "Have we any common ground?"

"Not so much as a dirt clod between us."

"We agree on Lucy. That she's beautiful and wonderful, and she ought to be happy."

He smiled, and her heart turned in her chest, it was that wicked. "I'll grant you that."

"There, you see?" She smoothed her skirts and wished pink were not her color. Lucy could wear dramatic colors while pink was so...so horribly dainty.

He leaned closer and for what seemed like an eternity they stood inches apart. Mere inches, and the longer he stayed silent, the more drawn to him she was. Falling into his black eyes, and it was all she could do not to touch his face, and then she was doing precisely that, her finger slid along the length of his crooked nose and then down to his mouth, and moved along his lips.

The air became still. Nothing but their breath between them. He tipped his head up the slightest bit and then his tongue touched her finger. She ended up with her palm pressed to his cheek.

"You," he said in that dangerous whisper that never failed to thrill her, "are a brat. A beautiful, sumptuous, vain brat who thinks there's not a man alive who can resist her."

"I don't think any such thing." She leaned toward him because she'd lost her mind, and he did the same, and when their mouths touched, it was as thrilling as the first time he'd kissed her.

More.

When he kissed her, the world fell away. She knew what they were doing was wrong, and that the way he kissed her was lewd, and that no proper young lady would let a man kiss her as if he meant to devour her.

This was how women ruined themselves.

CHAPTER FORTY-ONE

In the front parlor, Thrale leaned back on his chair and listened to Aldreth reading a letter from an uncle of his who was traveling in Europe. They were leaving tomorrow. All of them back to Bartley Green. There, Lucy would remove to Aldreth's but would accompany the duke and duchess when they removed to the duke's seat.

All four of the sisters were sitting on a sofa cater-corner to Aldreth and across from him. Thomas Sinclair sat with a glass of wine in hand, quiet for now. Lady Aldreth and the duchess both had needlework in hand. Bracebridge was slumped in a chair, an unread letter in one hand. Miss Sinclair had a novel open on her lap but was not reading. Lucy, with Roger at her feet, appeared to be counting the strands of silk in one of the tassels of her shawl.

Aldreth's uncle had a talent for description and amusing stories, a family gift, it would seem. Everyone in the room was smiling, even Lucy, despite her distraction. Bracebridge propped his feet on the fender, listening in his quiet way. The duke had an elbow on the mantle, and he was watching his wife.

As he listened and watched this gathering of friends in a parlor he had robbed of warmth and comfort, he wanted this for himself; the bonds of marriage and family. He plucked at the bottom of his waistcoat while he looked anywhere but at Lucy. None of these people were fools, and he had no desire to find himself obliged to explain himself to Aldreth or Cynssyr when he remained uncertain of what he ought to do in respect of Lucy. Any sort of declaration to her might be taken as interference.

Lucy's shawl slipped off her shoulders and landed in a puddle at the one side of her chair, and he wanted to fuck her again. Though he considered her looks secondary to what fascinated him, the fact was he wanted those long legs around him again, he wanted her breath in his ear, his mouth on her in places it oughtn't be, and he wanted her to put flowers in his room every day of his life.

He left his chair to pick up her shawl and hand it to her. "Mrs. Wilcott."

"Thank you, my lord."

Their fingers touched. He was aware the duchess was watching him. She was an observant woman, the duchess.

"Shall we take Roger for a walk?" He held out a hand.

Miss Sinclair said, "Shall I come with you, Lucy?"

Thrale met and held the duchess's gaze and willed her to understand, and she did, for she smiled and said, "Emily, do please help me with this." She held up her needlework. "Your fingers are so much nimbler than mine. I can never stitch as small as you."

"But—"

Bracebridge was glaring at her.

"Please," the duchess said.

"Very well."

He glanced at Roger. "Come along, old man. Mrs. Wilcott?"

She put her hand in his. Outside, with the noble Roger walking between them, having decided he could not allow her to leave here with him having said nothing about what he felt, he gathered himself. "Lucy."

"My lord."

He smiled through his tension. "You and I have embarked on an adventure."

"An adventure. Yes. I suppose that's so."

They arrived at the spot where Lucy had worked on the marigolds. New blooms were a dash of color amid the greenery. His groundsman had been back, for the lawn here was scythed and trimmed, new gravel laid down, the roses pruned to a less wild tangle. The bench had been scrubbed of grime. "Thank you for this.

For the memories of my mother. For beauty where there had been none."

"You're welcome."

He faced her and clasped his hands behind him. He was aware he could be ruining everything with his impatience, with his inability to let another moment pass without telling her how he felt. "Lucy. Lucy. I did not ask you here on a whim."

"No?"

"I've long thought I was no suitable husband for any woman."

"That is absurd, Thrale. You could not be more suitable."

"You know why." He held her gaze until she acknowledged him. "I was resigned to making a marriage that would do." He took her hand and raised it to his lips. "A year ago I thought you a beautiful woman and hardly more. When I came to Bartley Green, I had in mind that I might marry your sister. A vague notion, I grant you that. Then you. Lucy, you were not what I believed of you. In the time we have known each other I have come to admire you more than I can say."

She pulled free of his hand and fiddled with her shawl again. "I like and admire you, too. You can't think otherwise."

"You brought laughter into my life. Color where there was none before. When I understood the woman you are, I was in awe of you. I remain so. In bed, you are my match, and even so, I have endeavored to be a friend to you."

She looked up from her shawl. "You are my friend. You are."

He stepped forward and took her face between his hands. "In all my life I have never seen a more tender mouth." He swept a thumb over her bottom lip. He bent his head and touched his lips to where his thumb had been. No one could call that a proper kiss, and it wasn't one.

She drew in a breath, and the sound struck to the center of him. The sound made him think of sex, of warm skin, and damp mouths. He tightened his fingers on her shoulder and kissed her again, though he had no intention of doing more. She leaned into him and angled her head, and tension leapt between them.

He kissed her again and slid an arm around her waist while his other hand moved from her shoulder to side of her throat. She kissed him back, melting against him as she did. Tension sang between them, arousal, anticipation. Her mouth was soft against his and then she draped an arm around his shoulder and drew herself closer yet.

That gorgeous tension expanded in him, shivered through him, between them, and he was lost in this moment. She kissed like an angel, soft and sweet, put her arm tight around his shoulder, and settled her other hand on his upper chest, and she kissed him with a gratifying, shocking, marvelous enthusiasm.

He drew away, and found himself gazing at her, drinking in her bedazzled, hungry expression.

"Oh," she breathed. She swayed against him. "Oh, that was lovely. Kiss me like that again?"

He tightened his arm around her waist and kissed her again, and she opened to him, a surrender of herself to his arms and mouth at the same time she answered his passion, and it was fierce, the way she did that. "Marry me, Lucy. You're the woman I want. No other. Marry me. Be with me."

She took three steps backward. "I'm no suitable wife."

"Yet, you are the wife I want."

"Thrale."

"I love you, Lucy. I love you passionately and ardently. These are not words I use lightly. You know I would not say them unless I meant them. I love you. I've been in love with you for an eternity. I want to live the rest of my life with you. For you. Because of you."

She covered the lower part of her face so that all he could see of her was her blue, blue eyes.

"If you do not return my feelings, I hope you will allow me to court you properly and prove myself worthy of your love."

"Your worthiness is not the issue."

"I don't care what anyone thinks of you or says. I don't give that for women like Mrs. Glynn. They may say what they like and have all the outrage they require for their dislike of you, and it changes nothing about the woman you are or the woman I love."

Slowly, she lowered her hands. "You mean this."

"Marry me, Lucy. Be my wife. If you come to love me half as much as you loved Devil then there will be no luckier man in the world than me. No one luckier."

"Oh." Tears pooled in her eyes.

"I wish nothing more or less than to spend the rest of my life making you happy. You and that noble dog of yours." He saw her try not to smile, and fail at that. "Darling. Lucy, darling. Roger adores me. Can you be so cruel as to separate us?"

"I suppose," she said. "I suppose that when you put it like that, I cannot." She laughed, and walked into his arms, and wrapped her arms around him. "Don't think I do not love you. I do. I do, Thrale, I do. You know what I am, you know all my flaws, and you have been steadfast despite them."

His heart continued to jitter away in his chest. He could have lost everything, and he hadn't. "We can live here, or anywhere you like when I am not called to Town. Cynssyr won't object. Nor Aldreth, and if they do, bugger them."

"Yes, yes, Thrale. Exactly so. I daresay they will be relieved to have me off their hands."

He kissed her again, and she kissed him back. When they parted, a wicked grin lit her eyes. "All this," she said, "for my Milton?"

"I'll have the lawyers make an exception. The Milton will be your sole property." He put his arms around her, too. "I've my own paradise found."

About Carolyn Jewel

Carolyn Jewel was born on a moonless night. That darkness was seared into her soul and she became an award-winning author of historical and paranormal romance. She has a very dusty car and a Master's degree in English that proves useful at the oddest times. An avid fan of fine chocolate, finer heroines, Bollywood films, and heroism in all forms, she has two cats and two dogs. Also a son. One of the cats is his.

Newsletter
Sign up for Carolyn's newsletter so you never miss a new book!

Visit Carolyn on the web at:
carolynjewel.com | twitter: @cjewel | facebook: carolynjewelauthor |
Goodreads: goodreads/cjewel

EXCERPTS

LORD RUIN

C ynssyr glared at the door to number twenty-four Portman Square. "Blast it," he said to the groom who held two other horses. "What the devil is taking them so long?" He sat his horse with authority, a man in command of himself and his world. His buckskins fit close over lean thighs, and the exacting cut of his jacket declared a tailor of some talent. A Pink of the Ton, he seemed, but for eyes that observed more than they revealed.

"The Baron's a family man now, sir." The groom stamped his feet and tucked his hands under his armpits.

"What has that to do with anything?"

A handbill abandoned by some reveler from one of last night's fetes skimmed over the cobbles and spooked the other two horses, a charcoal gelding by the name of Poor Boy on account of the loss of his equine manhood; and a muscular dun. The groom had a dicey moment what with the cold having numbed his fingers but managed to send the sheet skittering to freedom.

"Man with a family can't leave anywhere spot on the dot," the groom said.

"I don't see why."

The door to number twenty-four flew open with a ringing crack of wood against stone. Of the two men who came out, the taller was Benjamin Dunbartin, Baron Aldreth, the owner of the house. He moved down the stairs at a rapid clip, clapping his hat onto his blond head as if he meant to cement it in place. The other man gripped his hat in one hand and descended at a more leisurely pace. The wind whipped a mass of inky curls over his sharp cheekbones.

"My lord." The groom handed Benjamin the reins to the dun. Before the groom could so much as offer a leg up, Ben launched himself into the saddle without a word of greeting or acknowledgment. Most everyone liked Benjamin. With his good looks and boyish smile, it was practically impossible not to. At the moment, however, Cynssyr thought Ben did not look like a man who cared for the family life.

"Come along, Devon," Benjamin said to his companion. He spoke with such force his dun tossed its head and pranced in nearly a full circle before Ben had him under control again.

Cynssyr's green eyes widened. "Have you quarreled with Mary?"

"Certainly not," said Ben.

"Well, you look like you've been hit by lightning from on high and still hear the angels singing. What's put you in such a state?"

"None of your damned business." The dun stamped hard on the cobbles, and Ben swore under his breath.

Cynssyr's bay snorted, and he reached to soothe the animal. "I should say it is, if I'm to endure such behavior from you."

"Devon!"

"Is this, by any chance, about Devon's letter?"

Ben's neck fairly snapped, he turned so quickly. "What do you know about that damned letter?"

"He wouldn't let me read it, but it must have succeeded. Camilla Fairchild is too young to be looking at a man that way." Cynssyr's mouth quirked and with the slight smile his austere features softened. When he smiled, he was about as handsome as a man could get, a fact not lost on him. He knew quite well the effect of his smile on the fairer sex.

Devon reached the curb in time to overhear the last remark.

Coal-black eyes, at the moment completely without humor, slid from Ben to Cynssyr. "Disgraceful, ain't it? Her mother ought to set the girl a better example." He, too, accepted the reins of his gelding from the groom. He glanced at the stairs.

"Do you think she will?" Cynssyr managed, quite deliberately, to sound as though he hoped she wouldn't. Christ, he hoped not. He fully expected to soon discover what Mrs. Fairchild's backside felt like under his hands. Soft, he imagined. Energetic, he hoped.

"You ought to know better, Cyn," Devon said. "Even Mary said so."

"You will be relieved to know that at lord Sather's rout Miss Fairchild's passion was as yet untempered by experience. I merely provided her some." His smile reappeared. "A regrettably small amount, to be sure."

"You know, Cyn," Ben said, "one of these days you're going to miscalculate and find yourself married to some featherbrained female who'll bore you to tears."

"What else have you done, Devon, that's made him such wretched company?" Cynssyr kept one eye on Benjamin.

"Not one word," Ben said, glaring not at Cynssyr but at Devon.

Devon stopped with one foot in the stirrup to gift the world with affronted innocence. "All I did was—"

"Not one!" Ben turned a warning glance on him, too. "Not a word from you, either, Cyn."

SCANDAL

The first thing Gwilym, Earl of Banallt, noticed when he rounded the drive was Sophie perched on the ledge of a low fountain. Surely, he thought, some other explanation existed for the hard, slow thud of his heart against his ribs. After all, he hadn't seen her in well over a year, and they had not parted on the best of terms. He ought to be over her by now. And yet the jolt of seeing her again shot straight through to his soul.

He was dismayed beyond words.

Beside him, Sophie's brother continued riding toward the house, oblivious.

She heard them coming; she left off trailing her fingers in the water and straightened, though not before he caught a glimpse of the pale nape of her neck. Just that flash of bare skin, and Banallt couldn't breathe. Still seated on the fountain's edge, she turned toward the drive and looked first at her brother and then, at last, at him. She did not smile. Nor, he thought, was she unaffected.

Nothing at all had changed.

"Sophie!" Mercer called to his sister. He urged his horse to the edge of the gravel drive. Banallt took a breath, prayed for his heart to stop banging its way out of his chest, and followed. He wasn't afraid of her. Certainly he wasn't. Why would he be? She was a woman and only a tolerably pretty one at that. He had years of experience dealing with women. "What luck we've found you outside," Mercer said, leaning a forearm across his horse's neck.

Anxiety pressed in on Banallt, which annoyed him to no end.

What he wanted from this moment was proof she hadn't taken possession of his heart. That his memories of her, of the two of them, were distorted by past circumstance. They had met during a turbulent time in his life during which he had perhaps not always behaved as a gentleman ought. They had parted on a day that had forever scarred him. He wanted to see her as plain and uninteresting. He wanted to think that, after all, he'd been mistaken about her eyes. He wanted his fascination with her to have vanished.

None of that had happened.

Banallt still thought he'd do anything to take her to bed.

Sophie lifted a hand to shade her eyes. "Hullo, John."

She was no beauty. Not at first glance. Not even at second glance. Bony cheeks only just balanced her pointed chin. Her nose was too long, with a small but noticeable curve below the bridge that did not straighten out near soon enough. Her mouth was not particularly full. Thick eyebrows darker than her dark hair arched over eyes that blazed with intelligence. The first time he saw her he'd thought it a pity a woman with eyes like hers wasn't better looking. Not the only time he'd misjudged her; merely the first.

She stood and walked to the edge of the lawn. Behind her, nearer the house, mist rose from emerald grass, and above the roof more fog curled around the chimneys to mingle with smoke. Havenwood was a very pretty property.

"My lord." Sophie curtseyed when she came to a halt. Her smile didn't reach her eyes. Banallt saw the wariness in the blue green depths. She didn't trust him, and she was still angry. Considering his reputation and their past interactions, a wise decision. She knew him too well. Better than anyone ever had.

Banallt relaxed his hands on the reins. Really, he told himself, his situation was not dire at all. He preferred tall women, and Sophie was not tall. In coloring, his bias had always been for blondes, and she was a brunette whose fine-boned features added to one's impression of her fragility. Delicate women did not interest him. She was in every way wrong for him. Havenwood might be a gentleman's estate, but despite the wealth and property, despite the fact that Mercer had important connections, the truth remained that Mercer and his sister were only minor gentry. Sophie's marriage had most definitely been a step down for her. His dismay eased. He would get through this ill-advised visit unscathed. He would tell her good morning, or afternoon, or whatever the hell time of day it was, express his surprise at seeing her, and be on his way, having just recalled an important engagement.

"You haven't changed," he told her. Good. He sounded stiff and formal. It was not in his nature to abase himself to anyone. Not even to Sophie Evans. His Cleveland Bay stretched its nose in her direction, remembering carrots and sugar fed from her hand, no doubt.

"You've met?" Mercer asked. His mount danced sideways, but he settled his gelding quickly. He was a competent horseman, John Mercer was. And far too alert now. Mercer was a dutiful brother looking out for his sister. Well. There was nothing for it. Banallt was here after all, and Mercer had reason to be suspicious.

"Lord Banallt was a friend of Tommy's," Sophie replied when Banallt did not answer. She pressed her lips together in familiar disapproval. Sophie had seen him at his worst, which was quite bad indeed. Legendary, in fact. Heaven only knew what was going through her mind right now. Actually, he thought he knew. It was not much to his credit.

MOONLIGHT

CHAPTER ONE

June 3, 1815, The ballroom at Frieth Hall, The Grange, North Baslemere, Surrey, England

By the time Alec McHenry Fall, who had been the third earl of Dane for a very short time, made his way around the ballroom, Philippa was by herself. She sat on a chair backed up against the wall, her chin tipped toward the ceiling. Her eyes were closed in an attitude of relaxation rather than, so Dane hoped, prayer.

Her position exposed the slender column of her throat to anyone who might be looking, which was almost no one besides him since the room was nearly empty. Her hands lay motionless on her lap with the fingers of one hand curled around an ivory fan, the other held a corner of a fringed shawl the color of champagne.

He continued walking, not thinking about much except that Philippa was his good friend and that he was glad to have had her assistance tonight. He stepped around the detritus of a hundred people jammed inside a room that comfortably held half that number. A gentleman's glove. A bit of lace, a handkerchief, silk flowers that had surely started the evening pinned to some young lady's hair or hem.

Dane stopped in front of her chair. "Philippa."

She straightened her head and blinked at him. Her shawl draped behind her bare shoulders, exposing skin as pale as any Englishwoman could wish. Her legs were crossed at the ankles and her feet were tucked under her chair. Dane was quite sure she smiled before she knew it was him. He didn't remember her eyes being quite so remarkable a shade of green. An usual, light green. How interesting. And yes, disturbing, that he should notice any such thing about her.

He grinned and reached for her hand. He'd removed his gloves for the night, but she still wore hers. "A success, my little party, don't you think?"

A concoction of lace, ribbons and silk flowers covered the top of her strawberry blonde hair, a fashionable color among the young ladies of society. That he was now the sort of man who knew such things as what was fashionable among the ladies remained a source of amazement to him. He'd known Philippa his entire life. Her hair had been that shade of reddish-gold before it was fashionable.

Philippa was no girl. She was a mature woman. Thirty-one, though she could easily pass for younger. Her features were more elegant than he had called to mind during the time he'd been away. The shape of her face and the definite mouth above a pointed chin balanced out her nose, and her eyes, as, for some reason, he was just noticing tonight, were striking. Her smile, in his opinion, came too rarely.

"My lord." Her eyes traveled from his head to his toes, and he quirked his eyebrows at that. She meant nothing by the perusal, after all. Another smile played about her mouth. "How dare you be so perfectly put together after dancing and entertaining all night."

Dane knew he was in splendid form. His clothes fit with the perfection only a London tailor achieved for a man of means. He wasn't a sheep farmer anymore, except by proxy when his steward forwarded the income, and he was inordinately pleased that Philippa had noticed the change. Made him feel a proper sort of aristo.

"I was about to ask you the very same question." He bowed, returning her smile with one of his own.

Philippa had agreed to act as his hostess tonight because he was a twenty-five-year-old bachelor, his mother was in Bath with his eldest sister, and he was alone at Frieth House for the first time since leaving four years ago. He made a mental note to send her flowers tomorrow. Was there even a florist in North Baslemere? Gad. He might have send to Guildford for roses. Pink or white, he wondered? Or perhaps tulips if they could be found.

"Flatterer." She opened her fan and waved it beneath her chin. Her eyes twinkled with amusement. He did like the sound of her voice. Definite, controlled. And yet, there was a fullness to the tone that made him wish she'd keep talking. "Do go on, my lord."

He laughed, but that he'd said such a fatuous thing embarrassed him. He'd been in London long enough that empty words came to his lips without thought. There was no good reason for him to flatter Philippa, particularly when doing so made him look a bloody damn fool.

Was it flattery if what he'd said was true?

The only other people in the room now were servants, most of them hired by Philippa on his behalf since he no longer made Frieth House his primary home. He'd come back to North Baslemere for a number of reasons. This was his birthplace, for one, and he had deep and lasting connections here despite the changes in his life. For another, Philippa was going to remarry, and he wanted to celebrate the happy event when she and her prospective groom formally announced their news.

"Not too tired to walk a little more, I hope?" He cocked his head in the direction of the terrace door and looked at her sideways. She'd taken a great deal of care with her appearance tonight. Something he hadn't noticed before, what with the excitement of a party so perfectly managed he'd had nothing to do but enjoy himself. Pink roses. "Did I remember to compliment your appearance?" This wasn't flattery, he told himself. "If I didn't, you have permission to shoot me."

"No, Alec, I don't believe you did." These days Philippa was the only person to call him by his given name. He rather liked the informality. From her. She held out her hand, and he took it as she rose. "A breath of air would be delightful."

Now that he'd spent time in London, he saw Philippa with a more experienced eye. She was not quite beautiful, but she had something that appealed. Her looks were in no way inferior, but her confidence, her utter satisfaction with herself as she was, made her interesting for more than her face and figure. During his time away, he had learned that even perfection was tedious in a woman one did not otherwise admire. She glanced at him, mercifully unaware of his inventory of her physical attributes. Christ. London and its courtesans had made him a letch before he was thirty. What business had he noticing her that way? Before she tucked her hand in the crook of his arm, she adjusted her shawl and in the process gave him a flash of bare shoulder. He hadn't seen her in an evening gown before, and, well, this close to her and with none of his earlier distractions he could see her skin was perfectly smooth and white from her forehead to her bosom.

They continued to the set of double doors that led to the terrace, leaving the servants to the task of cleaning up. If it were daylight they would be able to see the roses that had been his mother's pride while she lived here, before his sisters had given their mother grandchildren upon which to dote.

"I've asked a maid to make up a room for you," he said. They were outside now and crossing the terrace. He'd also never realized she was as delicate as she was, thought one also had to take into account the fact that he was a bigger man now, taller and broader through the shoulders than when he'd left North Baslemere.

"It's not so late," she said. "I'll walk home."

"Nonsense." He put his hand over hers. "I won't hear of it."

Philippa tilted her head in his direction. "I'm not sure that's wise, my lord."

"What isn't wise?"

"My staying the night."

"Why ever not? You're family." Even before the words were out, he understood, with a disconcerting thump of his heart, what she meant. He'd thought of her as an older sister for years and years. Twenty-five years, to be exact. But she wasn't his sister. Appearances were everything, and if she stayed the night, a youthful widow in the home of a London buck, there might be unpleasant speculation. A rather explicit image popped into his head. Him covering her, thrusting into her, while she held him tight against her naked body. Good God. Had he gone entirely mad?

"And yet, not family." She adjusted her shawl.

"If not family, then fast friends." Dane had the oddest conviction that he'd somehow stepped out of time and that now nothing was familiar to him. Not his childhood home. Not this terrace or the garden he'd grown up with. Not even Philippa, who he admired as a friend.

"Yes," she said, tightening her hand on his arm. "We are friends, aren't we? Lifelong friends." They stopped at the furthest edge of the terrace. She took a deep breath of the night air.

Dane who, by coincidence, happened to be looking down, saw the swell of her breasts against her neckline. In his out-of-place mood, he thought of sex. With Philippa. And that sent another jolt of heat through him.

Made in the USA
San Bernardino, CA
09 October 2014